SMALL
SECRETS

ALSO BY LUCY GOACHER

The Edge

SMALL SECRETS

LUCY GOACHER

THOMAS & MERCER

Text copyright © 2023 by Lucy Goacher
All rights reserved.

Published by Thomas & Mercer, Seattle

www.apub.com

Amazon, the Amazon logo, and Thomas & Mercer are trademarks of Amazon.com, Inc., or its affiliates.

ISBN-13: 9781662506291
eISBN: 9781662506307

Cover design by Faceout Studio, Molly von Borstel

Cover image: © elegeyda © Raggedstone / Shutterstock;
© Carlos Caetano / Arcangel

Printed in the United States of America

In loving memory of my own horrible Rosie

EPISODE 1: IT'S ALWAYS THE BOYFRIEND

'Do you like hearing about gruesome murders?' a woman asks.

'Good, because we *love* talking about them,' a man says. 'This is *All the Gory Details*, the true crime podcast.'

Music blares out – heavy on the drums and electronics, with the distant sound of sirens mixed in. As it fades away, the man's voice cuts back in.

'Hello and welcome to the first ever episode of *All the Gory Details*, a weekly podcast for those of us who hear about a violent crime in the news and think, *Hmm, I wonder if there are any uncensored photos on Twitter?* I'm Nate Blackwell, and I'm joined by my murder aficionado best friend, Stevie Knight—'

'Hi.'

'—who, I think it's fair to say, absolutely *hates* the idea of podcasts and had to be coerced into doing this with bribery. And beer.'

'Cheers to that. No, I don't *hate* podcasts, okay? I just think it's incredibly unlikely that anyone will actually ever listen to this one. So why are we bothering?'

'I think you'll be surprised. We talk about murder stuff all the time, it's normal for us, but there are loads of people out there who haven't got a possibly sociopathic best friend to do that with.

That's where we come in. We let them be a fly on the wall to our informative discussions.'

'Disordered ramblings, you mean.'

'Speak for yourself. You might live off vibes, but I know my facts. We'll be half accurate, at least.'

'But what makes you think anyone out there will be interested in what *we* have to say? We're probably introing to nobody.'

'*Or* we could be introing to millions. Schrödinger's podcast, my friend. Simultaneously a worldwide hit and a complete flop, and we won't know which one we are until long after we've finished recording. No pressure, though. It's just the future of our podcasting career that's at stake.'

'Ugh. Pass me that bottle opener. I need another drink.'

'So, podcasting. Each week, Stevie and I are going to bring our listeners—'

'If we have any.'

'—a new episode—'

'Recorded *very professionally* in my tiny flat.'

'—about a different true crime story, focusing on the good stuff that we all love. Which is, Stevie?'

'Bloody, gory, gritty murder.'

'Hell yeah. Now, as part of the bribery to finally get Stevie to record this podcast with me – because, trust me, she was *born for this*, even though she swears it's not her scene and she's currently glaring at me like she wants to rip my face off – I promised that she could pick the first murder we're ever going to talk about. No ifs, no buts – whatever murder she wants, that's our first episode. To be completely honest, I assumed she'd go for a heavy hitter, like Fred West or Dennis Nilsen and his stash of torsos in the wardrobe. You know, something *juicy*. But no. That's not Stevie's style. Instead of a big, famous serial killer, Stevie wants to start with—'

'The unsolved murder of Lauren Parker, a seventeen-year-old sixth-form student who died in the small town of Sandford in 2006.'

'And *why* do you want to start our murder podcast with a murder nobody's ever heard of before?'

'Because Nate and I both *lived* in the small town of Sandford in 2006. And in fact, we were two of the last people to ever see Lauren alive on the night she died. Wait, hang on, that sort of makes it sound like *we* murdered her.'

'Yeah, let's just throw in a disclaimer there, shall we? Stevie and I categorically did *not* murder Lauren Parker in 2006.'

'Or in any other year, before anyone tries to be clever.'

'Ah, so you *do* think someone's listening to this podcast!'

'There are a lot of human beings in this world, so . . . I'll admit it's a possibility that *someone* might listen.'

'Did you hear that, guys? She's starting to believe. Ow! And she threw a bottlecap at me.'

'And I'll throw another if I have to. Can we get back to this podcast I don't even want to be doing? I know that some people – Nate in particular – think you need to start a podcast with a bang, with the most famous and cool serial killer who ever existed. A clickbait murder, basically.'

'*Local man buys axe and gatecrashes his ex-girlfriend's wedding – what happens next will shock you!*'

'But sometimes the scariest, creepiest, most insomnia-inducing murders are the small ones that happen out of nowhere, in the middle of nowhere, to the girl next door when she's just on her way home. And that's what Lauren Parker was doing that night in 2006. She was on her way home, and she never made it back.'

'We have loads of favourite murders – Stevie likes a good cannibal story, and I'm partial to dismemberment, myself – but this was the first piece of true crime that was truly *ours*. It happened in *our* town—'

'—and to someone *we knew*, however distantly. That makes it personal. And also . . . more people should hear about it. I've never seen a documentary about Lauren, or heard her mentioned in a podcast. Her death wasn't glamorous. It didn't have the kind of resolution that makes for a good *based on a true story* movie adaptation. So if I *have* to record a podcast—'

'Which you do.'

'I want to start with Lauren. I want every listener we ever get to come back and listen to this story, *her* story, before anything else. Because she doesn't deserve to be forgotten just because she's dead.'

'I *knew* I couldn't start a podcast without you, Stevie. If it were up to me, we'd be elbow deep in decapitated heads right now, and every episode would be downhill from there. Right, set the scene for us.'

'Okay. It's Halloween in Sandford, which is a small town in Surrey where . . . well, not everyone knows *everyone*, but everyone knows enough people who know enough other people to cover basically everyone in town through association. It's the kind of place where there's one supermarket, a couple of schools, and you might not know someone's name, but you've certainly seen their face before.'

'Or if you haven't seen their face, you've heard their name. We didn't actually meet until we were . . . seventeen?'

'You were seventeen, I was sixteen. First term of AS levels.'

'Right. But I heard a lot about this mysterious Stevie who used to bring a wallet of CDs to parties and always ended up guarding the stereo like a feral cat.'

'He's exaggerating. By 2006, it was *definitely* my iPod and an aux cable.'

'That's all I knew about you. Stevie's from Sandford, born and bred, but I grew up in London and my parents only moved to town when I was about . . . eight, I guess? Then my mum died and I was shipped away to boarding school at the first opportunity – *thanks*, Dad – and there were a lot of summer camps and annoying Christmas skiing holidays, so it wasn't really *my* town for a long time. I didn't join the boys' school until just before our GCSE exams.'

'Because you got chucked out of boarding school.'

'Yeah, they don't like it much when you don't follow any rules – and also accidentally set fire to libraries.'

'Accidentally?'

'I may have been trying to impress a girl by reading French poetry and smoking. Neither of which I knew how to do, it turns out. Anyway, Sandford. We had separate schools, girls' and boys', and we didn't have any friendship overlap, not even when we both went to the same college. And I mean sixth-form college, not university.'

'Did you seriously just clarify something for an American audience in episode one of a brand-new podcast nobody's going to listen to anyway?'

'Yeah, I did. Deal with it.'

'So, *anyway*, we meet for the first time when Nate throws a party on the Friday before Halloween and invites . . . the whole town?'

'I didn't *invite* the whole town, but yeah, pretty much the whole town decided to attend.'

'I didn't really want to go, to be honest—'

'What!'

'Oh, come on, that's not new information. You know I wasn't into the whole crowded party scene, especially back then. Small talk with drunk idiots I don't even know? No, thanks. That's why I preferred to hang out with stereos.'

'*Ugh*, you've always been so infuriatingly cool.'

'Cool? *Me?*'

'Yeah! Aloof girl completely uninterested in everyone else at a party? Likes music? Plays guitar? Ripped jeans? Great eyeliner? *Cool!*'

'If you say so.'

'That's *just* what a cool person would say!'

'*Anyway,* back to your party. My friend really wanted to go, and there was a serial killer costume theme, so I thought, why not? So I grabbed some booze—'

'And your CD wallet.'

'—and headed all the way over to the edge of town, because Nate's family lived on the posh road by the woods.'

'Can you believe my ill mum wanted to move to the countryside for "a pretty view" and she ended up staring at nothing but haunted trees until she died? Nice one, Dad. No wonder I wrecked the house with a party the first chance I got. Taking that relaxing trip to Sardinia with my stepmum was a mistake.'

'You didn't wreck the house on purpose, though, did you? Not with your little brother there?'

'*Half*-brother, and Charles wasn't supposed to be around, anyway. He was meant to be with his grandparents, but they cancelled at the last minute. So, technically it's *their* fault he had his first beer at the age of nine. I told him to stay in his room, like a good babysitter. Maybe I should have got him a cage.'

'Like a dog?'

'Yeah. A bitey, annoying little chihuahua. Then he wouldn't have got out and tried to chat up girls after raiding Dad's bathroom for cologne. I swear, the damage to my nose was worse than

anything that happened to the house . . . So, I'm home alone –
apart from the yappy younger brother – and the party's in full
swing.'

'Everyone's there. *Everyone.* The weird stoner guys in the garden, kids from the year below hoovering unattended bottles, couples snogging on the sofas, emos moshing in the living room.'

'I bet you put a stop to that.'

'No way! I knew better than to mess with the emos and their
music. They're the real feral cats. So there are all these people, some
I know and some I don't, and . . . Lauren Parker.'

'She was there that night. At my party.'

'Along with just about every other young person in Sandford.
I didn't know her, not really, but I knew *of* her.'

'I didn't even know of her, to be honest. The first time I knew
she existed was after she went missing.'

'Really? I saw her around school corridors all the time when
I was growing up – she had a backpack covered in badges for different bands and gigs, and it used to catch my eye. But other than
that, she was kind of nondescript. Dark hair, a side fringe, maybe.
She was just another person in the crowd who happened to have a
backpack I was interested in. I'd never spoken to her. I don't think
we'd even ever been at the same party before.'

'We found out later that she'd come with some of her friends,
and none of them had any reason to think the night would end as
it did.'

'She hadn't mentioned being stalked or followed, or anything
that might suggest she was in danger or feared for her life in any
way. To them, and to her, it was just a normal night at a normal
teen party.'

'It wasn't supposed to be a *normal* teen party, though.'

'Oh, here we go. Nate's decade-and-a-bit-long grudge rears its
ugly head again.'

'My party was serial killer themed, I put it on the invite—'

'You mean the *bulletin* you posted on *MySpace*.'

'—but I guess nobody bothered to read it, because instead of a party full of real-life murderers, what we mostly had was normal clothes, the odd Ghostface mask, a few Freddy Kruegers, and *a lot* of sexy cats.'

'To be fair, cats *are* very efficient killers.'

'She literally said that while booping her cat on the nose.'

'What? It's a compliment. Rosie's a killing machine, aren't you? Such a vicious little murderer, yes, *yes*.'

'I don't understand cat people . . . Anyway, *I'd* made an effort with my costume, even if no one else had. I'd gone as Xander Tremaine, hippy cult leader from 1970s' San Francisco, complete with some flares I'd dug out of my mum's old things, a long wig, and a suede waistcoat with a fake severed hand sticking out of the top pocket. Oh, and about a pint of fake blood down my chest. But what did I hear all night? "Oh hey, you're Captain Jack Sparrow!" Honestly . . . One person got my outfit, though.'

'Hi, it was me.'

'Not only did Stevie get my outfit, but—'

'I had accidentally arrived in a matching one.'

'You should've seen her. Long floaty dress—'

'Courtesy of my mum and her part in my parents' Fleetwood Mac tribute act.'

'—flowers in her hair, a wicker basket full of mannequin limbs, and probably *two* pints of fake blood down her. Of all the killers in the world—'

'I'd accidently come as his wife, Sage Tremaine. If you don't know the Tremaines – aka the San Francisco Snackers – we'll definitely get to them in the future, but let's just say Xander founded a cult—'

'A free-love sex cult!'

8

'—and when he and Sage grew tired of one of the members, they would keep things fresh by cooking and eating them.'

'It kept the lunch bill down, too. A self-sufficient cult!'

'You can't say that.'

'You're the one laughing at it. So, anyway, Stevie and I spot each other, and I shout, "*Whoa, babe, Susan is, like, burning on the stove, man!*"'

'And that was it. Friends for life, instantly.'

'I don't know if anyone has ever randomly bumped into someone completely on their wavelength before, but it was like lightning for me and Stevie. We just got each other. It was like the party disappeared, and suddenly it was just the two of us talking about our favourite murders—'

'And cold-case theories—'

'And worst crime scene photos—'

'And saying how we'd want to be murdered, if we had to be. It was *amazing*. Then it got really loud—'

'That was when the emos *really* started moshing, I think.'

'—so we went to your dad's study to talk, and then I spot a file on his desk, casual as anything, about Jerry Daniels and the case against him. Jerry Daniels! The guy whose stepdaughter died in his pool! That's when you told me your dad was a swanky defence barrister in London who specialises in helping rich murderers get away with it—'

'Allegedly.'

'Uh, yeah, sure. *Allegedly.* But that was so cool! No wonder you were so into true crime – you lived and breathed it at home. You got the inside scoop!'

'I did – but trust me, it's not so much fun when you know your father is on the side of the accused rather than the victim. Especially when everyone knows the accused obviously did it. Allegedly, I mean. Don't sue me, Dad! Just kidding – he'll never be interested in me enough to hear a word of this.'

'After finding out about your dad, there was *no way* I was going back to pretend to be having a good time at that crowded party. I wanted crime scene photos, I wanted case details, and I wanted to know how these accused men had managed to escape conviction. I wanted *true crime.*'

'Ironic, right? If we'd just gone back to the party, we'd have witnessed the seeds of a new one in real time.'

'But we didn't go back. We swiped your dad's whisky and went all the way up to the attic to look at his archives. And we didn't come down until the next morning. And by then, everything had already happened.'

'I'm sure we passed her on the way up there. Lauren.'

'*Did we?*'

'Yeah, for sure. Like I said, I didn't *know* her, but I remember the dark hair, the side fringe. She caught my eye for a second.'

'Maybe time to throw in that *we didn't kill her, okay?* disclaimer again, huh?'

'I know it sounds bad that she was last seen at my house, but literally everyone else was at my house, too. Her friends, her year group, people who knew her—'

'—and people who didn't.'

'Exactly. *I* didn't even know everyone at that party. But I saw her. She was by the stairs, and she looked . . . not happy. Like, I know I didn't *know* her, but I could tell she looked sad. Like she'd been crying. And we just walked right past her as we went up.'

'I wish I'd noticed her. I would have stopped and talked to her, asked her if she was okay.'

'Would you, though? You didn't *know* her then. Her being sad or distressed probably wouldn't have fazed you either way. It didn't faze me. It's only after, with hindsight, that you realise things could have been different. But in the moment . . . She was just another stranger at my party.'

'You're right. But it's still hard to shake that feeling. That sense of guilt.'

'No, I get you. How do you think I feel? If I hadn't thrown that party in the first place, she wouldn't have come. And she wouldn't have been killed on the way home from it. Anyway, we went up to the attic, but the party carried on downstairs. Now, obviously, we weren't there for this bit, so we can't say for certain that it *actually* happened, but—'

'Oh, it happened.'

'Yeah? You're going all in on this theory already, are you?'

'It's corroborated. Guests said so. People saw them argue. Or if not argue, at least have a tense discussion in a corner.'

'Okay. Tell them what happened, wise, all-knowing Stevie.'

'Well, Lauren Parker was seeing a local bad boy called—'

'Nope. I'm cutting that bit out.'

'What?'

'You can't name him.'

'But it's a fact. It's on Wikipedia!'

'Yes, and so is the page summarising *defamation*, Stevie.'

'Fine! Lauren Parker was seeing a local bad boy called . . . well, I guess we'll just call him The Boyfriend.'

'Thank you!'

'And they had an argument at your party that resulted in him storming out. And then a few hours later, she was dead.'

'For legal reasons, I'm going to point out that those were two unconnected statements, and any link made between them is purely coincidental.'

'Almost two years of an abandoned law degree under your belt, and you're sucking all the fun out of this . . . But sure. Lauren argued with the secret bad boy boyfriend she hadn't even told her family about, and then later that night she was murdered. *Totally! Unrelated! Events!*

'Do you reckon he was *actually* her boyfriend, Stevie? I mean, he said he definitely was after she went missing, but do you think maybe it was more casual than that? And *worried boyfriend* has much better optics than *guy-who-was-using-her-for-sex-who-argued-with-her-the-night-before?*'

'I think that's probably it, yeah. For context, this guy was *not* a meaningful relationship type of guy. All the girls liked him – he had shaggy blond hair, he was in a band, he had these amazing green eyes that were like—'

'Okay, okay, we get it. You had a crush on him.'

'I did *not!*'

'For the benefit of the tape, I'm raising my eyebrows really, *really* high at Stevie right now.'

'All right, maybe I had a *bit* of a crush on him . . . But so did everyone else! He was one of those mysterious types who always had a different girl pawing at him. I'd seen plenty of girls crying in the loos over him – girls who thought they were the ones who could change him, but none of them ever could. That's why it was so weird when she went missing and suddenly he was all over the news as the worried boyfriend. He'd never been *anyone's* boyfriend before – at least, not in his eyes. So, I think you're right. For her, it was meaningful. For him—'

'Not so much. Until he was under the microscope, anyway. But we're getting ahead of ourselves. So, Stevie and I are alone in the attic, looking at old files and swigging whisky.'

'I don't recommend *any* teenagers swig whisky, by the way. It doesn't taste how you expect it to in the old film noir movies. And you start seeing double *fast.*'

'My party goes on without us. Some older lads had turned up, and they were the kind of lads who like to cause trouble in other people's houses. Things get broken, like the stereo – the emos were so annoyed – and a whole load of crystal glasses. Someone finds my dad's golf clubs, and the balls get hit into the woods while the clubs end up wrapped around a couple of trees.'

'What is it with boys wanting to destroy everything? I don't get it.'

'I don't, either. Maybe some of us never grew out of our cavemen brains? Anyway, Stevie and I are oblivious up in the attic, which is probably for the best, as there's nothing we could have done to stop it anyway.'

'In hindsight, we probably shouldn't have left your little brother downstairs to fend for himself with a load of gate-crashing thugs.'

'He was *fine*. He was probably the instigator of the destruction, to be honest. Bet he handed out the golf clubs to get me in even more trouble. So while he's irritating everyone downstairs, I dig out the best cases in the attic so we can look at the grizzly photos. It's nice.'

'We stay up almost all night looking at files, like the Stuart Brown case – the retired footballer whose wife was beaten to death with his own Golden Boot trophy. And then the next morning, we—'

'You skipped a bit.'

'Did I? *Oh*, the window? Well, I didn't see that, you did. Tell it, Nate.'

'So, at one point, I'm by the big attic window, just kind of staring into space . . . and I see someone climb out of the back garden – through the hedge and over the wall. I didn't really think anything of it at the time – you know, there were plenty of people milling around, I didn't consider it could be dangerous for someone to be outside alone, or that they were alone, even. It was only the next day that I realised that person was Lauren.'

'Her boyfriend had stormed out earlier that night, and then at some point after that she'd left on her own, too. She didn't tell her friends. She didn't take her bag with the badges on it with her. She just left.'

'We go downstairs the next morning – my brother Charles was literally sat between two passed-out stoners, watching cartoons and eating cereal with ice cream – and as the stragglers wake up, we realise Lauren's unaccounted for. Her friends had stayed over in a spare room, thinking she'd turn up somewhere, but she didn't. She'd left behind her phone, her purse, her house keys. Out of character stuff.'

'We said at the time – not knowing her at all, really – that maybe she'd gone home with someone, or gone after her boyfriend when he left early, or just had a weird turn and headed home without her things. There were possible explanations. This is not in any way meant as victim blaming, but people get drunk and wander off sometimes. It happens.'

'We checked my garden and the woods, just in case. I didn't even remember her leaving through the hedge at this point, but we still checked, just in case she'd gone to get some air and got lost. There was no sign of her. Stevie and everyone went home, and I sent Charles round to a friend's because he was doing my head in, and then it was just me, an enormous hangover, and a completely wrecked house. I mean, *wrecked*, for no good reason. I'm talking toothbrushes down the loo, broken beds – I don't want to know *how* they got broken, or what those stains were – shower curtains ripped down, paint thrown around the garage and over my dad's old Jaguar . . . Not to mention the puke everywhere, and the broken glass from all the cups and windows guests had felt the need to shatter. Between the hangover and the house, I was out of it until the Sunday. I didn't even think about Lauren – not until you and your friend came round to talk about it, and the police arrived five minutes later to *also* talk about it.'

'That was weird, wasn't it? Especially because you answered the door in rubber gloves and reeking of bleach.'

'Puke was *everywhere*, I swear. D'you know I found some about six months later in a plant pot? Someone had literally lifted the plant out, puked in the pot, and put the plant back in. That peace lily was never the same . . .'

'It was so weird to realise we were basically standing in a possible crime scene. Lauren was nowhere, she'd been officially reported missing, and your house was her last known location. I bet you were grateful your dad was a top defence barrister that morning, right?'

'As if he'd offer to defend me in court after what I'd done to the house! He'd have thrown me in the cells himself. Nah, luckily the police could see pretty quickly that I was a hungover husk of a boy who wasn't even capable of cleaning up puke properly, so by the time Dad and Christine – my stepmum – got home, the only thing I was in trouble for was being a stereotypical teenage house-destroyer. Plus I'd been with you all night in the attic anyway.'

'Yep. We told the police everything we knew, everyone who'd been at the party did, but nothing really helped. There was no sign of violence in the house – aside from all the teenage violence against windows – and you told them how you saw her leaving well before the night ended, but after her boyfriend had. Nobody could get a completely accurate timeline for her night, but it was certain that she left the party at some point on foot, in the direction of the road, without any of her things, and was never seen alive again. All those witnesses at the party, but nobody actually witnessed anything to help the investigation.'

'The police did their best. Maybe in a town with more murders and disappearances they could have been better, but they knew it was serious from very early on. They searched my house, they interviewed as many people from the party as they could, they searched for CCTV of any possible cars, but found nothing.'

'People did a lot, too. Posters, campaigns, searches through the woods. There were vigils. The church ran special prayer services. It made the regional news, too. You can dig up the old articles online – see them change from missing girl to murdered girl, always with the same image of her last ever school photo, with dark hair, side fringe, and plectrum-shaped earrings. And then the picture of her shoe on the ground. When she went missing, there was no trace of her, but then after two days—'

'Three.'

'—after three days, a dog walker found her shoe on the road. It was in the bushes, hidden in all the fallen leaves, but the dog found it, and there was blood, so the walker reported it and the police came to the area.'

'But she wasn't there. This was the road leading back towards town from my house—'

'So, the direction we know she left in.'

'—which means she must have been grabbed on the road, maybe bundled into a car.'

'Or a van.'

'Yeah, or a van.'

'Her body wasn't in that section of the woods, but the mood changed. Her parents got desperate. A shoe is one thing, but a *bloody* shoe? And no body? Not a great sign. Their TV statements changed, do you remember, Nate? They had all these theories about her being hit by a car that night and the driver covering it up, maybe keeping her alive somewhere, and they begged for that person to come forward. They just wanted answers about their daughter.'

'I couldn't watch that stuff.'

'Eventually, after a week, someone found the other shoe. It was sticking out of some bushes right near the road to a big old farmhouse, a few miles from Nate's. And that's where they found her. The house had been abandoned years before, so nobody lived there, but kids used to break in from time to time to drink, take drugs, that kind of thing.'

'Did you ever go there for that?'

'Excuse me, you want me to confess to *illegal activities* on a podcast?'

'I was just wondering! Stevie and I only became friends after Lauren's death, and there weren't any more gatherings at the farmhouse after that.'

'Hmm. I think I went once or twice. It wasn't really my scene – there was no stereo. My friend dragged me there a few times, I think, but I never, uh, partook in the festivities. Did you?'

'No, I never quite got in with the right crowd. Wasn't it mainly the stoners who went there? The stoners and the cool kids. I didn't actually know that place existed until Lauren was found there.'

'When that news broke, I think we all thought . . . you know, maybe it *was* drugs. Maybe she'd gone there with someone, taken too much, and . . .'

'But it wasn't drugs.'

'No. It wasn't. Lauren had been stabbed multiple times in the chest, probably an hour or so after Nate had seen her leaving the house. They said the injuries were violent and aggressive, but she was found lying on a sofa, like she was sleeping. Her eyes were shut, and she was arranged so she was holding a bunch of dead wildflowers. It was creepy, I heard. Like some kind of memorial thing. I don't know why the killer did that. Maybe it points to something personal – killing her violently, then regretting it? Trying to be, I don't know, respectful, somehow, at the end? Or maybe making her look so angelic was part of the fun for them. A power thing. I guess we'll never know, will we?'

'Yeah, spoiler alert – this case is unsolved.'

'There was no CCTV of Lauren with anyone, known or unknown, after she left the party. The trail goes completely cold between her leaving Nate's house and being found a week later in the farmhouse.'

'And because the farmhouse was used by kids as a hangout spot—'

'—it was completely contaminated with loads of different DNA samples, like multiple hairs on the sofa, fingerprints, cigarette stubs, cups, dried vomit.'

'And don't forget the used condoms.'

'Yeah, those too. The police matched some of the samples to kids who'd had run-ins with the local police before, but generally people didn't come forward to offer up DNA samples to prove they'd done *other* criminal activity that placed them right in the scene of a murder. Well, the place where a murder victim had been found, anyway. Because Lauren wasn't killed there.'

'Oh yeah, this bit's weird.'

'When Lauren was first missing, people went looking for her. We searched around Nate's house, then later that day her friends and family checked some other places. One of those places?'

'The farmhouse.'

'The farmhouse! And there was no Lauren on the sofa. Yet one week later—'

'There she was.'

'Yep. Someone moved her. They took her, killed her, then carefully, *carefully* placed her in that farmhouse, right in the middle of a cesspit of teenage DNA. It's clever. If they'd left their own DNA behind somehow, who would know? But from what I heard, she was clean anyway. No fibres on her, nothing to point to another location. Untraceable.'

'And whoever killed her got away with it. It's over a decade later, and no one was ever caught for this murder. She never got justice. It's awful.'

'Awful. I feel so sorry for her parents. They acted quickly, but it wasn't enough. They spent a week searching for her, giving interviews to the local news, pleading for their daughter to be returned to them, just to find out she'd been dead the whole time. Dead and waiting for them in a location they'd already searched.'

'Damn, Stevie. Did you *have* to pick such a jolly murder for the first episode? I thought we were going for something serious, here.'

'Sorry. This case has stuck with me. I always come back to it. I don't think it hits you the same because . . . like you said, Sandford wasn't *your* town. You moved there when you were a bit older, you went to boarding school, you weren't a part of it your whole life like I was. But I remember Lauren in the school corridors. I can see the wet missing posters peeling off trees in that week before she was found, and the fresh ones her family put up year after year, pleading for new information. We moved away, to uni, to London, and your dad came back to the city, too, but my family still lives there. Lauren's dad was their optometrist. Her mum was my mum's hairdresser. It's *weird.*'

'No, I get you. I don't like talking about it as much as you do, because . . . Well, it was my party. If I hadn't thrown it, and she hadn't come, then . . .'

'Then she might not have died.'

'Yeah. But then we wouldn't have become best friends either, I guess. Swings and roundabouts, right?'

'For me, it's that it's unsolved. Lauren's family never got that closure, but the town didn't, either. Like we said, small town, everyone basically knows everyone else. It's a tight-knit community. Safe.

But then, suddenly, it wasn't. Who killed Lauren? Was it a stranger, a drifter, someone driving through who saw a girl on her own in the street and did something impulsive? Or was it planned? Was she personally targeted by someone who knew her? Someone who loved her? Someone she trusted to get into a car with?'

'That's certainly what the police thought. There was only ever one major suspect in Lauren's murder – her boyfriend. He'd left my house before she did, but his friends had stayed. No alibi, just his mum saying she *thought* she heard him come in at about eleven p.m. and go to bed.'

'While a whole party of people remember them arguing, and her being left in tears. Her parents hadn't known she was seeing anyone, but when she was missing, this boyfriend was there all the time with them, joining the search, crying, saying how worried he was about her and how he wanted her to come home. He was very . . . visible.'

'And then her body was found.'

'Yep. And then he became very *invisible*.'

'Because he was at the police station.'

'Under arrest.'

'On suspicion of murder.'

'My crush on him ended right then, I swear.'

'You're not one of those groupies for death row prisoners, then?'

'Don't make me throw another bottlecap, Nate.'

'There was a fair bit of circumstantial evidence that stacked up against him. They were sleeping together, they'd argued, he'd left first in his van, and police knew she'd been killed and transported to the house, so the use of a car was kind of key to this. Police wanted to search his van, but—'

'—unfortunately it had been *stolen*, quite *inconveniently*, by *vandals*.'

'Who set it on fire and destroyed any evidence that may have been inside.'

'His DNA and fingerprints were found at the farmhouse—'

'But not on Lauren's body itself, Stevie, so they could only prove he had been there at some point, not narrow it down to that night, or one of the many gatherings he and his friends attended over the previous months. And there was plenty of other DNA found there along with his.'

'Police never found the murder weapon—'

'But it was believed to be a knife with a thin blade. Without it, they couldn't trace it back to an owner, or tie any particular DNA or fingerprints from the house to the murder. The DNA evidence against him wouldn't hold up in court – and you don't have to be the son of a defence barrister to know that.'

'Plus his mum insisted she had heard him come home that night, and nobody else could prove that she hadn't.'

'With flimsy DNA evidence and an alibi, Lauren's boyfriend was released without charge, and no other suspects were ever arrested or even interviewed after that. There was no way to trace who had murdered Lauren, what kind of car had taken her to the farmhouse, or where she had actually been murdered. So, as of today, nobody knows who murdered Lauren Parker back in 2006. Whether it was someone who knew her, or someone who didn't, they've walked free for thirteen years.'

'And in a few more, they'll have escaped punishment for her murder for longer than she was actually alive.'

'Whoa, Stevie. That's weird to think about.'

'I know. It's crazy that the person who killed her got to do whatever they wanted with their life – uni, travel, marriage, kids, career – but she never got the chance. She was dumped in a grotty farmhouse and left to rot, while the person who put her there could thrive. It's not right.'

'Yeah.'

'Do you think the killer thinks about it every day? Is it something they privately gloat about? Or have they repressed it, like it never even happened?'

'Who's to say? The psychology of all murderers is different, and we don't know the motives behind whoever did this to Lauren. If it was personal, they might think about it a lot, but if it was a drifter, someone who's done this before somewhere else, then—'

'Oh, come on, Nate!'

'What?'

'It wasn't a drifter or a random person. It was someone who knew her, and someone who knew *our* town. It was someone she trusted.'

'We don't know that. The police may have had a suspect, but he wasn't charged. There was no direct evidence linking him to—'

'Screw the evidence! Look at other cases – Kathleen Peterson, Reeva Steencamp. Both women who were murdered by romantic partners, partners who didn't even have the decency to confess to what they did. Isn't that what all of your dad's cases are about? Men accused of murdering their wives?'

'Not *all* of the cases . . .'

'Look, I know, we don't want to get sued. Fine. I'm not naming names, and I'm not saying anything for certain, but . . . come on. Come on! It's *always* the boyfriend, isn't it?'

'Stevie!'

'What? You wanted me on this podcast, and that's what I think. And it's a proven fact, too. Women are more likely to be killed by someone they love than someone they don't know. I thought you were a stickler for facts?'

'I am, but—'

'Then we're in agreement! Statistically, based on all the data we have, worldwide, about all female murder victims, this statement is true: it's always the boyfriend.'

'No. Not true. It's not *always* the boyfriend – it's just *most likely to be* the boyfriend. Statistically, I mean.'

'Oh, yeah, of course, Nate. Statistically. *Allegedly*. It's always—'

'Most likely to be!'

'—the boyfriend.'

'On that possibly libellous statement—'

'I said *allegedly*, it's fine.'

'—listeners, who do *you* think killed Lauren Parker? Stranger or boyfriend? Someone who knew her, or someone who didn't? Send us your theories, and if you enjoyed today's episode, please stab that *like* button, hit *subscribe*, rate, review, and share. Stevie and I will be back next week with my choice of murder – a certain serial killer from the Scottish Highlands, you know the one – but until then, remember to keep your wits about you, and trust nobody—'

'Especially not your boyfriend.'

'Stevie!'

'Bye, guys!'

CHAPTER 1

Thursday nights used to be podcast nights.

Nate and I would set up at my coffee table after work – him sorting the recording equipment and lining up his notes, me uncapping the beers and checking that his boring pepperoni pizza hadn't been 'contaminated' by my seafood with extra pineapple – and spend the next couple of hours talking about what we loved best: true crime. He always sat upright on the sofa, ticking things off his list, while I lounged sideways across my armchair, feet dangling, Rosie purring on my lap as I absent-mindedly stroked her ears while talking about the terrible things human beings do to each other. Even after almost four years and 194 episodes, that's what this podcast always was to me.

Thursdays with a friend.

But now I sit here alone, hunched over my laptop in the dark, digging through the *All the Gory Details* email account for things that will hurt me.

You should be ashamed of yourselves.

Stay on hiatus forever.

Overrated sellouts.

It was Nate's idea to set up this account. '*Audience participation is key to building a successful podcast,*' he said all those years ago. '*Let them feel like they're part of it, and like we're accessible. Like we're all friends.'*

The messages from friends are rare these days. They're still there, nestled amid the insults and the trolling. That's the weird, timeless nature of podcasting. *All the Gory Details* became infamous for all the wrong reasons, but not every listener has reached that part yet. Some are still working their way through, oblivious to the scandal, replying to our requests at the end of our weekly episodes for their local murder stories or theories about cases.

But when they reach the last episode – *Episode 194: Our Apology* – they'll know. And they'll resent us like the rest of our former listeners.

Rosie brushes against my ankles, and I scoop her up. She misses Thursdays, too – chasing microphone cords, hissing at Nate, glaring at him from her spot on my lap. I nuzzle her black fur, my dark blonde bob flopping around us like a curtain.

Nate wanted to keep going. *'We can get past this,'* he said. *'If we keep posting, we can change the narrative. People will forget. Please, Stevie – don't throw this away. I need you.'*

But I couldn't do it any more. I couldn't pretend that our tweets weren't swamped in insults, or that we didn't deserve them to be.

You can't wreck someone's life and still expect to enjoy your own.

Before this, I never struggled to leave things in the past. Bullies' insults? Too lame to remember. My childhood best friend, August, moving away and losing touch? It happens. Break-ups? When it's over, it's over. Things never rattled me. I was always on the same constant, chilled level.

But not with this.

No matter how many times I pack this feeling away in a mental box and hide it in the proverbial wardrobe, I still end up digging it out, peeling back the tape, and shaking every painful memory out across the floor.

Tonight is one of those nights.

I flip my hair back and scroll further down the emails. I haven't looked at these in months, but Nate has. Even the ones with the worst subject lines – YOU'RE SCUM. DIE. SCREW YOU – have been opened and read. If it were me, I'd have deleted them. But then again, perhaps there were worse ones that made these seem tame.

I delve into the Trash folder. Oh, wow. Yep, worse. Much, much worse.

And just what my guilty conscience needs.

I click through the emails that haven't auto-deleted yet, wincing at the threats, the Photoshopped images of our heads on famous mugshots and crime scene photos. Maybe we always received things like this, but I never really looked. This was Nate's area. So much of the podcast was Nate's area – the recording and editing, the intro music, promo, merchandise, sourcing sponsorship deals, running the social media accounts, sifting through listener responses, pointing me in the right direction . . .

All I did was turn up and speak without thinking.

It's strange that for someone so prepared on how to run a great podcast, Nate couldn't see how I'd doomed ours before we even posted the first episode.

You ruined that kid's life, the next email says. His childhood sweetheart was murdered, but YOU started a witch hunt against him just so you could get famous. You make me sick. Your whole podcast is insensitive garbage that profits from other people's tragedies. I hope you never post again. I hope one day someone murders YOU and your loved ones have to listen to podcasters laughing and joking about it like it's an episode of NCIS. I hope when they find your body in pieces in a dumpster, everyone—

I hit 'delete forever' and return to the safety of the list of insulting subject lines.

Gonna kill your cat

Stevie should get tongue cancer

Small Town Disappearance

Huh? I read the three words over again. What's one of the rare *nice* emails doing in with the Trash? I click it.

Hi, Stevie and Nate. I know you're on hiatus and everything (which I totally understand but also think was things getting blown way WAY out of proportion! You did nothing wrong!) but I was wondering if you'd heard the news about the girl who's gone missing in Dorset? Anna Farley? If not, here's the link. Interesting, right??

There's a link at the bottom of the email, after the phrase everyone used to sign off their emails with: Keep your wits about you, and trust nobody – especially not your boyfriend!

Maybe this person is using it ironically, and this is some trick where I'm about to open a hard-drive-eating virus, but . . . it seems genuine. And if not, a virus is probably what I deserve anyway.

I open it.

It's from what looks like a Dorset town's local news site: obtrusive ads popping up everywhere; a sidebar of articles about speeding limits and stolen lawn ornaments. I scroll through the paragraphs.

Last weekend, a teenager called Anna Farley went to a party with her friends in the rural town of Foxbridge, and never came home. Her friends don't remember her leaving, and the next morning, her bag and coat were found still in the house. There was no sign of her for days, until on Monday a dog walker . . .

I toss Rosie on to the sofa and clamber up in my armchair to stick my head out the window behind me. Above our narrow street of near-identical white terraces, the very top of one of Battersea Power Station's chimneys shines in the distance, poking out across the Thames through a gap between the large buildings of Churchill Gardens Estate. Three storeys below me – beneath several of Mrs Piastri's flower boxes – a familiar glow comes from the sunken basement flat. Nate's in.

And he's not going to believe this.

There's no time for boots. I rush down the stairs of my pokey attic flat in my socks, out the front door, and loop down the steps to Nate's basement flat. We've lived this way for a few years now, sandwiching our sweet, old landlady Mrs Piastri's townhouse in Pimlico from above and below. I knock for him as a train rattles across the tracks towards Grosvenor Bridge, balling my hands in my sleeves as I feel the bite of the early autumn air.

'Nate? Nate! Come on, open up. I need to talk to you!'

I keep knocking until he answers.

'Stevie?' He opens the door a little, pulling on a baggy jumper. 'What is it? What's wrong?'

'Nothing's wrong – well, not with *me* – but I just read something, and . . .'

His dark hair is tousled, and I register his boxers and bare feet.

'Oh! Are you . . . *busy*?' I nod to the slice of flat I can see behind him. Nate has always been the type to be frequently *busy*. 'I can come back another time.'

'No, no. It's fine. Really, I'm alone. I mean, I was just about to shower, but—'

'Great, because you *have* to hear this right now.'

I push past him into the flat, eager to get my feet on to a warmer surface, and hit the kitchen area immediately. It's like my place, but there are differences: his basement doesn't have the benefit of a separate bedroom, and he's a *lot* neater than I am. Usually, anyway. After pulling on some trousers, he quickly gathers a few things up from the table, the bed, and stuffs them away in a drawer, while I grab a beer from the fridge and offer him one. He shakes his head, but tosses me a bottle opener.

'What's this about? It's been a while since I've had one of your—' he checks his watch '—unannounced eleven p.m. visits.'

I take a gulp of beer, and pull my phone out of my pocket. '*Well*, earlier today someone tagged me in a tweet—'

He sighs. '*Why* were you looking at Twitter?'

'—saying that we never check our emails any more, so I decided to check our emails—'

He rubs his forehead. '*Why* would you check our emails?'

'So I could find *this*.'

I toss him my phone, the news article open on it. I drink as he reads it.

'There's a girl missing in Dorset?'

'Yep.'

'And? What's so special about that?'

'What's *special* is that the circumstances of this teenage girl's disappearance sound *exactly* like when Lauren went missing all those years ago in Sandford.'

'Really?'

'Yes!' My socked feet start pacing around the kitchen table. 'I'm talking same small-town vibe, same situation with a teenage girl going missing after a big house party on the outskirts, same kind of victim, even. And get this – a *dog walker* found one bloody shoe on the road *three days later*. That was Monday! Just like with Lauren!'

Nate jumps back as I pace past him, and sinks on to the edge of his bed. 'So?'

'I don't think these two disappearances are just similar. I think they're *the same*. I think whoever took Lauren that night has taken this girl, Anna Farley, too. I think the killer has struck again.'

I expect Nate to gasp, to smack his face, to be excited – but he isn't. He just shakes his head.

'Nah,' he says.

'Nah? *Seriously?*'

'Yeah. Girls go missing from places all the time, you know that. There are probably a hundred teenagers who've disappeared after parties like Lauren did. Doesn't mean they're all connected.'

'But this one *is*, I'm sure of it. I mean, come on, look at her. Look at her!' I clamber on to the bed beside him and scroll to Anna Farley's picture on my phone: long dark hair, a side fringe, the same kind of features as Lauren.

'Loads of girls look like that,' he says. 'Stick a long brown wig on you, and you'd look like Lauren, too.'

'But this isn't a wig. They're so similar, can't you see it? And look, there's an article about the dog walker and the shoe, with a photo. Look, Nate. Look! Even the blood stain is the same shape.' I toss my phone on the bed and clap my hands. 'It's. The. Same. Killer.'

He claps, too. 'No. It's. Not. Stevie.'

'Why isn't it? Give me one good reason! There's a clear link here.'

'Is there? Or do you just really want there to be one?'

'What does that mean?'

'It means . . . I think you just really want there to be a conclusion to Lauren's story that isn't "murder goes unsolved and podcasters accidentally set a horde of fans on an innocent man later exonerated by DNA evidence". Which I get, I do, but it doesn't mean you have to drag some missing girl from Dorset into it.'

'I'm not *dragging* anyone—'

'This is why I deleted that email, Stevie. You weren't supposed to see it. I knew you'd jump to conclusions if you did, so I got rid of it. Or tried to, anyway. Apparently you check the Trash now, huh?'

31

I shuffle away from him on the bed, kicking myself for forgetting which folder I'd found the email in. Messages don't end up in the Trash by accident. 'You've been policing what I read? What the hell, Nate?'

'Why does it matter? You told me you didn't want anything to do with the podcast any more, so why do you even care?'

He can't keep the anger out of his voice. It stabs me like a knife, finding the one spot of guilt I've managed to bury – and twisting it.

I rip it out. I can be angry, too.

'You have no right to delete emails that are addressed to me as well!'

'I do when I know they'll hurt you! I don't want you to see the threats or the trolling any more, that's why I do the emails and the social media. You don't have to see that stuff. But I know what you're like about this. I knew you'd go looking.'

'But that email *wasn't* a threat. Why hide a news story from me?'

'I just didn't want you to see it.'

'But *why?*'

'Because you need to move on from Lauren's murder and leave it in the past! And you can't do that if you're clutching at straws in the present. And Anna Farley . . . she's a straw, Stevie. I read the articles, too. It's a generic missing girl in a generic British town. It's not the same killer. You just *want* it to be.'

My beer is empty, so I get another from the fridge. I stay on the other side of the kitchen table, seething and looking anywhere but at Nate.

He's not like me. I never had much of our merch in my flat anyway, but I hid it away months ago. It was already boxed-up when the podcast fell apart, ready for the move to Logan's flat that never happened because we fell apart, too. I unpacked everything else, reassembling my records on the shelf and putting my toothbrush back in the bathroom cabinet, but the merch stayed hidden. I couldn't stand to look at it.

But it's everywhere here: a coaster on the table, a mug by the sink – a framed, stylised version of our logo sent by a fan, with that catchphrase beneath it.

It's Always the Boyfriend.

Listeners clung to that phrase. It became a long-running joke for us, to blame the boyfriend – whichever boyfriend, in whichever case. If someone wrote in about a crime story their partner had told them, we'd read it out and go, *Oh! Watch out for that boyfriend of yours!* It was a joke. A meme. Harmless fun.

But Lauren Parker's boyfriend is Googleable. I'd wanted listeners to know Lauren's forgotten story, but I hadn't considered how it would throw her boyfriend – Mike Edwards – into the limelight again, over a decade after he'd managed to shake off a whole town's suspicions.

It started with listeners discussing the case on social media. Someone name-dropped him, and then eventually someone else doxed him: current photos, place of work, home address. It started as harmless fun, too, until online spilt out into real life. People put posters up in his neighbourhood calling him a murderer. They sent photos of Lauren to him, scrawled with things like *how could you?* and *we know what you did.* He had to delete his social media accounts, move towns. But they found him again. They kept hounding him, punishing him.

Because, as I'd so confidently stated in Episode 1, it's always the boyfriend, isn't it?

Until it's not. Categorically. Months ago, back in Sandford, someone found the weapon used to kill Lauren Parker: a knife with a thin blade, with traces of her blood on it. And traces of another person's DNA. The killer's DNA.

And it wasn't The Boyfriend's.

All the Gory Details had never been top of any charts, but we had loyal listeners. We were alternative, with a cult following. Weirdos talking to the weirdos who were listening. But Mike's story of trial-by-social-media made the news, and so did our podcast. Suddenly we were bumped up the charts – through people listening out of curiosity, and hate. People mocked that first episode from four years ago, with me throwing an innocent man under the bus so matter-of-factly. Like it was nothing. Like I didn't care he had a life and a reputation and a private trauma he'd carried for over a decade.

And I guess I didn't care back then. Not really.

Because I truly did believe it was The Boyfriend.

But now I know better. It wasn't him, and that means it *was* someone else. And that someone else could have struck again.

I swallow a mouthful of beer – and most of my anger.

This isn't about Nate and me, or the failure of our podcast. It's about Lauren – and Anna.

'Okay, Nate. Fine. Maybe you're right and it isn't the same killer – but what if it *is*? What if it's him and we do nothing and that town never gets any answers? We know Lauren's case, and that's why it looks similar. Admit it, the only reason you hid that email from me was because *you* thought it was similar enough to get a reaction from me. Right? *Right?*'

'I suppose so, yeah.'

'Lauren's death never made the national news, and neither has Anna's. Those people probably don't realise there's a link – a potential link – between them, because they never heard of Lauren's case. But we could let them know. If it's the same killer, we could help. We could stop them looking in the wrong place.'

'Which is?'

'The Boyfriend.'

I return to the bed and pull up one of the local news articles about Anna's disappearance. There's a photo: parents with red eyes who haven't slept in days, and a boy of around eighteen standing beside them in a hoodie and ripped jeans.

'Maybe the police there will make the same mistake we did, and be so focused on the boyfriend that they don't consider anyone else. But we could make sure they do. We could make sure they do things right this time. *We* could do things right.'

Nate stares at his fingers, lacing and unlacing them. Now it's his turn not to look at me.

'You said I need to leave Lauren's murder in the past,' I say. 'Well, this is how I do that. I have to make up for accusing the wrong person by helping to catch the right one. Will you help me do that?'

'Damn it, Stevie.' Nate sighs heavily, like I've asked him to help me rob a bank, and swipes my beer. He nearly drains it. 'Okay, fine. I'll help you do whatever it is you need to do. Are we calling the police? Leaving an anonymous tip?'

'Not exactly.'

I shift, tucking my legs under me on Nate's bed.

A few months ago, this was normal for us – late-night visits, drinking beer, chatting by the soft light of his bedside table. But I haven't been down here in a while. We used to be in and out of each other's places every day, but the gaps have stretched to weeks now. We've both been busy – me taking on extra guitar lessons and session gigs, him with his bar job. That's what we told each other, anyway.

I got fed up with him always asking if I was ready to restart the podcast yet.

And I suppose he got fed up with me saying no.

But I miss our Thursday nights more than I ever thought I would.

'We used to read about true crime cases and then talk about them together. We would discuss what we already knew. But . . .' I take a deep breath. 'I don't want to sit back and read about what's happened to Anna. I want to go there, and find out for myself.'

'You want to . . . investigate it? In person?'

'Yes. With you.'

Nate stares at me. 'We don't do that. We've never done that. We follow it on Reddit or Wikicide and then—'

'But there *isn't* anything on Reddit or Wikicide about this. I checked. Nobody knows about it, because it's a tiny town in the middle of nowhere, and the papers are too busy talking about Destiny Davis, that missing little girl from Brixton.'

'Maybe there's a reason it's not in the news, though. Maybe everyone in town knows Anna's the runaway type, or she fell in with a bad crowd or something. Maybe she's got lost in the woods before. Or maybe the police know more than that article can tell us, and *they* know there's absolutely no link between this and Sandford.'

'Maybe,' I admit. 'Maybe I'm completely wrong and it's nothing to do with Lauren Parker at all, it's just a coincidence – but I have to know, and the only way to know is to go there. I *have* to investigate this myself. And I know things have been weird between us, Nate. I know that, and I'm sorry, but . . .' I give him a half smile. 'It just wouldn't be right if I went amateur sleuthing without my true crime buddy.'

Nate rubs his hands over his face, sighing loudly. 'Well, looks like Blackwell and Knight are setting off on their first caper, then.'

'Blackwell and Knight? Knight and Blackwell, you mean.'

'Oh, it's like that, is it? Okay, fine, Knight and Blackwell it is. But I do have one condition.'

'Name it.'

He takes a deep breath. 'You want to investigate this missing girl, and you want people to know about her, right? Well, I'll go with you. I'll help you look into it. *If* we make a new podcast about it.'

'A podcast? After what happened with the last one? Nate, I can't do that.'

'You can! It won't be like before, I promise. It'll be investigative. Whatever we find out, we tell people about. Whether you're right and it's the same killer – *unlikely*, by the way – or a completely different case, we can interview people, have theories, and maybe do some good. We can help.' There's a shaky excitement in his voice that I haven't heard for a long time. 'This could be how we fix things. We could get our reputation back.'

I shake my head. 'Nobody's going to listen, Nate. I saw the emails, remember? People hate us.'

'So let's give them a reason not to.'

I stare at my hands – detailed silver rings, long nails painted metallic black. I resist the urge to pick all the polish off, and fiddle with an onyx band instead, rotating it around my finger.

All the Gory Details was Nate's idea, right from the start. It was his baby. He's lurched from job to job for years, never quite figuring out what he wants, never knowing what was right for him. But the podcast received all of his passion. He put in the work, he researched the market, he'd engage with fans on social media. He made us what we were – until that stupid first episode came back to bite us this year.

I used to be angry at him for refusing to delete it. I listened to it a few months ago, to hear how bad the accusations were, but I couldn't finish it. I was so ignorant and indignant. So wrong.

But there was something about it. The graininess from our old mics. The nostalgia of our friendship. My irritation at being made to record a podcast at all, despite knowing I'd go on to willingly record nearly two hundred more episodes without ever suggesting that we stop.

The podcast was always Nate's baby – but it became mine, too.

I look up at Nate, and for a moment it's like we're back in his attic all those years ago – hippy costumes sticky with fake blood, his wig thrown in a corner, swigging whisky, poring over his dad's old cases by candlelight.

Him and me, on the brink of something incredible.

'Deal,' I say. 'Time to learn to be amazing investigative podcasters, I guess.'

Nate jumps up and returns with a notepad. 'Where do we start? Usually there are interviews, being on the ground, getting involved. Where did Anna Farley go missing from, again?'

'Foxbridge, in Dorset.'

He leans across the bed and starts writing. 'Okay, so we go there as soon as possible. Tomorrow? I bet Piastri will lend us the car. We ask around, get some statements, see what *we* can see.'

'We could join a search, if there are any going on.'

'Great idea! And it's a small town, so we can probably find loads of people with information about her, even if it's just character stuff to help build up a picture. That'll be good to make it more personal – more emotional. We could also try reaching out to people online, friends and stuff, see if there's anything on her social media, and . . .' He looks up at me. 'What? Why are you smiling at me like that?'

I hug my knees to my chest, grinning. 'Because I've missed this. I missed it a lot.'

Nate props himself up on an elbow, and smiles back. 'Me too. Glad to have you back, Stevie.'

◆ ◆ ◆

Hours later, when our plan of action is drafted, I let myself back into my flat and head to the window. I open it again and, with well-practised precision, drop my spare keys back down to him – I always forget to take mine. He catches them, waves, and we both close up for the night.

Rosie is asleep in my chair, my laptop still open on a dimmed news article about Anna Farley.

I hope I'm wrong, and Anna will turn up on her parents' doorstep alive and well in a few days. But if I'm right, and Anna is already dead just like Lauren was, then I want to help.

I have to.

CHAPTER 2

Sixteen seconds of 'Learn To Fly'. Twenty-three of 'Celebrity Skin'. Five of 'Try Honesty'. Seven of—

'Would you *stop* skipping the bloody playlist?' I slap Nate's hand away from 'When You Were Young'. 'You're driving me up the wall.'

'Fine,' he says – backhanding my knee in return. 'Put your feet down, will you? Who knows where those boots have been.'

I unfurl and shove my feet back on the floor of Mrs Piastri's old Mini. We help her out when we can – I do her shopping when her hip's playing up, and Nate uses the power of YouTube to blag enough DIY skills to fix her peeling wallpaper or leaky taps – so she didn't mind lending us the car. Not that the favours really count for much. I'm fairly sure Nate could charm his way to a stranger's car keys if he smiled hard enough.

'We're nearly there,' he says. 'Look.'

Nate turns off the main road and follows a series of winding lanes down towards Foxbridge. Like Sandford, the town is surrounded by countryside and woods and idyllic houses, then becomes denser and more concrete as you hit the urban centre. Newer housing estates circle Foxbridge, stretching up the slope of a hill in the north-east, while the middle of the town is more historic: cobbled streets, a church, rows of picturesque cottages.

No matter the area, every street has a poster with Anna Farley's face on it.

We head for the main visitor car park and get our things together. I would have been happy to explore the town and then record our thoughts back at the flat, but Nate wants the full immersive experience: interviews with locals, background noise, off-the-cuff thoughts. He fixes a portable microphone to the collar of my leather jacket, and clips his own to his chunky blue jumper, ready to catch everything. He pulls a small, professional-looking video camera out of the car boot, too.

'What's that for? You remember we're *podcasters*, right?'

'*Yes*, but it doesn't hurt to cover more bases. James Nash always posts video versions of his podcasts on YouTube now, with monetised ad breaks, and we'll get more traction on TikTok if we can include visual clips as well as audio.'

'I'm just now remembering why I hate podcasting,' I mutter, thrusting my hands in my pockets. 'Fine, but don't go shoving that in anyone's face without asking, okay?'

We set off into the town. It's sunny today, but it's the kind of October sun that makes the shadows icy by contrast. Orange leaves cling to trees, or lie in colourful piles in gutters and against walls.

Maybe this town is cute, sometimes: village fetes, firework displays. But there's an air of gloom, despite the sunshine. All the shops in the village square have the same poster in the window. The same girl's face.

It was like that in Sandford, too.

'Where should we— Ugh, Nate!'

He's right behind me with the camera, filming me look at a poster. I duck away.

'What? It was a good shot!'

'Ugh. These mics are weird enough as it is, but videoing is another level of cringe. I can't.'

'Okay, okay, I'm putting the camera down.'

'Thank you.'

'For *now*. I'm getting it out again if anything juicy happens.'

'Anything *juicy*?'

'Yeah, you know, like when I prove Anna's disappearance is nothing to do with Lauren's.'

I glare at him. 'I thought we were here to look into Anna's case as a team? For the podcast?'

'We are, we just have different theories about what happened to her, that's all. You think it's Lauren-related, and I'm going to prove it isn't.'

'I'm going to prove you wrong.'

'I look forward to seeing you try.' Nate grins at me – then drops it, his eyes drifting to Anna's missing poster. He clears his throat. 'All competition aside, let's go figure out where this girl is.'

Over the next couple of hours, we work our way around the main streets of the town, asking questions. My first attempt doesn't go well. Apparently marching into a post office and saying, '*Hi, we're podcasters, do you know anything about the girl who's gone missing?*' to the wizened old man working there who a) doesn't know what a podcast is and b) thinks you're accusing him of kidnapping, isn't the best way to start an investigation. Who knew?

Nate shows me how it's done when he targets the two middle-aged women who run the newsagent's. He strolls in under the pretence of buying a snack and smiles at them, his dark hair flicking out from under a knitted cap, bright blue eyes twinkling, head slightly tilted as they ring up his Wispa while he makes polite conversation. Then he makes a show of his smile slipping as he pretends to notice the poster on the wall behind them.

'What's that about?' he asks innocently. 'Is someone missing?'

And the ladies unleash their gossip from there.

'Such a sweet girl.'

'She wasn't the partying type. I don't know what she was doing all the way over there last weekend.'

'She wouldn't just wander off on her own. Too sensible for that. I should know, my brother was her primary school teacher.'

'I don't trust that boyfriend of hers.'

'Oh, no. Nasty boy, that Ethan. Used to come in here and steal sweets.'

'Now he steals cans of lager. Thinks we don't notice. *Nasty* boy. Where was he that night, eh? That's what I want to know.'

'And me.'

Thanks to Nate's *dazzling* smile, we leave the shop with a few recorded quotes and a local map marked with key information: the house Anna disappeared from, the road where her shoe was found a few days ago, and one of the ladies' numbers circled with a heart.

'I didn't realise the appeal of investigative podcasting was that you'd get to flirt with everyone you meet.'

'It's a little perk of the job, I suppose.' Nate winks at me, then points to another shop. 'I hope you were taking notes. You're up next. Burly bloke in the butcher's. Go flirt, girl.'

He isn't so smug once we get inside and see several rainbow flags and a signed photo of Kylie Minogue on the wall.

'Go flirt, *boy*,' I mouth, enjoying the wink far more than I should. Nate sighs, then approaches the counter with his winning smile, resting his elbows on it.

'Hey.'

As it happens, Nate was flirting with the *heterosexual* half of Goodison Brothers' Butchers, but we still manage to leave with some good information – and teasing material.

'Sorry that you weren't his type,' I say, patting Nate's shoulder. 'You'll find your prince one day.'

We hit the rest of the shops in the town square and end up in a cutesy café with *amazing* cheese toasties. We sit in the cobweb-decorated window in two mismatched armchairs, looking out at the orange bunting and hanging baskets and cobblestones.

And the missing posters.

'It's not the same killer,' says Nate, with a mouthful of cheese.

'Were you even listening to those people? It's just like in Sandford.'

'Nah. The boyfriend, Evan—'

'*Ethan.*'

'—Ethan, right, he's guilty as hell. Sounds a complete tearaway.'

'Everyone said that about Mike, too, Nate. And they were wrong then.'

'But maybe these people are right *now*. Look, I know it got us in trouble, but it *is* always—'

'Don't say it.'

'—*most likely to be* the boyfriend. You know that. So why can't it be true now?'

I put down my coffee – with care, as it's in a fiddly, may-break-at-any-moment cup – and pull Nate's notebook towards me. 'Multiple people mentioned the boyfriend, Ethan, has an alibi.'

'Pfft, those can be faked.'

'On the map, the distance between the house party Anna went missing from and the area where the shoe was found is almost identical to the locations back in Sandford near your house.'

'Coincidence.'

'The late-night prowler. That lady in the greengrocer's mentioned a car, *and* the guy in the bookshop did, too. Sleepy town, but a car driving around in the early hours. Scoping the place.'

'See, that just supports *my* theories, though, Stevie. Doesn't mean it's *your* killer. Could be my unconnected one who was doing the scoping.'

'Anna's social media. Her profile's public. The killer could have found her online and picked her out because she fits his type, and then stalked her that way.'

'Again, that helps my case for a randomer, too.'

I close the notebook and toss it on the table towards Nate. 'Why are you so closed off to this theory? I don't get it. To me it's so . . . obvious? Do you really not even think there's the *possibility* of it being the same killer?'

Nate goes to say something, then takes a bite of toastie instead.

'Why do you want it to be the same guy so badly?' he asks. 'We know how that story ends, and it's nowhere good for Anna. Is it so bad to be hoping for a happy ending instead?'

I ask myself the same question in the toilets, puffing my shoulder-grazing bob out of my face as I touch up my eyeliner. Maybe Nate's right to have this attitude. It's far healthier to be hoping for dissimilarities than to be cheering for signs that Anna is already dead.

I should want Nate to be right, too.

We head back to the car and drive to the Foxbridge equivalent of Nate's house that his newsagent admirers marked on the map. It's on the outskirts, just as Nate's was, with a big double-sided driveway and a garage, and all the hallmarks of a recent house party that went too far: bottles in hedges, a few boarded-up windows.

'Now, *this* is familiar,' Nate mutters.

We already know police searched the house and found nothing suspicious, just like in Sandford, so we didn't *need* to come here. But I thought it was important to see it.

And Nate thought it was important to video it.

'Go stand over there,' he says, holding the camera up. 'Walk mournfully, but with purpose.'

I make a rude hand gesture instead.

The shoe was found over a mile from here, and that's where several people told us the volunteers are focusing today's search. We drive on, park in a bridleway, and join the group of locals milling about between the trees. Just like in Sandford, it's a remote, rural road, surrounded by woods.

'. . . I know we've looked here before, but it can't hurt to try again,' says a man standing on a tree stump with a clipboard. 'Keep your eyes peeled for *anything*, okay? Clothing, fabric, anything that could be blood or hair. One shoe can't be all there is. Let's find something to help us find Anna today.'

The group has its instructions, and people pair off and fan out. Nate and I rush to catch the man with the clipboard before he joins them.

'Hi, my friend and I are from out of town. Are you in charge here?'

'Yes, I am. I'm Clive – family friend of the Farleys. Trying to do what I can.' He looks us up and down, lingering on the mics and Nate's camera. 'And you are?'

'Stevie, and he's Nate.' I decide to be direct. 'We're true crime podcasters. We heard about Anna's disappearance and thought maybe we could help. Can we?'

'True crime podcasters? Here, in Foxbridge? For Anna?' He darts forward and pulls us into an awkward hug, his clipboard poking me in the ear. 'Thank you! I've been trying to get Anna's disappearance out there in the press, but nobody's interested. That missing little girl is taking up all the headlines.'

'Destiny Davis?'

'Yeah, her.' He releases us and sighs. 'I don't mean to be rude. I *don't* blame people for trying to help her, she's only five, after all, and to lose your child in the playground is every parent's night-mare, but . . . Anna's important, too. She's just not newsworthy

46

right now.' He stares sadly at the locals picking their way through bracken. 'The police already searched all round here, and everywhere, really. But I think it helps morale to keep trying.'

'Is there anywhere you haven't searched?'

'Well, it's a big area. But I think between us and the police, we've covered most of it.'

'Any landmarks in the woods where she might be? Wells? Cabins? Ditches?'

'All checked. I even . . . I even checked the rivers. Nothing. I didn't want to find her there, not like that, but . . . at least it'd be an answer.' He clears his throat. 'I should go, make sure everyone's in the right area. Thanks for helping us. We really appreciate it.'

He heads off into the woods, and Nate raises his camera.

'What are you doing?'

'Getting him on video,' Nate whispers.

'Why?'

'Hello? Family friend, leading the search, happy to talk to the weird podcasters? He's probably the one who's killed her.'

'Really? You think Mr Helpful Clive did this?'

'Maybe!'

'Well, I don't remember him from Sandford, so unless he was a driver passing through back then, he couldn't—'

'Did I hear that right?' someone asks behind us. 'You're podcasters?'

Ethan, Anna's boyfriend, stands by a tree. He looks just like he did in the news article: a crew-cut fade, hoodie, ripped jeans. Times have changed and styles have moved on, but Ethan is the modern-day equivalent of Mike, even without the shaggy hair or baggy jeans.

There's a similarity in his eyes, too. The empty, haunted look in them.

'Yeah,' Nate says. The word is said politely enough, but I feel him bristle beside me. 'True crime podcasters. We're investigating the disappearance of Anna Farley – do you know anything about it?'

Ethan scoffs. 'Can't be very good investigators if you don't even know who I am.'

'We know, *Ethan*,' I say, thumping Nate in the ribs. 'We're trying to find out what happened to her—'

'And to *find* her,' Nate says.

'We've asked all around town, but we'd love to hear from you. I know it must be very difficult for you right now, but—'

'She went missing on Friday, around midnight. We were at the party together, and I was with my friends, I should have been with her, but I was with my friends, and I realised I hadn't seen her for a while, and . . .'

He doesn't stop. He spills out all the information we could ever need or want from him.

I know Nate is recording it on his mic, but he starts taking notes, too. He tilts the book at me, pointing to a word, underlining it: *REHEARSED*. I snatch the notebook away from him, shaking my head.

'. . . and that's all I know,' Ethan says, getting his breath back. 'She'd never run away, she wouldn't do that to her parents, so . . . so someone's taken her. But I have literally no idea who. She just . . . vanished.'

He turns away from us, rubbing his face.

If this is an act, Ethan is a fantastic liar.

I feel a twinge of guilt for even thinking it. Sure, this is a Gen Z heartbreaker who steals from local shops, once vandalised the war memorial with a graffitied penis, and is by all accounts a sarcastic little turd, but he's also just a teenager going through one of the worst things a person can go through.

48

I made Mike's life far harder than I should have. I won't do that to Ethan.

'Would you like to record something?' Nate asks. 'For the podcast, I mean. It can be question and answer, or—'

'You can use whatever you've already got. I know you were recording me. I saw you turn on the mic.'

'I wouldn't have used any of that without consent. It was mainly so we'd have a record of—'

'I'll give a statement as well. You can film it, too. For TikTok, right?'

Nate gives me a look that says *I told you so*, and raises the camera. Ethan fixes his hair, his collar, his eyes. He clears his throat – and smiles.

'Anna, babe, it's okay. I'm gonna find you. Wherever you are, I'll find you, and you'll be fine. 'Cause we're gonna grow old together, me and you. And we'll go to Tokyo, just like you wanted. I'm gonna find you. I'll find you.'

Ethan's smile stretches and stretches, shaking as the tears roll silently down his face. Then it snaps, and he turns and heads off into the woods, pulling his hood up, stuffing his hands into his pockets, head down.

And Nate's camera follows him.

The search itself is as fruitless as we knew it would be. Local volunteers comb the area until it grows dark, but all they find is Nate getting in their way, asking for their little recorded vox pops and snippets of any new information. Nate gets in my way, too, insisting on recording the sound of my boots in the crispy leaves, and our breathing as we walk.

'We need the podcast to be *atmospheric*,' he insists.

The search ends at nightfall. People head back to their cars, back towards town. And so do we.

49

I thought there would be more. Some scoop, some vital piece of information to make everything click for certain one way or another . . . But really, we have nothing.

Today is Episode 1 of a podcast that may never have anywhere to go.

I plug my music back in for the trip and curl up in my seat, getting comfy – but Nate turns the music off.

'That's even more annoying than when you skip it,' I say, reaching to turn it back on.

'Don't. We've got another stop to make.'

'Where?'

The dark roads snake through the trees, and I lose track of the twists and turns. Eventually Nate pulls into a lane, one without streetlamps, and we follow the glare of headlights until we reach a fence – one with a sign saying *KEEP OUT*.

Nate turns off the engine, and rubs his nose in the glow of the map on his phone.

'Some teenagers came into the café while you were in the loo,' he says. 'I asked them if this town has such a thing as an abandoned house where kids get together to drink and take drugs, and – after I bribed them by paying for three chocolate sundaes – they told me about this place.'

I scramble out of the car. It's pitch black, but the night is clear. Past the gate and off in the distance, the faint silhouette of an old farmhouse stands out against the sky. Slowly, Nate gets out, too.

'Don't get too excited,' he warns. 'The kids could've been lying, and anyway, we're not going to find anything in there. This place was already searched. I asked the volunteers earlier, and they said friends checked this place—'

'Last weekend? The day after she went missing?'

'Yeah, but that doesn't *mean* anything.'

'But with Lauren, she—'

Nate covers his face and grunts. 'Stevie, we're not here to find a dead body or anything like that. We're here so I can show you, once and for all, that it's *not* the same killer. Okay? Because if it was, she'd be in that farmhouse, because that farmhouse is just like Sandford's. And when she's not there, you have to drop this.'

'Drop it?'

'Not the *whole* thing, but the Anna-being-connected-to-Lauren thing. We leave that stupid theory behind and focus on the facts, on this being a separate case. All right? Are we agreed?'

'But what if there's another party house in this town? What if—'

'There isn't. I checked, and you can check again if you want to. But this is it. This is the thing that'll prove I'm right, and you're wrong. It's *not* the same killer.'

I zip up my leather jacket and flick my phone torch on. 'We'll see about that, won't we?'

The wooden gate is chained shut, so we climb over it as best we can in the darkness. We head up the track towards the house, dirt shifting beneath our feet, rocks threatening our balance.

'This is very *Blair Witch*,' Nate says, drawing level with me with his camera. 'How about a few snotty up-the-nose shots?'

I give him a playful shove, and he shrieks as he overbalances.

'What was *that*? Oh, just a bush. Bloody hell, that scared me . . .'

Eventually, our torchlight begins to touch the farmhouse. It's clearly deserted: cracked bricks, broken roof tiles, a rusted tractor lying on its side. The front door is boarded up.

Nate exhales, his breath misting in the torchlight. It's clear tonight, and cold. It's rural enough to see stars.

On another night, and in different circumstances, this would be nice.

'The kids said they usually get in round the back. Something about a broken door tied shut?'

We head around the back. I find the door and fiddle with the heavy chain looped from its handle to an old lantern bracket beside it, trying to get it open.

'Looks rusty,' Nate says. 'Nobody's opened that in a while. Definitely not in the last week.'

'Shut up and help me.'

'You want me to stick my fingerprints all over a *crime scene*? Are you trying to frame me?' Nate laughs, shining his torch and camera around, trying to see in through the grimy windows.

The excitement I felt in the car deflates out of me. This is ridiculous, isn't it? Why would the killer close up after themselves like this? Nate's right: nobody's been inside for weeks, if not months. The gate out front was locked. There's no way someone could have dumped a body here.

I'm not some hard-hitting journalist about to discover something incredible. I'm just a dumb podcaster chasing a hunch, because I'm selfish enough to want it to be true.

I tug the chain, hard, and the bracket disconnects from the wall – loudly, clattering on the old stone steps. The door creaks open.

I know there's nothing in there, but . . . it's worth a look anyway, right?

I raise my torch. I'm in the kitchen – a very outdated one – but there's an archway leading to another room on the far side. A living room. I enter it – nearly tripping on the old pizza boxes and beer bottles strewn across the floor. Nate was right about one thing, at least: this farmhouse was definitely used for local hangouts at some point.

I shine my torch around the room.

Old lamps, a bookcase, an armchair that probably has a family of mice living in it, a coffee table with rubbish all over it, a sofa.

A sofa with something on it.

'I can't see anything,' Nate calls from outside, his light blinding me as he scrubs at the dirty glass with his sleeve, making a hole in the years of grime. 'What about you?'

'I . . . don't know,' I say, trying to blink the glare out of the centre of my vision. I step closer to the sofa, focusing my light on it – waiting for my eyes to focus, too.

Blankets, definitely – heaped up, the folds of fabric mimicking shapes against the stained cushions. Shapes like two limp, bare feet. The curve of a body. Dark hair spread out across the armrest.

A face I already know so well.

'What's going on?' Nate calls, moving to another window. His light passes across my back, casting my shadow over the sofa, until he sees what I see. 'Is that . . . ? Oh my God.'

Outside, Nate stumbles away, swearing, and I hear him retch.

Inside, I stare down at the body of Anna Farley lying on the sofa, hands clasped around a bouquet of dead flowers – just like how they found Lauren Parker almost seventeen years ago.

At sixteen, I naively imagined that scene as angelic. In my head, Lauren lies on that old farmhouse sofa as though she's sleeping. Too pale, too still, but sleeping, like that painting of Ophelia floating with her handful of flowers. Beautiful, still. Perfect. She's just a girl who happens to be dead.

The reality is different. It's not serene or sanitised.

Regretting every movement, my eyes seek out the horrors of Anna's body.

Her face is grey, and wrong. The skin seems loose and disconnected, like a flesh fabric draped tightly over jutting cheekbones and sunken eye sockets, smoothed out but not quite secured at the chin. Either through blood loss or blood pooling, there's no colour to her.

The flowers don't cover anything. Five stab marks are gouged into her chest and neck. They're not pinpricks, but deep, angry wounds, the skin bruised around them, the cuts congealed and oozing. They're still wet; the body's slow rot making its way to the surface through them.

And blood. There's so much blood. It's soaked through her clothes, seeped into the sofa, and splattered on to her skin. Dried, crusty streaks are the only colour on her face. Her hands, arranged so neatly on top of the flowers, are dark, too.

She isn't clean. This wasn't quick. And her placement is no respectful tribute.

After seventeen years, I know exactly how Lauren Parker looked that night on the sofa.

But I wish I could go back to a time when I didn't.

CHAPTER 3

'I need to take a cheek swab now. Open your mouth, please.'

Sitting on the edge of the open boot of a police car, I do as the officer instructs me and let her take a sample of my DNA. She carefully seals the swab, and reaches for another.

'And now you, please,' she says to Nate.

'I didn't go in there,' he says, leaning forward with his hands between his knees.

'He's right. He stayed outside the whole time. I'm the only one who went in.'

The only one who disturbed a crime scene and probably trampled over a load of important evidence.

'We'll need fingerprints, too.'

'Anything you need,' I say.

When she's finished, Nate and I sit in silence.

The land around the farmhouse is abuzz with hi-vis police jackets, parked police cars, and heavy-duty lights. We're to the side of the house, kept away from the scene, but we can see the officers walking around, discussing things. An ambulance appears, but too late to do any good. The paramedics offer us warm drinks and blankets – perhaps it makes them feel better to care for *someone*.

An officer comes up from the driveway, a plastic evidence bag in his hand. Even with the reflected glare of the lights, I can see there's a shoe in it.

A shoe at the end of the driveway, just like with Lauren. I didn't even think to check.

I twist the plastic travel cup in my hands, wishing it had something other than coffee in it.

I've never seen a dead body before. Crime scene photos, sure, loads of them – but there's distance with a photograph. Faces don't quite look real; blood is always the wrong colour. You forget the horrific subject matter used to be a living, breathing person with hobbies and friends and a daily routine.

But Anna was real. I've spent the day learning about those hobbies, those friends, those daily routines, just to hammer it home.

Somehow, it would have been easier if she was one of the horror stories – the bloated victims of drowning; the faces torn beyond recognition by guns. But she wasn't. She was herself, still – an uncanny, ghoulish, hideously dead version.

A murdered version.

'I didn't think she would be in there,' Nate says, as the forensic team in their plastic suits head into the farmhouse. 'I . . . I didn't want her to be in there.'

He raises his drink, but can't swallow any of it. He's shaking.

I've never seen him like this before. Once, maybe. Back in Sandford, all those years ago. That Sunday when Lauren's disappearance became serious, and he was cleaning up after the party and the police arrived. Two nights before that, we'd pored over the horrific details in his dad's cases and discussed the goriest things we could think of.

It must hit him differently when it's in real life.

A man approaches us, wearing a suit beneath his coat. I can guess what he'll say already.

'Miss Knight? I'm Detective Inspector Chopra, and I'm the lead on this case. Can I ask you some questions?'

Nate and I already gave statements to the uniformed officers who first arrived on the scene, but we go through it again with Chopra.

Yes, we're true crime podcasters who were poking around to investigate. No, we're not from here. Yes, we both have alibis for last Friday night. And yes, we should have known better than to trample across a crime scene.

I should have known better.

'Miss Knight, what were you doing out *here* tonight? Why this town and this case? How did you know there would be a body here?'

'Because we've seen this before. This exact thing. The girl missing after the party, the shoe found by the road, the farmhouse. It happened in Sandford, our hometown, seventeen years ago. A girl called Lauren Parker died then. We heard about this case, and wondered if the same thing had happened to Anna. And it has.'

Nate crumples a little beside me, rubbing his face with his hand.

I continue. 'I know we're not detectives, but it's the same MO, the same everything as what happened in our town. It has to be the same person. They never caught them before, but there is new DNA, so maybe—'

'Lauren Parker, was it?' DI Chopra searches for her name on his phone. '*Oh*. This was the case in the news recently? That victim's partner was suspected, but then exonerated? After his reputation was ruined by two rogue podcasters? That's you, I presume?'

'Yes, but we didn't do it on pur—'

'And you think the same killer has struck again for the first time in nearly two decades?'

'Yes,' I say. 'Although maybe it isn't the first time. Maybe there were others, but nobody found a link. Anna didn't make the national news, and neither did Lauren. Others could also have gone under the radar. But it's the same killer. I'm sure of it. Lauren had flowers in her hands, too.'

Anna's hands were bloody – her fingernails rust-stained. Did she die instantly, or did she clutch at her chest? Did she try to stop the bleeding? Did she know she was dying and there was nothing she could do to stop it?

There's movement and shouting in the lane.

'Get off me. Get off me!' a man shouts, shrugging off an officer and running towards the farmhouse. As he runs into the lights, I see he's not a man, really – he's a boy in a hoodie and ripped jeans, his hair spiked up, and desperation on his face.

Ethan.

'Anna. Anna! Is she here? *Anna!*'

He runs past us and tries to get into the back of the house, but officers stop him. He must have seen the forensic team, the empty ambulance, because he wails. He falls to his knees and wails.

'I'll be back with more questions,' DI Chopra says.

He leaves us, and Nate and I stare in silence, watching Anna's boyfriend punch the ground, filled with anger and pain and confusion that has nowhere to go.

Did Lauren's boyfriend Mike do the same when he found out?

Every time a new person listened to our *It's Always the Boyfriend* episode, was he still trapped in his own private hell, reliving his own version of the worst day of his life over and over again? Or had he found peace, only for us to churn his trauma up again?

The paramedics comfort Ethan, trying to calm him – but the police officers have sterner looks. Chopra jots something down in his notebook.

There's no guarantee the police will find a concrete link. Months ago they found unidentified DNA on the knife that killed Lauren, but everything else about her was clean: the crime scene was contaminated with teenage DNA, but not her body or her clothes. What if it's the same here? Nothing to link Anna to Lauren, or to exonerate Anna's boyfriend for good.

What if nobody believes it's the same killer?

'I didn't think she'd be in there,' Nate says hollowly, still shaking. 'I'm sorry.'

'Sorry?'

'For bringing you here. For making you find her.'

'Oh. It's okay. I wanted to find her.' I rub my forehead. 'I didn't mean that. I meant, *if* something bad had happened to her, in the same way it happened to Lauren, then I wanted to help. But I didn't *want* her to be in there. I really didn't.'

'I know.'

'But at least her loved ones get an answer. Or part of one, anyway.'

Over in the ambulance, Ethan is hunched over, his hood up and his hands clamped over it.

'Nate, how are we going to explain this in the podcast?'

'The podcast? You still want to do the podcast?'

'Yes. More than ever.'

I see Anna's face again: too pale, too gaunt.

Will I ever stop seeing it?

'We found her. That means something, Nate. We have to see this through.'

Nate manages a sip of his coffee. He's coming back to himself a little.

'But, can we?' he asks. '*Should* we? This is an active case. Are we even allowed to talk about it?'

'I don't know. Maybe we can't go talking about what we saw in that house – but Anna isn't the only victim of this killer, is she?'

Nate chews on his bottom lip, and takes another sip of coffee.

'We need to go back to Sandford. We need to look at Lauren's murder again – and this time, we do it right. Because we didn't investigate it at all back then. We just told the story, and made the wrong conclusion at the end of it. But we can do it differently this time. Maybe we'll spot something new, something that could help. Maybe someone from our town now lives here, or there's some other connection we don't know yet. Maybe there are other murders to look into, and raising awareness of it with listeners will jog other people's memories about things that happened in their hometowns. While the police are investigating Anna's murder, we can go back to Lauren's. And maybe we can help to finally solve it.'

Nate fiddles with his cup. 'Are you sure you want to go back there?'

'To Sandford? It's home.'

'No, I mean . . .' He sighs. 'Poking around in Lauren's case is what ruined our podcast. It ruined an innocent man's life, too. Are you sure you want to churn all that up again?'

'The mess we made of it last time is *why* we need to investigate this, Nate.'

I fiddle with my favourite chunky ring – an ornate, Victorian-style wreath of roses surrounding a silver anatomical heart – and take in a deep, icy breath.

'My parents told me that Mike Edwards had to be hospitalised after he moved back in with his mum last year. It was a suicide attempt.'

'Oh. I didn't know that.'

'He did that because of me. Because of what I said about him on our podcast.'

'No. Don't—'

'He wanted to die because of lies *I* told.'

'It's not lying when you believe it, Stevie! You didn't do anything wrong.'

'I did. I ruined his life, and I deserve every single one of those threatening emails and insulting Twitter replies. I deserve worse than that. Whoever killed Lauren was happy to let Mike take the fall for it, and we spread that rumour like it was truth. We should have thought about it, evaluated it, but we didn't. We lapped it up just like everyone else in Sandford, and then broadcasted it to the world. We were wrong – factually *and* morally. I don't know if this new podcast will change the way any of those people think of me, but I need to do it to change the way I think of myself. Because unless I do something to help fix the mess I made, I'll never be able to forgive myself.'

'You're doing this to . . . make it up to Mike?'

'Yeah. I know he'll never forgive me, but I want to help find the person who ruined his life before I did. I *need* to. Otherwise I won't be able to move on with mine.'

Nate drains his coffee. He looks up, and I do, too: the stars we saw before are hidden in the glare of the lights. I shiver in the cold, my socked feet in plastic shoe covers because my boots were taken as evidence. Nate pulls off his warm knitted hat and puts it on me.

'If this is what you want,' he says, grabbing my hand, 'I'll do it. I'll go back to Sandford with you.'

We've never held hands before, we're not those kinds of people, but I squeeze his back.

I lean my head on his shoulder, closing my eyes so I don't have to look at Ethan crying, or Anna being stretchered into the ambulance in a body bag. I try not to think about the same happening with Mike and Lauren seventeen years ago.

I don't know if Anna is the only other victim of this killer since then – but maybe I can help make sure she's the last.

CHAPTER 4

Nate and I record our first Anna episode while it's still fresh, lacing in the local interviews and on-site recordings with the hindsight we now share – but I get Nate to promise not to post it until DI Chopra gives us the go-ahead. It's bad enough to be the podcasters who falsely accused an innocent man, but being the podcasters who wreck an active investigation by sharing sensitive information and giving the killer time to cover his tracks? No way.

But someone else from Foxbridge isn't so conscientious.

Anna Farley's disappearance didn't make the national news – but the fact that her body was found by two true crime podcasters does.

> TRUE CRIME SCENE: Podcasters help discover missing girl's body

> Podcasters swap mics for yikes in shocking crime scene discovery

> True crime podcasting duo find murder victim in rural town – but why were they there?

At first, it's just headlines, and we're two anonymous podcasters connected to a random death – but then someone IDs us, they find out which case we're 'famous' for, and the rumours begin.

It starts small scale: threads on our Facebook page, our Twitter mentions, our Reddit sub. Fans – we still have a few, I guess – look up Anna's disappearance and see exactly the same similarities to Lauren's as I did. Then it spreads among the true crime community, and to the comment sections underneath news articles. Views on our *It's Always the Boyfriend* episode spike. DI Chopra bats away a question about a link at a small press conference.

But we know. We all know.

Especially after Nate decides to release Episode 1 of our new Anna podcast regardless.

'*Seventeen years ago,*' Nate's voice says in the shareable teaser he released alongside it, '*Lauren Parker was murdered in the town of Sandford. She left a party and was never seen alive again.*' Lauren's old school photo fades out, and footage of boots – my boots, now impounded as evidence – walking through fallen leaves in the woods replaces it.

'*We made assumptions back then,*' my voice says, '*and it led to us – to me – blaming the wrong person. We can't undo the damage we did to an innocent man's life, but we can try to right that wrong.*'

Shots of Foxbridge, of its pretty cobblestone square and orange-leafed trees. And then me, from the back. Staring at a poster attached to a black lamp post.

'*Just days ago,*' Nate says, '*a girl named Anna Farley went missing after a party, in a small town just like Sandford. So we went there.*' Night-time. '*We looked around.*' The farmhouse. '*And we found something.*'

A split second of me with my phone torch through the dirty window, the room out of focus, and then the reaction caught on my mic: the sharp, horrified intake of breath as I saw Anna's body lying on that sofa.

It cuts away to a black screen.

'*Seventeen years ago, we got it wrong,*' I say. '*But we won't get it wrong this time. Join me, Stevie Knight—*'

'*—and me, Nate Blackwell—*'

'*—as we investigate two murders almost two decades apart, and do what we can to finally get justice for both of these young women.*'

Words fade in, stark white against the black: *When It Happens Again*, from the makers of *All the Gory Details*.

When we started *Gory Details*, I didn't think anyone would listen to it – and that was okay. Embarrassing, maybe, but okay. I didn't expect the fans, the catchphrase they latched on to, the requests for us to sell merchandise . . .

But this time, I *want* people to listen. I need them to hear about Anna, to stick around to hear the real story of Lauren. And I think they are, judging by the numbers on our streaming platforms, and the engagement on our Twitter teaser.

OMG I knew there was more to this!!!

So glad you two are back! <3

Stop profiting off other people's tragedies

Can't believe you'd interfere with a police investigation like this. Actually, I CAN believe it.

Attention seekers

Whose life are you gonna ruin this time?

Nate whacks my leg from the driver's seat, tutting.

'One, stop looking at Twitter because you *know* it always upsets you, and two, feet off the bloody seat!'

'They're brand-new boots, Nate. Virgin soles. They won't leave a mark anywhere.'

He tuts again, and continues on the A3 towards Sandford. I put my phone away, focusing on the episodes to come rather than the one already out in the world.

We left it a few days before coming back to Sandford. Nate needed to work some bar shifts – Mrs Piastri's flexible about rent, but not *that* flexible – and I needed some research time.

The Boyfriend – Mike Edwards – was the only person I ever suspected of killing Lauren Parker. It was a teenage hunch that solidified over the years when nothing popped up to contradict it, so by the time Nate and I recorded our episode about the murder, it was practically fact for me. There were never any solid alternative theories, either – the case wasn't interesting enough to warrant other podcasters covering it. And even when James Nash – a former detective turned investigative podcaster – did his own episode in the wake of the DNA evidence and Mike being exonerated in the court of public opinion, he was mostly just using it as an excuse to bad-mouth Nate and me in every way possible. He's hated us since we ranked higher than him on the *Best New Podcasts of 2019* list.

Even after all these years, the possible theories are the same as the ones we floated in *It's Always the Boyfriend*: stranger, local, or Mike.

Ruling out Mike – the only suspect the evidence ever pointed towards – doesn't exactly help. But I have a few ideas of where we *may* be able to find some information that does.

It's grey in Sandford today. It's raining in that heavy, oppressive way: large droplets plummeting straight down, hammering on the windscreen and bouncing off the ground.

Sandford has been grey for years. No amount of Christmas lights or summertime flower displays can cover the darkness of this town, however hard the local committees try. Perhaps the same will happen in Foxbridge. It was picture-perfect the other day, but the memory of missing posters and police tape will linger long after they're taken down.

We park outside my childhood home and run inside to look for umbrellas.

'Good thing you remembered your keys this time,' Nate says, shaking his wet hair like a dog. 'Where are your parents? Poland?'

'Lithuania. Apparently Fleetwood Mac is massive there. They get invited back all the time.'

My parents have always loved the spotlight, and the spotlight loves them – no other cover band goes quite so hard on replicating the tempestuous relationship of Lindsey Buckingham and Stevie Nicks onstage. After growing up in the front row, I *much* prefer being an anonymous session guitarist in the recording studio, and going back home to obscurity.

All the Gory Details changed that a bit, though.

I dig a large umbrella out of the stand by the front door for Nate, and head upstairs to my room. I definitely had a multicoloured umbrella knocking around here somewhere . . .

'This is like the olden days,' Nate says, twirling the big umbrella by its hooked handle. 'Hanging out in your room when it rains. I'm glad we've ditched the baggy low-rise jeans, though. Remember the wet hems?'

'They'd get ripped to pieces.' I dig through my drawer of old jeans, and pull out a pair. 'Look, ribbons! Why do I still have these?'

Even though I haven't lived at home since leaving for uni, my parents never changed my room. I took bits and pieces with me, but there's a childhood's worth of things still in here. Placebo posters on the walls; hundreds of CDs – and *cassettes* – stacked up on shelves; tubes of liquid eyeliner that are either dust, or teeming with enough bacteria to have created new life.

I check around for the umbrella, knowing that my habit of 'tidying' surfaces by scraping whatever's on them into the drawer below started long ago. Eventually, I find it – beneath a pile of old shag bands, and with a necklace caught in the spokes. I unpick it, and run my thumb over the pendant: the jigsaw piece with a dark gem on it, fixed on a black cord, with the word *best* punched into it.

The *nostalgia* of it! August and I bought these . . . what, *twenty* years ago? More? Me with the *best* piece, and her with the matching *friends*. We used to wear them all the time, until we got too cool. I glance at the photo collage on my wardrobe doors, looking for the picture. There. Us at the London Dungeon one summer, my hair a lot longer and blonder than it is now, hers dark and frizzy, both of us grinning as we stand either side of a hooded waxwork holding up a decapitated head. Wearing our necklaces.

'Ah, I remember that night,' Nate says, joining me at the wardrobe. He points to a photo beside the one of August – us at a party a year or so after Lauren's death, his skinny jeans even skinnier than mine, sharing popcorn together while we watch a gory movie nobody else in the room can even look at. August's family had moved away by then.

'That was that dodgy German VHS, wasn't it? I think Gary actually puked when it got to the bit with the fingers.'

'Yeah. Good times.'

I stare at the London Dungeon photo again. It's strange to think of now, but before Nate, there was August. We did everything together: terrifying the other girls at sleepovers with our horror stories, sneaking into 15-rated films at the cinema, piercing each other's ears – and nursing the resulting infections. We were inseparable.

But then a few months after we went to Nate's party and became a trio, she and her family moved away. We lost touch, as old friends do. I can't even remember the last time we spoke.

Now it's just Nate and me.

I toss the necklace back into the drawer. I bet August threw hers away years ago.

Nate and I set up our recording equipment like we did in Foxbridge, and head from my house into town. We have the same plan: talk to people, get some soundbites, visit the important locations in the story. But I don't know what the reception is going to be like.

I haven't been back here since *Gory Details* went on hiatus. Some locals always resented that our podcast had churned up the town's darkest secret, but others were happy for a few new true crime visitors in the pubs, and for the confirmation of their own beliefs. I wasn't alone in blaming Mike for the death of his girlfriend. Even after the police released him, a lot of the town turned their backs on him. Shopkeepers wouldn't serve him; people stopped talking when he entered the room.

Lauren Parker was our local murder victim – and even without a conviction, Mike Edwards was our local murderer.

He moved away to escape that reputation. I can only imagine how bad our listeners made his life for him to choose to come back.

We make our way around the old hotspots: pubs, cafés, the main shops. Places with the biggest gossipers. The old faces – who used to be much *less* old – all know us. Or me, anyway. I used to just be the weird girl in headphones, the daughter of the overzealous Fleetwood Mac tribute duo who won the talent show every Christmas, but now I'm Stevie Knight the podcaster.

Whether that's a good or a bad thing depends on the individual.

Mrs Davies in the bookshop doesn't want anything to do with us, but Mr Banks in the fish shop across the road waves us in.

'Heard the radio show is a-go again,' he says, beheading a trout. 'Excellent. Could you give this place a mention this time? You could tell everyone Lauren's last meal was fishcakes.'

'Was it?' Nate asks.

'No, but since when do you two let the truth bother you?'

We dash from building to building with our umbrellas, testing my new boots' claim to be waterproof. As expected, the locals don't have anything of value to share. They either have no clue about other possible suspects or suspicious activity – as confirmed by Mr Norris, the leader of the neighbourhood watch, who loves showing off more than he hates us, so was willing to check his records to confirm that no, *actually*, he didn't miss anything – or they cling to the only narrative they've ever known as confirmed by the women in Lauren's mum's old hair salon, who share their theories about Mike being a prolific serial killer of brunettes, or raising his secret love child Ethan to follow in his murderous footsteps.

It's almost a relief when we check in with the estate agents' – former classmates of ours, now married with three kids and *very* smug about it – who dig out some old records to confirm that nobody left town shortly after the murder except Lauren's parents and August's family, and as far as they know nobody from here has recently moved to Dorset with murderous intent, and had we considered the murder might have been committed by Victorian ghosts punishing teens for having sex out of wedlock?

'How could we have been so stupid?' Nate says when we escape back on to the street. 'Of *course* it was frigid ghosts. Duh.'

'Watch out, you don't want the ghosts to get wind of *your* sex life. You'll be executed on the spot.'

He kicks a puddle at me, and sighs. 'Now what? Nobody here knows anything.' He taps his camera. 'We've got a whole load of nothing.'

'*So far*. But I think I know someone we can talk to. Well, if he agrees.'

'Who?'

'Benkins' brother.'

'Again, *who*?'

'You remember Benkins, right? Ben Jenkins? Once locked himself in a bathroom at a party and redecorated all four walls with his own vomit?'

'Oh, *that* Benkins.'

'Yeah, him. Well, his brother's a couple of years older than us, and he's a mechanic now, or so Facebook tells me – but back then, he was a police officer.'

'Was he?'

'Yep. Started the summer before Lauren disappeared, but quit by the end of the year. And that's exactly the timeframe we have questions about.'

'Questions that a *serving* police officer wouldn't be able to answer?'

'Bingo. I know he wasn't a *detective*, but I remember him being involved in the searches of the woods and stuff. He's bound to know more about it than we did back then.'

Jon – although it's weird to call him anything other than 'Benkins' brother' – works at a garage tucked away behind the main shops, more for quick, dirty repairs than by-the-book servicing. We head in through the open doors, grateful to get out of the rain. There are a few mechanics at work, and a drill cuts over the loud radio playing in the corner.

'. . . *with Sussex Police advising those in the area to avoid Brighton Pier and the surrounding beaches until—*'

'Can I help you, love?' A burly man with a shaved head comes over, wiping his oily hands.

'I'm looking for Jon Jenkins? Does he work here?'

'Yeah, if you can *call* it working. Jonkins! Over here! Got yourself a couple of admirers.'

The man leaves, and Jon comes over to us, throwing some banter back to his colleague. 'Hi, how can I . . .' His smile fades as he sees the camera and the microphones on our coats. 'This is about Lauren, isn't it?'

Jon was always tall and thin, even when he was a kid in the primary school playground. But when he mentions Lauren, his face looks gaunt. Despite the tattoos on his arms, he seems like that kid again. He gestures to the radio, which has switched back to playing tinny music.

'Heard about that other murder last week. Just like Lauren's, they're saying. That's why you're here, isn't it? Because it's the same killer?'

'We think so,' I say, trying to be tactful. 'We have some questions. Would it be all right if we asked them?'

He scratches his short hair. 'I guess, but . . . I don't know what I can say. I did everything I could to help last time around.'

I didn't know Jon or his younger brother well at all, but people talk.

Jon didn't leave the police because he was bored.

We cram into a small office room – I'm *very* aware that my new boots are squeaking – and Nate sticks the camera in his face.

'Don't film me,' Jon says. 'This has to be off the record. Please.'

'That's okay, it is,' I say. 'You can be anonymous.'

'Good.' He sighs, and starts fiddling with a ball of elastic bands. 'What do you want to know?'

I resist the urge to say *everything*. 'Were there ever any other suspects aside from Mike Edwards?'

'Kind of. She was a seventeen-year-old girl, so they looked into all the local sex offenders and stuff.'

'Who were they?' I ask, grabbing Nate's closed notebook and opening it, pen at the ready.

'I can't name names, but they weren't proper suspects anyway. She wasn't, you know . . . She was stabbed, that's all. Nothing sexual.'

'Was there anyone else? Family members, friends? Local weirdos *not* already on a register?'

'Not that I remember. We thought she was missing at first, as in, *lost*. Like, we'd find her in the woods or something. But then they found that shoe.'

'Who found the shoes? The first one was a dog walker, and the second was a farmer, right?'

'Yeah, McClusky. His was the one off that road near the farmhouse, a mile or so away.'

'Does he still live there?' I turn to Nate. 'We could ask him some questions, too. I've always wondered about—'

'He died. About ten years ago, now.'

'Oh. Do you remember, was that his usual route? Did he walk there a lot?'

'I don't know, I didn't interview him. I didn't do the interviews. I was just . . . there. I helped with the searches, I looked around, I took notes.'

Nate shifts beside me. 'So, Mike really was the only suspect? How did the officers feel when you had to let him go?'

'Frustrated, I guess. We wanted to solve it. We wanted justice for her.'

'But how did you feel about *Mike*? Be honest – did *you* think you were letting a killer walk?'

'Nate,' I say, 'what are you on about? You know Mike didn't—'

'Because so many things pointed to him, didn't they?' Nate continues. 'His relationship with Lauren, his weak alibi, the way his van was found torched in that field outside town. Keys were in the ignition, we're they? How did the police reconcile that?'

'I don't know.' Jon scratches at his arm, not looking at us. 'I wasn't with the police that long. I found the body, and then—'

'Wait, *you* found Lauren?' I ask.

'Yeah. Well, I mean, I saw it first. They'd already checked the farmhouse the week before, but we were told to check it again after McClusky found the shoe. My boss told me to check the back rooms . . . and that's where she was. On the sofa.'

I swallow uncomfortably. 'I didn't realise you were actually *there*, Jon.'

'Yeah, I was. Wish I hadn't been, though.'

Before we got to the garage, Jon was probably laughing and joking with his fellow mechanics. Now, he's a shell. I know he's reliving it: the creak of the farmhouse floorboards, the dim light, the smell. The dead petals festering in a chest wound.

I know, because I've lived that sight, too.

Nate presses on about Mike, but I cut him off with a question of my own.

'Who torched the van?'

'Mike's van? We thought he did at first, but then . . . I don't know. Vandals, he said. We never caught anyone.'

'Did things like that happen in Sandford a lot when we were younger? Joyrides, destroying cars? Dumping them in fields?'

'A bit, maybe, with old bangers.'

'Mike's van wasn't an old banger, though. He used it for his band stuff. It had those cool decals on the side. What were they, flames? Creepy angels?'

'Something like that.'

'Why all the van questions?' Nate asks me, as though Jon isn't here.

'Tell you in a bit,' I say, because Jon *is* here. 'Jon, why didn't police find the murder weapon back in 2006?'

'I don't know. We looked, I swear. I heard it was buried somewhere, and it got churned up somehow during the construction work. They've torn that place down now and they're building a new house. I wouldn't want to live there. I . . . I don't even go out that way any more.'

Jon is so pale. He must have thought joining the police in Sandford would mean traffic stops, shoplifters, the occasional drunken fight. Instead he got the worst crime our town has ever known – and he saw it up close.

I don't blame him for quitting.

'I have to get back to work now. My boss is calling me.'

We know it's a lie, as the whirring of tools and the muffled jingles on the radio are the only sounds, but we take the hint. He walks us out, still not meeting our eyes.

'Jon,' I say, just before we part. 'I'm so sorry to ask this, but I *need* to know. You saw Lauren's body, right?' He nods. 'Her wounds, they were . . . like this?'

I point to the spots on my chest where Anna's injuries were: five deep, messy punctures on her upper chest.

'Yeah,' Jon says. 'Yeah, just like that. Exactly.'

When we're out and under our umbrellas, I turn to Nate.

'In 2006, everyone thought Mike torched his own van to destroy the evidence of Lauren's murder. But his DNA isn't on the murder weapon, so we know he didn't kill her. His alibi was genuine. He had nothing to hide. So either some local toerags just happened to vandalise the prime suspect's van, or someone did it on purpose. Someone who was very happy to let the police distract themselves with the theory that it's always the boyfriend.'

'You think the killer was trying to *frame* Mike?'

'Yep. And it basically worked, didn't it?'

Before Nate and I continue through town to the woods, we go to the church. The rain lets up a little as we get to Lauren's grave. I haven't looked at it in years. It used to be shiny and new, and surrounded by flowers and tokens and photos protected from the elements in plastic wallets. But it's been seventeen years, and time has worn away the sheen. The friends who used to visit have grown up and left town, or just stopped coming. Her parents moved away years ago, but I think they still visit. Christmas, birthdays. Death day. There will be fresh flowers here soon for her, rather than the old, shrivelled ones in the vase.

I get a flash of it: Anna lying on that sofa, dead flowers in her dead hands.

I stoop down and pull out the wet, mushy bouquet from Lauren's grave, feeling rose thorns stab my palm, and shove them in the bin on the way out.

We walk the long way to Nate's old house, following the posh road out of town: a lane that winds from the outskirts through the start of the woods, its twists and the trees between them offering lots of privacy. Too much, as Lauren discovered that night.

'I hate it here,' Nate mutters as we walk up the short driveway to the gates. He glares at the house – a big, mock-Tudor monstrosity. But I know it isn't just the architecture he has a problem with.

Back when we were teens, Nate's house had everything: huge TVs, games, snacks. The case files. But we hardly ever hung out here. Even if we could hide away from his brother Charles' pestering and somehow not disturb his stepmum Christine's near-constant and hyper-sensitive meditative yoga sessions, Nate was always on edge, eyes quick to flick to the door, waiting for his dad to come home and the cold, calm berating to start.

'Nathaniel, I told you to put these away in the garage. Don't make me ask again.'

'I won't tolerate grades like these, and neither will the top universities. No son of mine is going to a polytechnic.'

'How do you expect to join the law firm if all you do is laze about? You can't just waltz in with no education and demand a spot at the table. The Blackwell name can only take you so far.'

It was easier to go to my house.

Nate doesn't like to talk about his childhood much, but I know the basics: a mum sick with cancer who died too young, and a dad who remarried too soon after he was widowed – bringing along a half-brother who was born *before* Nate's mum died. It's no wonder Nate's avoided his family – and the memory of this house – as much as possible for almost two decades. It was cursed long before it became the last place Lauren was seen alive.

'Should we be here?' I ask, my hands wrapped around the gate railings. 'What if the owners are home?'

'I own it. Well, Dad does. He never got around to selling it. Too many memories, he said. More like he just can't be bothered.'

'Wow. Can't believe I'm friends with someone whose dad is rich enough to *forget* to sell a whole house – and yet I still have to buy my own drinks.'

Nate doesn't laugh. Looking closer, I can see the house isn't lived in. The bushes are too overgrown, and paint has peeled a little from between the timbers. A few roof tiles are missing.

'Shall we get some video?' I ask. 'For TikTok?'

'Not here.' Nate stuffs his hand in his pocket. 'Let's just get on with Lauren's walk.'

We follow the woodland roads until we reach the spot where Lauren's shoe was found, the Monday after she went missing. When this all first happened, Nate, August, and I came here multiple times, tiptoeing around the trees, looking for anything that might be evidence. We never found anything then, and we don't find anything now. But we have information.

'Nineteen minutes by foot,' I say, checking the time. 'But it would probably be longer, because it was pitch black, and she didn't have a torch. How did she find her way so far?'

'Maybe she wasn't alone? Maybe her killer had the torch, and they were talking together before he attacked?'

76

'Maybe.' I walk around the trees some more, digging through the leaves with my toe. 'The shoe always bothered me, you know.'

'What do you mean?'

'Losing a flat ballet shoe in the initial struggle, right here? Sure, makes sense. But the second one, outside the farmhouse? Bit careless from a killer who left zero DNA evidence, isn't it? How did he lose *two* shoes?'

'Maybe he didn't. Maybe Lauren realised she was in danger and left them there, as clues? So people might be able to find her.'

'Well, that's a horrible thought.'

'Everything about this case is horrible, Stevie.'

We continue to the farmhouse. The distance between it and Nate's house is greater than the equivalent distance between the party house and farmhouse in Foxbridge, and Sandford's is more remote: not just down a lane, but down several, over a narrow stone bridge, and then down a dirt track. Difficult to get to by road, but easy for kids on bikes to get there through the other side of the woods.

We walk down the track, but it's nothing like what I remember from the times I visited as a teenager. I knew it wouldn't be.

The farmhouse has been torn down, and in its place a house that's going to be even uglier than Nate's is being constructed. Metal fences close off the area, and behind them there are mounds of dirt, a half-constructed building, and heaps of materials.

'I'm glad it's gone,' Nate says.

'They should tear down the one in Foxbridge. Maybe they'll find the murder weapon in the ground there, too.'

Nate doesn't respond. He just stands there, staring at the spot where the farmhouse used to be.

I bite my lip. Something isn't right with Nate. I first noticed it at his house, when he didn't want to record like he did in Foxbridge, but it started earlier than that, didn't it? Pressing the Mike questions on Jon; following sluggishly behind me instead of steaming ahead with his camera. It's like his heart isn't in it today.

I let my eyes drift, wondering how to address this weirdness, and they settle on a tree. Words are carved into the bark, like a love declaration meant to last a lifetime – but there's no love in this.

IT WAS THE BOYFRIEND.

I miss the days when this case was that simple.

I miss being certain.

'Nate, what's going on with you?'

'Huh?'

'You're being weird. In Foxbridge, I couldn't stop you filming stuff and getting involved, but you don't even seem like you want to be here. So, what's going on?'

He sighs, and tugs his hat a little lower over his hair.

'Sorry. It's just . . . being back here. It's not good for me. This place was your home, but it was never mine. I couldn't wait to leave. The only good thing that ever happened to me in this town was meeting you.'

'Well, that's a lie,' I say. 'What about that time you found a bag of weed in the gutter over on Jones Street?'

He gives me a half smile. 'Okay, *two* good things. But that's still not much.'

I kick at a clump of sodden leaves. 'I don't really like being back here, either. Christmases, visiting my parents – that's all fine, because that's fun family stuff. It's everyday life. But the murder side of things . . .'

I follow Nate's gaze to the building site, imagining the farmhouse in its place. With a better idea than ever of what was inside it.

'I know this will make me sound like a psychopath, but for years I *liked* that we had this local unsolved mystery,' I say. 'I loved true crime, and true crime came to my doorstep. What more could a weird girl want, right? But since everything happened with the podcast, and especially since the farmhouse in Foxbridge, and finding Anna, seeing her up close . . . It's all too real, isn't it? It's not a strange story from the past any more.'

Nate is still staring at the house. 'It changes you, seeing something like that.'

'Yeah.' I consider telling him how I can't wash the smell out of my hair, how I can't sleep because I keep seeing her posed on that dirty sofa, her grey feet wilted against the fabric, her face like a mask – but I don't. 'I'm so glad you didn't have to see her up close like I did.'

Nate takes a deep breath. 'Stevie—'

'It's true, then?' a voice shouts behind us, making us jump. 'It *is* you?'

A man comes out of the woods from the direction of town, his Converse caked in mud and his clothes sodden. His cheeks are flushed an angry red, and his fists are clenched.

I step backwards, against the tree with its carving. He laughs.

'Still believe it then, do you? Think I'm gonna hurt you, like you said I hurt her?' He points to the building site. 'You never had a clue what happened there, did you?'

'. . . *Mike?*

'Oh, Mike? I have a name now, do I? Thought I was just the guilty boyfriend to you pricks.'

He looks so different now. Gone are the good looks, the shaggy hair, the bad-boy charm. His hair has been shaved away to nothing, and heavy bags distort the green eyes all the girls loved staring into back in high school.

I used to think he'd be a rock star, that he'd leave this town and never look back.

But our podcast made sure he couldn't.

I swallow the awkward lump in my throat.

'Mike, I'm so sorry for what I said in that episode. I didn't think, I—'

'Yeah, that's obvious. You didn't think about *any* of it. I had an alibi. The police let me go without charge. I had *nothing* to do with any of it. And yet people keyed my car with *murderer*. I lost my job. My friends. My life. *Again*. All because of you!'

He stomps forward – and so does Nate.

'Stay back,' Nate says, tossing the umbrella away. 'Don't go near her.'

'I'll go where I want. You can't stop me.'

'I can, actually.'

'Oh! Posh boy's been taking boxing lessons, has he? Did Daddy pay for those? Let's see if he wasted his money on you. The mental side of your education clearly didn't stick.'

I dart forward and grab Nate's wrist.

'Let's go, Nate.' He doesn't want to budge, but I tug him until he moves.

'Oh, running away, are you? Cowards. *Fucking cowards.* Falsely accuse me, and can't even look me in the eye? What happened to that apology, huh? What happened to making things right?'

This time, I'm the one who goes back.

'That's what we're here for, Mike.'

'Really?' He reaches forward, fast, and flicks the mic clipped to my jacket. ''Cause it looks like you're just trying to profit off Loz's death. *Again*.'

'That's not what we're doing,' I say, quietly.

'Yeah, it is. It's all you ever do. Chew people up and spit 'em out. Wreck lives and run off with your own good one. This isn't about Loz or that other girl, it's about *you*. It's about—'

'Help us,' I say. 'We're trying to do the right thing here. We want to investigate it properly, so help us. Let us interview you. Give us your side of things. Help us understand what happened that night, and what *you* think happened that night. Help us do the right thing. *Please.'*

Mike's mouth – lips cracked, stubble flecked with grey – moves, like he can't decide which words to voice. In his eyes, up close like this, I see a flash of who he used to be.

Then he spits at the ground beside me.

'Help you? I wouldn't piss on you if you were on fire. Leave.' The word is intense, his face twitching with rage. 'And don't fucking come here again.'

He storms off into the trees, heading back towards town. Back to whatever life he's been able to salvage since his name got cleared.

'Wait!'

I can't let the conversation end like this. I run after him, trying not to slip in the mud. Nate grabs for my arm, but I pull away, leaving him with nothing but my umbrella. The path to town curves round and back on itself as it descends, but I cut the corner and slide down a bank, through the overgrown bushes – and Mike grabs me by the shoulders at the bottom.

'Leave me alone,' he snarls. His grip gets tighter. 'Don't make me—'

'Someone torched your van to frame you,' I blurt. 'They wanted it to look like you were hiding something, so they stole your van and destroyed it.'

His fingers twitch. 'I . . . I could never prove it. Nobody would listen.'

'Well, I'm listening now. Did you ever find out who did it?'

'No.' Mike lets go of me and crosses his arms. 'Someone must've taken the keys from my bag.'

'Where? When?'

'I don't know. The . . . Thursday? It was before Loz was found. I went to one of those vigils for her, at the church, and then I went searching with some friends. When I got back home, my van was gone.'

'Who was there that night? Who could have stolen it?'

Mike shrugs, shaking his head. 'It could've been anyone. Loads of us used to go to those things when she was missing. The whole town. You should know. You were always there, too. Both of you.'

'Stevie!'

Nate catches up to us, glaring.

'Wait, I still wanted to ask you about—'

But Mike heads off down the path, his fists clenched. He doesn't look back.

'What was that about?' Nate asks, holding my umbrella over me. There's not much point: I'm already soaked. 'What did you say to him?'

'I asked him about his van keys.'

'Why?'

'Because they might be the best chance we have of solving this thing. He thinks someone stole his keys at one of the vigils. On the Thursday, he said.'

'So?'

'*So*, if the killer took the van to frame Mike, it means they were still in town six days after the murder. That means Lauren's murder wasn't a random act done by a random person passing through town, someone who hung out in the woods for a day and dumped her body in the farmhouse the following night. It was a local.'

'Well, it could still have been a visitor, but—'

'No. To frame Mike, the killer had to know who he was, and where he'd be. They needed to be able to get close enough to steal the keys. They needed to know where the van would be, and where to dump it. Nate, they needed to know where the *farmhouse* was.'

I start back towards the car, feeling a buzz inside me, a spring in my step – even though my boots are rubbing my feet to ribbons.

'We can throw out the other theories. Whoever killed Lauren and framed Mike knew both of them. And for all we know, we might've known the killer, too.'

◆ ◆ ◆

Mike must have dropped by my parents' house before following us to the woods, because when we get back, there's a message waiting for us on the car: *LIARS* is keyed into both sides.

'Piastri's going to kill us,' Nate says, touching the etched words. 'We'll be running errands for her for months, even after we pay for repairs.'

'*We?*' I joke. 'Aren't you the one with the rich dad? Couldn't he sell a house or two to cover the cost? Or let you pawn a diamond cufflink?'

'It's not exactly my dad's style to help me out of messes that he deems *self-inflicted*. That's what the money Mum left me is for.'

'Oof, that must be running dangerously low by now.'

He smiles. 'Don't remind me. That's why *we're* paying for repairs, okay?'

I chuck the umbrellas back in my parents' house then join him in the car, kick off my boots and wiggle my wet toes, wishing I'd brought spare socks. I grab my phone cable.

While I scroll through playlists, trying to find a good one to fit our oncoming brainstorming session, a radio presenter tells us about some major incident in Brighton. A body was found on the seafront earlier today, and local services are appealing for information from any possible eyewitnesses from the previous night, and offering support to those affected.

'You know something grim's happened when they're offering support to the general public,' Nate says, starting the car. 'Probably a decomposing corpse got washed up. See if you can find some pictures on Twitter.'

But when I hit a playlist – early 90s' grunge, classic – I don't go on Twitter. I open a new file and type in everything I can think of, letting the connections form, getting down threads of theory before they disappear.

There's no way a body on a beach could be as interesting as *this*.

EPISODE 10: MURDERY-GO-ROUND

'Do you like hearing about gruesome murders?'

'Good, because we *love* talking about them. This is *All the Gory Details*, the true crime podcast.'

Intro music plays – drums, electronica, sirens – before fading away.

'Hey, weirdos! Welcome back to another episode of your favourite murder show—'

'Bit optimistic with the *favourite* there, Nate.'

'—where we discuss all the disgusting stuff you *can't* talk about at the dinner table. And trust me, we've got a really sick one for you today. Before Stevie and I get started, I just wanted to say thank you to all the listeners who've reached out to us with their own local murder stories so far. We've had so many emails—'

'He means three emails.'

'Three and a half if you count that person who signed us up for an erectile dysfunction newsletter. Virus-ridden spam or not, we really appreciate the support we've had for this creepy little podcast of ours. Who knew we'd make it as far as ten episodes?'

'Not me. But apparently our three listeners—'

'Three *and a half*.'

'—like what we're about for some reason, so here we are. Ten episodes in.'

'And with plenty more horrific murders to come. We can probably keep going forever, Stevie. There will always be some new, weird, horrible thing happening for us to talk about. Did you hear the story about the girl who jumped off a cliff outside Brighton earlier this year? Turns out she was actually pushed—'

'—by her *boyfriend*. Yeah, I heard.'

'Bet you loved that one, didn't you?'

'I told you, Nate, it's *always* the boyfriend!'

'Is it hard to date guys when, you know, you're convinced they'll kill you?'

'Correction – I don't think boyfriends, by default, kill their girlfriends. But it's like when I'm walking home and it's dark. Any man I pass on the street *could* attack me, so I have to be aware of that, and protect myself as if they *will*.'

'Not all men are creeps, though.'

'I never said they were.'

'But you said *any* man—'

'In a line-up of ten ordinary men, one's a wrong'un. But I don't know which one. So I have to treat them like they're *all* wrong'uns. Get it?'

'Wait, are women at night thinking *I'm* a wrong'un?'

'Almost certainly.'

'Damn. What if I buy myself a T-shirt that says, *Good guy, not going to murder you*?'

'Then I'd think you were *definitely* going to murder me.'

'Oh. There's no winning, is there?'

'Not while men like murdering women, no.'

'*Some* men, not all – ow! I've got to stop letting you have bottlecaps.'

'Shall we get on to today's real-life wrong'un?'

'Please. Especially since no women were harmed by men in the making of this story. Although perhaps our killer was shaped into the warped and twisted individual they became by an unaffectionate mother who – ow! What was that for?'

'Don't blame women for men being killers!'

'What if it was legit bad parenting, though?'

'Then *Daddy* needs to take his share of the blame, too.'

'Ugh, I didn't realise this had turned into feminist podcast hour. For the tape, Stevie is scowling because she can't reach another bottlecap with her cat on her lap.'

'I'm not above throwing the cat, to be honest.'

'I jest, I jest. Feminism matters, and men are absolute trash. As this story will once again prove. So, it's 1998 in Blackpool, which is a British seaside town in the north-west. Think fish and chips, donkey rides on the sand, the Pleasure Beach theme park, a pier. All that stuff.'

'A man named Fred Barker is on holiday there with his wife and two kids. His wife is a bit ill—'

'Hungover from too much Lambrini in the arcade, more like.'

'—and the kids are young enough to be a bloody nightmare from dawn 'til dusk, so early on the Saturday morning, he takes them out to run off some energy on the beach.'

'The kids spot a carousel on the pier, and poor old Fred gets bullied by five-year-olds into making sure they get the first ride of the day. He and the kids wait for the shutters to be pulled up and the ride to open, and the ride . . . conductor? Engineer? – says the kids can go round and pick their horses straight away.'

'Yeah, Nate, health and safety wasn't really a thing in the nineties . . .'

'It's so early, there's no one else around. It's just the three of them.'

'But he and the kids aren't alone on that ride. On the other side of the carousel, on the pink horse his daughter really wants, is a person. A man. He's slumped forward, holding on to the pole, his head bent down over the horse's head.'

'That's what it looked like, anyway. But as Fred's daughter finds out when she goes to ask the man to let her have the pink horse, this man won't be going anywhere. Because not only is he duct-taped to the pole by the wrists, but he also—'

'—doesn't have a head.'

'I do love a beheading, Stevie. I really do. Luckily this little girl was young enough to not quite comprehend the horror of what she was looking at, so Fred was able to pick her up and get her away pretty fast. Unfortunately, his son wasn't so lucky. He'd picked out one of the carriages to sit in instead—'

'—and had managed to pick the one with a severed head in it. Can you imagine ever looking in *anything* ever again after finding a head somewhere? Laundry basket? Might be a head. Cutlery drawer? Head. Cat litter box? A head!'

'As if cat poop boxes weren't disgusting enough already. You realise Rosie's probably got faeces all over her paws, right? And you're just letting her rub it all over you?'

'If I'm destined to die from feline poop-related bacteria, so be it.'

'Stevie, gross. Anyway, the kids are traumatised – which is pretty standard for a holiday in Blackpool, I assume – and the police are called. Obviously the most obvious potential suspect is the ride . . . manager? – who is the only one with access to the key to the shutters, but—'

'He's the cutest, sweetest, most benign of grandpas who ever existed, so suspecting him would be like suspecting Father Christmas.'

'He also had a solid alibi of attending bingo that night and then going home with one of the regulars—'

'No droopy drawers for ol' gramps, I guess.'

'—which is maybe the more important reason for the police dropping that line of inquiry. And as we all know, locks can be picked.'

'The set-up of this murder, a man beheaded on a horse, it's got a real horror movie vibe, hasn't it, Nate? You'd think, oh, this is one of a series of funfair-related crimes, or hey, there's another headless chap over there in Southend-on-Sea! But no. It's just this one murder in this one place – and once you find out the identity of the victim, it actually becomes . . . a lot less horror, and a lot more Mafia.'

'The body – and the head, of course – belonged to Martin Jackson, a fifty-three-year-old *horse breeder*. And we're not talking farm horses here. These are racing horses, the best of the best. The kind of horses where a *lot* of money is involved. And when a horse doesn't perform as it should, that's a lot of money lost.'

'And a few of Martin Jackson's latest ponies—'

'Foals, Stevie. A baby horse is called a foal. Ponies are a different animal.'

'All right, fine. A few of Jackson's latest non-ponies had turned out to carry genetic defects, making them unable to race long term, as the owners discovered when the horses couldn't finish races and had to be, um . . .'

'Sent to the glue factory.'

'Nate! Vegans might be listening.'

'You think one of our three-and-a-half listeners is vegan? Leave a comment and let us know if you are, okay? So, we have a possible motive for murder, and a range of suspects in the horse racing world – and the criminal one. Because who gets involved in betting?'

'Gangs!'

'Who doesn't like it when horses who are supposed to perform suffer spontaneous heart attacks?'

'Vegans! And also gangs!'

'And gangs – or the kind of people who can employ professional killers – makes sense here. Because, you guys, beheading is *hard*. Unless you've got some kind of ninja blade, you have to saw. It's messy. Blood goes everywhere. It's not for the squeamish.'

'Why do you sound like you know this from experience, Nate?'

'We've both seen *Hereditary*, you know what I'm talking about. So, initially this is looking like some kind of hit to the police – but then the plot thickens.'

'Martin Jackson wasn't *just* a horse breeder. He was also a serial adulterer—'

'Which opens things up to not only the wife, but any former girlfriends, or those girlfriends' partners.'

'—*and* he was exposed just the year before for mistreatment of animals in his care—'

'Which brings in the anti-horse racing, vegan, Greenpeace-type do-gooders. Although could a vegan hack off someone's head? Isn't that against their ethos?'

'Do you think that's specifically in the code somewhere? *No meat, dairy, or eggs shall be consumed, and not one human head removed.*'

'*Fingers are fine, though.*'

'I don't know about the activist theory. It seems too graphic for that kind of group. Surely they'd graffiti his property or disrupt his practices, not brutally murder him in a fairground setting? Seems more like a mob message to me.'

'I like the idea of a vindictive ex. A woman scorned. Although she'd need help to move the body.'

'You don't know that, Nate. She could've been a strong, independent women who didn't need no man to help her mutilate and dump a dead body. Plus this guy was a former jockey in his youth. They're all tiny.'

'I'm imagining our girl boss killer carrying him princess-style to that carousel.'

'This is another one of those unsolved cases where we get to speculate. I like these ones. Nate doesn't.'

'I like an answer! I hate it when the ending's up in the air. Who's the killer and did they kill anyone else in the last . . . twenty-one years? We don't know. Can't tell you. All we can do is hazard a guess. Mine's definitely an ex, or the husband of an ex.'

'I'm going mob. Although . . . what about the wife herself? Maybe she had a boyfriend of her own, and they came up with the plan together to off Jackson and take his money for themselves? And they did it in such an outlandish way to throw people off the scent of a very unextraordinary motive?'

'Ooh, I like that. Or maybe it was that, but with an *Orient Express* twist! The wife and *all* the mistresses found out about each other, so teamed up to take him out together. One blow to the neck each.'

'Trussed up on a pretend horse after he took all of them for a ride.'

'Love it. So for once, not the boyfriend – but the *girlfriends!*'

'That's all we feminists want, Nate. The same opportunities as men.'

'What do you think, listeners? Who beheaded Martin Jackson back in 1998? And did those kids who discovered the pieces of him ever go on a carousel again? Thinking about it, those kids are grown up now. Kids, if you're listening to this, write in and tell us more! We'd love to get your memories about it.'

'You think one of our three-and-a-half listeners happens to be a bystander of the very crime we're talking about?'

'You never know, Stevie. Plus I bet we're up to a full four listeners by now. Maybe even five if the girl boss stuff went down well. As always, hit up our email with your theories, any ideas for cases you want us to cover, and any stories of your own you want to share. And remember to keep your wits about you, and trust nobody—'

'Especially not your boyfriend.'

'—*or* your multiple extra-marital girlfriends.'

'Bye!'

CHAPTER 5

It's always the boyfriend, that's what Nate and I said.

Throughout true crime, it happens again and again – husbands murdering wives; rejected men targeting their exes. Male rage. But Lauren Parker's murder wasn't an example of this happening again in Sandford in 2006: it was a killer *using* that stereotype to deflect the blame. Whoever killed her knew where the police would look, and who the town would suspect.

While everyone was staring at Mike, someone else was washing Lauren's blood off their hands.

But who?

There were many, many people at Nate's party that night. Was Lauren's killer there? Were they one of our friends?

Were they someone *Lauren* considered a friend?

What was the killer's real aim seventeen years ago? To kill Lauren and get away with it, or to punish Mike?

Who was the real target that night?

And if it was so personal, what does Anna and her identical murder have to do with any of it?

My doorbell rings in Nate's distinctive way – three times quickly, then once more – which means he's used his key and is on his way up.

Rosie stretches out her black paws on the sofa opposite me, flexing her claws.

She knows Nate's ring, too.

The coffee table is covered in notes and printouts, and both my laptop and tablet have dozens of open tabs. I'm not usually a planner – facts and figures are Nate's style – but I'm giving it a go. I made enough mistakes in Episode 1 of *All the Gory Details*. This time, I want to get those details right.

'Have you been following the news?' Nate asks, breathless, the second he comes in the door. 'About the murders?'

'Has DI Chopra gone public about the link now?' I click on my news tab. 'It's about time, everyone's known about it for—'

'What? No, not *that* murder. The one from Brighton. You know, a body found on the seafront? They mentioned it yesterday on the radio, when we were driving home. Remember?'

'Uh, yeah, I guess.' There's no breaking news headline about it online. 'What's special about that one? I thought it was someone who drowned?'

'No, that's just what I assumed it was. The truth is *way* more interesting.'

Nate grins and jumps on to the sofa. Rosie turns and hisses at him.

'All right, calm down.' He scoots right over to the edge, wedging himself against the armrest. 'Better, Satan?'

Rosie puts her head back down, but keeps glaring.

'Okay, so I looked into this Brighton thing a bit more, 'cause, you know, I was wondering if there were any pictures floating around, and . . . I found out some stuff.'

Nate leans forward, his hands clasped, his knees bouncing. I feel the same – an itchy, restless enthusiasm to talk about my theories of Lauren's death and Mike's framing. But if this Brighton murder has hooked Nate, it must be worth a detour.

I lean forward, too.

'What stuff?'

'It's Brighton, right? Seaside town. Amusements on the pier. A carousel.'

'Go on . . .'

'Well, the carousel . . . *operator?* – comes down to open up yesterday morning. Raises the shutters, which were locked overnight. Goes around, doing his health and safety checks. And finds someone sitting on one of the horses. Someone dead.'

This sounds familiar . . .

'It wasn't a drowning victim after all, Stevie. No, it was a *headless* victim, taped to the horse. And guess what? They found the head—'

'—on another part of the ride?'

'Yep, in a little carriage. Just like—'

'—that dude from, um, Blackpool. Back in the nineties. The pony breeder guy!'

'Foal breeder, but yeah. Martin Jackson, that was his name.'

It all comes back to me in a rush.

'How did you find out about this? It's in the news?'

'Nah, they haven't said about the beheading bit yet, but obviously there were people around at the time who saw it. Someone even shared a picture, look.'

He shows me his phone: a blurry, overly zoomed image of a pretty, gold-embellished carousel, and a figure in black slumped over a pink horse.

'And get this – police haven't confirmed the beheading stuff, but they *did* release the name of the victim. Ron O'Donnell. Want to take a stab at his occupation?'

'Not a horse breeder?'

'Yes, a horse breeder. Former jockey, too. It's a carbon copy of the *same* murder.'

'Whoa.' I sink back in my armchair. 'What did we think, it was a gang thing? To do with horse racing?'

'Or animal activists, *or* vengeful ex-girlfriends.'

'Gangs definitely makes more sense right now, though. There was probably something shady going on with this O'Donnell guy, too. Screwed over the wrong people, and they punished him in the same way.'

'Maybe. I think there are lots of theories for this one.'

'Oh, speaking of theories . . .' I grab my notebook again. 'I think Lauren's murder was definitely done by a local. So we need to figure out *who* in Sandford in 2006 would want to kill Lauren – or, potentially, why they hated Mike so much that they wanted to frame him for murder.'

Nate stills, his enthusiasm draining. He looks over the messy coffee table, the old portable hard drive plugged into my laptop. 'What's that for?'

'I've been trying to find old photos from when we were teens. You know I don't exactly have a filing system for anything. But anyway, I've got loads of ideas to work with for the new podcast.'

'Wow. That's great, Stevie, but . . .' He scratches his head. 'I don't think I want to investigate Lauren's death right now.'

I can't have heard him right. 'Sorry, what? We *just* started the new podcast about her.'

'About Anna.'

'No, Episode 1 was about Anna being killed by the same person who killed Lauren. Why would we *not* investigate Lauren's death? That's the whole point of the podcast. You want to scrap it?'

'I didn't say that.'

'Then what *are* you saying?'

'Lauren's murder is years old, and it's not going anywhere. There might not be anywhere *for* it to go, anyway. But here we have a contemporary murder, an exciting one, and I think the smart move is to focus on that first.'

'Stick with Anna, you mean?'

'No.'

'Then who? Are you saying a third girl has been killed? You found another victim, before Anna?'

'No.'

'Then what are you talking about, Nate?'

'Carousel, Stevie.'

'The Brighton murder? Are you serious?'

'Yes!' Nate's knees bounce again, his enthusiasm returning. 'Look, we don't know why Lauren's killer struck again in Foxbridge but it can't be a coincidence that they struck again, for the *first time* in nearly two decades, and then a week later, the carousel killer does the same. *That's* the connection we should be exploring. *That's* where the interest is.'

'Huh?'

'Anna Farley died, very tragic, but her death became news because *we* were there, right? And people connected it back to Lauren's. Well, I think Lauren's killer was inspired to kill again by the murder weapon being found this year – and then whoever killed Martin Jackson on that carousel in Blackpool twenty-five years ago was inspired to strike again *because* of it. I think one old serial killer has prompted another to try to one-up them.'

'But . . . the carousel murderer wasn't a serial killer. It was personal. It was to do with the business with the horses.'

'We don't know that. Maybe it was just a dude who really wanted to cut a horse breeder's head off. And now he's done it again.' Nate leans forward, his hands clasped. 'This could be gold, Stevie. Two killers trying to get back into the news, competing with each other to make the bigger impact. This could bring others out of the woodwork, too. And we could cover them all.'

'What is there to cover? I'll admit, it's interesting that there's been another carousel murder, but there's no proof of any link. It would be two episodes – Anna's, and this new carousel one. Done.'

'I bet other killers we've spoken about have struck again. We can explore that. We can make it a whole series about first-time killers doing it the second time.'

'But that's not what *this* series is about. *When It Happens Again* is about Anna and Lauren.'

'And it's not too late to change that. Even the title works! We can still pivot and keep it alive.'

'It *is* alive, though?' I gesture to my table of notes. 'It's an investigative podcast, and we have things to investigate. That's what our listeners are expecting.'

'But our listeners won't care if we change it. And this is better. More exciting. More *us*.' Nate scoots to the edge of his seat. 'Everyone loved that carousel story in *Gory Details*, and they'll love it again now. We can be the first to break this story, and we can float the idea of serial killers inspiring each other. *This* is what we need to focus on right now. This is how we break back into the podcasting scene, for real. Please, Stevie. Trust me on this.'

This is like four years ago, when he got the idea of starting a podcast and then hounded me relentlessly about doing it with him. He was convinced he could make it work – and he was right. He had so much hope back then. He read books about podcasting. He listened to *podcasts* about podcasting. He learnt the theory and put it into practice, and it was starting to pay off. We were steadily increasing fans over the years. We were selling T-shirts. I used to see them on the Tube, sometimes: girls with lip rings and headphones and an *It's Always the Boyfriend* top.

The only one I've seen since was on a rack in a charity shop.

Before Lauren's murder weapon was found at the old farmhouse site this year, Nate had even been approached by a small venue asking us to do a few live shows. But then the scandal got into the news, the events were cancelled, and we went on hiatus.

Not just the podcast, but Nate and me.

I used to love spending Thursday nights together. Us in my flat, the cosy lamps on, a beer or two to help me relax about the fact there was a microphone shoved in my face. I loved how we'd try to gross each other out with case details, how sometimes we'd laugh so much he'd have to cut it out of the recording.

I just loved being with him.

But for Nate, it was always about Mondays. He'd check the new episode's stats the moment he woke up, and spend the day promoting it and interacting with listeners on social media. He'd retweet the funniest comments, and post from the *Gory Details* account about how we were so glad people were enjoying it.

But on Mondays, there never was a 'we'.

I straighten up in my chair.

'No. I won't pivot the podcast on to Carousel.'

Nate sits back, too. 'We *have* to. It's what listeners will want, Stevie.'

'I don't give a crap what listeners want, *Nate*. This isn't about them, it's about helping to find who killed Lauren and Anna. It's about spreading the truth this time.'

'And what truth is that? That we went to Sandford and talked to about fifty people, but the only thing of value we got was the prime suspect assaulting you in the woods?'

'Assaulting me?'

'I heard it on the recording. Mike grabbed you when you ran after him, didn't he? He made you yelp. You were scared of him.'

'He startled me, that's all.'

'He's a thug. He's dangerous.'

'He's not!'

'He is! We were in town to investigate the murder of his girl-friend, and he told us to get out. He practically kicked us out of the place. He didn't want to cooperate. I know you feel guilty about how our listeners hounded him, but I think . . . I think they had good reason to. I think it's wrong to assume you can trust anything he says.'

I rub my forehead, laughing. 'What are you saying, Nate? That after all that, you actually think he *is* the killer?'

'I don't think you should rule it out. Not after the woods yesterday.'

'But what about the things that exonerate him? His van ended up torched because someone stole his keys—'

'No, he *claims* someone stole his keys.'

'—and his DNA was categorically *not* on the murder weapon.'

'Yeah, and no DNA was found on Lauren's body, either! He could've stolen that knife from someone who'd already used it, and worn gloves when he killed her with it. You don't know what happened, Stevie.'

'I can't believe you're saying this. We lost our entire podcast *because* we accused Mike. And now you want to accuse him all over again?'

'No, I don't. That's the point.' Nate digs his nails through his hair. 'You think Mike was framed? Okay, sure. Let's say we investigate that, and it turns out he wasn't. He *did* kill Lauren, but there's no hard evidence. What then? What happens to all your apologies to him, hmm? Do we have to go *back* to accusing him, or just . . . ignore it? Because believe me, Stevie, the optics are awful both ways.'

I roll my eyes. 'The *optics* won't matter, because Mike didn't kill Lauren.'

'He was aggressive yesterday. If he killed Lauren, and Anna, then we know what he's capable of. He could find out where you live. He could punish you for looking into this again. He could stop you.'

'Mike. Didn't. Kill. Lauren!'

'You don't know that!'

'No, I *feel* it.' I bang my chest. 'In here. He didn't hurt her, but someone else did. Someone blamed him for it. There is literally no harm in trying to find out who.'

'No harm? If it wasn't Mike, you're still stirring up the past, trying to find a killer who *we* may have known. And killers kill. You're putting yourself in the firing line.'

'That's ridiculous. And even if that was true, how is looking into Carousel any different?'

'Because it's not personal! It's a gruesome case that has nothing to do with us. It's safe.'

'Safe got us into this mess, Nate. We told stories, we didn't look into things, and we ruined someone's life. We possibly helped a killer walk free. I won't do that again. I have to do something to help. I have to find out the truth.'

Nate plays an audio clip on his phone.

'*It looks like you're just trying to profit off Loz's death,*' Mike's voice spits. '*Again.*'

'*That's not what we're doing.*'

'*Yeah, it is. It's all you ever do. Chew people up and spit 'em out. Wreck lives and run off with your own good one. This isn't about Loz or that other girl, it's about you.*'

Nate puts his phone down.

'I think Mike was right, Stevie. You're not doing this for Lauren or Anna. You're doing it for you.'

He says it with the sombre finality of a doctor giving a terminal diagnosis, as though he's won a painful argument – but he's wrong.

'Are you seriously accusing me of trying to profit off Lauren when *you're* the one worrying about podcast optics and listener engagement?'

He looks shocked. 'No, I—'

'If all you care about is topping charts and building hype, go and do Carousel on your own. Go chase the latest fun murder trend that'll get you those clicks. But I'm staying right here with Lauren – whether you think she's worth your time or not.'

I open my notebook and review my notes – keeping my eyes off Nate.

We've never argued like this before. The odd disagreement or butting of heads, sure, but never scowls and raised voices and expressions I can't read. But maybe we needed to do this, to clear the air. Maybe now Nate will stop for a minute and—

The door bangs shut, and Nate's boots echo in the staircase.

The flat feels horribly quiet.

The regret is almost instant. I pull up the window and lean out, ready to call down to him, to apologise as he unlocks the door of his basement flat – but he doesn't stop. He stomps down the steps of the house and heads off down the road, hands thrust in his pockets, not looking up.

He doesn't even want to be in the same building as me right now. And seeing the anger in his step makes me feel the same way about him.

My laptop dims from inactivity, and I turn the brightness back up. A folder from my old external hard drive is open, dozens of tiny image icons arranged across the screen in a grid. I click through them.

Nate and me at a forensics event at the Natural History Museum, hoods up on our white plastic overalls, swigging beer in front of a microscope.

Nate and me in Sandford Library, posing with armfuls of true crime non-fiction books.

Nate and me on a night out at uni, his arm around my waist, some girl's lipstick around his mouth.

August and me in front of my parents' mantelpiece in 2006, me in my bloody 1970s' Sage Tremaine dress, and August in her equally bloody Millicent Potter Victorian gown.

'*Girl power!*' we joked, making Spice Girls-style peace signs.

I sink back in my chair. August and I lost touch long ago. She moved away in 2007, just after Christmas, but we swore to stay best friends forever – like our old necklaces said. But it didn't work out that way. I ended up going to a different university. We made different friends. Chose different paths. Now, I can't even remember the last time we spoke.

I pull out my phone.

Time to change that.

CHAPTER 6

I wander around Paddington Station, pulling my scarf tight against the morning cold and resenting the one-and-a-half-inch gap of bare skin between my boots and checked trousers. I scan the arrivals board again. August's train should be here soon.

The YouTube ads on my phone have ended, so I focus on the screen again.

It didn't take James Nash long to find the best way to capitalise on the hype around Anna Farley's murder – and the best way to hurt us while doing it.

Filmed in 4K, Nash sits in a hard-backed chair in his study, grey hair neatly swept to the side, addressing sombre questions to the guest sitting opposite him.

Mike Edwards.

'When did you first realise that Stevie Knight had accused you in the podcast?'

Mike shifts in his seat. 'I didn't know anything about the podcast for ages. I'm not into that kind of thing. I wasn't before Loz's death, but after it . . . I hate all that stuff. So, I think it was . . . 2020? Late that year, maybe? That's when the trolling started.'

'What was that like?'

'DMs, mostly. Saying I was a murderer. Saying I deserved to die. Asking me why I did it.'

'And how did that escalate?'

'They found out where I worked. Posters started going up on trees – like missing posters, but with my face, and saying MURDERER on them. And one time I came out and my car had been vandalised. Someone had keyed KILLER on it. People in my town started to believe the crap in that podcast. It didn't matter that I hadn't put a foot wrong at work, or that I helped people carry their shopping home. Everyone just believed the lies. And it cost me everything.'

'What did you lose, Mike?'

'My job. My friends. My . . . my girlfriend.' He wipes his face with his sleeve. 'I moved towns, but they found me again. I went back home, to Sandford, and it was just like before I left – everyone staring at me, everyone thinking I was a killer. But I'm not a killer. I want justice for Loz more than anyone on this planet. More than them.'

'More than who?'

'Those podcasters. The ones who do this just for clicks. They don't care about Loz, they just care about the story. If they really cared, they'd have come to me first, because I knew Loz the best. But they didn't. And now they want to use Anna Farley's death like they did with Loz. I listened to their episode about her.' The snarl on his face shows how much he enjoyed it. 'It made me sick. They interviewed her boyfriend in it. Where was my interview? Where was *my* benefit of the doubt?'

'Do you worry they'll ruin other lives with their careless accusations?'

'Yeah, I do. They don't care about facts. I was innocent, I was *never* put on trial or convicted, yet they go on their podcast and spout off about me anyway. They don't care about people. Those two, they'll trample on anyone they have to. They'll—'

'Oh my God! Stevie!'

I look up, yanking down my headphones.

August rushes towards me from the ticket barriers, her dark curls flying against her leather jacket, her smile as wide as it used to be when we'd reunite in Sandford after family holidays.

I grin, and rush to her, too. We collide in a hug – the same as always, her taller than me, holding each other tight as we half sway, half stumble from foot to foot – and laugh. Her pulled-down headphones play in my ear: Placebo, like always.

'Wow, this is so weird,' she gushes, pulling back. 'How are you? I *love* the hair.'

'And I love yours.'

'Thanks! Took me thirty years, but I finally realised I *wasn't* supposed to try to brush my curly hair straight every morning. Are those new Docs?'

'Yeah, and they hurt like they hell. When did you get the nose piercing?'

'Oh, years ago. That hurt like hell, too. Got infected. Pus for weeks!'

'*Cool.*'

She checks the big raised clock on the wall. 'Okay, I've got to be at the court in about an hour. You still okay if we combine our chat with a cab to the Old Bailey?'

'Definitely.'

'Cool, let's grab a drink for the road. I'm guessing you're still a night owl who'd rather be horizontal at this time of day, right?'

'Yep.'

'Me too, to be honest. But unfortunately, even the weirdo lab girl has to be a functioning member of society sometimes. Well, *ish.*'

We set off for a coffee shop, trading jokes about bedtimes, our boots making the same sound on the floor.

I thought this would be awkward. I expected her to be stand-offish, to have become some unrecognisable adult who no longer fits in with my lifestyle of casual shoes and lazy mornings and rock music. But August is the same August as always.

At different universities, we drifted apart. Long emails turned to texts, and then texts turned to the odd Facebook like. Our long-held plan for a gap year travelling to the true crime hotspots of the world turned to half-hearted proposals of '*oh, we* must *meet up again soon!*' that neither of us ever tried to arrange.

The other night was the first time we'd actually spoken in years. We texted a little to arrange this mini-meeting, we small-talked, but I had no idea she'd be so—

'Sorry I don't have time for a proper visit,' she says as we join the drinks queue. 'We're just massively snowed under at the lab right now. I'm talking samples up to our ears. After I give my evidence, I'm heading straight back for more tests.'

'I still can't believe you *actually* went into forensics. It's *so* cool. I know we used to talk about it, but it always seemed like a silly dream back then.'

'It probably was a silly dream, to be honest. But after my family moved away from Sandford, things were rough. I didn't make a single friend at my college – I guess I was always the odd new girl to the other kids – and uni wasn't much better, so I had a *lot* of free time for studying. Being the weird loner definitely paid off, career-wise.'

I feel a fresh stab of the guilt I've tried to ignore since I was eighteen.

August and I always planned to go to the same university, but Nate didn't get in. I chose to go with him to my second-choice uni instead.

'It's not too late for you to live *your* silly dream,' she says. 'The police are always recruiting, and I know you'd be the best hard-boiled detective – with or without the alcoholism and murdered wife. We could get our little crime-fighting duo back together.'

'Trio. I'd catch the bad guys, you'd prove their guilt in the lab, and then Nate would get them put behind bars in court. Remember?'

'Oh yeah, it was a trio for a little while, wasn't it? But you've got to admit, it was *our* dream long before he came along.'

Was it?

'So, no Nate today?' August asks after she orders our drinks. 'How come? I thought you two were still joined at the hip.'

'He's . . . busy.'

'Oh. Well, his loss is my gain. This'll be just like old times. The *really* old ones. How is Nate, by the way?'

'Uh, he's fine. Yeah. He's good.'

I assume. We haven't spoken since our argument in my flat. I keep getting halfway down the stairs to apologise, but I stomp back to my flat every time. I won't apologise for wanting to do right by Lauren, or for not wanting to chase a true crime trend. He's doing that without me, anyway. I've checked his Twitter – more than I should have, maybe. He posted about the carousel beheading in Brighton hours after we fell out over it, and has been pushing our old episode about the Blackpool carousel murder ever since.

I can't argue with his logic, however soulless it feels: that episode has been getting more hits than ever.

'I've met his dad in court before,' August says.

'*Really?*'

'Yep. He was actually there for my first ever forensic report a couple of years ago. Almost as terrifying in the courtroom as he was when we were teens. Remember when we went back to Nate's that time and he told us off for wearing our shoes in the house? It was like that, but multiplied by a million.' She shudders. 'Dude's a menace, seriously. Does Nate look even *more* like him now? Is he all grey too?'

'No, luckily. He says he got his mum's hair gene, rather than his dad's prematurely white one. Other than that, I'd say he's still a bit of a clone, yeah. But the opposite of an evil one.'

Nate's dad – although I can't say I've seen much of him over the years, since he and Nate aren't exactly on bring-a-friend-round-for-dinner terms – was always a straight-backed, strong-eyebrowed, white-haired glarer of a man, the kind who could make you reconsider all your life choices with a single stare. Nate has the same features as his dad, but softened: hair solid black and floppy rather than harshly combed back; his strong jaw blurred with a dusting of stubble rather than sharpened with a straight-edge razor.

Maybe that's why the other day was so upsetting: for the first time since I've known him, Nate's expression looked as severe as his dad's.

'Are you okay, Stevie?'

August's hand touches my shoulder, and I feel myself warp back through the years to the Sandford of my childhood – to sharing a scarf on the cold playground; to air-guitar duets in my bedroom; to lying awake together and telling murder stories in the dark.

I know that, even now, I can tell her anything.

'We had an argument,' I say as our drinks arrive. 'But it doesn't matter. Let me get this.'

I reach for my card, but she slaps her own on to the payment machine.

'Business expense,' she says.

'Can you get away with two different coffees as a business expense?'

'Sure. My boss loves me. Got my boots reheeled while I was here last year, too. Walking counts as a travel expense, Stevie! Not today, though.' We take our drinks – mocha for me, Americano for her – and she heads for the taxi rank. 'I think we probably both know from experience that talking murder in a crowded commuter train isn't the best idea, right? Not everyone wants a live podcast experience featuring a special guest. So, what was this argument with Nate about?'

I sigh. 'Like I said the other night, we're investigating Lauren's death – for real this time – and we were going to make it a new podcast series, but suddenly Nate doesn't want to. He wants to focus on another case which has nothing to do with it.'

'But he couldn't get enough of Lauren's murder back in the day. Why doesn't he care now?'

'I don't know. Well, maybe I do. He thinks if we poke around too much, someone might try to stop us. Especially if I'm right, and Lauren's killer is someone we knew.'

'You think we knew the killer?' August's grey eyes go wide – with excitement.

'Yep. I think they were there that night, at Nate's party. But, um, *not* the boyfriend. Obviously. I've learnt from that mistake.'

We get into either side of a black cab and buckle up. Our morbidly curious Google searches of car wrecks as teens had a lasting impact.

'Old Bailey, please,' August says, 'and then . . . whereabouts in London are you, Stevie?'

'Pimlico, near the railway bridge – but I'll make my own way home. You don't have to—'

'Old Bailey and then Pimlico, please! Expenses, remember?'

The driver pulls out of the rank, and August turns to me. 'Can I be honest?'

'. . . *Yes?*'

'I never listened to your podcast. I mean, I heard a bit. Most of the first episode. But it wasn't really for me, so . . . yeah.'

'Oh. That's okay. Don't worry about it. *Most* people haven't listened to it, either.'

'I just thought I should come clean, as I don't really know the ins and outs of what's happened with it. Just that you blamed Mike, and then you got in trouble for it.'

'That's all you need to know, really. Good summary.'

'So weird that they only recently found the murder weapon after all those years.'

'I know, right?'

'Do you think it was *really* well hidden, or did the police just screw up at the time? You know, one guy was asked to check a certain bush, but didn't?'

'Maybe. We actually spoke to Benkins' brother—'

'Jonkins! I remember him.'

'—and he was an officer back then. He was there when they found her, and he was . . . not okay about it. So maybe—'

'*He* was the killer!'

I laugh. '*He* wasn't at Nate's party. Wait, was he? I don't actually remember.'

'I think I still have that hard drive with everyone's photos on it somewhere. Maybe at my dad's house?'

'Seriously? You have all our friends' old photos from then?'

'Yeah, I used to pester everyone for copies. I had the weirdest feeling MySpace would crash one day and we'd lose everything. So, I was half right. I'll get my dad to post the drive, and then I'll stick it all on a shared folder for you.'

'August, you're a lifesaver! I couldn't find anything from the party in my files, just us before it.'

'The photos your mum took in the kitchen? Us doing our ironic Girl Power schtick?'

'Yeah, those ones.'

111

'We looked damn good that night, to be fair. So, someone we know is a killer?'

I stare at August for a moment, then grin.

'What?'

I shake my head. 'It's just *really* nice to talk to you again.'

As the taxi makes its way around Hyde Park and past Buckingham Palace – and the driver's eyes give us a range of eavesdropped emotions in the rear-view mirror – August and I discuss everything: the possibilities of Lauren having an ex-boyfriend or a stalker; which classmate could have been capable of murder; the motives for framing Mike; why Lauren left the party that night, and who may have lured her to the street.

'Should we talk about the elephant in the room?' August asks as we get clogged in the Trafalgar Square traffic, somehow wedging her boots into her black leather backpack along with the thick folder already there.

'Which is?'

'That less than a week ago you found a dead body?'

The taxi driver's eyes pop in the mirror, but he manages to keep his attention on the road.

'Dead people are my world. Not that I'm a pathologist or anything, but I've been to post-mortems. Sometimes the samples I analyse come from under the fingernails of murder victims. It's all quite . . . ordinary for me. Horrible, but ordinary. It's part of the job. I mean, today I'm giving evidence about a child beaten to death by his parents. It's grim, but that's my everyday. How do *you* feel about it, Stevie? And don't just say you're fine, because I know that's not true. How are you really?'

I bite on my thumbnail. I used to chew my nails down to the skin when we were younger, but not for years now. I broke that habit years ago.

I pull my hand away.

'I keep seeing her, everywhere. Especially when I'm trying to sleep. I can smell her. And . . . I know this is irrational, I *know* that, but part of me feels like I made it happen. I read about Anna's disappearance and I thought it sounded like Lauren's, I *wanted* it to be like Lauren's, and then it was. Exactly. It's like, by me going there, I sealed her fate.'

'I get that. But someone else would have found her there if you didn't.'

'I know. But it wasn't someone else. It was me.'

August reaches over and squeezes my hand.

'Nate thinks it's my fault that she's dead.'

'Excuse me?'

I rub my nose. 'I mean, he didn't blame *me*, but he thinks the way we covered it in our old podcast, and the way the case got back into the news this year with the recovered murder weapon and the DNA test and Mike having his name cleared . . . He thinks all that made the killer want to do it again. We caused this.'

August looks away as our taxi turns on to the tree-lined street beside the Thames, falling leaves glowing like embers in the morning sunlight. She shakes her head. 'Typical Nate.'

'What do you mean?'

'Making himself the centre of things, as usual.' August scoops her hair up and twists it into a clip. 'If it was something to do with your podcast, it would have happened *years* ago. And that murder weapon was always going to clear Mike's name when it was found. Who says Anna Farley's death has to have anything to do with you? There are plenty of reasons the killer could have struck again.'

August reels off the theories that I've been scribbling in my notebook for days, her eyes alight with purpose. I think of Nate trudging around Sandford behind me, uninterested, trying to move away from Lauren's story at the first possible chance.

But August gets it. She always gets it.

Guilt gnaws at me. We started drifting apart the moment her family moved from Sandford – but I did nothing to prevent it.

When I texted her the other night, the last message on our thread was from her over three years ago.

And yet she still ran to me in the train station like we'd only been apart a week.

'Why won't Nate podcast about this?' August asks, removing her nose ring. 'Lauren Parker's case has always been *our case*, and now there's a whole new layer to it. Do you think it got too real for him when you found Anna's body? Did he take it worse than you did?'

I remember him running off to vomit, and the way he shook while we sat in the boot of the police car.

'Yeah, he was a mess.'

'Makes sense. He was kind of weird after they found Lauren, too – he didn't want to poke around the farmhouse, remember? I guess he's more of a "read about it online" than a "go and see for himself" kind of person. Maybe he just needs some time to come around? He seemed fine with Lauren's death in your podcast. It wasn't an accurate portrayal of the story, but it was certainly a jolly one.'

'I don't know if time is the problem. He said something about covering this *other* new murder being the smart choice to get our reputation back.'

August rolls her eyes. 'Making himself the centre *again*! Why is he like this? Follow the damn story you were meant to, Nate.'

She unzips her leather jacket, revealing a neat blouse. With her hair up and her boots swapped for heels, she looks utterly professional.

'You scrub up really well.'

August laughs. 'I try my best. We know what juries like, and that's *nerds*.' She puts on a large pair of glasses, and taps the side of the frame. 'Clear glass. People just trust science more when it comes from someone in glasses.'

I fiddle with my chunky heart ring, twisting it around my finger. Our taxi heads north just before Blackfriars Bridge, taking us away from the water and back into the dense city streets. The spire of St Paul's Cathedral pokes out above the cluttered buildings, stalking us at every crossroad.

'What do you mean about Nate making himself the centre of things all the time?'

She sighs, pushing her glasses up her nose. 'He likes to be the centre of attention, that's all. Hence roping you into the podcast.'

'Roping me in?'

'I *know you*, Stevie. You were the best guitarist in the county and looked like a ready-made rock star, but you never even considered starting a band. The spotlight has never been your scene. At heart, you're still the freak who I used to spend lunchtimes in the library with, seeing what horrific photos we could sneak past the school's search blocker. Nate's the kid who'd be doing cartwheels on the cafeteria tables.'

'That's going a bit far.'

'Is it? Even if I hadn't listened to the first episode, I'd still know that starting the podcast wasn't *your* idea. Why did you agree to do it?'

'Because I like talking about murder, you know that. And he said I could pick whichever murder I wanted for the first episode, and I wanted Lauren's. I wanted to raise awareness about it.'

'Okay, very noble. But why did *he* want to start a podcast in the first place?'

I think about it. 'To . . . be a podcaster, I suppose?'

'And that's what I mean, Stevie. He wanted people to listen to him, to notice him. Just like he wanted *you* to notice him that night at his party.'

I frown. 'What do you mean by that?'

'Ugh.' She smooths her hair, sighing. 'It doesn't matter.'

'It *does*. What do you mean? Tell me.'

'We were the weirdos at school, Stevie. We got called witches. Someone once accused me of using their dead cat in a *potion*. We did our history project in Year Seven on Jack the Ripper, with *photos*.'

'Yeah, and?'

'*And*, we just so happen to get invited to a Halloween party which is serial-killer-themed, where the host's costume matches yours, *and* you end up in a study with a load of confidential case files spread out on his very professional father's desk?'

I blink at her. 'Yes? That's what happened.'

'Yeah, but I don't think those things happened by chance.'

'Again, what?'

She sighs. 'The main reason I couldn't stand listening to *All the Gory Details* was because that first episode was completely wrong. Not the Mike stuff, or even the weird Mandela Effect thing where you both seem to remember him and Lauren arguing at the party. What I hated most was that Nate had gone all those years letting you believe you'd had this magical, coincidental meeting, when really he orchestrated the entire thing. He and I had maths together at college. He invited me to the party, and made sure I'd bring you. He even asked what we were going to wear. I thought he was just being friendly, but he dressed to match you, Stevie. On purpose. Because he wanted you to notice him. And it worked.'

'No, that can't be right. Nate wouldn't lie about that, he . . .'

I trail off, thinking about Foxbridge. Thinking about Nate charming those ladies in the corner shop with his focused smile, his bright blue eyes, his head tilted to just the right angle to get the information we needed.

I think of his party, the glut of snogging couples and moshing emos and popular kids smashing up glasses, and the way we gasped in disbelief when we noticed our similar costumes.

I think of the glow from the candles in that attic, and their soft reflection in the big back window. It's quiet up there, muffled. Nate and I are laughing, joking – then we lock eyes over crime scene photos, and both look away.

'Central Crime Court,' the taxi driver shouts, pulling up outside a big stone building.

August leans forward and pays the driver for this fare and on to my flat.

'Obviously you and Nate *are* amazing friends,' August says, 'but it's always bothered me that he never told you he staged your meet-cute. I mentioned it back then, but he just laughed it off and changed the subject. I'm guessing you also don't know he asked me to get us more drinks from the kitchen and then whisked you off upstairs without me?'

'What? You went for some air. We didn't ditch you.'

She raises her eyebrows at me. 'Yeah, that's not true. I came back with three Smirnoff Ices, and you were gone. But it's fine. Water under the bridge. And I only had to put up with a couple of months of being the third wheel before I moved away. That was a silver lining, for sure.'

She says it in a jokey way, but it isn't a joke. There's a bitterness there – the bitterness I was half expecting this morning before we met up. But it has a very different source.

'*Anyway*, it was so great to see you again, Stevie. Sorry about the rushed chat, but I'll get those photos to you when I can. Good luck with your investigation. I'm sure you and Nate will figure everything out together.'

She gives me a smile and leaves the taxi. She turns back and waves as she walks away, her heels clicking on the pavement. Now she's the adult I expected her to be.

'Can I have a minute, please?' I ask the driver, and hop out, too. 'August, wait!'

She turns, the wind tugging free a few strands of dark hair, and I bundle into her with another hug. She's even taller now.

'I'm so sorry about making you feel like a third wheel. I . . . I didn't know that stuff about Nate. I thought we were all friends. Equally.'

'So equal you wrote me out of the story of Lauren's death.'

The guilt stabs at me again.

August was at the party. She was there the next morning when we searched the woods. We were at Nate's together when the police arrived. It was her idea to poke around the road where that dog walker found the shoe. We went to the vigils together. She was there for all of it.

But Nate and I described it like it was all about the two of us.

'I . . . I didn't know if you'd want to be mentioned in that first episode of *All the Gory Details*. Nate said not to. We hadn't talked in a long time, and—'

August hugs me back. 'It's okay, Stevie. Really.'

'I wasn't trying to cut you out. Not then, or . . . at uni. It's just that we didn't talk for a while, and I felt awkward, and that snowballed until suddenly it was years later, and—'

'I get it. You don't need to feel bad. I didn't exactly try to reach out that much, either.'

I pretend to glare at her. 'Yeah, why didn't you? So rude.'

She laughs. 'We'll call it even, then. But I *do* need to get to court now.'

'Of course!' I spring back. 'Sorry, sorry. Go. But, um . . . I'd love to talk more about Lauren's case with you sometime. If you want to.'

August tucks her hair behind her ear, and smiles.

'I was hoping you'd ask me that.'

I turn towards the taxi, but come back again.

'Just one more thing. What was that about the Mandela Effect?'

'Yeah, it's a weird thing in your podcast. You and Nate both *swear* that Mike and Lauren had this blazing row and Lauren cried, but it didn't happen. I was down there all night and didn't see it, and no one else saw it, either. They chatted, kissed, and he went home. That was it. How'd you and Nate get it so wrong?'

I can't answer that – for August, or for myself when I'm back in the taxi. I cross my legs on the seat, draining my cold mocha that I forgot to drink.

'So, you like murders then, eh?' the taxi driver asks in his gruff voice when he turns off The Strand, the white stone and spires of the Law Courts disappearing behind us as we return to the river.

'Sure do.'

'I heard about a good one last night. One of the cabbies told me. So, out on Hampstead Heath, right, there are these two suit-cases, and no one knows why they're there. They've been dumped. And they're the big, old kind, with stickers on it. Vintage. And they open them up, right, and there are bodies in them. Just shoved inside. And those bodies had been—'

'Burnt prior to being put inside, with their arms and legs bound with garden wire.'

He blinks in the mirror. 'Cor, how'd you know that?'

'I've heard it before. Two teenagers had been vandalising a guy's garden, and he went mental and torched them in his garage. Drove all the way to London to get rid of the bodies, but didn't realise an old receipt inside one of the suitcases would help the police identify him. That's an old one. 1960s, wasn't it?'

'Nah.' The driver stares at me in the mirror, other cars beeping at him as he pauses at a green light. 'It only just happened. They found two burnt lads in suitcases *last night*. Are you saying that's happened before?'

I tug my phone out – Mike's face in James Nash's high-production-values YouTube series still frozen on the screen – and scroll down the list of *All the Gory Details* episodes. I find what I'm looking for.

Episode 43: Unclaimed Baggage.

It *has* happened before.

But this time, there's no way it could have happened again.

EPISODE 43: UNCLAIMED BAGGAGE

'. . . so remember to use the code *TASTYDETAILS* for twenty per cent off your first *Hi Tasty* order.'

'That's *TASTYDETAILS* for cheaper, tastier dinners. We love them!'

'Okay, ad break over.'

'*Finally.*'

'Stevie! Don't anger the sponsors.'

'Let's just get back to the murder.'

'Fine. So, Nigel Smith – having beaten his former students to death with a spade and burnt them in a can in his back garden – stuffs them both into a couple of old suitcases and drives the five hours to North London to dump them somewhere far, far away from home.'

'Now, you're probably thinking this is the work of someone in a panic, right? He was a meek little maths teacher who was hounded for *years* by these boys, and one day he snapped and attacked them, and then had to scramble to find a way out of it. He hadn't meant to do it. He regretted it. He was *sorry*.'

'Well, listeners, you'd be *wrong*. Old Nigel drove to and from Hampstead Heath in a state of utter calm. His wife made him sandwiches for the trip. He stopped in to see his sister in Kettering on the way there. He dumped the suitcases and returned home as if nothing had happened. He was back at school in Harrogate by Monday, wearing the same tie as always.'

'This wasn't a man wrecked by guilt. This was a man who'd taken his revenge fantasy to the extreme, and he liked it.'

'But in the same way as he'd like a book of tricky maths puzzles, or a long walk on the beach, Stevie. He murdered two boys in a brutal way and desecrated their corpses, but he got it out of his system. I don't think he was about to start murdering students left, right, and centre. He had one night of extreme cruelty, and that was it. He packed it all away in those suitcases and left them in London.'

'Do you really think so, Nate? I don't think people do things like that *once*. I think the floodgates would have opened if he hadn't been caught.'

'No, I truly think he was one and done.'

'Two and done.'

'Well, yeah, *technically*. But can't you understand where he was coming from, even a little? Obviously he shouldn't have killed those teenagers, but they weren't *just* teenagers – they were vandals. Stevie, they made his life a living hell. Are you really saying you can't imagine lashing out against one – or two – specific people just once?'

'I can't imagine beating them to death and burning their bodies, no. Are you saying you can? Red flag, red flag!'

'*No*. I just mean . . . I've been bullied before, right? In boarding school, I wasn't posh enough, and then in Sandford, I was *too* posh. Kids can be cruel. I can see how somebody could be pushed over the edge like that, but just once. Are you a truly bad person if it's just once?'

'Yes! Absolutely! You write a snotty letter to their parents, you don't *murder* them, Nate.'

'Oh crap, really? That's where I've been going wrong all these years.'

'So, moving on from Nate's apparent love of revenge fantasies, the police are closing in on Nigel. He's still trimming the hedges in Harrogate, teaching maths, whistling as he walks the dog. He doesn't realise that detectives have traced the receipt left in one of the suitcase compartments, and they're coming for him.'

'That sounds a bit too exciting. It's the sixties – no computers, not a lot of talking between different departments – so it's slow. It takes weeks. But first they ID the kids, which points back to Harrogate as the place of the murder, and then they start working on the receipt.'

'It's so funny to me that this is how they got him. Basically, they have a fragment of a torn receipt – which was a printed form with all the details written by hand from a café. And the order was for tomato soup, an egg mayonnaise sandwich, and a cup of tea.'

'The police literally went around every café in town asking if anyone remembered that order – and loads of them did. *Oh yeah, that's Nigel. Comes in all the time. Likes to dunk his sandwich in his soup.*'

'Imagine, Nate, your big murder plan being foiled because you eat egg mayonnaise sandwiches with soup. That's so embarrassing.'

'They'd get you for always ordering extra pineapple on your seafood pizzas.'

'I like my fish to be *tropical*, okay? They'd get you for ordering the wankiest, most disgustingly healthy smoothie on the menu – to go with your greasy burger.'

'It's called enjoying a balanced diet, *Stevie*. So, the weird soup habit gets Nigel caught.'

'He *nearly* got away with it, too. He was just Mr Smith the maths teacher, the nerdy one with glasses and a nice garden. Even though police investigating the boys' disappearance interviewed him because of the vandalism he'd reported time and time again, he wasn't a suspect. He managed to convince them he'd seen the boys walk to the train station the night they disappeared. Just because he wasn't a creepy guy in a trench coat, the police believed him.'

'It's no wonder he was so calm about the whole thing, really. Even when he was arrested, he cooperated.'

'What was it he said when they asked why he did it?'

'*I was tired of them breaking my gnomes.*'

'Not the gnomes, Nate! Won't somebody please think of the gnomes?'

'I kind of love that he said it. It's so . . . quietly unhinged, you know? Aside from one outburst of extreme, calculated violence, everything about the guy was completely mundane. No fuss at the trial, no angst. He just went away and served his time until he died.'

'That's got to be the ultimate relief for the families of victims, right? The killer gets caught, he confesses, it's an easy conviction, and then he gets a decade or two of utterly horrible imprisonment before dying of – hopefully – incredibly painful natural causes.'

'It's like capital punishment, but without anyone having to flip the switch.'

'Exactly. So many of the families in these stories *don't* get that. If something's unsolved, they're always wondering where the killer is, or if he's hurting someone else. There's never any justice of closure. At least the families of these boys got that. In the circumstances, that's practically a happy ending.'

'I don't know, hearing your sons were killed by a maths teacher for gnome abuse can't be the best feeling in the world.'

'Stop ruining my attempt to wrap this up on a positive note!'

'Okay, sorry, sorry. But wouldn't you be *embarrassed* if that was the reason for your death, Stevie? I'd want mine to be for something cool, like I fought back against a burglar, or got shot with a crossbow on a camping trip because I flirted with someone's girlfriend. What about you?'

'I'd rather I just wasn't murdered at all, to be honest?'

'You're no fun. Conversation killer. Ow! *Stop* with the bottlecaps. You're pushing me to the brink of shoving you in a suitcase. Motive – pelted with bottlecaps by the deceased.'

'Worth it. Right, I'm done. Join us next week for . . . did we decide yet?'

'No, but it's your turn to pick.'

'Oh, good. We can go back to something horrific and unsolved.'

'Your favourite. So, as always, let us know what you thought of the episode, and make sure to redeem your twenty per cent discount with *Hi Tasty* by using the promo code *TASTYDETAILS*.'

'It's okay, Nate, I think they heard you the first fourteen times. *Hey!* You can't throw my own bottlecaps back at me.'

'You underestimate my power. So, lovely, weirdo listeners, that's us done for the week. Whatever you do until we next see you, remember to keep your wits about you, be kind to gnomes, and trust nobody—'

'Especially not your maths teacher.'

'Right, let's go get some dinner. I've got the strangest craving for soup and egg mayonnaise . . .'

CHAPTER 7

I leap out of the taxi the moment it stops and rush down the steps to Nate's flat. I knock on the door.

'Nate? Are you home?'

The curtains are closed. I knock again – more obnoxiously – and don't stop.

'Nate!'

'*What?*'

I pull back my fist as the door opens and Nate appears, his hair a mess of black and half his face covered in creases. He's in his underwear, and an *It's Always the Boyfriend* T-shirt.

'Stevie?'

'Hi. I'm guessing you haven't checked the news this morning?'

'No? I *was* having a lie-in after a late bar shift, but . . .' He rubs at his eyes, and blinks at me more consciously. 'What's happened? Is this about Lauren? Did you find out something?'

'No, it's not about her. You were right, Nate. There *is* a link between Anna's death and Carousel – but not old killers inspiring each other in the present. It's more than that. Last night on Hampstead Heath someone found two suitcases, and in them—'

Kids skip along the street above us, laughing, rattling their toys against the railing as their mother pushes a buggy.

'Can we talk about this inside?'

'Yeah, of course.' Nate starts to open the door further, but pauses. 'Does this mean we're back on speaking terms, then?'

'Speaking-about-murder terms, yes. I still think you were an absolute wanker the other day.'

'That's fair, to be honest. Sorry.'

I smile. 'The apology helps.'

Nate lets me in, smiling too, and he pulls on trousers while I fill up the kettle.

'Stevie, I still stand by what I said before, just not the way I said it. Lauren's case *is* dangerous, especially if you're right and we knew the killer when we were kids—'

I hold up a hand to stop him.

'Oh, you're done with Lauren, too?' He exhales. 'Good. I don't want to stir all that up again, it's much better that we—'

'No, *I'm* still looking into Lauren, just not with you. August said she'd help.'

'*August?* Really? I didn't know you still spoke to her.'

'We reconnected. I was just with her. She's a forensic expert witness in court cases now.'

'Wow. I never knew she had it in her.'

The things August said about Nate in the taxi this morning bubble up again – but now isn't the time.

'So, Hampstead Heath,' I say. 'A taxi driver told me that two suitcases were found there last night, or early this morning, and each suitcase had a teenage boy in it. Burnt to death. Hands tied with garden wire.'

'How does a taxi driver know all that?'

'Cabbies share stories. I checked the news. Like with Anna and Carousel, the detail is vague – *bodies found on Hampstead Heath*. But it confirms part of the story, at least.'

'Weird. It's just like that double murder from the sixties, isn't it? Nigel . . . Smith? The schoolteacher who killed those kids.'

'Yes, it *is* just like it. Exactly like it.' I widen my eyes at Nate, waiting for him to wake up. 'Just like Anna's death was exactly like Lauren's, and Ron O'Donnell's in Brighton was just like Martin Jackson's up in Blackpool. Identical murders, years apart. You thought those killers were striking again to get in the news—'

'To one-up each other, yeah.'

'—but that doesn't work for Hampstead Heath. It *can't* be the same killer striking again, because—'

'Oh shit.' Nate sinks on to the edge of his bed. Now he gets it. 'Nigel Smith died in prison.'

'Yeah, in 1982. *Forty-one* years ago. And he confessed to killing those boys. It was done and dusted. Case closed. He killed those boys on Hampstead Heath in the sixties – but he didn't kill the ones who were found there this morning. Somebody else did that. And I think they did it that way on purpose.'

The kettle boils, but neither of us go to fill the mugs.

'You think someone copied that murder? They recreated it?'

'Yeah, I do. But not just that one.'

As Nate sits, I pace his kitchen.

'I think whoever killed those kids and dumped them on Hampstead Heath did the same thing to Anna Farley, and to O'Donnell. I think they're all the same killer. The same copycat. He's just copying *different* murders each time.'

Nate doesn't speak.

'Think about it. All three of these murders – the original ones – were one-offs. Someone was killed in a distinctive way, and that was it. Never again. Why would the killers do it again now? It doesn't make sense. But *this* does. Someone is recreating famous British murders – and so far, they're getting away with it.'

Nate exhales, his bedsheets clenched in his fists. 'You're right. Lauren's death was personal, we know that. We don't know how or why, but it was. You were trying to figure out why her killer would go after Anna seventeen years later, and now we know. It *wasn't* the same killer. It's someone else entirely – someone who killed her just because she fit the hallmarks of Lauren's case.'

Nate runs his hands over his chin, scraping his stubble. He laughs.

'I *knew* the real podcast story wasn't with Lauren. Told you so.'

'*Typical Nate*,' August's voice says again in my head. '*Making himself the centre of things, as usual.*'

Nate grabs his laptop and notebook and heads to the table.

'Okay, so, three different cases recreated pretty much perfectly, right? The police aren't exactly going to release confidential information to the press, but as far as we know, the killings are like for like. Right?'

'Right,' I say, shaking off August's words.

'Immediately they've got a few things in common.' He starts a list. 'One – British. All happened in England. Two – old. Nothing more recent than 2006, which, I'm sorry to say, is basically classed as ancient history now. Um, what else . . .'

'Three – different *types* of death. We've got stabbing with Anna, beheading with Carousel, and fire with Hampstead Heath.'

'Weren't those teens beaten to death with a spade first? Or was it the fire that finished them off?'

'I can't remember.' I slump into the seat beside him, scraping my hair back. 'Bloody hell. They were *teens*, Nate. Someone just killed two teenagers, and they don't even have a misguided reason for it.'

He writes a 4. 'Maybe the type of victims is a factor? Teenage girl, older man, two older teen guys. That's different every time, too?'

'And luckily there are only so many combinations.'

Nate scribbles this down, while I hug my knees.

I think of Anna, as I often do: face pale grey and streaked with blood, feet curled limply against the sofa. So young. I don't need police confirmation to know that the boys found on Hampstead Heath this morning would have been around the same age.

'We need to tell the police about this,' I say.

'They must already know. They're not clueless these days. It's not like back when Ted Bundy could get away with it by moving states, or the Yorkshire Ripper could be interviewed by the police nine times before being arrested. There's probably some automated database search that cross-checks all case elements against old ones to look for similarities.'

'But they might not know Anna, Carousel, and the suitcases on Hampstead Heath are linked to *each other*. And that if there's been three of these copycat killings already, there could easily be a fourth. We need to warn them, so they can coordinate the search.'

Nate taps his pen on the table. 'Okay. And then we need to warn the public.'

'Warn the public?'

'Yes! Do you *really* think the police will admit there's a copycat serial killer out there? No, they won't – but *we* can.'

Nate leans in close.

'We know the original murders, and we were *there* to find Anna, the first of the copies. We're involved. We should—'

'Wait.' I sit up, staring at Nate's notes. 'What if Anna *wasn't* the first of the copies? It only *got* in the news when it leaked that we were the ones who discovered the body.'

'Huh.' Nate searches Google for *UK murders 2023* – and gets about a million hits about knife crime. 'Ugh, that's a lot to wade through.'

'Just go to Wikicide. You can sort it by newest murders first, can't you?'

Nate types in two letters and his most frequently visited Wikicide page link finishes itself: Lauren Parker. He picks the homepage from the list, and clicks it.

ERROR: WEBSITE OFFLINE UNTIL IDIOTS WHO LISTEN TO STUPID PODCASTS STOP MESSING WITH THE ARTICLES

'Ugh, this guy,' Nate says, rolling his eyes. 'Curtis Templeton. You think he'd be grateful for the extra traffic we give him, but no. He's taken the whole website down.'

'Back to trawling through Google results, then.'

'Not necessarily.' He checks the time. 'Screw it, let's just go visit him in person.'

'Visit him? We don't even know where he lives.'

'I do. He runs a bookshop over in Hackney Wick. It's listed on the website, down at the bottom where . . . Well, it's not here right now. As you *may* be able to tell from the way he calls his visitors idiots, he wasn't really the responding-to-emails type. I went over there to ask him some stuff.'

'When was this?'

'Ah, well, it was earlier this year when . . . you know, we weren't really hanging out much. I wondered if he knew anything about that new DNA evidence in Lauren's case.'

I fiddle with my twisted serpent thumb ring. We stopped talking for a while because that was *all* Nate wanted to talk about. That, and using whatever information he could find to restart a podcast people no longer wanted to listen to.

'And did he know anything?'

'No, but he did enjoy tearing the podcast to shreds in person, so I'd say he'll be fairly pleased to welcome us back.'

Nate disappears into the bathroom to get ready, and I make myself a coffee. I glance at Wikicide's angry new homepage. I knew Nate was making the most of Anna's murder and the second

Carousel killing, but I had no idea he was driving enough extra traffic to crash a website.

There's a Twitter tab open at the top of Nate's browser, and the notification count ticks to 157. I check Nate's profile.

Poll! Battle of the psychopaths?? Which recent murder shocked you more?

I'm not saying I want to see more photos of the headless horseman, but I'm also not NOT saying that. DMs open.

Police have urged people not to speculate about the recent murders in Foxbridge and Brighton. Sure would be a shame if people joined me in speculating in the replies right now . . .

The page updates before my eyes.

The plot thickens! Two burnt bodies found on Hampstead Heath in two suitcases. Where have I heard this one before?? #AllTheGoryDetails

He's tweeted it *while* brushing his teeth.

August was right: Nate loves to be in the centre of things. Even now, when we're technically just going by the word of a random cabbie, he's tweeted out a link to Episode 43 like our theory is fact. And his tweet is already on its way to getting another 147 notifications.

I squirm at the replies: that reaction video where Brenda from Bristol exclaims: 'You're joking – not another one!' A gif of Michael Jackson eating popcorn. A pretty girl with skulls in her username: OMG, this was one of my favourite episodes!!

Murderers usually have a reason for what they do. Their MOs are carefully thought out and often personal: reminiscent of childhood trauma, or a reworking of a past experience. Serial killers have favourite methods and weapons. They're creatures of habit. Their crimes, however barbaric, are meaningful.

But what meaning is there in copying someone else's murder? In killing a girl who looks like a victim from the past, or a horse breeder who lived near a seaside carousel? Why kill two teenagers – *kids* – for no reason?

What kind of person could do these things? And what else could that person be capable of?

'Ready to go?'

I swap back to Wikicide, pretending I haven't seen Nate's tweets.

It isn't my style to use social media the way he does, but maybe this time, it's for the best.

If there's no pattern to the murders except for them all being copies, anybody could be next. At least Nate's method might give them some warning.

CHAPTER 8

We head north-east across London to The Murder Emporium. I walk along with Nate, scanning the signs of vape stores and phone repairs and bland coffee served behind grimy windows – and almost miss the bookshop entirely. It's a single door between shops, and it opens immediately on to a narrow staircase leading down into a dark, dingy basement.

'Are you sure this is where people come to read about murder, and not where people come to *be* murdered?' I ask.

'Pretty sure, but we'll see how this goes, I guess. Maybe we'll catch Curtis in a particularly bad mood.'

The walls of the staircase are plastered with posters of serial killers – both fictional and real – and there's a *mind your head* sign at the bottom with the image of an axe and some spurts of blood next to it.

That might have made me laugh before I discovered Anna's body in the farmhouse.

The shop itself is stranger than I imagined. Second-hand books are stacked right up to the low ceiling on rickety shelves, while too-bright strip lights blink out of time with each other, uncomfortably overcompensating for the lack of windows. There's a line-up of famous mugshots behind the till in the corner, and amid the many books – fiction, true crime, biographies of serial killers – there are stacks of rolled-up posters, and plastic pots of badges. I pick out a few: FRED WEST GARDENING SERVICES; AN APPLE A DAY KEEPS HAROLD SHIPMAN AWAY; ED KEMPER, MEET MY MOTHER-IN-LAW.

On the few spare patches of wall there are letters framed behind glass, each with different handwriting and signatures, but the same addressee at the top: CURTIS.

'That one's from Dennis Rader,' a deep voice says behind me. One of the mugshots on the wall isn't a mugshot at all, but a man sitting in front of it. Curtis stares back at me, black hair long and straggly and greying.

I gulp, and realise what he said. 'The BTK Killer wrote back to you?'

'Yep. They all write back to me.'

Curtis stands up. He seems too big for the small basement: tall and broad, he slouches through necessity, his open flannel shirt revealing a stretched wrestling tee of Chris Benoit beneath it.

I'm guessing his interest in Benoit is less his WWE career and more the fact he killed his wife, his son, and then himself back in 2007.

Curtis comes towards me, pointing at other framed letters around the room.

'David Berkowitz. Peter Sutcliffe. Ian Huntley. Manson. Bundy. John Wayne Gacy. He was my first. I was nine. He did that painting for me.'

Curtis says it wistfully – or as wistfully as his monotone voice will allow – like a teen reminiscing over a selfie with BTS, not a grown man thinking about the time a convicted killer and sex offender wrote back to his younger self for, I presume, all the wrong reasons.

'I like talking to them. Sometimes they say everyday stuff. Other times you get to hear their side of things.'

'Do you need to hear a serial killer's side of things?' I ask.

'For full context, yes. You don't learn much from one-sided podcasts where the hosts don't even do their own research, and are proud of it.' Curtis looks at us pointedly.

'Typical Curtis,' Nate says, tutting – like they're old friends having a bit of banter. 'You love a good dig at *All the Gory Details*, don't you?'

'Is it a dig if it's true?'

'There he goes again! Always getting the last insult in. I do love our little get-togethers, Curtis.'

I know this tone well. It's the one Nate uses when someone doesn't thank him for holding a door open, or when he's around someone he can't stand: overly friendly, pushing straight through smarm to sarcasm.

I remember the first time I heard it: him, August, and me picking through the lane where the dog walker found Lauren's shoe all those years ago.

I didn't realise you were coming too, August. Great. I love it when it's the three of us.

I didn't pick up on it back then, though.

Curtis rolls his eyes. 'Why are you here, Blackwell? I'm guessing it's not to purchase something educational. And why'd you bring this one with you? She's even more clueless than you.'

'Clueless?'

'Yeah. You did accuse the wrong person in your first ever episode, right? And then profit off it with merchandise and sponsorship deals? And then heap more inaccuracies on top of it with every new episode?'

I cross my arms. 'I didn't always get the facts perfectly right, but Nate—'

'Was hardly a fountain of knowledge himself. You mixed up the dates in the Richard Ramirez episode, you spent an hour pronouncing Joachim Kroll's name completely wrong, and don't get me started on the utter hack job you did on Jeffrey Dahmer.'

'You seem to know a lot about our podcast for someone who hates it so much.'

'Well, *someone* had to try to correct all your mistakes in the comment section. Too bad you or your gullible fans never bothered to read it.' He mocks our voices. '*Trust nobody – especially not us, as we're completely unqualified idiots.* James Nash is so much better. Now there's a podcaster you can trust. No fluff or pointless chat with him, and he actually looks into the history and motivations of his killers rather than making jokes about them. You two should listen, and take notes. Or even better, go back on hiatus. Permanently.'

Okay, now I get why Nate can't stand this guy. I open my mouth to retort, but Nate steps in.

'Curtis, you're right. We should have tried harder. We should have properly studied your articles every single week and put together episodes that were informative, honest, and respectful. We didn't do that, but we've learnt our lesson. For our new podcast, we want to be better – but how can we, when we can't access *the* best murder database on the internet? I don't trust any website but Wikicide, do you, Stevie?'

The Nate Blackwell charm offensive is underway – and I join it.

'I can't even think of another website to use as an alternative. That's why everyone's been visiting yours, Curtis. Because it's the best.'

Curtis looks between us, then barks out a laugh. 'Whatever it is you came here for, you won't get it by arse-kissing.'

He stomps over to tidy a shelf, laughing to himself. I follow him.

'Okay, fine. You don't like us – and to be honest, I don't like you either. But you *are* an expert at true crime, and we have some legitimate true crime questions that you might be the only person who can answer. So are you going to let us ask them, or are you going to be so stubborn and unpleasant that you don't even get a look-in on the unfolding-before-our-very-eyes true crime story that we're working on right now?'

Nate catches my eye. '*Nice,*' he mouths.

Curtis pauses, a book half slid on to a shelf. 'Okay, I'll bite. What's the story?'

'There's a serial killer recreating past murders in the present,' I say. 'It's a c—'

'Copycat killer, yeah, I know. Anna Farley, Ron O'Donnell, and the human remains found over on Hampstead Heath.' He looks between us, and smirks behind his hair. 'Oh, have you only just realised?'

'We thought the first two were the original killers striking again,' Nate says, 'but . . . Wait, how did *you* know it was a copycat?'

'Hello?' He points at himself. 'True crime expert. The first two were *too* on-the-nose to be legitimate second murders, and the suitcase murders are clearly a recreation because Nigel Smith died—'

'In 1982, we know.'

'—*and* because they were found in completely the wrong location.'

Nate and I frown at each other. 'No, they weren't. They were found on Hampstead Heath, just like the original kids.'

'*No,* you just think that because you got it wrong in your podcast. Timmy Renshaw and Michael Green weren't found on Hampstead Heath.'

I can never remember the names in old cases, but Curtis reels them off from his mental encyclopaedia like they're family members he's known all his life.

No wonder he hates our podcast.

Sighing, Curtis moves to a different shelf. He hunts through the books and pulls one out for us, finding a specific page.

'Nigel Smith's biography,' he says. 'There, see? ". . . *while the garden vandalism was a fun after-school pastime for Michael and Timothy during their younger years, it was a hobby that would eventually lead to the boys being killed and dumped in suitcases in Hampstead Heath Square, a small communal garden in a sleepy North London street.*" Hampstead Heath *Square*. It's like nobody even bothers to read the whole name.'

'That's so weird,' I say. 'I *always* thought it was Hampstead Heath.'

'Me too.'

'All it takes is for one website or podcast to get it wrong, and everyone who copies them gets it wrong, too. I'll give you something, though – you definitely weren't the *first* to get it wrong. For once.' Curtis puts the book back where he found it. 'It does say a lot about our so-called copycat, though.'

'How do you mean?'

'He's clearly not a proper true crime aficionado, or he'd know it was Hampstead Heath Square. So he's not as smart as he thinks he is. Nigel Smith would be rolling in his grave if he knew someone redid his murders and did them wrong. I'd be embarrassed if it were me. Wouldn't you?' He looks us up and down, and then laughs. 'What am I saying? You'd probably take it as a compliment.'

Curtis grabs a stack of books and skulks around the room, returning them to the correct places. Nate and I stay where we are, whispering.

'This killer wants attention,' I say. 'He wants people to look at his work and know what he's referencing.'

'He's showing off.'

'Yeah. But he got the location wrong for the Suitcase Murders just like everyone else.' I look around the room. There must be books on hundreds, probably even thousands of old murders that would appeal to the killer. From the big, glamorous, caught-after-a-seven-year-manhunt kind, or the small, creepy, keep-you-up-at-night kind, there are so many to choose from.

'What if whoever's doing this is picking murders made famous, or more famous, by the true crime community? Lauren's case exploded this year and suddenly everyone knows about it. Carousel was always a strange one, but James Nash did that in-depth look at the horseracing motive a few years back. And it's practically a rite of passage to look up that photo of Nigel Smith and his wife standing in their front garden with their holiday suitcases and the gnomes. Nate, what if the killer is picking these murders because people like us have made them famous?'

Curtis is back at the counter. He leans against it, watching us with his head tilted, his long, dark hair hanging limply over his shirt.

In another life, this could have been a record shop. He could have had signed letters from rock stars, not convicted criminals. His T-shirt would've had a band on it, not a WWE wrestler-turned-murderer. We may even have been friends.

But how people love true crime is a spectrum, and he and I are at different ends.

'Curtis, you know more about true crime than we do,' I say.

'I'm glad you can admit it.'

'The thing is, we're idiots who care. But we came here because we thought you might be able to help us.'

'You want me to join your little sleuth squad?' He pulls a dorky double thumbs-up. 'No thanks.'

'Yeah, we *definitely* weren't asking that,' Nate mutters.

'Have there been any other possible copycat murders recently? I know you keep track of these things, for your website. Has anything else of note popped up?'

'Well, well, well. Look who finally wants to *learn* something.'

He looks so smug I can barely stand it – but that's just what he wants.

'Please help us, Curtis. You're smart, we're dumb. You guessed this copycat link days before we did. We *need* your help. And . . . we'll do whatever you want in exchange for it. You want us to pay you? Buy books?'

'Name-drop you in future episodes of the podcast?'

Curtis is still, his arms crossed and a little smirk fixed on his face. Then he shifts on the counter, making it creak.

'All right, I'll give you my expert opinion. The killer is escalating. Murder one, Anna Farley – basic. Good attention to detail in copying the events of the case, but the murder itself is nothing to write home about. A few stabs to the chest. Blah. Boring. Anyone could do that.'

I think of Anna's blood-sodden clothes, the way her hands had been manipulated to hold the dead flowers – and the gaping wounds on her chest.

I couldn't do that.

'But then we get the headless carousel, and that's much more exciting. Not only *because* of the beheading, but the public nature of it. The killer had to sneak around CCTV cameras, pick locks, generally put themselves more at risk to stage a spectacle. And it worked.' He gives Nate a knowing nod. 'You can imagine the rush, right? Must have felt amazing.'

'Uh, sure . . . And this latest one?'

'Two victims, bludgeoning and burning, leaving the bodies in a public place. Now *that's* a good double murder.' Curtis rubs his chin. 'I wonder if he's trying to say something through the choice of cases. Two unsolved, one done and dusted. Not sure of a link there. We'll have to see what's next.'

'And what do you think could be next?' I ask. 'Will it escalate further? Or return to something more . . . sedate?'

'More boring, you mean? I hope not. Well, if it were *me*, I'd do something really iconic. I'd want to show what I can do – and what I know. Maybe do a Philip Burns and hang a load of Scouts from an oak tree during a camping trip, or choke a woman to death with her own severed foot like Ernest Williams did in 1946. Ooh, or the Newcrest Hall fire, where the illegitimate son of an earl locked the family and all their servants inside and then torched the place. Honestly, there are a *lot* of good ones . . .'

He stares off into the distance, smiling, and Nate mouths three words to me: *what a psychopath.*

'I don't know a lot about those ones,' Nate says. 'If only there was a website, run by a literal genius in the field of murder, that I could visit at any time to tell me all about all these amazing crimes in great detail . . .'

'Fine,' Curtis says, 'I'll open the website again. But *stop* sending links and overloading it with your grubby fans who mess up the articles. The edit function is so people with real information can add to the entries, not so idiots can post their theories like they're fact.'

'Okay, I'll tell them to stop. Thank you!'

'Is that a good idea?' I ask. 'I hadn't thought of it before, but . . . won't it give the killer ideas? You're giving him step-by-step details on how to recreate these murders. What if he's been using the website already?'

'If he was using my website, those suitcases would have been dumped in Hampstead Heath Square last night like they should have been. Giving people false information is your area, not mine.'

The insults are easy to shake off now.

'Wait,' I say. 'The killer *did* dump the suitcases on Hampstead Heath, even though that was wrong. Do you think he knew it was wrong? Did he do that on purpose, to make some kind of state-ment? Or did he not know any better?'

Curtis sighs. 'We'll have to wait for another few murders to be sure. This guy's got potential to be a prolific, once-in-a-lifetime figure in true crime. There could be books on him. He could inspire *others* to be copycats. This could be the start of something that makes a worldwide impact. I could end up with a letter from him on my wall!' His eyes shine with possibility, then dim. 'Be a real shame to find out it's just some idiot who believes everything he hears in podcasts.'

◆ ◆ ◆

Nate and I head home, and make some phone calls on the way. Going through the 101 non-emergency police line, we get put through to the Dorset, Sussex, and Met forces, and we even leave a message for DI Chopra on the number he gave us.

'Tell him that we were wrong about Anna Farley's death. She wasn't killed by the same person who killed Lauren Parker, she was killed by someone *copying* Lauren Parker's death, and we think that person has killed other people using different copied methods as well. Please, have him call us back as soon as possible.'

The operators and officers we speak to are all polite and take down everything we say – but I don't know if they believe us. I'm not sure I would have believed claims about a copycat serial killer a day ago, either.

Nate is right: we have to get the word out. If Curtis is correct and the killer is escalating, it won't stop with four victims. The methods won't stop with stabbing, beheading, and bludgeoning.

There are many terrible ways to die. After nearly two hundred episodes, Nate and I know that only too well.

In the evening, Nate comes up to my flat with recording equipment and pizza and we sit together, like we always used to on

Thursday nights – but this time, we're not trying to entertain with stories of murder.

We're trying to prevent new ones.

After Nate leaves, I lie in bed with my fingers in Rosie's fur, staring up at the ceiling.

Lauren Parker's murder in Sandford in 2006 wasn't a big story. Then earlier this year, because of the murder weapon being found and me wrongly blaming Mike, her death was put in the spotlight.

Lauren's murder is famous because of me. She's as well-known now as the Suitcase Killings and Carousel because *I* drew attention to her.

And that means Anna Farley is dead because of me, too.

CHAPTER 9

The boys in the suitcases on Hampstead Heath are identified as Joshua Pinkham and Kenny Jones, two nineteen-year-olds from Liverpool. Their parents cry in their TV interviews, clutching football shirts that'll never be worn again, pleading for anyone who has information about what happened to their sons to come forward.

All they know so far is that the teens were playing football in the park with friends, and then never made it home.

'Hey, look at this one,' Nate says from the sofa, showing me his screen. It's another piece of fan art: us reimagined in classic Sherlock Holmes style, with deerstalker hats and pipes and magnifying glasses, and Nate sporting an enormous moustache. *A Study in Podcasting* it says below, in fancy lettering. 'Cute, right? I'll put it on our Instagram.'

I press my thumbnail between my teeth, resisting the urge to bite.

We posted our latest episode of *When It Happens Again* two days ago, and Nate has barely looked away from his phone since then. In between his bar shifts and the lessons with my regular guitar students, we were *supposed* to be trying to figure out what Mimic – as Nate decided to call him – might do next, but Nate is more interested in what fans send him.

I scroll down list after list of British murders, hoping something will jump out at me – but nothing does. Or rather, *everything* does. So many murders could be recreated in the present for maximum drama, but there's no way to guess what could be next.

This felt personal before, back when it was us, Lauren, and Anna. I knew where I was then: theories about killer classmates or party-crashing strangers; old leads to help solve a new murder. I had been there, seen it, lived it. But this . . . this is overwhelming. A killer in three counties, with four victims, and three different styles. No firm link between murders. No CCTV or leads released to the press. Nothing.

The killer could live hundreds of miles away, or next door. He could be one man, or several. He could be completely unaware of *All the Gory Details*, or he could have listened to every single episode.

Perhaps he listened to our new episode of *When It Happens Again*, where Nate and I revealed the link between the three cases and made his work as Mimic official. Perhaps it's scared him off, now he knows people are on to him.

Or perhaps it's made him want to do it more.

Nate smiles at something on his phone, and taps out a reply. I chew on my nail.

Nate gets a rush from podcasting. He always has. That's what August meant about saying he centres himself – as an extrovert, he thrives off attention. He encourages the drawings and the memes because he loves seeing the impact he's had on our listeners. He replies to people's comments because he wants them to send another.

Does Mimic feel the same? We covered Anna's death, and now we've covered Carousel and the Suitcase Murders, too.

If Mimic feeds off fame like Nate does, should we be giving him what he wants?

'Okay,' Nate says, sitting up on the sofa and clearing his throat. Rosie glares at him from the armrest. 'I've been checking out coverage of these three cases over the years. Lauren's death didn't pick up until this year, we know that, but Blackpool Carousel and the Suitcase Murders have both been in documentaries, and podcasts, and Nigel Smith even had that drama adaptation a few years back – the one with Michael Sheen, remember?'

'That doesn't really narrow it down, does it?'

Nate sighs. 'No. But at least so far the murders have all been cases we know. We'll be on the backfoot if he picks something new next.'

I put my laptop on the table, and stretch in my armchair. Nate and I are reversed today: me upright and rigid, him sideways on the sofa.

'What are we doing here, Nate?'

'Researching?'

'No, I mean . . . What are we trying to achieve by doing this? We're trying to raise awareness, I get that, but you and I can't change anything here. Whether we read up on every old case or listen to every single podcast in the world, we're not going to suddenly predict the next attack, or stumble across the killer's name somewhere. We have no idea what DNA evidence the police might have, or what they're doing to connect these murders. Doesn't it all feel a bit pointless?' I chew harder on my nail. 'And dangerous?'

Nate sits up. 'Dangerous?'

'You said before, *ages ago*, that you didn't want to look into Lauren's murder because we were too close to it.'

'Yeah, true.'

'But how is this any different? This killer is taking his inspiration from real true crime cases, and you and I are part of the true crime community.'

'We're just *a* part of it, though.'

'Not when it comes to this case. We're the ones covering it. You've always covered it, even back when I thought everything was about Lauren. *When It Happens Again* started out about her, but now it's about *him*. Doesn't it freak you out that the killer probably wanted someone to find the link? He could have been watching your Twitter, waiting for the moment it happened.'

Nate wraps his arms around himself. 'Okay, that *is* creepy.'

'I just feel . . . useless. I wish we had some ballpark for what we should be looking for. Is the killer going to go back decades or just years? Will he target women or men? Gay or straight? Old or young? What race? What political affiliation? What story?' I rub my forehead. 'I hate not knowing. And I hate that, for all we know, the next one could have happened already.'

I go back to my scrolling of famous murders, the metallic varnish on my thumbnail chipped and jagged.

His seven victims were all nurses . . . a newborn baby smothered in an alleyway . . . the three men were found in their tent with deep stab wounds . . .

I used to read these articles like they were movie reviews: is it exciting enough? Will I get my gore fix? Does the story have a compelling villain? I knew it was real, but it never felt *real*. There was a distance to it, especially if the photos were retro and all you saw of the victims was one headshot. They were figures from the past, and long dead. They had become legend.

But there was nothing exciting about seeing Anna in that farmhouse. The deep, congealed wounds on her chest weren't something cool to gawp at – and neither are the images of Ron O'Donnell sitting headless on that carousel. Joshua Pinkham and Kenny Jones are loud and vibrant and alive in videos taken just hours before they were dumped, beaten and charred, on Hampstead Heath in suitcases.

For years, I only cared about the best stories.

I didn't consider the innocent lives that were taken in exchange for them.

I check the news websites for any updates. There aren't any. It's still grieving relatives, pleas for information. I've seen too much of this lately. Joshua and Kenny's families, Anna's, the O'Donnells – and before that, Destiny Davis' mother clutching a framed photo of her daughter, begging for her safe return after she was snatched from a playground and . . .

I can never remember the names or dates of individual cases – but Curtis can, and his website has a search function. I go to Wikicide and search for articles containing the word *playground*.

There are several hits: teen killers who hung a classmate from the swings; a school shooter in America who targeted his old teachers.

And Dillan Jones.

. . . after serving two years for the sexual assault of three girls, Jones was released from prison and moved to Swansea to live with his mother. Soon after her death in 1987, Jones abducted five-year-old Tanya Meadows from a local playground and took her to his home, where he strangled her to death with his mother's tights. Jones was briefly interviewed by police, but was never considered a suspect. Tanya Meadows remained a missing person until 2004, when the now-deceased Jones' home was cleared out as part of the Channel 5 show Extreme Hoarders. Her body was found buried in old newspapers beneath Jones' mother's bed, and was partially mummified. The episode never aired.

There's an image of Tanya Meadows: dark braids with fluffy hairbands; glowing cheeks.

So much like Destiny Davis, with her big grin and impossibly cute Afro puffs.

'Nate, read this.' I send him the link and watch as he reads it – confusion on his face at first, and then understanding.

'This could be Destiny Davis, right?' I ask. 'Taken from a playground, same demographic—'

'But Tanya wasn't found for years, and Destiny's only been missing for weeks. How would he recreate that?'

'I don't know. Maybe he's playing the long game? But the thing is, nobody knows when Tanya died. Dillan Jones died without mentioning it to *anyone*, so he could have kept her alive for days, weeks, *months* before strangling her. And that means—'

'Destiny could still be alive, too.' Nate sits up straight, his eyes big. 'We should record a new podcast episode. Now.'

'No, we should *tell the police*.'

'Okay, fine. Call them, and then we'll record. How didn't we spot this before? Wow, this is a scoop. This is huge.'

Nate starts planning out the episode, his knee bouncing with excitement.

My knees don't bounce at all.

I don't want this to be real. I don't want the person who stabbed Anna, beheaded O'Donnell, and burnt Joshua and Kenny to have hurt Destiny Davis, too – but it's the only lead we have. How do I get the police to listen to it?

DI Chopra never returned our call, and there's nothing in the official statements about the murders being linked. The copycat theory we phoned about the other day might be being investigated in secret – or it might have been ignored entirely.

I can't take the chance on a tip line again. I need to talk to someone who'll take me seriously.

I scroll down my messages – way, *way* down – and find an old thread: Logan Jeffries.

For two years, this message thread used to be alight with dinner plans and in-jokes and *I can't wait to see you*s, but it slowed to a stop months ago. The last messages on the screen are abrupt and terse: cold words about the arrangements for returning each other's things, and cancelling the van that would have moved me from my flat to his.

Hi, it's Stevie. Can we talk?

I send the text and wait, eyes fixed to the screen, holding the phone almost painfully tight.

I don't know if he'll respond. Maybe he's blocked my number. Maybe he's changed his. Maybe—

Of course. What's this about?

I exhale.

Something important. Are you free now?

There's a pause, the little *typing* dots coming and going.

I can spare a few minutes. Outside work, one hour?

Perfect.

'I'm going out,' I say, heading into my bedroom to pull on my boots and leather jacket. I think about reaching for lipstick, but don't.

'Where?'

'This is too important for a phone call. I need to tell someone about Destiny in person.'

'Where, though? Her local police station?'

'Um, Logan's.'

'No,' Nate says immediately, standing up. 'Not him.'

'Yes him. He's a *detective*, Nate. He'll have contacts he can pass this on to, and they'll take it more seriously when it comes from him.'

'But is he going to take it seriously when it comes from us?'

'When it comes from me, he will.'

'Oh. So when you say *you're* going, you mean without me?'

I fiddle with my zip. 'I think that's for the best. Don't you?'

Nate bites back a retort, and shrugs. 'Yeah, I suppose me calling him a dickhead to his face probably won't help. He is one, though.'

'I know you think so.'

'I *know* so.' Nate shoves his hands in his pockets. 'I don't understand why you'd want to see him again after all the things he said to you.'

'That was months ago. Besides, we're adults. Adults can talk about things, even with some awkward history. If you actually *dated* women instead of redeeming one-night free trials, you'd know that for yourself.'

'Fine. But if he upsets you again, just leave. Call me, and I'll hotwire Piastri's car and come get you. Seriously. I'll bop him on the nose.'

'You're going to steal an old lady's car so you can punch a police officer in the face?'

'If I have to, yeah.'

I smile. 'Good to know.'

I grab my bag, and Nate reaches for his things from the sofa. There's a hiss, and a shout.

'Ow! She just scratched me.'

While Nate indignantly rubs his arm, I go and kiss Rosie's head. She purrs.

'You know that's her favourite way of saying goodbye to you.'

Nate grumbles something under his breath.

Out on the street, Nate hesitates before heading down to his basement flat.

'I mean it about Logan, you know. You don't have to go if you don't want to face him. I could go. You don't have to see him.'

'I do.' I shiver in the cold air, wrapping my arms around myself. 'Whatever happened between him and me, he's still the only police contact we have. I'll take a few minutes of awkwardness if it helps Destiny Davis get home safe.'

'Do you really think that's a possibility? Honestly?'

'Yes. Absolutely.'

But the state of my thumbnail tells a different story.

CHAPTER 10

I know the walk to Lavender Hill police station well: across Chelsea Bridge, through Battersea Park, and then down into the streets. For a while, this area felt like it would be home – like I'd one day have a go-to takeaway place, and know which pub served the best Sunday roasts and which one had the worst toilets. But it never became my home.

I pop into Logan's favourite coffee shop and leave with two drinks and a pocketful of biscotti. Then I head for the side of the police station, tucked away behind a corner. Our old spot.

I haven't been here in a long time. Not since—

Logan is already there: hair still braided and knotted on top of his head; suit still incredibly well fitted. The familiarity of him, here, hurts my chest in a way I didn't expect.

I packed up our relationship into a mental box a long time ago, and I've never felt the need to go poking around in it. In fact, I tried to forget the box was there at all.

But I suppose I did that for a reason.

We look at each other's hands, both of us carrying two cups from the same café, and laugh.

'Thanks for remembering my order,' he says, 'but you *really* shouldn't have.'

'I was feeling particularly thirsty, what can I say?' I balance both drinks in one hand and fish out the biscotti for him.

'No way.' He reaches into his own pocket. 'Millionaire's shortbread.'

We swap favourite snacks and the other's drink – resting the spares on a ledge – and take a few sips.

'New boots?' he asks, gesturing with his own smart shoe.

'Yep.'

'I like them.'

'I don't. I'm still breaking them in. How's work?'

'Busy, you know how it is. A lot of stress.'

I used to help him unwind, back then: strong drinks in pokey little bars; laughter as we stumbled into the lift to his flat; the steam from his walk-in shower . . . That would have been our everyday life now, if things hadn't fallen apart like they did.

I had so wanted that to be our everyday, once.

My next sip is more of a gulp.

'How are you, Stevie?' Logan tilts his head in his familiar way, two braids flopping across his forehead. 'I've wanted to ask a few times – *lots* of times – these past few months, but . . . you know.'

I do know. But some things said during arguments can't be taken back.

'I'm okay.' A lie. 'Stressed. Very stressed. Not really sleeping at the moment.'

'Yeah, finding a dead body for the first time will do that to you.'

'You heard about that?'

'I think *everyone* heard about that. Your new podcast about Mimic – *When It Happens Again*, right? – is all over the news. Six months of *not* googling your name, and you ended up on my news feed anyway.' He takes a bite of biscotti. 'So unfair.'

155

I smile. 'Sorry about that. Next time I stumble across a crime scene, I'll try to keep it out of the papers.'

'Thanks, I'd appreciate it.' He brushes a few crumbs from his mouth, and his face turns serious again. 'Jokes aside, are you all right? Officers are offered counselling if they see something like that, and they're trained for it. How are *you*? Really?'

'I'm . . .' I sigh. 'I don't know.'

'Is this just because of what you saw? Or because you're spearheading a viral copycat serial killer theory that you probably should have left to the police?'

I scrape my hand through my hair. 'Wow, I really *have* been on your news feed, huh?'

'You can't stumble across a crime scene and then drop a grenade about a new serial killer, and *not* expect people to talk about it.' He takes a sip of coffee. 'I assume that's why you're here? To ask me questions about this Mimic of yours that I'm not allowed to answer?'

'Kind of. Sorry.'

'It's okay. Trust me, after how we left things . . . I wasn't expecting this to be a social visit, anyway.' Logan puts his coffee on the ledge, freeing his hands. He presses them together. 'So, what questions would you like me to *not* answer for you today?'

I put my coffee down, too. We used to play this game when we were together: me ever curious about his cases; him teasing me with sideways answers. But sometimes he'd let something slip.

'I reported the copycat theory two days ago, but no one's called me back and there's been no mention of it in official statements about the murders. Is it being investigated?'

'I imagine the official statements are official statements for a reason, and they'd tell the public more if they felt it necessary. Next question?'

'Are the cases being investigated as the work of copycats individually, at least?'

'I don't know, because they're not my cases.'

'Are there any leads on who might be behind these murders?'

'If I knew, I would quite literally lose my job if I told you. But you already knew that, didn't you? From last time you asked.'

Logan's casual friendliness splinters, exposing the echoes of arguments I thought we'd left in the past.

'This again?' I sigh, shoving my hands in my pockets. 'I should never have asked you to look into Lauren's files, and I'm sorry. I just wanted – *needed* – to know what was going on with that DNA evidence. But I shouldn't have put you in that position.'

'*You* didn't, Stevie.'

He fixes me with a knowing look – and I look away.

'*Just ask him about the DNA,*' Nate said six months ago, over and over, as the trolling started and our podcast stats fell to nothing. '*We need to get ahead of this. It can't be hard for him to access old Sandford files, can it? See what they know. Is the DNA a match to anything? Do they have any leads or suspects? Just ask him, Stevie. Ask him!*'

'We were trying to do the right thing,' I say to Logan's shoes.

'We both know that's not true. You wanted to end that podcast, once and for all, but he wanted to revive it. He was clutching at straws, trying to find anything that would get you back in front of that microphone and back into the charts. He didn't care if I lost my job because of it.' Logan pauses. 'He didn't like that you were spending those free Thursday nights with me instead.'

I didn't want to talk about this. I threw everything about Logan and our relationship into the box, sealed it, and drop-kicked it into the recesses of my mind, precisely so I *wouldn't* have to talk about this. But all those memories spill out now.

Nate and Logan's sarcastic little comments to each other whenever we hung out together.

Logan's possessive hand on my waist or my leg whenever Nate was there.

Nate bringing up in-jokes and stories from our past that Logan wasn't a part of.

Logan shutting Nate out of our plans.

Nate crashing those plans.

Logan bad-mouthing Nate.

Nate bad-mouthing Logan.

Logan breaking down after too many drinks, crying, shouting: '*Why can't you see it? He's trying to split us up. He wants you for himself.*'

And the ultimatum, some two or three or four identical arguments later, right before we were about to move in together: '*I can't do this any more, Stevie. It's him, or me. You choose.*'

And I sealed up the box, and chose Nate.

'Did he put you up to coming here?'

'*What?*'

'It was Nate's idea, wasn't it?' Logan says his name with as much dislike as ever. 'Try to get some information out of me for the podcast? An exclusive scoop for the two of you to laugh about?'

'No.' I meet his eye again, returning its anger. 'It was *my* idea. He didn't want me to come at all.'

'Ah, I see. He wanted you to stay away from me? Well, nothing's changed there, then. He must be livid you're spending time with someone other than him. Did you have to sneak out, or is he around the corner, watching?'

I clench my fists in my pockets, resisting the urge to grab my shortbread and go.

The good times with Logan were *great* – but by the end, there weren't enough of them to stay for. No matter what I said to make him feel secure, it was never enough.

When your partner keeps accusing you of not loving them, eventually it comes true.

'I didn't come here to have this argument with you again, Logan. This isn't about us or Nate, and it's not even about you. I don't want any information from you – I have information *for* you. But if you don't want to hear it, I'll try my luck with another station.'

The anger drains from Logan's face, as it always used to. He softens, a silent despair in his eyes as he realises too late what he's said. He chews over an apology, trying to find the words – but we both know they won't change anything. There's no point any more. Not now.

Like he said, this isn't a social visit.

He clears his throat and picks his drink back up, like nothing happened. 'What information?'

'Mimic has struck three times, right? Foxbridge, the Brighton carousel, and Hampstead Heath.'

'According to your theory.' He takes a non-committal sip. 'Go on.'

'All three original cases were British murders from the past which have been recreated in exact detail. I think it's the same killer, and he'll strike again. He wants to do famous cases, things that are shocking or horrific. He's inspired by these cases. And . . . I think I might know what he's going for next. I think he might have taken Destiny Davis.'

Logan taps his cup. 'What makes you think that?'

'There's a Welsh case from the eighties where a little girl – Tanya Meadows – was snatched from a playground and never seen alive again. She was found *decades* later when the killer's house was being cleared out on one of those TV shows about hoarders. She was found under the bed, partially mummified.' I pull up an old picture of Tanya on my phone and show him. 'Logan, she looks a lot like Destiny. Just like Anna Farley looked like Lauren from my hometown.'

Logan scrolls up and down the page on Wikicide.

'Okay, there *are* similarities – but Destiny Davis isn't my case. None of them are.'

'But you can make people aware of this, can't you? I know you can't say, but *if* the police are already linking these murders together and looking for one killer, this line of inquiry could be vital. And they'll take it seriously if it's coming from one of their own.'

Logan hands the phone back to me.

'Are you sure about this, Stevie? If I'm going to stick my neck out, you have to be sure.'

'I'm sure enough.' I pick at a loose chip of nail polish on my thumb. 'I don't have police resources or information, but I know what I saw in that farmhouse in Foxbridge. Everything about Anna Farley's disappearance and death was just like Lauren Parker's. And the same goes for Carousel and the Suitcase Murders. The two men were taped to *pink* horses, both times. Those guys, Joshua and Kenny, they were beaten and then burnt, weren't they? Hands tied with garden wire? The police haven't said, but I bet there was a receipt in one of the suitcases, wasn't there? A food receipt, for tea and egg mayonnaise sandwiches and tomato soup?'

'You know I can't say anything, Stevie. And it's not my case.'

'*I know*. But these things are specific, and they're recognisable within the true crime community. Destiny Davis' disappearance sounds *a lot* like Tanya Meadows'. I hope it's nothing to do with her and she'll be found safe and sound, completely okay, but . . . What if it *is* the same person? And what if she ends up hidden under a bed somewhere?'

'Then . . . we'd feel absolutely terrible about not trying to find her.'

I think about stepping closer to him, occupying the space that was mine six months ago – but I don't. 'I know you didn't trust me before, but trust me now. Get this information to someone who can do something about it. Let me help Destiny. Please.'

'You don't need to beg me,' Logan says. He smiles sadly. 'I'll pass it on.'

'Thank you. Really.'

We stare at each other for a moment, thinking things we don't know how to say. Or that we don't want to say.

'Bye, Logan.'

I pick up my drinks and head towards the street.

'Stevie, wait.'

Logan holds my arm. He lets go as our eyes meet, his fingers grazing across my wrist.

'It was never that I didn't trust you,' he says. 'I just couldn't trust Nate.'

By the time I step into Battersea Park again, my memories of Logan are back in their box, the edges resealed with tape.

If it helps Destiny Davis and puts a stop to these murders, the awkwardness was worth it.

My phone buzzes, and I pull it out as I walk. Messages from Nate pop up every second.

Someone just sent me this video
It's going viral
I think it's legit
Some kids in Birmingham broke into a warehouse last night
They found this

A video loads on the page, and I sit on a bench to play it – angling the last of the daylight away from the dark screen. It's a screen recording of a TikTok video, a live one, and four teenage boys – five, as one's filming – are breaking into an old warehouse somewhere at night.

'Got a tip off about some good stuff here,' the recorder says. 'Let's go hunting, lads.'

They smash a window, laugh, and clamber inside. Their phone torches hit dusty machines and old crates and empty corners – but as the camera pans around, there's something in the background.

The camera swings back to it.

'What's that?' the guy with the phone asks. 'Jake, come over here.'

The torches return, glaring as they hit the camera, and the video is blurred and jerky as the teenagers go deeper into the warehouse.

Finally, the camera slows.

There's a table set up, a circular one with a white tablecloth and a cake stand, with chairs placed all around it. Chairs with people in them.

'What the fuck?' one of the boys asks, laughing. 'Creepy mannequins.'

'Did they make clothes here or something?'

'Dunno. Smells rank.'

'Go touch one, Jake.'

Jake, in a baseball cap and hood, goes over. They all laugh, and the camera moves for a better angle. Jake reaches out, and touches the arm of one.

'Ew! It's soft. Must be rotten.'

'Kiss it!'

'Yeah, snog it!'

'No!'

The camera swings just in time to show another boy shove Jake towards the mannequin. He stumbles across it, and the chair topples over backwards. The mannequin falls – limp arms smacking against the hard floor – with Jake on top of it. The boys all laugh again.

But Jake doesn't. Jake screams. *Screams.*

He claws his way up, pushing against the mannequin, and staggers away – before vomiting.

'What's wrong with you?' the guy with the camera asks. He pans back to the table and the toppled chair. The mannequin's head is detached from its body, and lies about a foot away from it.

The camera gets closer.

Close enough to see the torn stitches hanging from the stub of the neck.

Close enough to see the shine on the protruding eyes.

Close enough to see that it isn't a mannequin.

The guy recording screams, too. He turns and runs, flicking the camera around to selfie mode.

'They're dead people, man!'

The video ends, but I've seen enough.

I don't need to Google anything. I don't even need to double-check our old episodes.

I know this one. Every murder fan knows this one.

Before crime scene photos and post-mortems and detailed reports, there were old-timey charcoal sketches in newspapers. The most famous is of an empty table with five chairs around it, as though the people sitting in the chairs are having tea together. But the people aren't right. There are stitch marks on their limbs. Their eyes bulge. Their heads loll to the side. It's a cartoon, but I've always been able to read between the lines and see the real horror of it.

And now I've seen it for real.

A grizzly crime from 1823 where five women were beheaded and dismembered, their body parts swapped and sewn back together, and the new combinations arranged around a table in an abandoned building, ready for an unsuspecting visitor to find them.

Frankenstein's Tea Party – held again two hundred years after the first.

EPISODE 81: FRANKENSTEIN'S TEA PARTY

'The thing that always gets me is – do you think the prostitutes were dead *before* or *after* they were dismembered?'

'Sex workers, Nate.'

'Right, right, sorry. Do you think the *sex workers* were dead before they were hacked up?'

'I really hope so. But judging by what was done to them afterwards, I'm not sure the killer would have been so kind.'

'They were snatched over a series of nights, right? What if the killer kept them somewhere together, maybe chained up or in cages, and worked on them one by one?'

'Ugh. Imagine being the last girl standing, knowing what he'd done to the others. Seeing your new friends get murdered and maimed one by one.'

'Do you think he had a filing system? Like, did he put all the left arms in one box and the rights in another, or was it all in one big pile?'

'And did he have a plan? Was it a random mishmash of *this* now goes *there*, or was it systematic? Did he think, oh, this girl's hot! But she'd look hotter with *that girl's* legs.'

'*Sheila, babe, I love you, you know that, but we just can't get around the fact that you have cankles. It's a deal-breaker for me. I'm sorry. Nothing can change it. Ooh, unless . . .*'

'*Extreme Makeover: Body Horror Edition.*'

'What would you get replaced? I might go torso. Swap out with one of those gym guys.'

'Isn't this a kind of metaphysical question? If you're diced up into limbs, head, and torso, and everything's mixed around – which part is *you*? The brain, or the heart?'

'Oh, good point. Head, I'd guess – but the torso is the biggest part, isn't it? You're not attaching a torso to a head, you're attaching a head to a torso, plus other assorted bits. Huh. I guess if you think about it, the five torsos were the people, and all the other parts were the interchangeable accessories. Like with Lego.'

'I think the scale of this one is so baffling. Five bodies. *Five.* Where do you keep them? How do you transport them? How do you lure them over in the first place?'

'It was probably that classic – although not yet popularised – Jack the Ripper method, right? Our killer could get prostitutes—'

'*Sex workers.*'

'—to follow him anywhere, because he promised to pay them if they did.'

'They're such a vulnerable community, even now.'

'Yep. Obviously we don't have a lot of hard details about this case, as it was well before documented post-mortems, but one account of the scene stated that two of the women were so malnourished, they almost looked like skeletons. *Skeletons.* Let's be honest – if I was already selling my body for money and I was on the brink of starvation, I'd probably follow a guy straight into a dungeon and let him lock me in a cage for a bit of bread. Hell, I'd turn the key.'

'You heard it here first, people. Nate Blackwell will do *anything* for a mouthful of bread.'

'I mean, I'd rather not end up dead with someone else's limbs sewn on where mine used to be, but yeah, pretty much.'

'It's the eyes that get me. Plucking out people's eyeballs and shoving them in other people's sockets. Yuck.'

'That's *difficult*, too. We've got someone here who's capable of carting five women around, he can cut bodies into pieces with relative ease, rearrange eyeballs, *and* he's a whiz with a needle and thread.'

'Sounds like a catch! A man who can darn his own socks.'

'*And* who has his own hobbies that get him out from under your feet most evenings. Bliss.'

'The perfect husband. Oh gosh, I wonder if he *was* anyone's husband?'

'Maybe that's part of the motive. Married to some ugly nag, so he wanted to have a go at making his perfect woman out of prosti— *Ow!* Okay, okay, *sex workers*. Sorry, I just forget. It's always the P-word in the articles. But yeah, maybe that cellar was his *Build-A-Babe Workshop*.'

'I'd generally assume women are more attractive *without* other people's decaying hands attached to them, though?'

'Don't be *necrophobic*, Stevie. We'll get angry emails. *Ha!* Caught the bottlecap that time.'

'I'd love to interview whoever did these murders. What *was* he going for with this? Was it honestly some weird sexual fantasy where he'd created – in his eyes – some gorgeous women to have high tea with—'

'*More cucumber sandwiches, Verity? Or how about a Cherry Bakewell? Don't worry, it won't go to your hips.*'

'—or was that scene just the result of a psychopath who was a bit too interested in Mary Shelley's *Frankenstein* and wanted to have a go at reassembling various corpses, and female sex workers were simply the easiest material to get hold of? It's *so annoying* that we'll never know.'

'Unless the killer is listening right now. If you're the two-hundred-and-something-year-old murderer of these women, email us! We'll love to hear from you.'

'And all you regular life-spanned listeners who *aren't* murderers, why do you think he did it? Or do you think it was more than one person?'

'And which body part would *you* happily swap with a prostitute?'

'Sex worker!'

'Join us next episode where we'll be discussing the famous—'

'—and disturbing—'

'—case of Nick Curry, who vanished one evening while walking home along a canal, and turned up again in several plastic bags on the other side of the country.'

'Two dismemberments in a row? I need to stop letting you pick all the murders.'

'Until then, make sure you keep your wits about, and trust nobody—'

'Especially not your boyfriend who's *really* into Victor Frankenstein cosplay.'

'Laters, prostitutes!'

'*Nate!*'

CHAPTER 11

The most disturbing thing about the farmhouse in Foxbridge was how ordinary Anna Farley looked on that sofa. Despite the colourless skin, the congealed blood, and the deep wounds in her chest, she still looked like the girl from the missing posters. She was recognisable as a person.

The video of Frankenstein's Tea Party is the opposite.

Hunched over on a bench in Battersea Park, I let the video loop on the screen, searching for the worst, most horrific parts, even though my brain begs me not to. I can't help it.

Eyes that point in different directions flashing in the torchlight.

An arm made of three flesh tones.

The deep, jagged crosses of thread that puncture the skin – the skin itself tearing away, little by little. Oozing.

Five figures at the table, all just as butchered as the others.

I don't want it to be real, but it is. The bodies, the horror done to them, the table with its cute little tea party cake stand. It's there, exactly like it should be.

Just like all the other Mimic murders.

Nate calls me, and I answer.

'Curtis was right, wasn't he?' he says breathlessly. 'The killer's escalating. *Five* victims. Dismemberment. The staging. It's a classic. He's really gone for it this time.'

'Yeah.' I can't think of any other words.

'I can't believe he did this one. Do you think it's more than one person? Multiple killers working together? Or one guy with a lot of planning? I just looked up the industrial estate where it happened. That factory's been empty for years. He could easily have got a generator and a couple of freezers and taken his time there. He might have been working on this for a while. Are you on your way back? We need to record about this now. We can break the news ourselves if we're quick enough. And it's another one from our podcast, too. Should I tweet about it? Get ahead of everything? Stevie? Can you hear me? Hello?'

'I'm here.'

'Are you okay?'

Am I? I'm not squeamish, but I feel nauseous. My heart is pounding.

'I . . . can't talk right now. I'll be home soon.'

I hang up and force myself back on to my shaky feet, aiming for home – but I can't outrun the anxiety pulsing in my chest. I flick back to the video and play it again, my hands cupping the horrors on the screen.

Five victims, just like the original. Dismembered and put back together, just like the original. Placed around a table with food on it, just like . . .

No. *Not* like the original.

I find the old charcoal newspaper drawing on Google: five women around an empty table. I check the text: an empty table.

So why has this one got a cake stand on it?

My phone rings again.

'Logan?'

'Can't talk long,' he says, his voice low. 'Need to tell you something.'

'Is this about those bodies in Birmingham? Nate just sent me the video. Did you know about this before? It's Mimic again, it's—'

'Stevie, listen. I talked to a mate working on the Hampstead Heath case, and what I'm about to tell you has to stay between us, okay?'

My brain, so full of reassembled limbs and horror, takes a moment to clunk back on to the Suitcase Murders – which now seem tame.

'What is it?' I ask.

'Promise me you won't share this anywhere.'

'I . . . I don't know what I'm promising. You said you couldn't tell me *anything*.'

'Yeah, I did, but this concerns you.'

'What?'

'Just promise me you won't leak this, Stevie.'

'Okay, okay, I promise. What's going on?'

'There *was* a receipt in the suitcase. It—' His voice changes, becoming loud and jovial. 'Yeah, I'll be inside in a minute! Just chatting with my mum.' He whispers again. 'Sorry, colleague spotted me. I really shouldn't be telling you this.'

'But please do.'

He exhales down the line. 'The receipt in one of the suitcases. You said it would be about soup, but it wasn't.'

'What? It's *supposed* to be about soup. It was Nigel Smith's weird food order, and that was how they caught him, because—'

'Stevie, the receipt was for a seafood pizza with extra pineapple.'

'But . . .' My breath catches uncomfortably in my throat. 'That's *my* weird food order.'

'I know it is, Stevie. But what the hell is it doing on a piece of paper in a suitcase with a dead teenager?'

'I . . . I don't know. Logan, what's going on? Why would it be there? Who would—'

'I'm sorry, I have to go. My boss is here. Don't leak this, please. *Yeah, yeah, love you too, Mum! Bye!*'

Logan hangs up. I stand with the phone to my ear, my hand shaking.

There's a child watching me from the top of a climbing frame in the playground, unashamedly staring in that way children do.

He's about the same age as Destiny Davis.

I flip my collar up and keep walking, avoiding the eyes of joggers and pedestrians on the path. I cut through a row of trees and across the leaf-strewn grass to get away from them.

What kind of impossible coincidence is this? Did the copycat put their own weird order on there to personalise it and it just happens to be the same as mine? Or . . .

I look at my phone again. The old newspaper drawing of Frankenstein's Tea Party is on the screen – the women and their empty table.

Listeners loved the Frankenstein's Tea Party episode. People made fan art based on it, and it became one of our in-jokes: the five women around a table, enjoying a feast of cucumber sandwiches and Cherry Bakewells. We made a joke about that in the episode.

'*More cucumber sandwiches, Verity? Or how about a Cherry Bakewell? Don't worry, it won't go to* your *hips.*'

People used to send us memes based on it: Ted Bundy waving a tiny sandwich at the cameras; Jodi Arias' intimate photos with a glacé cherry protecting her modesty; O.J. Simpson in court holding a tiered cake stand in each gloved hand.

'*We share the best ones on our Instagram, so be sure to follow us there!*' Nate used to say.

I watch the video again, and pause just before one boy pushes another into one of the bodies. There's a shot of the table – not brilliant quality, but visible. I zoom in.

There's a pretty cake stand on the table, one with multiple tiers. There are tiny sandwiches on it, and iced tarts.

Cucumber sandwiches. Cherry Bakewells.

A joke from one episode on a table surrounded by dead women. My order on a receipt in a suitcase with a dumped body.

It's not a coincidence. It can't be.

◆ ◆ ◆

I don't bother knocking; I unlock Nate's door with his spare key and go right in. He's sat at his kitchen table, his phone on a tripod.

'—and the police can't overlook this any more, no way,' he says to the camera. 'A fourth event is confirmation. Mimic is real. Someone is out there recreating famous murders, and it won't stop here. Someone has to do something.'

I shut the door, and Nate turns to me.

'Stevie! Stevie's here. Come join us. It's a livestream.'

I walk behind him. The screen shows us, and the many reaction emojis of the people watching it. Shocked faces turn to hearts, with comments.

Stevie!

She's here!!

Marry me Stevie

'I was telling them about the latest murders.' He says it to me, but he barely tilts his face away from the screen. 'Stevie and I are going to record a new episode, right now, and we'll get you all up to speed on the details. And this new crime scene . . .' He shakes his head. 'If you've seen the video going around, you know what I mean. If you haven't . . . I hope you've got a strong stomach. This is a bad one. It's Episode 81, friends.'

The emojis return to shocked faces.

Frankenstein's party????

I KNEW IT

Those poor women

'Stevie was just visiting an anonymous source for us. She has connections.' Nate taps his nose. 'What did you find out?'

My mouth is dry. 'I . . . I can't tell you right now.'

'Ooh. Did you hear that, friends? Sounds like we've got a podcast exclusive coming later tonight.'

YES

Stevie + Nate back again!!

It's always the boyfriend, Stevie!

The comments keep popping up. How many people are watching? Who are they?

I used to worry about nobody listening to the podcast. I never thought to worry about the kind of people who would.

'I know you've all got questions,' Nate says, 'and we're gonna answer them. Leave a comment, and Stevie and I will – *no!*'

I hit the 'End' button.

'What did you do that for? I wasn't done.'

'Nate, he's copying us.'

Nate blinks at me. 'Huh?'

'Mimic isn't copying iconic British murders – he's copying *our version* of iconic British murders. The table in that warehouse in Birmingham has got Cherry Bakewells and cucumber sandwiches on it.' I open his cupboard and pull out one of his *Gory Details* mugs – the one with a cartoon of the table on it, where the women are swapped out for famous killers. '*These* sandwiches. They weren't in the original, we made them up as a joke. But they're in the copycat version.'

Nate stares at the mug. 'Maybe it was just a mistake. Other people have called it a tea party before. Like Curtis said, Mimic already got Hampstead Heath and Hampstead Heath Square mixed up, like loads of people do. It's a coincidence.'

'It isn't. Logan just told me that the police *did* find a receipt in one of the Hampstead Heath suitcases, but it wasn't for soup and mayonnaise. It wasn't Nigel Smith's favourite meal, it was mine. Seafood pizza with extra pineapple. There's no way the killer could get that wrong by chance. That's *not* a coincidence.'

'We mention pizza in that episode.'

'We do?'

'Yeah. Episode 43: Unclaimed Baggage.'

Nate pulls down his phone from the tripod and plays Episode 43, skipping through fifteen seconds at a time. I hear the episode in snippets: laughter; Nate's fact-giving voice; my speculative one; *pizza*; Nate's *ow* as a bottlecap hits him.

He skips back.

'*Imagine your big murder plan being foiled because you eat egg mayonnaise sandwiches with soup. That's so embarrassing.*'

'*They'd get you for always ordering extra pineapple on your seafood pizzas.*'

'*I like my fish to be tropical, okay?*'

We sit in silence, letting it sink in.

Nate scrapes his hands through his hair. 'The killer's . . . referencing us. It's a little Easter egg. A nod to the podcast.'

'He's listened to our podcast. He's got his ideas from us, from the things we said. Nate, we put all these horrific murders on a plate for him, and he's gone through and picked the ones he likes best.' I gnaw on my nail, biting off chunks. 'We inspired him.'

Nate swears, and grabs a whisky bottle and two glasses.

I drain mine before he's even filled his. He pours me more.

'I should have known,' I say. 'I'm *so stupid*. No other podcaster covered Lauren but us. Her murder was our first episode, we got our catchphrase from it, and it's what ended the podcast, too. It's *our* murder. Of course whoever did it had listened to us.'

'We couldn't have known that. Other people covered it, too – after everything happened with the DNA. James Nash did.'

'He only did that to mock us for how wrong we got it.' I down my drink again, and Nate copies me. 'Nobody cared about Lauren's murder before. We're the reason people still know about it. If I hadn't insisted on talking about it in that first episode, Anna Farley might still be alive. All these people might still be alive.' I start on my other thumbnail. 'We don't even know who those poor women in the warehouse are yet. But they're dead because of us.'

'No, Stevie. This is on Mimic, not us. It's not our fault he's latched on to us like some . . . some obsessive fan. You heard Curtis the other day.'

'He's no fan of ours.'

Nate does a half smile. 'I know, he bloody hates us. No, I mean how he talked about serial killers, and the letters he had framed on his walls. It's hero worship for people who *shouldn't* be worshipped. Maybe the killer's one of those? Some . . . fame-hungry weirdo who thinks one-upping other killers will get him noticed?'

'He doesn't just want to listen to the podcast – he wants to be *on* it.'

'A starring role.'

'And he's got what he wanted.' I claw my hair back. 'What was the first thing we did after we went to Foxbridge and found Anna? We recorded an episode of *When It Happens Again*.'

Nate swears. 'And I jumped on Carousel as soon as I could. We took the bait. We're already two episodes in, and I've spent days promising a third. I already publicised the Tea Party for him. We did just what he wanted. We saw a sniff of something in the news, and we—'

'It wasn't in the news.' I grip my glass tight. 'Anna's disappearance went unnoticed because of all the press about Destiny Davis being abducted from the playground. We only found out about it because of—'

'The email.'

Nate finds it.

Hi, Stevie and Nate. I know you're on hiatus and everything (which I totally understand but also think was things getting blown way WAY out of proportion! You did nothing wrong!) but I was wondering if you'd heard the news about the girl who's gone missing in Dorset? Anna Farley? If not, here's the link. Interesting, right??

Keep your wits about you, and trust nobody – especially not your boyfriend!

S x

'It sounds like a normal listener,' I say. 'Some cool, fun person who's listened to every episode. A fan.'

'I know it does. But why would they send us this? How would *they* have heard about it? It doesn't say, *hey, check out this thing happening in my local area.*' He does a quick search. 'And we never heard from them again. They did this one email, then nothing. That's *weird.*'

'So the killer saw we hadn't noticed Anna's disappearance, and they put us on the right track.'

'They almost failed. I deleted this, remember? I didn't want you to get sucked into Lauren's case all over again.'

I laugh. 'And now we've been sucked into something much worse.'

We paste the killer's email address into Google, but nothing comes up: no similar social media handle, nothing to lead us back to a person. We hunch over Nate's phone and write out a reply to the original message – three words that take us far too long to type, and even longer to send.

Who are you?

But a minute later our message bounces back: This email address does not exist.

I don't need more alcohol, but I do want it. I drain another glass, letting it burn my throat. I pretend that's why my eyes are watering.

'Nate?'

'Yeah?'

'Everything's happened in order so far. Anna, Carousel, the Suitcase Murders, the Tea Party. That's the episode order.'

'Shit, you're right. It is.'

'I checked before I got here.' I bite down on my nails, wishing I didn't have to say it. 'Our Tanya Meadows episode is number 177.'

A girl next door. A family man. Two teenage boys. Five women.

None of their deaths are fair. I feel the weight of all of them – the lives only lived part way, all because of us and our stupid podcast.

But Destiny Davis is a child.

And wherever she is now, it's because we gave the killer the idea.

'It's okay,' Nate says, touching my back.

'No, it's not.' I wipe at my smudged eyeliner, sniffing. 'She's probably already dead. And we caused it. We should never have done this stupid show in the first place.' I get up and stomp around. 'What were we thinking? We weren't qualified to talk about this stuff. We should've left it to James Nash. Instead we charged in and got the facts wrong, accused innocent people, turned murder into entertainment.'

Nate smiles a little. 'Well, duh. That's what true crime is.'

'But should it be? Look at Curtis with his basement of shrines to serial killers, and this killer trying to emulate them. It's not normal to like this stuff.'

'When have we ever been normal, though? That's not us.'

'But why did we think that was something to be proud of? Liking real-life horror stories doesn't make us cool or interesting, it makes us freaks. We should've kept it to ourselves.'

'No. You're not a freak, you're just aware of how messed up some human beings are. And you help people. We always get emails from people saying that you make the scary stuff less scary, and you always give good advice about how people can protect themselves. You do *good* with the podcast.'

'Nate, we took *Hi Tasty* sponsorship and ran ads in episodes about sexual assault and child murder.' I flop back on his bed, covering my face. 'We deserve this.'

'In that case, I deserve it, not you. I organised the sponsorship. I did the merchandise. I made you do the bloody podcast in the first place.' I feel him flop on to the bed beside me. 'I dragged you down with me. I'll take the blame.'

I sigh. 'I wish you could. But all the things I said on that podcast were my own fault.'

'And mine were mine.' He swigs some whisky from the bottle, and passes it to me. 'Sucks to be us, I guess.'

We lie there, passing the bottle back and forth, long enough for the room – and my thundering panic – to become hazy and dimmed. We're safe down here in the basement, cut off from the world by the locked door, the closed curtains, and our phones being on the other side of the room. There's a buffer between us and the horrible things being done in our name.

'Why do you think Mimic's doing this?' I ask – blasé, like we're discussing the weather.

'To be famous.' Nate takes another swig. 'Wants his own episode. Maybe his own letter on Curtis' wall.'

'He'd need to be caught for that.'

'Oh, yeah. That's probably *not* part of the plan. Maybe he wants to be like Jack the Ripper. He'll do all these disgusting things and then just stop one day. Leave people guessing.'

'I wonder what's more appealing to a murderer like this. Do you actually *want* your name to be remembered? Are you more or less of a legend if you completely get away with it?'

'I'd want the glory.'

'You answered that *way* too fast.'

'Sorry, it's just . . . if I was putting all this effort in, I'd want the credit for it. Imagine doing all this and getting away with it, then someone else claims it years later. Not worth the risk. *I* want the accolades.'

'*Accolades?*' I slap his arm, and take the bottle. 'To be fair, you do have a lawyer dad who'd probably get your sentence down to ten years or something.'

'Five for good behaviour.'

'Exactly. Peasants like me would have to hide in the shadows.'

'Would you do a deathbed confession, though?'

I have some whisky. 'You know what? No. I'd let the truth die with me.'

'Ooh. Okay, that's *cool.*'

I pass the bottle back. 'If whoever's doing this wants to be famous, why haven't they been in touch? Apart from that first email, I mean.'

Nate raises an eyebrow. 'Are the big murders not enough of a statement for you?'

'Yes, obviously. But I mean . . . Zodiac and BTK and Son of Sam wrote letters and stuff to the police, and the Golden State Killer used to taunt his victims over the phone.'

'The ones he left alive.'

'Right. But they drew attention to themselves. Why isn't our guy doing that? If we hadn't jumped on covering this, and given him a name, would anyone even be aware of him?'

180

'Maybe he *is* leaving messages, but the police haven't revealed it. Or . . .'

'What?'

Nate passes me back the bottle. 'Maybe we're the message. He left your order on that receipt, and our Tea Party meme in the warehouse. Maybe Anna and Carousel had references to us, too. The police just didn't know what they meant.'

'We're dumb. Anna's death being like Lauren's *is* the reference. What's more stereotypically *Gory Details* than that case? It's basically our trademark. Us going there and finding her was the biggest message he could have left.'

We're down to the dregs of the whisky. I pass the bottle to Nate and lean back against the pillows, staring up at the ceiling.

'Nate . . . why us? Why our podcast?'

'I don't know.' He sighs. 'We made jokes, and we weren't *serious* podcasters, but I don't think we did anything to encourage violence. We never acted like murder was good and everyone should do it.'

'Maybe we did. Not intentionally, but maybe we did.'

I bite the inside of my lip, and pick at my nail varnish. Suddenly Nate's flimsy front door feels less secure.

'Do you think he knows where we live?'

'What?'

'He picked our podcast. Is it because he likes us, or because he doesn't? What if we start saying the wrong things about him? Will he come here?'

Nate touches my hand, stilling my picking. 'No.'

'He's done four of our murders so far, and Destiny Davis could be the fifth. Where does he stop? How does he stop? What's a big enough spectacle for him?'

'Don't think about it. The police will catch him before then. It'll be okay.'

'What if he ends where we did?'

'Our last episode before the stuff with Mike happened this year was . . . uh . . . the Victorian murder twins, right?'

'No. It was our apology episode, where we announced the hiatus. It was about the death of our own podcast. What if he recreates that?'

'He won't.'

'Are you joking? What better way to become notorious within the true crime community than to kill two of their own?'

'Stevie, that *won't* happen.'

'You don't know that.' The ceiling swims – but not from the alcohol. I squeeze my eyes shut, and force my palms against them. 'This person – people – whatever – has done so much already. They're capable, strong, they can pick locks, evade CCTV. They can snatch kids in broad daylight. And we have no idea who they are. We're probably as good as dead already.'

'No, Stevie. *No.*' I feel the bed shift, and he gently tugs my hands away. 'I won't let that happen. I will never let anything bad happen to you. *Ever.* You hear me? Stevie, look at me.'

I open my eyes. Nate's turned on to his side to face me.

'You're not alone in this,' he says. 'It's our mess, and we're in it together. We'll deal with it together, too. Just like we've always done.'

Our faces are close on the pillow. He reaches out, and softly presses the tears from my cheeks with the sleeve of his jumper. He rests his hand on my shoulder.

'I will always keep you safe. Always. I promise.'

Maybe it's the whisky on our breath or the horrors of the crime scenes that are still burned into our retinas, but something about this is like that night up in the attic. The two of us in the glow of the soft light, shadows around us, the attic door locked to cut us off from the party, sharing our deepest, most morbid thoughts together – and not for a second feeling ashamed.

That was seventeen years ago. We didn't know each other then. We looked at each other over his dad's case files, and looked away.

We don't look away now.

His lips are softer than I'd imagined. I roll my body to meet his, and his arm scoops around my back, touching the skin beneath my jumper, pulling me closer. The familiarity of him is different beneath my fingers: stubble rough and jagged, wavy hair impossibly soft. The same Nate, but in new ways.

He's warm, and comforting, and solid. He's something to cling to.

And I cling hard.

Nobody gets me like Nate – especially tonight. Whatever I feel – the shame, the guilt, the fear – he feels it, too. My stupid, thoughtless words inspired a murderer, but so did his. We made this mistake together. Now we're bound by it – our words scattered over crime scenes, and the two of us tangled up in the trauma of it.

There is no me or him any more. Not tonight.

Down here in the basement, there is only *us*.

I hook my leg over his, pressing against him, pulling at his top. His lips move to my neck, his breath hot and as desperate as mine, pushing his weight into me as he clutches a handful of hair, and slides his other hand inside my bra.

'*Why can't you see it?*' Logan shouts in my head, eyes stinging with tears of frustration. '*He's trying to split us up. He wants you for himself.*'

I block him out. That was before, and this is now. This is new.

'*It's always bothered me that he never told you he staged your meet-cute,*' August says again. '*He dressed to match you, Stevie. On purpose. Because he wanted you to notice him. And it worked.*'

I stare at the ceiling, my fingers threaded through Nate's dark hair and my leg wrapped around his.

We're alone now, bonded by true crime – as we were that night. Nate ditched August. Locked the attic door behind us. Brought a bottle of whisky up for us to share.

Is this what he wanted that night, too? To get me alone? Did he want to press me against the hard wooden floor as the party thumped below us, crime scene photos he knew I'd be interested in scattered around, our skin sticky from the fake blood on the costumes he made sure were matching?

Is this what he's wanted ever since? To get my notch on his bedpost?

And if he does, what happens to us tomorrow?

'Stevie,' Nate breathes against my cheek, seeking out my lips again.

I wish I could be back in this easy moment with him, not caring about what might come after.

But I turn my head away, because I do care.

I crawl out from under him and sit on the edge of the bed, breathing deeply. I rub my hand across my mouth.

'Sorry,' Nate says, sitting up behind me. 'Too weird?'

'Too . . . drunk.' I give him a half-smile over my shoulder. He's tousled and flushed. I am, too. I look away before my body makes me reconsider, and scrape my hair back. 'What are we going to do about these murders?'

Nate sits on the edge beside me – at a respectful distance, with his hands on his knees.

'We talk to the police again, and we tell the world.'

'That he's copying our podcasts? Admit we're the reason nine people are dead?'

'Yes. We have to own this, Stevie.'

I sigh. 'James Nash is going to love this. Surely the height of true crime incompetency is inspiring a serial killer? At least we'll finally have outrun the Mike scandal. We'll just be remembered for innocent people dying instead.'

'Hey, all publicity is good publicity.'

We sit in silence for a moment, waiting for another bit of gallows humour to rescue us. But it doesn't come.

'It's late,' I say, standing up. 'I should go.'

'You don't have to, Stevie. You can stay, if you want.'

I can't look at him. I focus on grabbing my leather jacket and keys and bag from the table.

'If it makes you feel safer, I mean,' he says, standing up, too. 'You can have the bed. I'll keep watch from the floor.'

'Like a guard dog?'

'I suppose, yeah.'

'Thanks, but I think Rosie is more than capable of protecting me from any intruders.'

'Well, in that case, she'd better not let me down. Not that anyone's *actually* going to try to kill you in your sleep.' He cringes, scratching his head. 'Didn't mean to add to the worry, there.'

'It's okay. I think we're probably safe for another murder or two, anyway.'

I head to the door, and Nate grabs the handle for me.

'I'm sorry about earlier,' he says softly. 'If it made you uncomfortable, or you felt weird, or—'

'No, I didn't. I mean, I *did*, it was, um . . . unexpected, but . . .'

I scratch my neck – then pull my hand away, remembering how his lips grazed there.

They're smiling a little now, Nate's head dipped, his blue eyes shining at me from beneath a wisp of dark hair.

I could reach up and smooth it back. I could drop my things and wrap my arms around him and push him backwards to the bed, and stay there with him until this whole thing blows over. I want to do that so, so badly. I want to be back where we were, our bodies slotted together as though they were built for each other, and not turn away from him. I want to claim him.

But he's not the kind of guy to be claimed.

'Goodnight, Nate.' I hug my things tighter to my chest.

He straightens up and opens the door. 'Night, Stevie.'

He watches from the steps to make sure I get into my flat safely. We wave at each other, I shut the door, and then I'm alone.

I lean back against the door, covering my face as the memories come: the arguments with every boyfriend I've ever had; the comments from our listeners.

Did you guys ever date?

There's sooooo much sexual tension in this episode

Navie forever! <3

I keep a box in my head just for Nate. It lies in pieces now, the cardboard ripped and the tape torn off, all its contents scattered through my mind. I gather them up: the electric jolt through my skin when he'd brush against me in taxis or in crowded venues; the painful volume of my headphones when I knew he'd brought a girl home to our halls at uni; the sparkle of his eyes that night in the attic as we talked murder; the cowardly way I looked down and missed the moment.

'*You didn't sleep with him, did you?*' August whispered to me the next morning. '*You know he's a total man whore, right? He only wants one thing. He'll date you then dump you when he gets bored.*'

'*Don't be stupid,*' I said indignantly. '*I don't like him like that anyway. We're just friends.*'

I tape the box back together and stuff the old memories inside – along with the new ones. The taste of Nate's lips. The pressure of his body against mine. His heartbeat.

I wind the tape around, again and again, tight enough to suffocate whatever's inside, and put it at the back of the cupboard.

But I know the tape is already peeling off.

I climb the stairs to home, and slump into my armchair in the gloomy flat. Rosie rubs against my ankles and I scoop her up – but she squirms away as I kiss her head, jumping down and skittering off into the bedroom.

She must be able to smell Nate on me.

I still can.

I pull out my phone. I should call Logan, tell him about the link to the podcast. But perhaps that's a conversation for the morning, when I don't have the taste of whisky and Nate in my mouth.

There's a message from August on my screen.

Hey! Just got the package my dad sent with my old hard drive in it. I'll send you the photos when I get home from work.

And then another.

Here's the link to the shared folder. Hope this helps!

I click the link. It's a neat folder – the opposite of my filing system – with specific sections for certain dates and parties. I open the one for Nate's.

It's just like I remember: the dark decor, masked students, drinks everywhere. Photos of the emos moshing in the living room – a vase perfect in one photo, then shattered in the next. The patio covered in a haze of smoke, both from the stoners' weed, and their breath in the cold air. My own breath catches as I get to the ones of the kitchen. Nate and I chat in the background, comparing outfits, getting lost in atrocities and gore as we discuss our favourite murders – August standing awkwardly beside us. Nate and I are both so young, so fixated on each other.

For different reasons.

Lauren Parker is alive in the photos, her dark hair as shiny as I remember it. She sits with friends, she's in the background of a few shots, and then she's gone. Forever.

I click through some other albums, seeing if I can find more of her from other nights.

Everyone here has been able to grow up. I know from social media that this guy moved to Australia, that girl had two kids before she was twenty, and those two are still together. We've had seventeen extra years to work on our smile lines, for wiry greys to spring up on our heads. Some of the guys have lost their hair; some of the girls have caesarean scars. Life has moved on.

But Lauren will always be the same.

I don't recognise this party. It's Mike and his friends, somewhere messy with old plastic tablecloths and camping lights and a dirty sofa . . .

I shut my eyes for a moment, trying to squeeze away the memory of the creaking Foxbridge floorboards, the stained fabric, the flowers in Anna's bloody hands. I focus on the lights, the people. The signs of life.

The photos are from the farmhouse.

It used to be *the* place for teenagers to hang out in private, before death meant it was boarded up and abandoned. Before Lauren ended up posed on the very sofa where her friends now sit, laughing.

After Lauren's death, the only people who went there were kids looking for scares.

Mike and his band are jamming, smoking, lounging around. Other people loiter, or sit on the floor, playing cards, chatting. It must be summer: the doors and windows are open wide, people standing outside, looking at the stars. I click past a shot of one of the stoners blowing a smoke ring – then click back to it. He's the focal point, but there's something in the background, just round the side of the farmhouse.

Two people together, a guy and a girl. Hair both dark, one of his arms on the wall behind her, the other on her jaw. Her bag is down by her side, the badges I remember seeing around school all over it.

Lauren.

The guy stares at her, saying something, his head tilted and his bright blue eyes scorched red in the camera flash.

I check the metadata on the photo. July 2006. It must have been an end-of-term party, something that drew more people than usual to the farmhouse. It was before Mike and Lauren got together later in the summer. Maybe this is how they met. But first, she met someone else.

Nate.

His hair was longer than it is now, he hadn't finished growing yet, but it's him. I know that jaw, those eyes, and that expression. I was on the receiving end of it earlier. I know how his fingers feel against her face, and how he'll scoop his arm around her waist to pull her close.

I cover my mouth, the tastes of tonight souring as vomit threatens to join them.

I search the photo for errors, wanting it to be faked or Photoshopped, for it to be some joke, but I know it isn't. It's real. This happened. I can't deny it – and neither can he. Not any more. Not ever again.

Nate knew Lauren.

Nate *kissed* Lauren.

So why has he spent the last seventeen years lying about it?

CHAPTER 12

'*So there are all these people, some I know and some I don't, and . . . Lauren.*'

'*She was there that night. At my party.*'

'*Along with just about every other young person in Sandford. I didn't know her, not really, but I knew of her.*'

'*I didn't even know of her, to be honest. The first time I knew she existed was after she went missing.*'

I pause the podcast on my tablet, and pull my phone back to my ear.

'You're sure it was Nate in that photo you found?' August asks, amid the noise of her Monday morning journey to work in Oxford.

'Yes.'

'Definitely?'

'*Yes.* Nate knew Lauren, and he lied about it. He's still lying about it. Why would he do that?'

'Are you sure he actually remembers? Maybe he was drunk that night, and it ended up a blur.'

'I know Nate, and he doesn't look drunk there. How drunk do you need to be to forget a human being entirely?'

'Incredibly drunk,' August admits.

'He said he didn't know the *dead girl* who went missing *from his party*. He pretended he'd never even heard of her. I remember him doing it the morning after, when we looked around for her. *What does she look like again? What was her name?* I pull my knees up in bed, hugging them. 'I mean, what the fuck, August? Why would he lie about something like that? Unless—'

'*No*, Stevie. I'm sure there's a reason for it. Something mundane and stupid.'

'Like what? What mundane reason is there to pretend you didn't snog a murder victim a few months before she died?'

'Uh, because he didn't want *you* to know he snogged her?'

'Huh?'

August sighs. 'It's like I told you before – Nate wanted you to notice him that night. You did, and you spent the night together—'

'Not like *that!*'

'But he *wanted* it to be like that, obviously. He didn't pull out the vintage whisky and matching murder costume because he really wanted to be friends with you, Stevie. Bringing up the fact that he'd probably shagged Lauren some time earlier wouldn't have done much to win you over.'

'They slept together?'

'Probably. He had a reputation back then. You know, confident new boys do well with girls who don't already know what they're like. She went with Mike, and his reputation was even worse. It obviously didn't matter to her.'

I rub my face, wishing I wasn't the nauseous kind of hungover.

'But nothing ever happened with Nate.' Excluding last night – the taste of which lingers, no matter how many times I brush my teeth. 'He could have admitted it so many times over the years, because he wasn't trying to impress me any more. He had nothing to lose by coming clean. But he kept lying to me.'

'Wouldn't you do the same?'

'What do you mean? I'm not a liar. I especially wouldn't lie about something as important as—'

191

'That's my point. Let's say I'm right and Nate did a quick lie the morning after his party because he didn't want you to find out he'd hooked up with Lauren before. Suddenly that innocent – well, innocent*ish* – lie turns into something bigger because Lauren hasn't just wandered off or gone home early without telling anyone. She's a missing person now, and that lie seems like it means more than it did. If he admits it, the fact that he lied in the first place becomes suspicious. So he doubles down, and sticks to the lie.'

'But when you see that photo of them, it's the fact that he's *still* lying about it that's suspicious.' I scrape my hair back. 'And that's not his only lie.'

I skip through the podcast, and play August another part – the part about the farmhouse, and whether we'd been there before.

'*No, I never quite got in with the right crowd. Wasn't it mainly the stoners who went there? The stoners and the cool kids. I didn't actually know that place existed until Lauren was found there.*'

'How do you know that's a lie?' August asks.

'Because the photo was taken *at* the farmhouse. The farmhouse where Lauren's body was dumped.' I scrape at my nail varnish, tearing off jagged strips. 'The girl Nate swore he'd never met was found at the location he swore he'd never been to. Are you're saying that's *not* suspicious?'

'Forget what I'm saying – what are *you* saying, Stevie? You think Nate killed Lauren for some hook-up-related reason, then dumped her back where they'd done the deed?'

'I . . . I don't know.'

'It's *Nate*. He's an arrogant tosser, but he's not a murderer. For one thing, he'd never be able to keep the secret.'

I vaguely remember something he said last night as we passed the bottle back and forth.

'I wonder what's more appealing to a murderer like this. Do you actually want your name to be remembered? Are you more or less of a legend if you completely get away with it?'

'I'd want the glory.'

I lean back against my pillows. I hate mornings, with their sharp light, crisp air, and the fog of grogginess that clings to my eyelids.

'Am I being an idiot?' I ask.

'Definitely.' August laughs, the beeps of a pedestrian crossing in the background. 'And besides, you *know* he can't have done anything to hurt her. You two were locked up in that attic together all night. If he'd left for a while, you'd have known.'

I only went into that attic once, but I remember it so well: the creaky boards, the large circle window overlooking the back garden, the faint film of dust on everything. We found a pile of old velvet curtains and got comfy on them, and sat up talking all night.

Almost all night.

'I fell asleep,' I say.

'What?'

'We stayed up talking for a long time, but I fell asleep. I don't know when, but I remember it being dark, and then when I woke up again, it was light. I always assumed Nate had done the same, because we woke up together, but . . . he might not have.'

'He could have gone downstairs while you were sleeping.'

'And come back up before I woke up. I'm a heavy sleeper. I wouldn't have known.'

For a moment, the only sound is the traffic passing her by in Oxford.

'But he probably didn't leave,' August says – too brightly. 'You were his focus, and he was with you all night. And even if he wasn't, what could he have done? He wouldn't have had time to go find Lauren on the road and do anything to her.'

'August,' I say – slowly. 'What if she wasn't on the road?'

'What do you mean? She disappeared from the road leading back to town. That's where her shoe was found.'

'But how do we know she was ever there? Only one person ever said they saw her leave the house, and that person was—'

'Nate.'

I bite on my nails. Hard. 'Nate said he saw her from the attic window, but I didn't. He didn't say anything about it at the time.'

'He didn't even say anything about it the next day. We searched the house with him for ages. Wasn't it only when the police came that he remembered her leaving?'

I skip through Episode 1 again.

'*We checked my garden and the woods, just in case. I didn't even remember her leaving through the hedge at this point, but we still checked, just in case she'd gone to get some air and got lost. There was no sign of her.*'

My mouth feels tangy and wet, like I'm about to be sick.

'So he knew Lauren, he knew the farmhouse, he could've left the attic during the night, and Lauren may never have left the house. Do you still think I'm being an idiot?'

August swallows uncomfortably, and doesn't answer.

I continue. 'Lauren's friends checked the farmhouse for her the day after the party, but she wasn't there. She was killed somewhere, and moved there later. Saturday night at the earliest. We went to Nate's house on the Sunday, didn't we?'

'Yeah.'

'He was cleaning. With bleach.'

'Yeah.'

'If Lauren *didn't* leave like he said she did that night, she could have still been in the house somewhere the next morning. I know we looked around for her, but—'

'We were looking for places a girl might be. Not a body.'

I hunch over, holding my head. Don't be sick. Don't freak out. Too late for the last one.

Nate and I have matching outfits and matching smiles in the candid photo of us in the kitchen that night. That's how I remember it: rose-tinted, the warm feeling of being understood. Laughter and smiles and twinkling eyes.

He was so different the next time I saw him, on the Sunday. He was pale, stressed, reeking of bleach from cleaning up after the party. A different Nate. I've only seen him like that once since: when we sat outside the farmhouse in Foxbridge, Anna's body arranged just how Lauren's had been.

I thought he was like that because, like me, he'd just seen his first dead body.

But maybe it was because it reminded him too much of his first?

'. . . you need to move on from Lauren's murder and leave it in the past! And you can't do that if you're clutching at straws in the present. And Anna Farley . . . she's a straw, Stevie. I read the articles, too. It's a generic missing girl in a generic British town. It's not the same killer. You just want it to be.'

Nate was sure Anna's murder wasn't connected. He told me time and time again, and Mimic has proved him right.

But how could he have been so sure, unless he *knew* who had done it the first time?

'He wanted me to stop looking into Lauren,' I say. 'I had to drag him back to Sandford to investigate. He . . . he even tried to swing things back around to *Mike* being the killer. And then when Carousel happened, he couldn't wait to leave Lauren's case in the dirt. Why would he do that? *Why?*'

'Stevie,' August says quietly. 'Do you really think Nate is capable of something like this?'

I bite my nails again. I can't make myself say it. 'We have no way to know what really happened. I can't just *ask* him. Lauren was stabbed five times in the chest. If he did it once, he could do it again. He could—'

'You don't need to ask him.' August sighs. 'Just, hold on a minute. I need to get to my office.'

She lowers the phone and I hear her enter the lab building: passes beeping, colleagues throwing out greetings, doors clicking shut.

'Okay, back,' she says. Despite the closed door, she's hushed. 'Look, you don't need to interrogate Nate about this, because there's a way to check it without him ever knowing we suspect him.'

'How?'

'The DNA on the murder weapon. There was Lauren's blood on it, plus unidentified DNA from the killer. It wasn't Mike's—'

'But it could be Nate's.'

None of this seems real. If things had gone even a little differently last night, I could still be down in Nate's flat with him. I wouldn't know any of this.

I stare at the ornate, anatomical heart ring on my finger – the one Nate bought for me a few birthdays ago.

I left last night because I didn't want things to change between us. But that change I could have coped with.

'Stevie, I know this is a lot to ask right now, but can you get me a sample of Nate's DNA?'

My mouth goes dry.

'Hair is good, the strands must have the root still attached, or something like a toothbrush would also work. Can you do that for me? I don't have access to the sample from the murder weapon, but I think I know an officer or two who might be willing to unofficially bend the rules a bit.'

'I know one who might help, too. Logan Jeffries.'

'Good. This won't fly in court, so we need to unofficially check the DNA, then, if it matches, we approach the police with the photo of Nate and Lauren and your new statement about not being able to give him a firm alibi that night. That should be enough for them to run their own tests and get that match.'

'Are you sure?'

'Yes. But we need that sample first. Can you get it?'

I kneel up in bed and look down through the window towards Nate's flat.

'I have a key. When he goes out, I'll go in and find something.'

'Be careful, Stevie. Look, for all we know this has *nothing* to do with him and it's a story you two can laugh about together later – *ha-ha, remember that time I thought you murdered someone? Such fun!* But . . . you're right. He *could* have done this. And because he didn't tell the police the truth earlier, it's up to us to rule him out. I'll come to London tonight. Pimlico, right? We'll go for a drink, away from the house, and I'll take the sample back with me. Even if he sees us, we're just friends catching up at the pub.'

'But what if he suspects something?'

'He won't.' She pauses. 'It'll be okay, Stevie.'

I sigh, rubbing my face. 'Thank you for helping me, August.'

'You don't have to thank me. Best friends forever, right? I'll always have your back.'

After she hangs up, I sit frozen in bed, staring at the wall.

Could Nate *really* have murdered Lauren? Could he have plunged that knife into her chest five times, so hard it splintered ribs? Hidden her body somewhere in the house? Moved her? Arranged her with flowers, angelic and obscene, in the very farmhouse where they first met?

I can't imagine it. Not *my* Nate, with his soft jumpers and bright eyes and the seventeen years of history between us. He couldn't hurt anyone.

But how I feel doesn't matter.

I need to be sure.

CHAPTER 13

After a strong cup of coffee and a deep clean in the shower, I feel more human. And rational.

This doesn't have to be a big deal. Sure, my best friend lied about knowing a girl whose murder was never solved, he didn't want me to look into her death again, *and* the alibi I gave him for the night she disappeared has a big chunk of time missing from it – but that doesn't mean Nate *actually* had anything to do with it. It's some weird self-preservation thing, like August said initially. That's all this is. Crossed wires. Coincidences.

I glare at myself in the steamy bathroom mirror, water dripping from my hair. *His DNA won't be a match for the murder weapon, Stevie. It won't. Get a grip.*

Later, when my hair's towel-dried, I'm dressed, and I've swiped on some eyeliner, I find myself back in August's shared folder of photos.

I go through the albums of Nate's party, seeing that night through different people's lenses. After he and I went to the attic, the party raged – things were broken, couples claimed bedrooms, the drinks caught up with the drinkers. Nate's little brother Charles flits between social groups, trying his luck. But eventually, things mellowed. People slumped on to sofas and plush rugs to talk about politics or indie bands or university first choices. That's where

August ended up: wedged between a couple of boys in Green Day T-shirts, looking bored out of her mind.

Lauren disappears from the albums around 1 a.m., an hour or so after Mike. Lots of people left around that time, either summoned home by parents or because they didn't want the lecture in the morning. But her friends stayed. They lie together in a spare bedroom – thinking Lauren must have found a room with Mike, or locked herself in a bathroom somewhere. They didn't know to be worried yet. A photo of the emos moshing – and about to break the stereo – shows her bag tucked into a corner where she left it.

Would she *really* have left the house without it? Wouldn't she have . . .

Behind the moshing teenagers with their blurred bodies and whipping hair, there's a slice of the first floor, just above the staircase. Someone's walking along, from left to right – brown boots stepping along the hallway. Familiar brown boots. I go back to the photo from the kitchen: Nate and me talking, smiling together in our matching, bloody hippy costumes.

Same boots.

The timestamp on the stair photo is 2 a.m.

I can't see a face, I can't see any more than brown boots, but it's enough.

Nate *did* leave the attic. He left the attic around the time Lauren was last seen alive.

The doorbell rings – three times quickly, then once again. Nate's ring.

He's coming up.

I leap up and slide the lock on the stair door. I can't see him, not now.

This is the third lie I've caught him in. First he didn't know Lauren, and then he didn't know about the farmhouse. Those could be explained away, but claiming the alibi of being in the attic all night?

I hear his steps on the stairs. He bangs into the door, the handle moving, and swears.

'Stevie?' he calls. 'You locked the door by mistake. Open up.'

I stand on the other side of it, trying not to breathe.

He's right there. He's always been right there. Nothing about him has changed since I looked at the photos – but what I know about him has.

'Stevie!' He thumps on the door. 'I've got my kit here, and some snacks. Hurry up, will you? I know you're in there.'

He's the same old Nate. And I need to pretend to be the same old Stevie.

I open the door. 'Sorry, I was brushing my teeth.'

'Since when do you lock this door?' He dumps his black duffel bag on the table, and tosses me a brown paper one from the bakery. 'You're not still thinking Mimic's going to come for you next, are you?'

'Uh, yeah. I just wanted to feel a bit more secure.' The thought of food makes me feel sick. I push the bag away from me on the table, and scratch my head. 'What are you doing here?'

He frowns at me. 'Recording, remember? We need to get the word out about Mimic copying our podcasts.'

My brain has been so full of Nate, I haven't had much time left to panic about that. It hits me again now.

'I thought we were going to go back to the police first?'

'I know. I already did. I couldn't sleep last night, not for hours, so I made some calls. Actually managed to get through to Chopra in Dorset, too. Told him everything, but he didn't give much back. Just said he'd look into it. Once again, we won't know if anyone's actually listened, but—'

201

'I could ask Logan.' After the last twelve hours with Nate, I grab Logan's name like it's a rope thrown into the dark pit I'm trapped in. 'He knows someone working on the Suitcase Murders. He could confirm any wider links.'

'Great. Absolutely ask him.'

I pat my pockets for my phone.

'Uh, here,' Nate says, getting it from the coffee table. It's next to my tablet. The screen's still on. 'What's this?'

'August sent through the photos from your party,' I say, grabbing it and flicking through to a different photo. 'I asked for them back when we still thought Anna was killed by the same person as Lauren. I thought something might jump out.'

'And did it?'

'No.'

I'm not brave enough to meet Nate's eye. Did he see his own boots at the top of the stairs? Did he see that I'd seen them?

'I'll text Logan, then.' I step away and tap out a message. Some stupid, impulsive part of me wants to tell him about Nate, but I resist it. Logan hates Nate enough to arrest him on the spot, even without proof.

'By the way, I found our mistake with Carousel,' Nate says, lugging his bag across the room. 'Mimic tied O'Donnell to a pink horse in Brighton, because that's where we said Martin Jackson was found in Episode 10. But I checked the original – Jackson's horse was blue. So that's another gory detail we got wrong.'

Nate sets up our recording equipment at the sofa – the same routine as always.

Things have been normal for seventeen years. We've had the odd disagreement, but nothing he's done has ever given me reason to suspect he'd be capable of murder. Why does that suddenly change now? There were plenty of people downstairs around the time Lauren went missing. It wasn't just Nate.

It probably wasn't Nate.

No, it *can't* have been Nate. Because what motive could he possibly have had?

This theory doesn't work at all. And the second we check the DNA, it'll confirm it.

I glance at a mug on the draining board. 'Do you want a drink?'

'Coffee would be great.'

I boil the kettle and polish the mug all over with a cloth – rubbing away any fingerprints. Once filled, I pull my sleeves down over my hands and carefully carry it over to the table without touching it.

'Thanks,' Nate says, sticking his head up from plugging in cables. 'Any response from Logan?'

'Not yet.'

He sighs, and takes his coffee. 'Looks like it's definitely up to us to get the word out, then.'

He sips his coffee – marking the rim with his saliva, and the sides with his fingerprints.

The hard part's done. I don't need to sneak around his flat or go through his things to get a sample of his DNA: he's offered it to me. All I need to do is carefully put it in a bag and deliver it to August, and then I can stop worrying about this stupid theory. We can go back to being Stevie and Nate, and I can forget that I ever doubted him.

We can go back to the important things.

Nate sets the mug back down, and stares at me.

'Stevie, what's going on?'

I hug my arms a little tighter around myself. 'What do you mean?'

'You're acting weird. Weirder than usual, I mean.' He smiles a little, then it fades. 'You've hardly looked at me since I got here.'

I stare at my feet. 'It's a stressful time.'

'I know it is, but it was a stressful time yesterday, too. And you didn't have a problem looking at me then.'

I can still feel the pressure of his hand on my back, his body against mine, his fingers caught up in my hair. I wish he hadn't mentioned it. I've been trying so hard to forget it.

Because all I can think about is if Lauren felt those things, too.

'We should talk about it,' he says, getting up from the floor. 'You should know that I—'

'It's fine. We don't need to talk about it. It was a mistake, that's all. It won't happen again.'

Half up, he sits back down on the sofa instead. 'We'll just forget about it, then?'

'Please.'

'Okay. It was a mistake that never even happened.' He takes another sip of coffee – another deposit of DNA. 'Glad we sorted that out. Now, we just need to sort everything *else* out.'

Microphones plugged in, he sets up a camera tripod.

'What's that for?'

'We need to make an announcement about what's happening with Mimic.'

'But the police—'

'Might keep things close to their chest. We don't know. But we *do* know other people are going to get hurt by this psycho, and we need to warn them somehow. I don't care if it interferes with their investigation – people deserve to know what's going on out there.'

I glance at his stuff. 'So, what's your plan?'

'We go for it. A full episode of *When It Happens Again* where we lay out what we know, plus some kind of to-camera announce-ment we can get going viral on social media. We can't risk this getting swept under the rug. The true crime community needs to know the truth – but so does the general public.'

'Is this the best way to do it?'

'Of course. Come sit next to me. Look, we'll both sit and record the podcast here, with the video footage as well if we need it. We can edit something from it. We make the announcement today, and then—'

I see myself frown in Nate's viewfinder. 'Couldn't we just send a tweet? Or email this to a newspaper? Why do we need to do all this?'

'I told you, for maximum impact. We need to get the word out *now* in the biggest way possible, not wait for some news intern to check their email. The more people we reach, the more we can help be on the lookout for this guy.'

'But we'll be putting the spotlight on to us.'

'It's already there, Stevie.' He gets his phone down and shows me. 'We're back in the top ten most listened-to podcasts – for both *Gory Details* and *When It Happens Again*. Our Twitter is exploding. And the Facebook group is getting hundreds of new interactions every day. People are looking at us. We have their attention. Let's put it to good use.'

I pick at my nail varnish. There's barely any of it left. 'This is just what the killer wants, though. He's doing this for attention, to be noticed. Should we be giving him that attention?'

'You'd rather not say anything, and let people die?'

'No, obviously not! But . . . is this right? Isn't it . . .' I sigh. 'Isn't it what all those trolls and James Nash accused us of? Capitalising on other people's trauma?'

'Stevie, I'm doing this to *help* people. And this involves us. It's *our* tragedy. We caused it, remember – not on purpose, but through what we said. We can't take that back. We can sit on this information and wait for James Nash or Curtis bloody Templeton to throw us under the bus and say it's all our fault, or we can claim it. We can own up to this and say, yeah, we inspired this psychopath, but we're trying to make it right. We're going to help stop him and save lives. This is the right thing to do.'

The passion in his voice gets me, and I push my doubts about him aside. Whatever awful thing Nate may have done seventeen years ago, it's in the past – but Mimic is happening now. This is our mess, and we have to own it. Together. We can't let anyone else die in our name without doing something.

Nate takes charge. We sit together, Rosie on the back of the sofa beside me, and tell the story so far. We list the references to *All the Gory Details* left behind at the crime scenes – including the information Logan gave me about my pizza order being linked to the Suitcase Murders, although I make sure we gloss over *how* we know about it – and own up to the mistakes we made when we recounted the stories. We plead with the police to believe us, and with the public to be extra cautious. And I plead with Mimic.

'Stop this. We don't want anyone else to die. I don't know if you love us or hate us, but we're not on your side. You're not a leg-end of true crime – you're just an unoriginal thief who doesn't even have their own ideas. Nobody will remember you. We will *never* say your real name. You are not one of us.'

'And we're going to do everything possible to catch you,' Nate says.

I stare at him in the camera – serious, confident, but calm enough to stop any viewers or listeners becoming hysterical. They're safe with him.

And so am I.

He cares about people. I believe the things he says, the pleas for help. Maybe in the old days of the podcast we were careless, we *did* brush off the emotional side of things – but not any more. This is real, and we both know it.

He's too soft to have done anything to Lauren. He returned to me in that attic just as innocent as he left it.

We both lean back. Rosie hisses, and jumps away.

'You did great,' he says, smiling. 'I'll need to edit all this together, but I think we've got everything we need. Thank you for doing this with me, Stevie.'

'As if I had a choice.' I smile back. 'This is a killer we created *together*.'

'A murder baby.'

'I wouldn't go that far.'

I stretch my legs out, almost hitting Nate's coffee cup.

I twist the heart ring around my finger, sighing.

'Can I ask you something?'

Nate turns to me, planting his elbow on the back of the sofa and fixing his blue eyes on me. 'Anything.'

Say it. Just say it, Stevie. Get it out of the way.

'Have you ever lied to me, Nate?'

I stare at him, trying to see through the swirls of blue to whatever secrets lurk behind them. Give me a reason for it, Nate. Come clean about knowing her, and tell me why I don't need to worry.

He looks down for a moment. 'Yes.'

My body tenses.

'I lied to you earlier today.'

Today? I sift through the loose strands of conversation floating in my head. We didn't talk about Lauren, did we? Not like that?

'You said what happened last night was a mistake, and I agreed. But I don't agree.' He looks up again – his face a little closer to mine. 'I've wanted that moment with you for as long as I've known you. And . . . I think you have, too.'

He cups my cheek and kisses me – not desperate like last night, but soft, slow. His fingers brush down to my neck and gently rest there.

Like they did on Lauren's neck in the photo of them at the farmhouse.

I've wanted that moment with you for as long as I've known you, he said.

He did throw that serial killer party just to get my attention. He dressed to match me, took me on a house tour that accidentally showed me his dad's case files, he took me to the attic where there were more. It was the perfect meet-cute for a true crime fan.

But I fell asleep. I ruined the moment he was trying to create between us. When I woke up, would it still be there? Or would I be hungover and not interested and never see him again?

I couldn't think of a reason why Nate would want Lauren dead – but maybe there isn't one. Maybe it was never about Lauren at all. Maybe it was about me.

Because what better way to solidify a relationship with a girl who loves true crime than to deliver a homegrown case to her on a platter, and then spend the next seventeen years bonding over it?

CHAPTER 14

I've never been scared of Nate. Even when I found the photos of him and Lauren and my mind jumped to murder, I thought of it as something in the past – a dark, half-buried secret about a single event. I didn't think of him as a threat.

But now his hand is on *my* neck. He's in *my* flat.

And I know what he's capable of.

I push him away – hard enough for him to know it's not me, it's him – and scramble up off the sofa. I don't want to be anywhere near him.

'Stevie, what—'

'It *was* a mistake,' I say, disguising my disgust as being about what just happened between us, not what happened seventeen years ago. 'I . . . I don't feel that way about you. There's nothing between us.'

He sits up straight, a little hardness creeping into his features. 'You're the one who kissed me last night. I didn't start it.'

'You did today. We said we wouldn't talk about it. I thought we'd left it in the past.'

'In the past? Stevie, it happened *last night*. You want me to forget it, just like that? I know you haven't. You kissed me like you meant it. I know the timing's not great, and I shouldn't have just done it like that, but you feel it too. I know you do.'

'I don't.'

'Then what was last night?'

'A mistake! It should never have happened.'

'But it did. It did, because *you* started it. Do you really expect me to believe it meant nothing to you?'

'It didn't.'

'I don't believe you, Stevie. Okay, maybe I'm wrong, maybe it's all in my head, but—'

'I don't *like* you, I don't *want* you, and I *never* have.' I back away and cross my arms – angrily, and protectively. 'And I think you should leave.'

Nate comes over to me. 'Stevie, I—'

'Don't touch me!'

He steps back. 'I wasn't going to.'

I want to scream, but I can't let on why. And screaming won't get him to leave any faster.

'I'm sorry,' I say. 'I'm tired and stressed, and I can't deal with this right now. We were drunk last night, but we're sober now. Last night doesn't count. I want us to forget about it.'

'But—'

'Forget about it, Nate.'

He opens his mouth to say something, but swallows it. 'Fine. You never kissed me, and I never . . . tried to kiss you again. It's gone.' He grabs his bag and packs up his equipment, the camera still recording. 'Well, I'll get this lot edited then, I guess. Thanks for the coffee.'

He heads to the sink and turns on the tap, but I rush and stop him.

'I'll do that.' I grab the mug handle through my sleeve. 'Just . . . go and get the word out, like we said.'

I can't look at him. He loiters for a moment, then touches my arm.

'Stevie—'

I flinch, and he pulls his hand away. He sets his jaw, and shoulders his bag.

'Right. Bye.'

When he leaves, I lock the door behind him.

◆ ◆ ◆

I already showered this morning, but I shower again. I brush my teeth once, twice, more. I can't get clean. I feel itchy, like ants are crawling beneath my clothes and biting me all over.

How many times did we check the woods back in Sandford all those years ago, looking for clues? And exchange theories once her body was found? He was happy for me to suspect Mike, and to accuse him on the podcast.

Mike. Nate is the one who tried to frame him. *He* stole Mike's van and torched it. *He* started the rumour about Mike and Lauren arguing at the party. He wanted me to think it was Mike all along. He never wanted me to look anywhere else, so I didn't. He kept my eyes where he needed them.

On him, but not in the way they should have been.

We spent hours recording the podcast, and it gets dark quickly at this time of year. I put my hand in a plastic bag and turn it inside out around the mug, preserving the traces of Nate left on it, and put it in my bag.

I thought the DNA would clear Nate's name. That's what I was hoping for.

I'm not sure I have any hope left.

When it's time to leave to meet August, I check out the window: Nate's lights, glowing on to the steps.

It used to be perfect, him living downstairs. We could pop in and out of each other's flats. We were always accessible. Now we're too accessible. After kissing Rosie's grumpy head, I leave my lights on and creep down the stairs, opening and closing the front door as quietly as possible.

I never mentioned I was meeting August tonight. That's for the best.

Once I get past our railings and down the road, I feel better. I breathe in the cold night air, letting it calm me as I wind my way through Pimlico.

I have the DNA, and I'm meeting the person who can test it. If this is a theory built on paranoia and fear, I'll know. If it's true . . . I'll know.

And I have to know.

I shove on my headphones, trying to block out the thumping of my heart with drums and heavy bass. I pass shops and news-stands, and can't help but read the headlines.

MIMIC STRIKES AGAIN

Five Killed in Warehouse Massacre

Frankenstein's Second Tea Party

This is what Mimic wants: exposure. Fame. Glory. And we're giving it to him freely. He probably follows us. He's glued to the stats just like Nate is, refreshing to see the latest hits, checking the comments for what people think about his latest project.

I feel a stab of nausea. Did Nate do the same when we first posted Episode 1 of *All the Gory Details*? Did he get a kick out of *it's always the boyfriend* taking off as a catchphrase when he knew it wasn't true? Did it make him feel special for getting away with it for so long?

He probably hated it when people stopped listening.

I stop in the middle of the street, and someone swears at me as we almost collide.

Anna Farley died just like Lauren did. As in, every last detail was recreated.

Who could recreate it better than the person who *actually* murdered Lauren?

It never made sense for someone to start a killing spree based on our podcast. We did okay, we had loyal fans, but we were never one of the big hitters. We were niche. Our listeners spiked, and then dropped, around the time the murder weapon was discovered and Mike was acquitted in the court of public opinion. We never recovered from that. Nobody wanted us to.

Except for Nate.

If he killed Lauren, why couldn't he have killed Anna, too? Sent that email and left it in the Trash for me to find? Borrowed Piastri's car early and killed Ron O'Donnell in Brighton the night before we went to Sandford? Killed Joshua Pinkham and Kenny Jones and dumped them in suitcases on Hampstead Heath to get things rolling? Charmed five women with his blue eyes and beautiful smile and killed them, butchered them, sewing them back together in the most ghoulish way possible? And setting up a tribute to our podcast on the table in front of them?

Kids don't want to wander off with strangers. But Nate isn't strange.

Destiny Davis would have trusted his smile.

I start walking again, past vintage boutiques with mannequins whose limbs are mismatched, and flower shops where the beautiful window displays seem to wilt and rot as I look at them.

My breath catches. Nate made a point of not wanting to look into Anna's disappearance in Foxbridge, but he's the one who suggested we restart the podcast. He brought the video camera. He found out about the farmhouse. He sent me in there. He stood back behind the window and let me walk in to find her.

'*You want me to stick my fingerprints all over a* crime scene? *Are you trying to frame me?*' he said back then, laughing.

He didn't get anywhere near it.

He didn't have to give his DNA.

Did he do this?

I turn down a different street, aiming for a different bar.

I can check this. Easy. You can't work bar shifts until the early hours of the morning and still be a serial killer. It's not possible.

I just need to check the dates.

The bar Nate works at is hip and slick, a huge cocktail menu served in neon-lit corners and TikTok-ready backdrops. It's early, but it's still busy. I grab a member of staff as he walks past with a tray of empties.

'Hey, do you know what shifts Nate has worked recently?'

'Who?'

The guy brushes me off and disappears behind the bar. I spot Patrice at the other end of it, and go to him.

'Patrice!'

'Stevie. Long time no see.' Nate's boss smiles – then doesn't. 'Nate not with you?'

'No. I came to talk about him, actually.' I scratch around for an excuse. 'He's been seeing this girl and she's got it in her head that he cheated on her a few times, on certain nights. I'm trying to keep the peace. Could you just check for me if he was working those nights? I'd really appreciate it.'

Patrice blinks at me. 'How should I know?'

'Don't you have a record of who works which shift?'

'I do – for my employees. Maybe you should try with Nate's current place of work, wherever that is.'

Now I blink at Patrice. 'He . . . doesn't work here any more?'

'Not for weeks. Left us in the lurch.'

'When was this?'

He checks. 'Over a month ago. Seventeenth September.'

Before Lauren. Before Destiny Davis' disappearance. Before any of it.

Nate doesn't have a job any more. So when he said he was at work, he wasn't.

He was busy somewhere else.

Somewhere he didn't want to tell me about.

'Didn't he tell you? Maybe he really *is* having that affair. Wait, where are you going?'

Back out on the street, I clutch my bag more tightly.

We're past coincidences now. Nate told me he worked late the night before Carousel. I remember it. But that was a lie. Everything has been a lie.

I have to get this DNA to August. Now.

I cut through the residential streets to get to the pub. It's my usual route, past a leafy private garden in a quiet square – but tonight, it makes me think of Hampstead Heath, and the two suitcases Nate put there.

I wish I could stop thinking. Stop imagining it.

Teenagers beaten and burnt. A man decapitated. Anna stabbed in the chest, looking right back at him. And those five women brutally dismembered.

A snippet from our first ever episode replays in my ears: '*I'm partial to dismemberment, myself.*'

I cover my mouth, gripping the garden railings for support.

He's always loved the gory stuff. He's always made a joke of it. I did, too, but not like that. It came too easily to him. He was more into the details than the personal side of the cases. He didn't care about the victims, just what was done to them. That's the part he liked.

More than I realised.

I keep walking. Get to the pub. Give August the DNA. Go back home and hide. Don't answer the door. Lock it from the inside.

Tell someone.

I fish out my phone. Logan has replied to my text about Mimic being inspired by us – Is that why your pizza choice was on the receipt? Shit. I don't know the details, but I'll look into it.

I feel like laughing. That isn't even relevant any more. We haven't inspired Mimic; we *are* Mimic. It's been Nate all along.

I send some new messages.

Need to talk to you.

Call me as soon as you get this.

Important.

I hesitate, then type out a fourth: I think Nate –

Someone grabs me, shoving their hand over my mouth as they haul me backwards through a gate into the darkness of the garden.

It's pitch black, and I can't move. I try to scream, but the hand gets tighter, clamping my jaw shut, their other arm pinning my hands to my chest. I drop my phone and dig my nails – my bitten, useless nails – into the person's arm, trying to force it away. I can't. Music blasts in my ears as I kick and squirm and try to break the hold of the person behind me. But they're too strong.

I can't see, can't hear, can't shout for help. I can't even breathe.

Then the arm loosens. I can get away, I can—

My attacker jerks my head to the left, and stabs a knife into my throat.

EPISODE 124: CHRISTMAS Q&A SPECIAL

'Do you like hearing about gruesome murders?'

'Tough, because today we're drinking Baileys and answering your questions. This is *All the Gory Details*, the Christmas Q&A special.'

The theme music plays – but instead of sirens in the background, sleigh bells ring.

'Ho-ho-*hello* and welcome to this very special Christmas episode of your favourite murder podcast, *All the Gory Details*. As always, I'm Nate Blackwell—'

'And I'm Stevie Knight.'

'—and today we'll be answering the questions you lot sent in to us after last week's episode. And we've definitely had some good ones. Start us off, Stevie?'

'Okay, this one is from Judith S in Manchester. *Hey, Nate and Stevie—*'

'Everyone always puts my name first.'

'—*long-time listener of the show here. Firstly, I just wanted to say that you two make Monday mornings bearable, and your episodes make all the scariness in the world seem a little less scary.*'

'Aw, that's sweet.'

'*My question is – if you were a serial killer, what would your MO be?*'

'What? That took a dark turn.'

'Judith S from Manchester, you're a wild one. I like it.'

'What would be my MO? Gosh, I don't know. Stevie?'

'Um . . . Ooh, I know. So, obviously, I don't *actually* want to kill anyone, but if I *had* to – it'd be people who play music from their phone speaker instead of wearing headphones.'

'That *is* annoying.'

'And it's never good music, either! Nobody wants to listen to your tinny dubstep, *Graham*.'

'What would you do to them?'

'Oh, something ironic. Like strangle them with a headphone cable, or turn their brains to mush by blasting them with an industrial-strength speaker.'

'Wow.'

'Again, not something I actually *want* to do, but . . . you know. If needs must. What about you, Nate?'

'Hmm. I don't know *who* I'd kill, but I've always loved those stories where bodies get found in gardens years and years after the victim was first killed. So, that. I'd bury people in my back garden, or under the garage floor, or whatever, and then keep it a *complete* secret. Then I'd die, or the grandkids would come round to help me out because I'm so old and frail, and they dig up the garden and find a load of bones. And suddenly cute old Grandpa Nate has a dark side.'

'I like how yours is explicitly linked to you having grandchildren, despite the fact you've never had a relationship longer than five minutes.'

'Hey, don't be mean! I'm sure I've got to seven minutes before. Six, at least.'

'Next question!'

'Okay, okay. Oh, this one's kind of connected, actually! *Hi, Nate and Stevie* – see, told you – *did you two ever date? Or would you ever date? Love the podcast! Cate.*'

'Why does everyone always ask us this? We. Are. Friends.'

'I think the first bit is new, though. No, we're not exes, we've never had a drunken fumble, it's always been strictly platonic between us.'

'Obviously Nate's a good-looking guy—'

'Aww, thanks!'

'—and any woman would be *lucky* to have him – aside from the bodies he'll be stashing in the garden for the grandkids to find – but we've always had that friend vibe. And that's how it'll always be. So *stop asking*, okay?'

'You know we have a ship name, right?'

'Do we?'

'Yep. And I'm sorry to tell you this, but my name comes first again. If we were together, we'd be Navie. If they put you first, we'd be—'

'State? As in, look at the state of our listeners and their gossip. Next question?'

'Go ahead. Read out another question for Navie.'

'Okay, here's one. *Stevie and Nate* – Ha! I got one! – *what do you think is the worst way to die? D.*'

'Crap, that's a good one.'

'Is it, Nate? Surely the answer is every single way, except dying in your sleep?'

'But some ways are worse than others, right? Burning to death seems grim – suffocating from lack of oxygen *before* you burn to death doesn't sound so bad. It's all in the situation, I think.

Anything that's over with quickly, I don't mind so much. It's the slow, painful, lingering stuff that freaks me out.'

'Really? I'm the opposite.'

'You *want* the torture?'

'No! But at least if something's slow, it might not happen. Maybe there'd be a rescue, or you could find a way to escape somehow. And you'd have time to think about it and make peace with the idea.'

'What's worse for you, then?'

'The quick stuff. So, if I was just grabbed and pulled into a park and someone slit my throat before I could even react . . . You can't fight that. You're dead and you know it, but you can't do *anything* to stop it. All you can do is stand there until you can't stand any more, feeling all your blood spurt out of you. That's terrifying to me. That would one hundred per cent be the absolute worst way to die.'

CHAPTER 15

I can see myself in the preview screens dotted around the *Morning Chat* studio: checked shirt collar tucked neatly into my jumper, hair curling softly against my forehead, eyes popping against the blue of the backdrop.

They're going to eat this up on Twitter.

'Our next guest,' bubbly blonde Janie Anderson says, 'is here to talk to us about the *awful* murders that have been happening across the country this month.'

Ken Radcliffe nods, his Botoxed forehead attempting a concerned frown. 'We've all heard the rumours, haven't we? But *are* these murders the work of a copycat? Where is the killer getting his ideas? And what old cases might be next?'

'We're joined today by Nate Blackwell, host of the hit true crime podcast *All the Gory Details.*'

The live camera switches to me, and I give Janie my best smile. 'Hi. Happy to be here.'

'And we're very happy to have you.' Janie smiles for a bit too long, and Ken clears his throat. 'Uh, your co-host couldn't be here today, could she?'

'No. *All the Gory Details* – and my new podcast, *When It Happens Again* – are joint projects that I run with my friend, Stevie

Knight. Unfortunately she's under the weather at the moment, but I know she's upset to miss this. She's watching from her sofa with a tin of soup.' The lie comes so easily, rolling off my tongue after so many years of practice. I look straight to camera. 'Get well soon, Stevie.'

'So,' Ken says, 'your podcast is all about murder, is that right?'

'Yes. It might sound weird to a lot of viewers, but there's a huge community of people who love to hear about old crime stories, things like serial killers or smalltown murders, and that's what Stevie and I did in our original podcast. *All the Gory Details* has 194 episodes covering all sorts of murders.'

'But why *do* people like listening to those stories?'

'There are lots of reasons.' A montage of black-and-white photos of famous serial killers starts to play on the green screen behind me. 'Some people like to be scared, others find it reassuring to know what people are capable of, and how they might be able to protect themselves. If there's a story where three individual women died but the fourth managed to escape, that's something to remember if you're ever in that situation. I think, as human beings, many of us are fascinated by the worst parts of the human psyche, and what we're capable of. Hannibal Lecter wouldn't have featured in five movies if we weren't.'

'I do like those films, don't you, Ken? The one with the pigs! Ew!'

'Now, Nate, you've been following these recent murders closely, haven't you? You were one of the first to link them together?'

'That's right. Some murders are *very* recognisable – it's like remembering the plot of a film. So, the . . .' Can you say beheading on daytime TV? '. . . uh, *discovery* of a body on a seaside carousel with the same injuries as another one from decades previously is something that stands out. At first, Stevie and I thought perhaps these were separate serial killers who all happened to be striking for the second time, but once we got to three and then *four* cases, ones where the original perpetrators were long dead, we knew it had to be connected. *When It Happens Again* is our new podcast detailing these murders.'

'And you were personally involved in the discovery of the first victim, weren't you?'

'Anna Farley, yes.' The TV monitor changes, showing the muted footage of the farmhouse. 'We heard about a missing girl, and the case sounded just like something that had happened in our hometown of Sandford when we were teenagers. We went to Foxbridge, to see if it really was following the exact same pattern, and that's how we found her in a farmhouse. That's where our local victim, Lauren Parker, was also found in Sandford in 2006.'

The video sweeps across to the sofa – nothing but a censored blur lying on it.

Janie leans forward, her hands clasped on her knee. 'What was it like to find her?'

'Shocking,' I say, emphasising the word. 'Worse than I could have imagined.'

'Can you tell us more about the murders so far?'

'Of course. After Anna Farley and Ron O'Donnell on the Brighton carousel, Mimic – that's the name I coined for the killer – came to London . . .'

I reel off my snappy summary – and Janie and Ken eat it up. This is going well. The camera focuses on me, switching to the presenters' shocked faces every so often, my name and *All the Gory Details* stuck to a banner at the bottom of the screen.

I wish I could see the Twitter trends right now. *#MorningChat* trending with *Nate* and *All the Gory Details* and *he's cute, though??*

Or maybe it's not like that at all. Maybe it's *where's Stevie??*

I rest my hand on my arm, pressing against the itching scratch beneath my jumper.

'Why do you think Mimic is doing this?' Ken asks, his eyebrows trying their best again. 'What's the motive?'

'Fame, we think. It's a downside to true crime podcasting, but some murderers are so notorious, they become celebrities in their own right. They get letters in prison from fans. Love letters, even.'

'Would *you* write to a prisoner, Janie?'

'No!' She giggles. 'Well, I suppose it depends on what he'd done.'

'And how often he uses the prison gym?'

'Stop!' She playfully slaps Ken's arm.

I try not to let my face twitch. Back to me. Move the focus back to me . . .

'If these murders are connected, why haven't the police made a statement about it?'

I sigh dramatically. 'I couldn't tell you. From the start of this, Stevie and I have told the police everything we know about it, but they've never got back to us.'

'Do you think that's because it isn't true? The murders aren't connected?'

'Oh, they are connected, whether the police admit it or not. Stevie and I know for certain.'

It's ominous and tense and ripe for a follow-up question.

'Before you go, we have one last thing to ask.'

Crap.

'Which murder could be next?'

I almost smile. 'We think we know already. But . . . I'm not sure if I should say. It might interfere with the investigation.'

'It won't,' Janie says, waving her hand.

'Tell us, Nate.'

Janie and Ken lean towards me, their eyes big and excited for a scoop.

'Well, this may be difficult to hear, but . . . Destiny Davis. I think Mimic is the person who took her from that playground.'

Janie and Ken exchange shocked glances, and someone in the production team hastily throws up an image of Destiny behind me.

'Well, uh, um.' Ken scratches around for the right words, drawing out the moment. 'What makes you think that?'

'The disappearance – and, unfortunately, the murder – of Tanya Meadows in 1987. She was taken from a playground, and found dead two decades later under her murderer's bed.'

'Oh, no.'

'I hope it's not the case, or that the killer can be caught before this happens. But it follows the pattern perfectly.'

Ask me about the pattern, ask me about the pattern . . .

'Well, let's hope it's nothing to do with poor little Destiny Davis.'

'Nate, thank you so much for coming in today.'

No. Not yet.

'After the break, we'll be back with a farmer whose cow has *two* sets of udders!'

'Is one semi-skimmed, Ken?'

'Wait and see! Maybe it's—'

'Sorry,' I say loudly, 'but there's actually one more thing I *need* to say.'

Janie and Ken glance at each other, then at a producer – who puts a thumb up, his eyes on a tablet.

'Uh, yes? What's that, Nate?'

'This killer, Mimic, doesn't just *know* true crime – he listens to podcasts about it. My podcast. He's recreating, in order, murders from *All the Gory Details* episodes.' I pause dramatically. 'He's a fan.'

Janie gapes at me, and touches her ear. 'Is . . . is that true?'

'Yes. I wouldn't lie to you, Janie. That's how I know about Destiny Davis. The crime he's recreating comes later in our series than all the others we've had so far. He's building up to it.'

The producer with the tablet waves to Ken, making a continue motion with his hand. *Good.*

'That's awful. Truly terrible. Uh, Nate, do you have a message for the killer who's using your podcast for evil?'

'I do.' I sit up straight, finding the camera lens – and my light. 'Whoever you are, and wherever you are, Stevie and I want you to stop this. It's not too late to do the right thing, and return Destiny Davis to her mother. If you do that . . . we'll talk. I'll give you a spot on the podcast, in your own words. But you have to let Destiny go. Please.'

◆ ◆ ◆

Janie and Ken love it. The producer grabs me during the ad break – '*The engagement numbers are off the charts! Can you come back as a show regular with updates on the case?*' – and my phone is alight with notifications in the dressing room. I timed it just right: the scheduled tweets and episode launch happening just as I finished my segment. It's maybe a bit too early in the morning to have made an impact in America yet, but it will.

I scroll down the replies.

These murders are to do with YOUR podcast??

Gory Details homegrown serial killer, let's go

OMG we've been listening with a killer all this time

So proud of you Nate!

#LetDestinyGo

I pull my hat on and leave the TV studios, a spring in my step. My phone continues to ding with retweets and emails for other press events – TV, radio, YouTube series, even a message from James Nash about a possible collaboration.

I always thought Stevie was the thing people loved so much about the podcast.

But look at how much I can achieve without her.

CHAPTER 16

I've always hated James Nash. His supercilious tone, the too-perfect teeth, the lowness of his voice when all his guests speak louder. But we have different audiences – *All the Gory Details* was always cult stuff, the weirdos in society, while his podcast was all facts, quite dry, and educational. If you want to learn stuff – *really* learn stuff – *Gory Details* wasn't the podcast for you. You don't trust two people in a flat, you trust the former investigator who's been on every true crime documentary Channel 4 ever put out. You trust the *expert*.

But for once, that expert is me.

'*I'll send a car for you,*' Nash said last night when we spoke on the phone, his voice too bloody quiet, like he was some millionaire in a film noir movie hiring me for a case. I can pay my own way and I don't want his stupid car – but a free ride is a free ride.

After checking my hair in the mirror – I'll need to top up the dye soon, as the silver is almost showing – I head out of the flat.

Someone's at the house's front door.

'Are you the taxi?' I ask, shouldering my bag. The person – a woman with brown curly hair and dark eyeshadow – jumps as she spots me. She's vaguely familiar.

'No. Um, hi, Nate.'

Oh *shit*. 'August?'

'Yeah. Hi.'

'Wow. Been a long time, huh?'

'Yeah. Years. How are you doing?'

'I'm good. You?'

'Good. I, uh, heard about everything with the podcast. Must be a stressful time for you.'

'Oh, yeah, yeah, of course. Super stressful. But I'm getting the word out, so.' I shrug. 'That's what I'm doing now, actually. I'm meeting with James Nash for a guest spot on his podcast. Got a few other engagements lined up, too. What is it you do now? You're a lab assistant or something?'

'Senior forensic analyst.'

'Oh. Good for you.'

She stands awkwardly, then she points at the house. 'I was looking for Stevie. Is she around? I haven't heard from her in a couple of days.'

I move my bag to the other shoulder. 'Uh, she's sick. I don't think she's seeing anyone right now.'

'Really? We had plans the other night, on Monday, but she never showed.'

'Plans? What plans?'

'Just a drink.'

'Well, I suppose she felt too ill to go. Can't really slam shots while puking your guts up, right?'

'I guess not.' She shifts from foot to foot, and glances up. 'Do you have a key to her place? I'd really like to see her, just to make sure she's okay.'

'She's fine,' I say, making a point of walking to the road.

'Are you sure?'

'Yeah, course. I popped in earlier. She's just . . . keeping to herself right now. Stress, you know. But she's fine.'

I cross my arms. Conversation's over, August. Take the hint. She does. 'Okay. I'll keep trying her phone, then.'

'Great idea. I'm sure if she wants to talk to you, she'll respond. Well, I've got to go. Nash's sent a car for me.' I open the door to the taxi, but stand and wave before getting in. I keep waving. 'It was nice to see you. Bye, August!'

She glances back up at Stevie's attic windows, sighs, then heads down the steps and to the street.

'Tell her to contact me, okay?'

I nod. That's never going to happen, but she doesn't have to know.

◆ ◆ ◆

On YouTube, James Nash's episodes are done from his wine-red study, the kind with shelves of leather-bound books, dark wood, and deep shadows in the corners. It gives that glamorous library feel of late-night microfiche and 3 a.m. case breakthroughs.

But of course, it's a set.

'I can't *actually* have people come to my house,' he explains, ushering me through the Greenwich studio and into one of the chairs at the table. 'And production is a lot easier this way.'

There are three cameras set up – one on him, one on me, one on the both of us – and two microphones on the desk.

'It's a shame your partner couldn't be here today,' Nash says, settling into his own chair. One of the three crew members rushes up to check the lighting, and picks a fleck of fluff off his suit.

'Yeah, she's sad to miss it. So, what's the plan here?'

'To cover the Mimic story. You're involved in it, obviously, but so am I. I worked on the Blackpool carousel case. It was one of my first. Maybe together we can get some insight into this serial killer.'

We start recording, and Nash immediately makes it clear this is *his* podcast. I don't mind, though: I know my voice will be louder than his when it airs, in both ways.

'A lot can change in a week, can't it? In my last episode, my guest Mike Edwards – the man falsely accused of murdering his girlfriend Lauren Parker in 2006 – was here to discuss how the real murderer had struck again, almost seventeen years later, in the very similar case of recent murder victim Anna Farley. Now, it appears the similarity between the two women's deaths was due to Anna being killed by a copycat killer, dubbed Mimic, who has since copied three other cases that we know of.

'But what *does* connect the murders of Lauren and Anna is my guest today, Nate Blackwell, co-host of the *All the Gory Details* podcast.'

'Hello.'

'Nate, you claim that all four of the replicated murders – Anna Farley in Foxbridge, Ron O'Donnell on the Brighton carousel, Liverpudlian teenagers Joshua Pinkham and Kenny Jones on Hampstead Heath, and the five as yet unidentified women in Birmingham – are inspired by episodes of your podcast. What brought you to this conclusion?'

It's a more direct question than I was expecting – but this is no *Morning Chat with Janie & Ken.*

'Well, firstly the initial murder that caught my attention, Anna Farley's, was incredibly similar to Lauren Parker's, which Stevie and I covered in Episode 1 because it was a case from our hometown. Lauren was just a year older than us.'

'Indeed, that was the episode in which you falsely accused Mike Edwards of murdering his girlfriend.'

Nash stares at me, unblinking. I grip my knee under the table.

'Technically that was *Stevie*.'

'Between you, you said – and I quote – *it's always the boyfriend.* That became your catchphrase, didn't it?'

'Yeah, but—'

'Heavily implying Mike had something to do with his girl-friend's death. And then earlier this year when DNA evidence ruled Mike out, you issued an apology and went on hiatus.'

'That's right,' I say through gritted teeth.

'Good, I just wanted to clarify that for our audience.'

There's a slight twitch in the side of Nash's face which is hidden from the main camera – a smirk. He's enjoying this.

'Please, continue with why you think your podcast is the inspiration for this new serial killer.'

'Well, Lauren's case was *ours*. Yes, we made mistakes in how we represented it, but all things considered, it was a small murder in a small town, and people forgot about it. We were the only podcasters who covered it. And it was our first episode.'

'Like it was the killer's first murder?'

'Exactly. Each murder has been discovered in episode order – one, ten, forty-three, eighty-one – and there are references to the podcast in the crime scenes.'

'You're referring to the body on the carousel being found on a pink horse, the dumping location of Hampstead Heath instead of Hampstead Heath Square for the Suitcase Murders, and the items on the table during the so-called Frankenstein's Tea Party?'

He somehow makes it sound dull. 'Yes. Those are some of the references to things Stevie and I said. It means the killer listened to our episodes.'

'And these are things you got wrong, correct?' The half-smirk is back.

'We . . . made inaccurate statements, or didn't get facts quite right.'

'Or made jokes. I believe you had a merchandise line themed around the original Tea Party murder?'

'We did.'

'And you thought that was appropriate?'

'It's a case from two centuries ago. It's not like there were any survivors or relatives to offend.'

'But you didn't *only* talk about murders from two centuries ago, did you? That's why you had to end the podcast – because you accused an innocent man, and ruined his life.'

I think of the hatred on Mike's face as he shouted at us in the woods, and the jagged lines of *LIAR* that he keyed into Piastri's car.

'I've apologised many times for the way fans reacted to our first episode.'

'And will you be apologising again for the way one fan has reacted to your podcast as a whole?'

I glare at him, the smug prick. 'Excuse me?'

'Your podcast has inspired a killer to such a degree that he's worked in references to your own mistakes in the crime scenes. How does it make you feel that your style of bad-taste jokes and sensationalism has resulted in the deaths of nine people in the last two weeks? Are you proud?'

Shit. This is why I'm here. He hasn't invited me as an expert – I'm the buffoon for him to make fun of. The dunce in the corner. A dying animal to poke with a stick.

But I can snatch that stick back.

'As I've said in every interview so far, I'm appalled by what's being done in the podcast's name. That's why I've used every appearance to try to speak to the killer.' I stare at the camera, twitching my cardigan a little to show off my *#LetDestinyGo* T-shirt. 'I don't support you. You're not a hero or a legend. But if you safely return Destiny Davis to her mother, you can be.'

'I see you're wearing a slogan T-shirt – *Let Destiny Go*. You're selling them as merchandise on your shop, aren't you?'

'A hundred per cent of the profits are going to children's charities in the UK.'

'Is it conscionable to sell something like that? Aren't you profiting from other people's—'

'You have a deal with YouTube, right? Episodes drop there first, and then as an audio recording later. You get money for that, right? From the deal, and from the ad revenue?'

'Yes. I channel that money into being able to pay my guests—'

'And don't you try to flog your book at the end of episodes? It's all over your social media, too. *James Nash: The Coldest Cases*. That's about real people. Is that conscionable? Aren't *you* profiting from other people's tragedies? Aren't you profiting right now by hosting *me* on this show?'

Now I'm wearing the smirk.

Nash takes a careful sip of his water. 'That's the issue with true crime, isn't it? The blurred line between education and entertainment. Nate, why do you think, out of all the true crime podcasts available, this serial killer would choose to reference yours? Particularly as before a few weeks ago, *All the Gory Details* was . . . let's be honest, a failed podcast mired in scandal.'

I want to punch his perfect teeth out – but instead, I do a little smile.

'Your guess is as good as mine. What makes anyone enjoy certain podcasts more than others? It's personal preference.'

'That's true. Although, I do find it interesting how you assume the killer is referencing you in a positive way, and that they're a fan. To me, it seems more that this person is humiliating you, highlighting all your mistakes and inaccuracies.'

'They were *small* mistakes.'

'But that's what the killer's latched on to so far, correct?'

'I suppose so.'

'So perhaps it isn't inspiration at all. At least, not in the way we'd usually interpret it. Perhaps it's more about sending a message.'

'Yeah? What message is that?'

'That sometimes true crime should be left to the experts.'

I take an angry sip of water. I want to storm out, but I'm on camera. And Nash would surely leave that in the edit.

One of the crew passes Nash a note and whispers something that I can't hear. He reads the paper several times, then places it on the table. We resume.

'Nate, what's the future of *All the Gory Details* for you and Stevie? Where do you go from here?'

I take another sip. 'We'll keep trying to help with our new investigative series, *When It Happens Again*. Hopefully the police will catch this killer, and nobody else will have to die.'

'But what about the original podcast?'

'Well, I'd like to restart it. Despite the things that have happened in our name – but *not* supported by us at all – I think we can do good by sharing more stories, and using our platform to help others. That's what I want for the future. To do the right thing.'

'I gather you're not aware of the tweet your co-host just posted, then?'

He passes me the piece of paper: a printout of a tweet from Stevie's Twitter account.

> Hi everyone. Nate and I started All the Gory
> Details four years ago to share our love of true
> crime with the world, but I can't in good con-
> science do that any more. I'm leaving the pod-
> cast and logging off social media for a while.
> Love you all. Stevie.

The paper shakes a little in my fingers, but I steady them. Keep it together, Nate. Forget about kissing her, and baring your soul to her, and having her push you away like you meant nothing.

Forget everything from two days ago. You've got this.

I sigh. 'I was hoping she'd wait until we'd had more time to talk about it. She's felt very unsettled by Mimic – I think we can all understand that, right?'

'Certainly.'

'And she hasn't been herself for a while. I hope she takes the time she needs to heal, and that she'll join me again for the podcast someday. But right now, we have to respect her privacy.'

Nash purses his lips, and I smile behind my water glass. He was hoping to rattle me.

Too bad for him that I'm used to keeping secrets.

I keep my inner smirk as we wrap up the podcast and say our curt goodbyes, and I can finally be alone. I stand in the car park, the evening darkening around me, and check my own Twitter.

DON'T GO STEVIE

Take all the time you need, but come back soon!!

You and Nate together is what made the podcast

I shove my phone in my pocket, and tug my hat on.

For so long, it's been Stevie and me. The two of us. And now it isn't.

It won't ever be again.

I rub my face, resisting the urge to scream into the night.

I went too far. I shouldn't have done it. I shouldn't have touched her. Anyone else, but not Stevie. I shouldn't have—

'Nathaniel Blackwell?'

I pull my hands away and turn. Two women are in the car park with me, in suits and long coats. Holding up badges.

I gulp. 'It's Nate, actually.'

'Ah. Well, Mr Blackwell, I'm Detective Chief Inspector Gates and this is Detective Inspector Hughes. We have some questions we were hoping you could answer for us.'

Despite the cold, my skin burns. I feel trapped suddenly, pinned against the studio building with the only exit route blocked.

'How did you know where to find me?'

'You've been sharing your media engagements on Twitter. When you weren't at your home in Whitaker Road, we checked today's tweets. James Nash's manager gave us this address.'

'Oh. And what's this about?'

Hughes stifles a scoff. 'The serial killer you claim is terrorising the UK? We're from Homicide and Major Crime Command. Our squad is investigating the murders, and we have a few questions.'

I blow out a breath. 'Okay, good. I've been trying to get the police to take this connection seriously for over a week now, but nobody would talk to me. I'm glad you're ready to listen.'

I walk with them to their car, and we drive from Greenwich into the heart of London, to their base at Charing Cross Police Station. Sitting in silence in the back of the car, I check Stevie's tweet again as we pass the Tower of London, the turrets that oversaw countless executions illuminated behind the spindly autumn trees.

Everything's going to be fine.

CHAPTER 17

I've never been in a police interview room before. It's small and beige, not as glamorous as some of the ones you see on TV, and Gates and Hughes – one statuesque with neat, cropped black hair, the other short, blonde, and smiley – are more pleasant than the hard-faced detectives in police procedurals.

Then again, I'm not here as a suspect, am I?

After we go over the murders in full – which, after a *Gory Details* episode, a TV interview, two radio phone-ins, three Zoom meetings with newspaper reporters, and a terse afternoon with James Nash and his punchable teeth, I'm thoroughly sick of recounting, to be honest – Hughes pulls out some glossy photos and slides them across to me.

They're of the Tea Party table – cropped to not show the bodies. These photos actually do justice to the spread, unlike the blurriness of the TikTok video those teens shared. It's all crisp and clear: the dainty cucumber sandwiches, the iced Cherry Bakewells with their shiny fruit.

'Yep,' I say, nodding. 'It's exactly what we said in the podcast. Cherry Bakewells and cucumber sandwiches.'

'Like this?' Hughes passes another image – a screencap of one of our Tea Party shirt designs.

'Yeah. Wow, they're even arranged in the same order on the table.' I look up. 'You do believe he's copying us, then?'

'It appears so.' The next image is of a piece of torn paper, old style, with a handwritten food order on it. Stevie's.

'We mentioned that in our Nigel Smith episode. It's—'

'Ms Knight's favourite pizza topping, yes. You mentioned that in the initial statement you gave over the phone.'

Gates taps the image. 'But this information was never made public. So how did you know it was there?'

I rub my hand along my jaw, feeling the Velcro rip of my stubble.

'I . . . know a police officer, and I asked them to look into it for me.'

Gates puts her pen to her notepad. 'Which officer?'

I open my mouth, ready to throw Logan under the bus – but I reconsider. For now. 'It's actually Stevie's contact. You'd have to ask her.'

'We've tried. She won't return our messages, and she wasn't home either when we made a house call.'

'Really?'

'Is she out of town?'

'She could be. She's going through some things, so she might have gone back to Sandford, or gone to stay with a friend. Or maybe she just didn't feel like answering.'

'Didn't you say on TV she was ill?'

I rub at my nose. 'Yeah, but I wasn't going to air her laundry on TV, was I? She's obviously a bit upset right now. It's a lot to deal with. Maybe she just doesn't want to talk to anyone at the moment.'

'But you've been in contact with her?'

'Of course.' I pull out my phone. 'Here we go. On Monday we recorded our latest episode of *When It Happens Again* – the episode about the Tea Party and our connection to it – and then I told her later that night that we had the *Morning Chat* appearance booked for the next day. She said, *Go without me.* There, see? And then she turned down the other appearances, too. She's just keeping to herself right now.'

'Okay, well, we'd like to speak to her, too, when she's available.'

'I'll tell her,' I say, smiling.

It's out of character for Stevie – true-crime-loving, wanted to be a detective when she was little – to not cooperate with the police. We all know it.

Only I know why she's not talking.

'Has the killer been in contact with you, or Ms Knight, since these murders began? Have you had any interaction?'

'No. Nothing.' They stare at me. 'Oh, actually, yes! Someone emailed us the link to Anna Farley's disappearance, to get us to notice it. But that's it.'

'Can we have that email address?'

'Sure. I tried to contact them, but the message bounced back.' I read it out to them, and forward the message.

'What about your social media? Any strange or threatening messages there?'

'Not that I've noticed, but our engagement has been way up these past few days. Something could have slipped through the cracks.'

Gates scribbles something, then underlines it. 'So, why you? Why this podcast?'

'James Nash asked me the same thing on his show earlier. I don't know. We were just the unlucky one the killer picked.'

'Unlucky, or lucky?'

'Sorry?'

'TV appearances, news articles, guest spots on other people's podcasts. And *All the Gory Details* is back in the charts, isn't it?

You've got two podcasts in the top ten. I'd say you're doing quite well out of this.'

Hughes points to my T-shirt. 'Merch, too. How'd you get that organised so fast?'

'It's a simple design,' I say, pulling my cardigan around me. 'Pretty easy to print and have delivered in a couple of days. And it's not *merch*, it's a fundraising T-shirt. All proceeds go to charity, whatever happens to Destiny.'

'Sounds like good publicity to me.'

I narrow my eyes. Suddenly this interview room feels like the ones in the movies.

'What exactly are you implying?'

'Oh, nothing. It's just that if anyone has something to gain from theming their murders around a particular true crime podcast, it's the podcast. Wouldn't you agree?'

'I don't *like* what's happening. I didn't ask for any of this to happen.'

Gates nods. 'Sure, of course not. You're just very clearly benefiting from it.'

'I'm making the best of a bad situation.'

'By giving a murderer who most probably craves attention *more* attention? You're a true-crime expert, aren't you? So why would you do that? Surely you'd know it would lead to more killings?'

'*Or* it can raise awareness, people will be extra cautious, and there will be *fewer* killings. Which would you prefer, officers?'

'We'd prefer no deaths at all, but it's a little late for that, isn't it? Tell me, Mr Blackwell – how was it you came to discover the body of Anna Farley when the area had already been searched by local police?'

I wish I hadn't finished my drink already. My throat is tight and painful.

'I asked some kids if there was a local drinking spot somewhere, like where Lauren's body was dumped. It was a guess.'

'A very lucky guess. Oh, sorry – *unlucky*.'

'Can anyone vouch for your whereabouts throughout September and October?' Hughes asks.

'What? Why?'

'Answer the question, Mr Blackwell,' Gates says. 'Where were you on Friday the sixth, Sunday the fifteenth, and Wednesday the eighteenth of this month?'

'I . . . I can't remember what I did.'

'Really? This is just the last few weeks.'

'It's been a busy month.'

'Yes, it has rather, hasn't it?'

'Taken a few trips, Mr Blackwell?'

'A couple.'

'To Foxbridge?'

'Yes.'

'To Brighton?'

'No.'

'How about Hampstead Heath? Or Birmingham?'

'*No.*'

Hughes slides two more photos of the Tea Party across the table to me. This time, the victims aren't cropped out. Their rotting skin shines in the flash of the camera, their heads lolling at strange angles, threatening to tear at the seams.

They can't stare accusingly – not when their bulging eyes no longer point in the same direction.

'Jennifer Green, thirty-seven, and Gemma Nichols, twenty-three,' Gates says, pointing at them one by one. 'Identified yesterday by their dental records. Rough sleepers who haven't been seen since early September in Leicester and Coventry. Made any trips to those cities, Mr Blackwell?'

'Absolutely not.'

'Are you sure about that? We have a team combing CCTV as we speak. And if you're on it, well . . .'

I clench my fists on the table. 'If you're going to accuse me, just do it. Stop pissing around with these questions.'

Gates and Hughes glance at each other, smiling.

I shouldn't have said that.

'Mr Blackwell, we'd like to take a DNA sample.'

'Why?'

'Just as a matter of course. It'll help rule you out of our investigation.'

'I don't need to be ruled out, because I clearly had nothing to do with it. This is being done *to* me.'

'We'd still like that sample.'

'You can't force me to give it to you, though.'

'No, we can't. Not yet.'

'At this point, it's completely optional. But you should be aware that withholding a DNA sample looks rather suspicious.'

'As does not answering our questions.'

'And not having an alibi.'

I rub my clammy palms on my jeans, and sit up straight. 'I want to speak to my solicitor.'

Less than an hour later, Gates and Hughes escort him into the interview room.

Dad.

He bursts in, white hair carefully combed back as always, dark eyebrows stern, his suit impeccably pressed.

'I'd like to speak to my client alone.'

The officers leave, but he doesn't drop the sternness. It's not an act just for them.

'Nathaniel, what is going on here?'

I sigh. 'There's this serial killer, and—'

'I know that. I meant, what have you *said*, and why didn't you call me sooner?'

'I didn't know I needed to. It started off friendly.'

His eyebrows get even sharper, somehow. 'It *always* starts off friendly, Nathaniel.'

'Nate. My name's Nate.'

He sits down opposite me. 'What have you said to them?'

'Nothing, really. I might have . . . got a bit upset when they implied *I* killed everyone.'

He shakes his head. 'Did you learn *nothing* from me? You never speak to the police. You call your solicitor, you say no comment, and leave. What were you thinking?'

'I was thinking that it wouldn't be a problem! I wanted to seem helpful. But then they were asking about alibis and DNA samples and stuff, so . . .'

'You are under *no* obligation to cooperate with them in any way.' He stands up. He hasn't even taken his coat off. 'Come on. We're leaving.'

I follow him – pocketing my plastic cup as I leave.

Gates and Hughes are waiting outside. Dad talks over them before they can say anything.

'My client is leaving. He has answered your questions, but he is under no obligation to answer any more. If you wish to speak to him again, it will only be in my presence. Good night.'

He sweeps off down the corridor, his long black coat billowing behind him. I crush the cup in my pocket, and follow him.

Charles is in the waiting area – hair blond like his mum's but combed back like Dad's, and his face more smug than stern. He chews on gum, grinning, in a smaller version of one of Dad's suit and coat combos. The second Blackwell at the family firm.

At least one of Dad's sons turned out like he wanted.

'What did they get you in for?' Charles looks me up and down, smirking. 'Crimes against fashion?'

'You're the one wearing a coat from H&M Kids. The girls' section.'

'Hey, this is Savile Row! You look like you've been robbing charity shops.'

'How would you know? I thought *Mummy* does all your shopping for you?'

'Quiet, both of you. Get in the car.'

Dad marches on ahead to the Jaguar parked outside, while Charles and I glare at each other. He spits his gum at me. I mess up his hair.

'Boys!'

We separate, still glaring, and grab the car door – the same one.

'I'm older – and *way* taller – so I get to go in the front.'

'You're the *estranged* one. You go in the back. We're just dropping you off on the way home.'

'Aw, little baby, still living at home.'

'I've got a separate floor while my own place is being renovated, you *bell-end*. Not my fault they turfed you out as soon as they could.'

'I turfed myself out, actually. Couldn't stand being around a little blond git any longer.'

'*Boys!* Charles, sit in the front. Nathaniel, in the back.'

Charles sticks his tongue out at me before swaggering into his seat. I get in behind him, and kick it.

Dad starts the car.

'Nathaniel—'

'It's *Nate*, Dad.'

'*Nathaniel*, you need to be honest with me. Not just as my son, but as my *client*. What do they think you've done?'

'Nothing. They were just . . . fishing for stuff.'

'They think he murdered all those prostitutes up in Birmingham.'

'Sex workers,' I say, like Stevie would. Like Stevie *used to*.

Don't think about her right now.

'Did you murder those women, Nathaniel?'

'No!'

'Are you sure?'

I roll my eyes. 'I don't think that's something I'd forget, Dad.'

'Well, this is a big case. There are plenty of former police chiefs and politicians at the club, and they're very worried about this Mimic person.'

'They are?'

'Yes. It's shaping up to be one of biggest public panics since the Yorkshire Ripper, and it's all down to a podcast, of all things. And my son is in the middle of it.'

I squeeze the shards of plastic in my pocket. There's no pride in his voice, no sense of, *hey, awful that people are dying, but look at you topping the podcast charts and being interviewed on* Morning Chat! *That's my boy!*

I was a disappointment to him when nobody was listening to the podcast. Now people are listening, and that's not good enough for him, either.

'They'll want to catch someone, and fast,' he says. Charles nods beside him – sycophantic little shit. 'They probably have no other leads, so they thought they'd try to pin it on you. Don't give them the ammunition for that.'

'I won't.'

'You already did by talking to them, *genius*,' Charles says. I kick his seat again.

'But I didn't tell them anything incriminating!' I scratch behind my ear. 'Because there isn't anything incriminating to tell.'

'Hmm.' Dad's eyes flick to me in the rear-view mirror, again and again, as he drives through Westminster and back along the Thames to my flat. But he doesn't say anything. Not until he pulls up outside.

He gets out, and so do I.

'Stay there, Charles.'

Charles huffs, but does as he's told. No wonder he's always been the favourite – even before he was born.

We wander away from the car, parallel with my place. I shove my hands in my pockets.

'So, which associate are you going to hand me over to? Not Charles, please.'

'None of them. You're my *son*. If anyone is going to represent you, it'll be me. I'm the best in the firm.'

'Wow. Well, hopefully you won't have to do much representing anyway. This whole thing's just been blown out of proportion. Like you said, they probably don't have any other leads.'

'Yes, quite.' He puts his hands in his pockets, too. 'I ask all my clients the same question on the first day I meet them, because how I approach a case is intimately linked to their answer.'

'What's the question?'

'What are you hiding that needs to be kept hidden? Because I can't protect that secret for you if I don't know what it is. Nathaniel, if you *are* involved in this, I need to know now.'

I know Dad's cases well: overprivileged men committing crimes, and their swanky barrister helping them get away with it. I've seen the photos of the beaten wives, the dead mistresses, the pedestrians killed in drunken, career-ending hit-and-runs.

He thinks I'm no better than they are.

'I don't have any secrets, Dad. And it's *Nate*. It has been for years. Maybe one day you'll care enough to remember.'

I cross the road, and hear him get back in the car. As it pulls away, Charles sticks his middle finger up at me.

I start heading down to my flat, but sink on to the steps instead. I bury my head in my hands, clawing at my hair.

This day has just been reminder after reminder that I'm out of my depth. People like James Nash will never take me seriously, no matter how many journalism night classes I take, not after all the mistakes on the podcast. And I've made another, haven't I? I tried to spin it to my advantage, build hype, go viral – capitalise on the deaths that were putting us in the spotlight. Yeah, some people love it. The *Morning Chat* crowd, the fans of *Gory Details*. But the normal people, the *police* . . . They see it differently.

I've drawn attention to myself. I shouldn't have done that. I should have emptied the Trash and kept us out of Foxbridge. I should never have let Stevie take Anna's disappearance and run with it.

I stare up at her flat. The light's on, glowing against the white brickwork around the windows. I used to love looking up there, seeing if she was home. Sometimes during summer I could hear her music coming through the open windows. That's how it was this last summer, when we weren't talking. I'd come out and listen to it, trying to imagine what kind of mood she was in. Was she hurting? Did she miss Thursday nights as much as I did?

I had her back, for a while. For a couple of weeks, and then for a magic five minutes.

But I fucked it up.

I cover my face again. I can't forget those last words she said to me.

'*I don't* like *you, I don't* want *you, and I* never *have. And I think you should leave.*'

I tried to talk to her, but she screamed at me not to touch her.

When I did touch her, gently, after I thought we'd resolved it, she flinched.

She flinched.

All these years, I knew she was off-limits. I had a shot, and I missed it. It was back then, in the attic. Before the stuff that happened after, and the stuff that's happened since. It was just us, the perfect moment, and I should have kissed her, but . . . I got scared. I looked away.

And I spent the next seventeen years pretending I wasn't in love with her.

Until two days ago. I gambled everything on showing her what a pathetic, lovesick loser I am, and ruined almost two decades of friendship in the process.

No wonder she won't talk to me now.

But why hasn't she talked to the police?

I look up at her flat again. The light's on and she's home. Not replying to my texts, I get. But didn't August say she hadn't heard from her either this morning? And why wouldn't she respond to the police?

Did I mess her up worse than I thought?

I get out my keys, and head up to her door. I ring three times, wait a beat, and then ring again. I head inside and up the stairs.

This isn't an ambush. It's not about me or us, but her and how she is. If she's okay and she just won't talk to me, fine. But we're in this murder narrative together, whether she wants us to be or not. We're co-hosts – or we were, before she left – and we co-share the weight of this.

I don't want to go through this alone. But more than that, I don't want Stevie to either.

We can't fix this by not talking to each other.

The top door is shut, as usual. I can't hear any music from inside, or footsteps. I knock, and listen. There's no called response, no hasty *go away!*

But there's a weird noise. A scratching. A yowling.

I try the door, and it opens. It isn't locked this time.

Rosie screeches at me, throwing herself against my ankles.

'Stevie?'

I check around the flat, Rosie almost tripping me up with every step. Nowhere in the living room. Not in the bedroom. Not in the bathroom.

Not in the flat.

Rosie yowls again and digs her claws into my trousers, climbing up my leg.

Her food bowl is empty. Licked clean. The brown bag of millionaire's shortbread I brought round two days ago is still on the table, the corner chewed open, discarded crumbs scattered around. This side of the stair door has tiny scratches all over it at the bottom, the paint torn away in chunks.

I grab some cat food from the cupboard and Rosie wolfs it down, almost inhaling it. I check around the flat, my heart hammering in my chest and my ears and every vein in my body.

Her toothbrush is in the bathroom. Charger and eyeliner still in the bedroom. Her bag and phone and tablet are gone.

She's gone.

Stevie hasn't been ignoring me – she's missing.

CHAPTER 18

I sit opposite Gates and Hughes again – but this time we're in my flat, and things are much, much worse.

'You're sure she's been missing for two days?' Gates asks, pen poised over her notebook.

'You don't have to answer that,' Dad mutters beside me, his fingers laced together on the table. 'You can always say no comment.'

'They might need a *little* more than no comment to help find Stevie, don't you think?' I scrape my hair back, sighing. 'Two days, yeah, I think so. I saw her on the Monday, that's when we recorded our latest *When It Happens Again* episode about Mimic, and then she went out in the evening. I saw her through the window there, going down the steps, but I didn't see her come back. I haven't seen her since.'

'Where was she going?'

'I don't know. To see musician friends, maybe?' I scratch my head. 'Wait, no. August. She was meeting a friend called August, I think. August came here this morning saying Stevie hadn't showed up to something they'd planned, and she hadn't heard from her. I didn't think anything of it at the time, I thought Stevie wasn't talking to *anyone*, so . . .'

Hughes takes a sip of tea, then frowns at the mug I pulled randomly from the cupboard.

Frankenstein's Tea Party.

'I thought you showed us a text from her?'

Gates flips back in her notebook. '*Go without me*, in response to your *Morning Chat* booking. That was that night, wasn't it?'

I find it again, my fingers shaking as I scroll by the unanswered messages I *thought* Stevie had been ignoring. 'Yeah, around ten. I don't know what time she was meant to meet August, but it must have been earlier than that. But August said she never made it.'

'Who is this August?'

'August Parsons, an old friend from Sandford. They only recently got back in touch.'

'Can we have August's contact details?'

I give them what I know – name, date of birth, a flash of her LinkedIn profile. It's a long time since I've had her number in my phone. She was Stevie's friend, not mine.

I twist my own mug in my hands, trying to stay calm.

'Mimic got her, didn't he?' I sigh. 'She said she was scared he'd come after us, but I said he wouldn't. I told her she was safe, and that I'd be there for her. But I wasn't. I let this happen.'

'We can't say for sure what's happened to her yet,' Hughes said. 'We'll need to check with her friends and family.'

Stevie's parents don't know yet. They're off in Europe on their Fleetwood Mac covers tour. How do I tell them that their only child is missing?

'She hasn't wandered off, okay? I thought she didn't want to be around me, I thought she was ignoring me, and that would've made sense. But Stevie would *never* leave her cat like that. She was starving.'

Rosie's eyes glow from beneath my bed. She was so thankful for the food, she barely even scratched me when I carried her down here.

'Stevie's missing, not hiding.' I press on my closed eyes, my head bowed. '*Fuck*. She's probably already dead.'

The bodies in the warehouse. O'Donnell beheaded on the Brighton carousel. Joshua and Kenny beaten and burnt and stuffed into suitcases. Anna Farley, the stab wounds in her chest just as deep as Lauren's.

We've talked about worse things on the podcast.

What would he deem bad enough for Stevie?

I scratch at my neck. Why Stevie? Why her on her own? Why not me?

'Mr Blackwell,' Gates says, 'you said yourself just a few hours ago that Stevie had been keeping to herself. Was that usual for her?'

'No. I mean, she's an introvert who likes her own space, but it's not like her to ignore texts. I should have realised something was wrong when August said she missed their drink, but I didn't twig. I didn't realise it was a problem yet.'

'And why is that? Why didn't you realise?'

Hughes checks out the illustration on her mug. 'Your podcast was always a two-person show. Didn't you think it was strange she'd leave you to do the media duties alone?'

'Weren't you worried by the fact she suddenly wasn't replying to your texts as she usually would? Didn't that strike you as odd? Or worrying?'

'Didn't it ring alarm bells?'

Dad clears his throat slightly, but I don't need the hint. I hear the shift in tone, too – like the previous interview, there's an accusation hidden in the questions. But no comment means less chance of finding Stevie.

'She was stressed, like I said. She wasn't sure we should be so in the spotlight.' I wring my hands on my lap. 'She thought we were giving the killer what he wanted, the publicity, and she didn't want to do that. We had an argument about it.'

'An argument?' Gates notes that down. 'How did it end?'

'Badly.'

I think of kissing her, and it being completely different from the night before. She'd grabbed at me then, hands clinging to my hair, pressing herself against me. But the next day, she was cold and blank and nothing.

The only passion in her was when she shoved me away, and when she flinched.

Why did she do that? What changed?

Dad presses his foot on to my toe, hard.

'I mean, not badly between *us*. We were both stressed, and the disagreement was about the situation. We weren't angry with each other.'

'Was this argument by text?'

'No, in person. We were in her flat to record the podcast, we argued about Mimic, and then I left.'

I can't tell the full truth – not when Gates' pen is darting across the page, underlining, circling. I don't want to see her write: *ego hurt from being romantically rejected, didn't check up on best friend for two days. What a pathetic loser.*

'So there's no record of it?' Gates asks. 'We only have your word that an argument ended happily hours before Ms Knight went missing? That's a little convenient, isn't it?'

Okay, so maybe Gates will write something worse: *ego hurt from romantic rejection, killed her as revenge.*

'Don't answer that,' Dad says.

I know how it looks. Hours ago, they saw the podcast's resurgence as a motive for me being the murderer. Now Stevie is missing, and I'm the last person who saw her alive.

It's not exactly a winning combination for a guy trying to prove his innocence.

'Look, we had a heated discussion, I left, and then she went out. I texted her to tell her about the TV stuff, and she replied saying I should do it without her. I – *stupidly* – thought she just needed space. From me. And I was trying to gloss things over in the media appearances.'

'Like when you said on James Nash's newly posted YouTube show that you knew of her decision to leave the podcast? When actually, she may not have sent that tweet at all because she's been missing for two days? That kind of glossing?'

'No comment,' Dad says.

'Did you even try to contact her directly yourself? You have a key to her flat, correct?'

'I do, but I didn't think she wanted to see me.'

'She was scared a serial killer might target her, and you didn't think to check on her?'

'Don't touch me!' she shouts again in my head, flinching. Staring at me like I'm a stranger harassing her on the street.

'I wanted to respect her privacy. That's all.'

I regret a lot of things in my life. Being too scared of another rejection to chase after Stevie is just another one for the list.

But it's the most important one.

Footsteps rush down the front steps, as they've been doing all night as police officers traipse from Stevie's flat to the street – and they continue down mine. There's a loud knocking on the door, and Hughes gets up to answer it.

'DI Jeffries, Lavender Hill Police Station,' Logan says, flashing his badge.

'Serious Crime is handling this case, Detective.'

'That's fine, but I know the missing person.' He looks past Hughes to me. He doesn't look annoyingly cool today – he's unpolished, with scuffed shoes and jogging bottoms under his smart coat, like he dressed in a hurry.

'I know him,' I say. 'He and Stevie used to . . . He's her ex.'

Gates nods Logan in, and I feel something I never thought I'd feel around him – relief.

I've hated all Stevie's boyfriends over the years: the long-haired musician, the stupid barista, the tattooist who spent half his free time in the gym. But I hated Logan the most. Couldn't stand him.

Because I'd never seen Stevie as happy with anyone else.

But right now, none of it matters. Not the petty jibes we used to aim at each other, or the jealousy I'd feel festering in my gut as I found someone else to chat up in the bar, one eye always on them.

Stevie never knew. I played that role well – the guy who was interested in every woman but her. But Logan could see through me. It wasn't just dislike we shared. It was rivalry – some deep, primal, pathetic male rivalry. And he made the mistake of letting it get to him.

But neither of us have her now. She's gone, and there's nobody who'll understand that feeling more than Logan.

Once again, Stevie is the link. But this time, it unites us.

Logan shuts the door and pulls up a chair at the table next to me. 'I got most of the details upstairs.'

He scrolls through some texts on his phone, and shows me three blank boxes.

Message deleted

Message deleted

Message deleted

'I was on a run, so I didn't check my phone for a couple of hours. By the time I did, whatever she'd sent me had been deleted. I asked her about it, but she didn't reply.'

'What time did she send the messages?' Gates asks.

'Um, 19.53.'

'Stevie was supposed to meet her friend August on Monday night,' Gates says, 'but Stevie never showed.'

'August Parsons?' Logan asks. 'I got a message from August at work this morning. It said she wanted to talk to me about Stevie, urgently. I phoned her back a couple of times, but she didn't answer.'

'I saw her this morning, too,' I say. 'She was here. She wanted to go up to see Stevie, but I said no. I didn't want to disturb her, and I was on my way out to see James Nash anyway.'

Logan shares August's number, and Gates calls it.

'Her phone's turned off. DI Jeffries, when did you last hear from her?'

'The text was at 10.23 a.m.'

'And what time was she at this property?'

'Uh . . . Eleven? She was outside, and I got in a taxi. I don't know where she went after that.'

Gates purses her lips. 'Do you have the contact details for the taxi driver?'

'No.' I feel an extra flutter of panic. Was I the last person to see *two* missing women, now? 'James Nash sent the car. I'm sure you can trace the driver through him.'

Gates notes this down, and the detectives at the table glance at each other.

'You think Mimic got her, too, don't you?' I ask.

'Possibly.'

'*Why?* Stevie's on the podcast, but August doesn't have anything to do with it. She's an old friend, from years ago.'

'It might not be about the podcast,' Logan says. 'Stevie wanted to tell me something. If Mimic realised both she *and* August had information, maybe he decided to go scorched earth on them both.'

'But what could Stevie know about Mimic that I don't? She never mentioned anything to me. And how would *he* know they knew?'

Nobody can answer that.

Nobody can answer anything.

Gates and Hughes go to check on things upstairs, and Dad steps out to make some calls. Logan and I sit in silence at the table, not looking at each other.

There's nothing to say. Neither one of us has the faintest idea who Mimic is, or what he could have done with Stevie.

Well, that's a lie. I have ideas about that – ideas I keep pushing away, that keep forcing their way back into my head.

The woman found in two halves in a well.

The woman chained to a concrete block and thrown in the river.

The woman dissolved in a tub of acid, with nothing but her hand remaining.

I can see it: the blue plastic tub, the red slime floating on the top of the liquid. A hand – delicate, beautiful, with silver rings and metallic polish – resting against the edge, preserved.

'I thought this killer admired you,' Logan says dully. 'I thought he was trying to prove he's your biggest fan.'

'So did I.'

'How could you let this happen to her?'

He stands up, hands shaking like he wants to do something with them that he knows he can't. He backs away from me.

'If you hadn't forced her to do this podcast, this never would have happened.'

'I know that.'

'If she's dead, it's because of you. You should have protected her. She trusted you. If she hadn't been on her own that night, and if you'd just bothered to check her flat the next day, maybe she would still be—'

'I know, Logan!' I shout, standing up so fast my chair falls over. 'I messed up, I know. I let her down – but I don't care how much you hate me for this. It doesn't matter.'

'It doesn't matter?'

'No. Because however much you hate me, it's *nothing* compared to how much I hate myself.'

When Logan leaves, Dad comes back inside the flat. I can already tell by his face that I've made a mistake.

'What happened to no comment, Nathaniel?' he asks.

'No comment is for men with something to hide.' I pick the chair up, and grip the back of it. 'I know they think I could have had something to do with it, Dad. I'm not stupid. But I can't *not* cooperate.'

'And I can't keep you from being charged if you continue giving them ammunition.' He pulls on his tailored coat and tugs the lapels. 'Still, at least I can get a head start on our case for the trial. All we'd have to do is present the jury with an alternative narrative, and one walked right in tonight.'

'What do you mean?'

'Logan Jeffries. Didn't you say it's always the boyfriend?'

I lie in bed after everyone's gone, staring at the glow of dawn on the ceiling while Rosie sleeps curled up against my foot – the comfort a compromise, like two enemies huddling together for warmth in a blizzard.

These murders are not a tribute to us. It seemed like they were, at first – a greatest hits of *our* podcast because we told the stories so well.

I think back to Curtis Templeton and his creepy bookshop full of serial killer autobiographies and personalised letters. What was it he said when we were first talking about a copycat?

'He's not a proper aficionado, or he'd know it was Hampstead Heath Square. So he's clearly not as smart as he thinks he is. Nigel Smith would be rolling in his grave if he knew someone redid his murder and did it wrong. I'd be embarrassed if it were me. Wouldn't you?'

The references are to the things we got wrong. It's not a cheeky nod to us, an informal little *omg, look at them, so cute how they made it their own!* It's putting our errors on display in the worst, most visible way. It's putting our names under brutal murders and saying we caused them.

Like Nash said, it's humiliation. It's hatred.

I was just so pathetically desperate for praise that I didn't even realise.

CHAPTER 19

A few weeks ago, Stevie and I wandered around Foxbridge and saw the posters of Anna Farley's face stuck to every tree and lamp post: *have you seen this girl?* She was everywhere.

Now Stevie is everywhere, too.

Podcaster Who Inspired Copycat Killer Goes Missing is too good a story for the news outlets to ignore. Stevie's disappearance gets splashed over front pages and prime-time news slots, and becomes a trending topic online. The Mimic case was already going viral, but this sends it into overdrive. YouTube becomes wall-to-wall videos with clickbait titles and misleading capitalisations:

True Crime Podcaster MISSING. Is Stevie Knight DEAD?

PODCASTER latest victim of SERIAL KILLER

WHERE IS THE BODY??

The thumbnails are the channel hosts looking shocked or worried against a picture of Stevie, either greyed or crossed-out, with grabby overlaid text: EXCLUSIVE! REVEALED. BODY FOUND?

She has her own hashtag on TikTok. *#StevieKnight* brings up Gen Z girls sharing theories over a background of screenshots of Google Maps or Wikicide articles, speculating about where Stevie was taken – the police managed to trace her route through the streets of Pimlico on CCTV, but she disappeared in a black spot – and what may have happened to her.

None of it is good.

I tweet out my own pleas – did any locals see anything? Has there been any suspicious activity or sign of her anywhere? – and it gets flooded with messages. People tag their friends, and they get talking. Speculating. They forget to untag me, and that I can see every reply.

Did you see this??? She's a victim now too.

OMG!! Not Stevie!! She was the best one!

I know. Do you think she's dead already?

Can't be alive. I wonder what murder he's doing for her?

Maybe she's in a cellar somewhere with Destiny Davis.

Or in a grave.

Ooh! Buried alive would be so cool!

Is this what I sounded like a week ago? Stoking the fire of Mimic theories: which murder will he do next? How far will he go? Which episode of *All the Gory Details* do you want to see in real life the most?

I knew this was serious. I knew innocent people were dead, and that it would get worse. But I just couldn't stop myself.

Getting that first comment on a tweet or listen on a podcast is incredible. It's that immediate gratification – a hit of dopamine that shoots straight through you, buoying you up, inflating you with confidence.

But one isn't enough. I need more, always. Gotta top it up. More engagement, more listens. Yeah, a hundred likes, great – but wouldn't two hundred be better? What about a thousand? And once you hit a thousand, the next tweet's got to get the same. If it goes down, so do I – deflating, every last shred of confidence trickling away into the air until I'm back to where I was: sad, alone, and insignificant.

I chased the high, and I used innocent victims to get there.

That's not a kind of fame I feel good about.

It doesn't make sense. If the killer changed his routine and went after Stevie because she knew something, what did she know? And how does he know about it when I don't?

I can't find the answers online, not when everywhere I look people are assuming the worst and getting clicks from it. Some of those YouTube videos have hundreds of thousands of views, and channels group them together into playlists: *The Stevie Knight Murder Case.*

No. She's only dead if they find a body. Until then, she can still be fine. She's still out there.

What's he HIDING? one of the YouTube videos says on the thumbnail, next to a picture of me – a shifty one, where I'm pulling up my coat collar to hide from a camera. *LIAR.*

James Nash doesn't go in for clickbait. He doesn't have to. As someone with professional journalistic clout, he's invited on to serious radio shows to give his opinion.

'I'm afraid what we're seeing in the UK right now is the result of years of carelessness within the true crime community. It used to be that we'd only ever hear about murder from verified journalists in newspapers or TV reports, or as part of genuine investigations. But now that anyone can tweet out a theory or start a podcast, the discussions that used to happen in pubs and workplaces between friends have become amplified across the internet. Serial killers have become rock stars, their images worn on T-shirts and printed on to mugs to be sold for profit. Podcasts like *All the Gory Details* have glamorised murder to such an extent that, culturally, we can no longer separate true crime from crime fiction. How can anyone be shocked that a person with narcissism and a damaged mind would see murder as a quick way to fame?'

I close the radio app, and keep walking. James Nash is an arrogant know-it-all and I hate hearing his voice. I hate it even more than talking to Curtis Templeton.

But when your best friend is *missing: presumed dead*, you've got to make sacrifices.

I head down the creaky stairs to The Murder Emporium bookshop which is, naturally, deserted. Curtis is sat behind the desk, lined up with the serial killer mugshots on the wall behind him like always. He looks up from his book on the Essex Eaters, and sighs.

'You again.'

'Yeah, me again.' I pull out my phone and flash a Wikicide page. I clear my throat. '*Mimic, as yet unidentified, has claimed the lives of eleven people, including Stevie Knight, host of the failed podcast* All the Gory Details.'

'And?'

'I asked you to take this down! Why is it still here?'

He rolls his eyes. 'Fine, I'll edit it so it doesn't say *failed podcast*.'

'You know that's not what I mean. Stevie isn't dead, she's *missing*. Same with August. There's a difference.'

'I'm just reporting the facts.'

'That's not a fact, Curtis. Not unless you know something I don't.'

'It's a fact based on what we know about the killer so far. Anna Farley disappeared for a bit, then turned up dead.'

'That's because in our hometown, Lauren—'

'Those Franken-women in Birmingham had been dead for weeks.'

'Yes, but that case required a *lot* of—'

'And Destiny Davis has been missing even longer. She's got to turn up partially mummified, right?'

'That might not happen. Maybe he doesn't kill kids. Maybe he just wants to scare people.'

'Won't kill kids, but will stab a teenager in the heart and chop five women to bits? Face it, everyone he's taken is dead. It's just a case of when they'll be found. And in how many pieces.'

Angry tears sting at my eyes, but I don't want him to see them. I turn away, staring at the rows and rows of books.

'There are plenty of cases where girls go missing and wind up dead later on,' he says, heaving himself out of his chair. 'You've covered enough of them yourself.'

He walks around, tugging books from the shelves.

'Casey Matthews, 1993. Missing for three weeks until she was found in her boyfriend's car. Or her head was, anyway. Irene King, 1958. Missing for twenty years before she was found at the bottom of a canal. Polly Perkins, 2017. Missing for two years until construction work started on her family home and she was found in bags under her stepbrother's floorboards. Louise Jones—'

'Stop it! Just stop it, okay? This is Stevie we're talking about. *My* Stevie. She's not a name to rattle off, she's a person, a human being, and she deserves better than that.'

'Didn't ever stop you before, did it?' He snaps his book shut. 'Why is she any different from the people you've talked about on your podcast?'

'Because I know her!'

'*Knew* her.'

'She's not dead!'

'Then why would the killer have bothered to take her?' He goes back to his chair. 'You're deluding yourself, Nate. Your friend had passion, I'll give her that, but she's no different from the rest of the names on my website. One of these days she's going to be found, and people will make their own podcasts about *all the gory details* of her death.'

'They're talking about her already. She's already a story to you people.'

Curtis smiles nastily. 'You reap what you sow, I suppose.'

I want to grab the hardback book on his desk and break his skull with it, or plunge a pen into his jugular, or strangle him until he goes blue and bloated and desperate – but I bury those impulses as far down as I can.

I save my rage for the person who really deserves it.

◆　◆　◆

Stevie's parents are back in the UK. They call me several times a day from Sandford, asking me questions I can't answer – who would do this? Why was Stevie the one targeted? What am I doing to help find her?

I hate feeling so powerless.

'*We are investigating it, Mr Blackwell,*' Gates and Hughes say every time I contact them. '*Try to keep your head down, stay off social media, and stay out of the press. Don't do anything to stoke the flames. If we get an update on Stevie, we will tell you.*'

But I can't sit by and do nothing. I can't sleep knowing Stevie isn't all those floors above me. I can't bear the thought of her never being there again.

I sit on the edge of my bed, holding up my phone, and start livestreaming.

'I know you're watching this,' I say, staring at the camera lens. 'Maybe not right now, but eventually. You love it when people talk about you, don't you? You love being the centre of attention.'

Emojis and comments flash up on the screen, but I don't read them. I stay on the lens. I don't break eye contact with him.

I have to make this count.

'But you're not the centre of attention right now. Stevie is. Taking women and kids isn't impressive. It's weak. It's *pathetic*. If you want people to be scared of you . . . come for me. I'll do a trade. You bring back Stevie, and you can have me. That'll get you noticed. Nobody will be talking about Stevie then, they'll be talking about *you*. The real you, not the one hiding behind other people's murders. Be original. Let Stevie go, and come get me.

'You know where I live, right? I'll be waiting.'

I end the live. The flat is painfully quiet. I sit on the edge of the bed as the flat darkens and my phone battery fades, scrolling and scrolling through social media to see if there's any reaction from him.

So far, he's never said anything, never *done* anything. It's like the murders happen out of nowhere, and all we know about this killer is what we've assigned to him – that he's a narcissist; that he hates us. But why doesn't he want to be *seen* somehow? Why doesn't he want to gloat?

I sit up all night in the dark, waiting, hoping, but nothing happens. Nothing but notification pings from hysterical fans or obnoxious YouTubers and advertisers – '*You called him out! We at* Smashed! Phone Repairs *would love to collab with you on this. How do you feel about challenging Mimic to meet you outside our Shoreditch location?*'

At some point, I fall asleep – but I only know that because I wake up, bleary and exhausted and empty-headed, to the sound of sirens rushing past the flat.

Not just one vehicle, but three or four.

I scrub the grogginess from my eyes and head outside. The blue lights flash at the end of our long street, reflecting off windows and cars. They've converged on a street corner, one with a small alleyway that tucks behind a shop. An officer in a hi-vis jacket winds police tape around a lamp post, sealing off the area.

'What's going on?' I ask him, my breath icing in the air.

'This is a crime scene, sir. Please stay back.'

I head to the other side, walking around the parked police vehicles. It's 3 a.m. and too late for much of a crowd, but a couple of people are here, looking distressed.

'What happened?' I ask a man who's consoling a woman, her box of chips open and uneaten in her shaking hand. 'What did she see?'

'Body,' she says, shivering beneath her boyfriend's jacket. 'Down there.'

I step around them to get a view into the alleyway. Police are gathered nearby, a car is parked almost across it, the tape restricts access – but I get a glimpse.

A woman lies on the ground between a couple of bins. She's face down, her blonde bob matted with blood, and her legs twisted. She's wearing checked trousers. Boots. A leather jacket.

Stevie's jacket.

I run at the alleyway, pushing past officers, kicking one, knocking over a bin, and fall to the ground next to Stevie.

I touch her hand – skin ice cold, the heart ring I got her still on her finger, and smeared in blood.

I scoop her up in my arms, pulling her to me, and kiss her cold, dead forehead.

My Stevie.

EPISODE 159: COMING UP NEXT – MY DEATH!

'I remember this one happening.'

'I don't. I was too busy being neglected at boarding school, I think.' ·

'Well, *I* remember it. I was only nine, so it was the first time I properly realised that celebrities weren't untouchable. Because, as a kid, you see presenters on TV every day after school and you think they're so . . . special. And then one of them gets their throat cut in an alleyway round the corner from their house, and you realise that stuff like that can happen to *anyone*. Nobody's safe.'

'True – although in this case, technically Valerie Sparks was killed *because* she was a celebrity. Being famous for having a big smile and teaching kids how to make rocket ships out of empty loo rolls and sticky-back plastic sounds like the safest career in the world, but nope. Crazed fan. Big knife. Over.'

'I've never understood people who do this. You *love* that celebrity, they are *everything* to you. What does killing them achieve?'

'It's the ultimate possession. If they can't have the celebrity, no one can. Valerie had a boyfriend who she lived with, she was about to get engaged, they were planning on having a family. Crazed fan doesn't stand a chance of an actual life with her.'

'Why's it got to be so weird, though? Just admire someone from afar! Why does it always have to be about *sex* with you guys?'

'Hey, there are female stalkers, too! Jodi Arias, Madeleine Winter.'

'I know, I know. I don't condone it, not at all, but in a way I can . . . *understand* lashing out after romantic rejection? Break-ups are traumatic, feelings get hurt, crimes of passion, all that stuff. But—'

'Hold on, do I need to send your boyfriend a warning text right now? *Ow.*'

'But what I can't understand is hurting someone who doesn't even know you exist, because you never even *tried* to pursue them. It's like this guy made a fiction of their relationship all in his head, and then killed her because it wasn't true. Can you imagine that? Having your throat cut open by someone you don't even know because you don't love them back? What are you even thinking in that moment?'

'*I can fix this! All I need is an empty bottle of washing-up liquid, forty-seven toilet rolls, a pipe cleaner, a glue stick, and a bloody miracle.*'

'And don't forget the glitter.'

CHAPTER 20

Hands grab my shoulders, pulling me back, while others try to gently tug Stevie away. But I don't want to let her go. I won't.

I cling on, tighter. People shout in my ears. There's a scuffle behind me.

'What's going on here? *Nate?* Nate! Let me through, please.' Someone pushes past the others, and crouches down to my level. Logan. 'Nate, it's not her. It's not Stevie. I promise.'

I look down at the woman in my arms. Blood mattes her hair and covers her skin, shiningly wet in the dull light of the alleyway. Logan moves his torch, aiming at her face.

Brown eyes, pale skin, eyeliner, a blonde bob, the outfit, the ring, but . . .

Not Stevie.

I'm holding a dead woman, but it isn't Stevie.

I release her and let myself be hauled backwards by officers. My hands are bloody, my clothes ruined. I gape at Logan.

'I . . . I thought it was her.'

'I know. So did I.'

He nods at the officers, and they let me go. I stumble back against the wall, and slide down it to the ground. I glance back at the body.

'Who is she?'

'She had ID on her. Zara Kelly. She's an influencer, but she looks different in her pictures. Longer hair. Different clothes. She lives around the corner.'

'Where?'

He points in the opposite direction from home, towards the shops.

I turn away, hunching over. 'This is Mimic.'

'Are you sure?'

'Are you joking? It has to be. We talked about something like this on the podcast. A children's presenter killed by a fan back in the nineties. Her throat was cut in an alleyway near her house.' I hug my legs, wishing I didn't have to smell the blood on me. 'That's what this is. It's that murder. Only he's dressed her up like Stevie to send a message. To punish me.'

'Punish you for what, Nate?'

'For calling him out online. I said nobody cared about him, they only cared about his victims. I told him to bring Stevie back, and take me in her place.'

'And you got another innocent woman killed because of it.'

He was kind at first, I realise. Getting me away from the body, trying to calm the situation. But the usual venom is back in his voice.

I don't need his judgement to add to my own.

'I messed up, I know. I shouldn't have done it. I should have shut up like everyone told me to. I just wanted to do *something*. I had to try.'

Logan shakes his head, but he doesn't say whatever it is he wants to. He pats my shoulder, harder than he needs to.

'Stay here, okay? Don't move.'

As Logan walks away to talk to the other officers, I bury my face in my knees, my hands clamped over my head.

That body over there could have been Stevie. It *should* have been Stevie.

Why wasn't it? This murder fits her perfectly: a famous woman killed by a fan she didn't even know. It doesn't make sense for this to *not* be Stevie. It's the perfect opportunity.

Unless he's saving her for something worse.

What if this is just a taster? A little preview of what he can do. Maybe she's still alive somewhere – or maybe her body is stashed somewhere just like Destiny Davis' probably is. Maybe I'm supposed to find her rotting, or unrecognisable.

Maybe he wants me to one day *wish* it'd been her I found in this alleyway.

Or maybe I'll never find her at all. I'll never know what happened to her, or who did it. No closure. No answers.

No Stevie.

I go to wipe my eyes, but my hands are stained with a stranger's blood. It's all over me, dried into the grooves of skin and stuck under my nails. I pull down my sleeve and scrub at it, trying not to cry or scream or tear myself to pieces.

I caused this, me and that stupid podcast. Not just this death, but all of them. I made Stevie host it with me. She didn't want to, but I forced her to. I asked and asked and asked until I wore her down, and now here we are, a string of deaths to our name.

If someone hates the podcast enough to do that, why didn't they just kill *me*? Why bring others into it? Why take Stevie?

It should have been me.

I deserve this. I always have. Ever since that night in Sandford when I—

Logan crouches down in front of me.

'I'm not sure if you should be on your own right now. Is there someone you can go and stay with? Someone you trust?'

'No.'

'Really? What about your father? Your friends?'

'There was only ever Stevie.'

Logan sighs – a mix of pity and vindication.

I heard the arguments he and Stevie used to have when they were together. I saw the possessive way he'd touch her when I was around, staking his claim to her as though we were rivals and I was about to pounce on her at any moment.

Ridiculous, really, considering it took me a cowardly seventeen years to tell her how I felt.

I was never a threat to him.

Logan takes a sharp breath, resetting his face into something professional.

'Nate, I understand why you did it, but you contaminated a crime scene.'

'Sorry.' I wipe my face with my sleeve. 'I just . . . I thought it was *her.*'

'I know. I'm going to have two officers escort you back home, and they're going to take a cheek swab, just as an elimination sample in case we find any of the killer's DNA, and they'll also need your clothes, just in case any important evidence has transferred on to them. Okay?'

I nod, wiping at my face again.

'Gates and Hughes are on their way to take over. They may need to speak with you, but I'll explain what happened here, so hopefully they won't need to.'

'Thanks.'

'We're doing everything we can to find her, Nate. I promise. Just . . . lay low. For real this time. Okay?'

'Okay.' He helps me to my feet, but I can't help looking back at the would-be Stevie. A mimic of her. 'That's Stevie's favourite ring. Can I have it, to give to her when she gets back?'

'It's evidence, Nate.'

'Oh. Yeah. Of course.'

Logan hesitates, then leans in close, whispering. 'You didn't hear this, okay? But Gates told me they've found DNA at multiple crime scenes so far. All we need is a match, and we'll catch the bastard who did this. And we'll get Stevie back. You can give the ring to her then, okay?'

I nod, and let myself be pushed out of the alleyway.

How we both felt about Stevie used to make us hate each other. At least now we're united in hating Mimic more.

After the officers are gone, I bolt the door and shower until the water runs cold. I scrub at my nails and my face, but I can still smell it. It's like it's bubbling up through the plughole around my feet, hot and sticky, clinging on to every guilty, shamed part of me.

I caused this death, and I contaminated the crime scene. I could have destroyed key evidence. I've probably made things *harder*.

I can't sleep. Rosie can't either. I try, but all I can think about is the alleyway at the end of the street. Have they moved that woman's body away yet? What happens to her blood on the pavement? Do they hose it off, or leave it there for when the rain comes?

The next day, I stick to my word. I don't leave the house. I don't post on Twitter.

I don't do anything to make this worse.

Curtis does, though. By 9 a.m., a new Jane Doe is listed on Mimic's page. Another badge of honour for this freak. James Nash tweets, too.

Some people are learning far too late that true crime is NOT entertainment.

I spend the day pacing around the kitchen table like Stevie used to, playing our old podcasts, the smell of blood and decay still all over me. Rosie lurks on top of the wall cabinets, staring down at me from the shadows. If the killer's saving Stevie for something, what is it? The answers must be in here somewhere, but I can't find them. I can barely focus on the words. Every sarcastic comment, every laugh, every time we bounce off each other, it's like someone squeezing my trachea.

She messaged Logan just before she disappeared, and the killer got hold of her phone and deleted her messages. What had she said? What had she found out that she couldn't tell me?

Something changed overnight between her kissing me and then me kissing her the next morning. She was twitchy, nervous. I put it down to Mimic as a whole, but was there something specific? Did she get a lead? A bit of intel from somewhere? Something she didn't want to – or couldn't – tell me? Something she had to keep secret?

But then, why did she tell August?

I'm not a big drinker, working in bars can do that to you, but I swig from half-empty spirit bottles as I make my circuits. It dulls everything a bit.

The police are on this. Logan said DNA has been found at all the crime scenes. The killer *has* to slip up eventually and be caught on CCTV somewhere, or by an eye witness. We just need that one moment to give us a suspect worth investigating, and we'll have him. This will all be over.

All the pieces for a good, fulfilling true crime story are here. We've had the sick murders and the abduction of the heroine, and now it's time for the big finale. The killer will slip up and be spotted. There'll be a chase, a race against time. Stevie, beautiful and whole and unharmed and *alive*, will be rescued, and the killer will be caught. We'll learn his tragic backstory: abused as a child by his bully of a father; a traumatic head injury that compounded his sociopathy.

At the end of the story, listeners will cheer – but not for him. Nobody will care about him.

We'll all be cheering for Stevie.

My phone lowers and raises the podcast volume as notification pings come in. I grab it, and pause the episode. Is it the police? The killer? Stevie?

No. They're Twitter notifications. I'm being tagged in comments.

Why would you post this??

What's going on?

WHO IS THAT ON THE PODCAST

What? The podcast?

Someone's posted a link. I click it, and it opens an episode of *All the Gory Details*. Episode 195.

But there was no Episode 195. We stopped at 194, our apology.

This one was posted today. Just now.

It's titled *A Message from Stevie*.

I hit 'Play'.

Silence – but not true silence. It's the static, gravelly sound of recorded silence, picking up the dust in the air, the faint creaks of floorboards, and fainter breaths. Then, noise.

'*No!*'

I cover my mouth, trying not to scream the same.

That's Stevie. *Stevie.*

'*No. Please, please, no. No—*'

The last word doesn't end – there's a hideous cracking sound, and it becomes a scream, terrible and desperate, full of pain and fear.

I hunch over my phone, knuckles white as I grip it, wanting it to be over but also not wanting it to end.

Because while she can scream, she's alive. If she keeps screaming, then—

The episode ends. It cuts her off.

She *was* alive. At some point, she was conscious and alive.

But who knows how old that recording is?

Perhaps it's the last scream of a dead woman.

CHAPTER 21

The killer hurt Stevie, recorded it, and used our *Gory Details* login to upload it. Stevie's phone and tablet went missing with her. I always did the uploading, but she had access. Sometimes she'd tweak the episode descriptions, or check on the stats.

Now the killer can do that, too.

But the recording is a clue. Maybe there's something in the background that can be enhanced, like a train in the distance or the noise of a street, or maybe the IP address it was posted from can be traced. Maybe Gates and Hughes can identify the killer from it somehow.

Maybe this is how we catch him.

Someone knocks heavily on the door, and I jump. Rosie does, too – hissing as she sinks further into the shadows on top of the cabinets. It's dark now, and late. I creep to the door, and check the peephole: white hair; dark, stern eyebrows. Dad.

'Nathaniel,' he says as I open the door. 'We need to talk.'

'Did you hear about the podcast? I'm just about to call the police. The killer recorded Stevie screaming and uploaded it. Has there been much digital evidence in your cases? Is this the kind of thing they can trace?'

I gesture for him to come inside the flat, but he stays at the door.

'You want to talk out here?'

'No, in the car.'

'The car? Why?'

'Because I have something to show you, but we have to drive there.'

I stare at him. 'I don't understand. Just tell me?'

'No, come with me. We'll talk on the way. Please, Nathaniel.'

He never says please. Something must be very wrong. I grab my keys and follow him out.

'Is it Charles? Has something happened?'

'No, it's not that.'

'Then what?'

'Just . . . wait.'

Charles isn't in the car this time, so I sit in the front. Dad starts up the engine, his hands tight on the steering wheel.

'What's this about? Tell me.'

Dad pauses for a moment, like he's thinking up a response in court. I saw him in action a few times when I was younger, back when I wanted to be him. He was deadly, but calm. He didn't fly into rages, he'd just fix people with knowing looks, as if burning them with infrared lasers.

'I've been defending clients for decades now,' he says, his eyes on the road. 'My clients are often those with successful careers or famous names, and they have reputations to protect. I can't protect them from bad news, but I can try to soften the scandal.'

'What do you mean?'

'I have people in the system who tell me things, and I tell them things in return. If I ask, I can flag certain cases with certain police officers. I can know ahead of time about damning evidence, or an imminent arrest. I know if a DNA match has come up on the system.'

'So?'

'So . . . Nathaniel, the police have matched you via DNA to six crime scenes.'

'*What?*'

'They're going to arrest you – but if you cooperate and hand yourself in first, the judge may look more favourably on you when it comes to sentencing.'

'Dad, *what?* What crime scenes? What are you talking about?'

'They know.'

'What do they know? Tell me!'

'They know that you're the one who staged those copycat murders. The Mimic is you.'

I think I'm going to be sick. I grab the dashboard, steadying myself.

Dad is still driving, hands tight but his attention on the road. All business.

'I didn't do that. Why do they think that?'

'Because your DNA was found at every crime scene. Sometimes I can get clients out of one piece of DNA evidence, maybe two, but six? That's not a lab error, that's a provable fact. They've got enough to convict you on this alone.'

'How did my DNA get there? I don't understand. I haven't killed *anyone*. You don't believe this, do you?'

'What am I supposed to think? I told you, I always ask my clients what secrets they're hiding – and they always deny the thing they're accused of. The DNA evidence against them doesn't get thrown out because it wasn't a match – it gets thrown out because I call it into question. I rip apart the people who collected and analysed it. I make the jury doubt the science. But what jury will doubt six pieces of evidence linking you to so many murders?'

This can't be real. I was there, in the alleyway, but . . . that's it. I didn't go in with Stevie to find Anna. We never went to Brighton, or Hampstead Heath, or the warehouse in Birmingham. There's no way my DNA can be in all these places – unless someone else put it there.

'Dad,' I say, my voice shaking like it did on the day Mum died. 'I've been framed.'

He scoffs. 'They all say that.'

'It's true! I didn't kill anyone. Why would I? That's not me, you *know* that.'

'No, I don't. I don't know you at all, Nathaniel.'

I claw at my hair, remembering the way Gates and Hughes sat across from me in the interview room, their friendly questions turning to barely veiled accusations.

I'm a *fucking* idiot. These murders started, and I restarted the podcast. I made it all about us – new episodes, more tweets, engaging with fans, doing the livestreams. I went on TV. I went on James Nash's show. I milked the situation as much as I could.

All this time we've said that Mimic wants fame.

That theory still checks out if *I'm* the one getting famous from it.

'Someone's framing me. I'm not lying, Dad.'

'Nate, there's *evidence*. You've been caught, and you have to turn yourself in. You can't keep denying this.'

'But I didn't do it! I couldn't hurt anyone, I'm not like that.'

'I haven't forgotten all the boarding schools you got kicked out of. Expelled for breaking a nose.'

'He started it.'

'Expelled for starting a fire.'

'That was an accident. I didn't mean for it to—'

'Expelled for stabbing a boy with a compass.'

'It was only in his hand, and he deserved it. He used to bully me about . . . about Mum.' I shake the memory away. 'That was years ago. I'm not like that any more. You really think I could kill five women and swap their heads around? *Me?*'

'I don't want to believe that, no – but what choice do I have?'

'You can *choose* to believe me.'

'How can I, Nathaniel? Six crime scenes. *Six.* Foxbridge, Brighton, Hampstead Heath, Birmingham, Pimlico. And not just from this month, but from seventeen years ago.'

'What?'

'Lauren Parker in Sandford. It was *your* DNA on that knife. No wonder you were so keen to blame that poor boyfriend of hers in your ridiculous podcast.'

This can't be real.

'No. No, I . . . I never saw a knife. I never *touched* a knife. That thing's been in the ground since 2006, it was *lost*, and . . .'

I dig my nails into my temples. None of this makes sense. How did the killer do this? *How?*

'Dad, I swear I didn't do this. I *promise.*'

He sighs, eyes straight ahead still.

I haven't been watching the road. Dad's car sweeps around Parliament Square, the heavy stone buildings of Westminster pressing in around us. He's taking me to Gates and Hughes at Charing Cross Police Station.

'Dad, you can't turn me in! I'm innocent.'

'If that's true, then we'll be able to prove it in court. But you can't avoid this. They're going to arrest you, one way or another. You have to cooperate.'

'I can't go to prison, Dad! I didn't do this. And Stevie's still out there somewhere. She needs me!'

'If they arrest you and the murders continue, then they'll know it wasn't you. Cooperating helps your case.'

'You think the person who's framed me with six planted DNA samples is going to keep going once I'm charged? Are you kidding me?'

The tourist sights of Whitehall flash past the window – the Cenotaph, Downing Street – and up ahead, Nelson's Column gets

taller by the second. Dad turns on to the Trafalgar Square round-
about, and passes the lions, the fountains.

We're close.

'I can't go in there, Dad. I'll never come out again. There's
DNA, there's the fame motive . . . How do I fight that?'

'We'll find a way, if a not-guilty plea is what you want to do.'

'Of course that's what I want! I'm innocent, Dad! *Not guilty!*'

'So prove it!' Dad screeches to a halt at a red light next to the
National Portrait Gallery. One right turn, and we'll be at the station. 'Prove it to me. Tell me one thing that'll stop me thinking my
first-born son is a serial killer.'

He turns to look at me now – not stern, but desperate.

'I . . . I can't. But I didn't kill any of them. And I'd never hurt
Stevie. Never.'

'I wish I could believe that.'

Frustrated tears sting my eyes. 'I wouldn't. I *couldn't*. I . . . I *love*
her, Dad. And I can't abandon her.'

The lights flick to amber, and I make my decision. I unclip my
seatbelt and open the door.

'Tell my landlady to feed the cat,' I say, as a car beeps behind
us. 'Someone *needs* to feed the cat.'

'Nathaniel, get back in the car. If you run, you'll look guilty.'

'I look guilty anyway, though, don't I?'

'Please. I can't protect you if you do this.'

I swallow hard. 'And I can't protect Stevie if I'm in there. I *have*
to run. Bye, Dad.'

'Wait!' He lunges across the seat and grabs my hand – and
presses something into it. His wallet. 'PIN is your mother's birthday. Get out as much money as you can, then toss it. I'll say you
stole it.'

A different kind of tears sting me now. 'Thank you.'

'Be careful, *Nate*. Go.'

I slam the door and dart on to the pavement by the gallery, narrowly missing a bus as it thunders past. Dad looks at me desperately, then turns right, still heading for the police station.

And I run.

As far as the police know, I'm a serial killer. They'll trace my phone and my cards. They're probably at my flat already. Dad gave me his wallet, but he'll still play by the rules. He'll go to the police and tell them exactly where I got out, and where I might go.

I need to be fast.

I push through the crowds of Leicester Square and jump on the first cash machine I see: dipping into my overdraft to scrape *£300 from my account, and hammering in Mum's birthday to get £1000 from Dad's. They'll be able to trace these transactions easily. I can't use the cards again. I can't use my phone, either. I turn it off in my pocket..*

With the money stuffed away, I try to put as much distance between me and Charing Cross Police Station as possible. I use the late-night crowds of the West End to my advantage, tagging on to the backs of rowdy groups until there's a side street to slip down. From there, I burrow through the smaller roads, past closed shops and closing restaurants, avoiding anywhere a police car could patrol. I don't know where CCTV cameras are – everywhere, probably – so I keep my head down and pick up the pace until I find a pub – a packed, stuffy one. I get inside and my eyes dart around, searching. I make my way through the tables like I'm trying to get to my friends – scooping a long tweed coat from the back of a man's chair, and a pair of glasses from the edge of a table – then loop back around towards the bar. Two older men are there, arguing about politics, one of their wallets just to the side. I snatch it, and dive into the bathroom.

I didn't learn much at boarding school, but nicking things from the posh kids just to mess with them was a skill I never forgot.

The coat is too big, but it doesn't matter. I pull it on, and try out the glasses. They're round and too strong for my eyes, so I punch out the lenses and throw them in the bin. I check the wallet, and pull out a few more notes to add to my collection. I haven't used cash in years, like a lot of people these days. I'm lucky to get this much.

Being on the run would've been a lot easier in 2006.

I toss the wallet at a barman on my way out – '*Hey, I think someone dropped this?*' – and pull up my collar as I hit the street. I orientate myself: the nearest Tube station is Bond Street. I stop in a shop on the way, grabbing a couple of touristy caps from the rack – one black and one white with '*I love London*' on them – and get a couple of prepaid phones, plus chargers. I pay in cash, buy a Tube pass in cash, and pick a train at random, heading west across London on the Elizabeth Line with my head and cap down, manspreading in my seat, chewing imaginary gum, trying to make everything about me look different.

When I exit the train at Southall, there are no police waiting for me at the station. No one approaches me on the street. It's dark and late and panic starts to set in.

I want to go home, but I can't. I can't *ever* go back.

Not until I clear my name.

CHAPTER 22

I find a grotty hotel and check in with a plastic bag of the cheapest supplies I can find, then spend the next few days sitting on the least-stained part of the bed, watching an old TV as the situation gets worse than I could possibly have imagined.

It starts with an update on the news in the early hours of Sunday: '*We're hearing reports that police have been called to an address in London in relation to the recent string of murders perpetrated by the so-called Mimic murderer.*'

The next update, there's more information: '*The address is believed to be Whitaker Road in Pimlico, very close to where the last victim, influencer Zara Kelly, was found just over twenty-four hours ago.*'

Then there's a reporter on the scene – tired and concerned in the pre-dawn darkness, face lit by the flickering lights of police vehicles. He's standing with his back to my house. A police officer climbs up the basement steps, his face ashen as he passes a pet carrier to a colleague. Inside, Rosie's eyes flash, and she's taken in to the main house. I get a glimpse of Mrs Piastri at the window – her frail hands shaking as she closes the curtains.

'*So far it appears that something very serious has occurred at the property behind me, believed to be the home of Stevie Knight and Nate Blackwell, the two hosts of the podcast which has allegedly inspired the killings that have gripped the nation for the last week. As you'll remember, Stevie Knight has been missing for six days, since Monday the twenty-third of October. At this time, it's not clear whether Mr Blackwell is still inside the property. More when I have it.'*

Video footage shows a forensic team going down the steps to my flat.

They come and go, zipped evidence bags in their arms.

And then, finally, the camera zooms past the reporter to catch the careful climb of two plastic-clad people carrying something up the stairs. A stretcher with a body bag on it.

A small one.

DCI Gates, more exhausted than I've seen her, runs the press conference later that day.

'I can confirm that the Metropolitan Police last night identified a suspect in the case referred to in the press as the Mimic Murders. This includes the deaths of Anna Farley in Foxbridge, Ron O'Donnell in Brighton, Joshua Pinkham and Kenny Jones who were found on Hampstead Heath, and the five women found in a warehouse in Birmingham, two of whom have been identified as Jennifer Green and Gemma Nichols. The same person is believed to be responsible for the disappearance of Stevie Knight, a podcaster whose series appeared to be the inspiration for the murders, her friend Dr August Parsons, and Destiny Davis, a five-year-old missing since September.

'I can confirm that, through DNA analysis, the main suspect in the case is Nathaniel Blackwell, a white male in his thirties. He is also linked to the unsolved murder of seventeen-year-old Lauren Parker from 2006. While my officers acted swiftly, we were unable to arrest Blackwell, and his whereabouts are currently unknown.'

Gates pauses, a photo of me appearing on the screen behind her.

My headshot's now a mugshot.

'Upon searching Mr Blackwell's property, officers discovered more DNA evidence linked to the crime scenes. I can also confirm that

human remains were recovered from the property. Although a full identification is yet to be performed, I can confirm that the remains are of a child matching the description of Destiny Davis.

'Blackwell is to be considered armed and incredibly dangerous. We are appealing to the public for any information about his whereabouts. If spotted, do not approach this man under any circumstances.'

I had to run.

I'm not an idiot. I know it makes me look guilty, but there's no explaining away DNA evidence that puts me in multiple crime scenes. There's definitely no explaining away DNA evidence in my flat, or human remains. Even I couldn't explain it, until I remembered Stevie's spare key. The killer has her, and her things. A key to my flat. I thought at first they must have planted the things – blood, a body – after Dad picked me up on Saturday night to turn myself in, but I realise now it was a day earlier.

I woke up to police sirens heading down my road, and I went out to find Zara Kelly in that alleyway, dressed in Stevie's clothes, wearing the ring I gave her. While I was busy contaminating the crime scene, the killer contaminated my flat. He must have hidden Destiny under my bed, like in the Tanya Meadows case. And I came home, and didn't realise.

I felt like I couldn't get clean. I scrubbed and scrubbed at my nails, but the smell of Zara's blood wouldn't go away.

It wasn't Zara's blood that haunted me. It was Destiny, long dead, and stuffed underneath my bed as I tried to sleep.

Even Rosie noticed it. She wouldn't sleep on the bed any more. She stayed up on the cabinet, staring.

Police confirmed the victim's identity on the second day. The media keep showing the same shots of her mother – hurrying out after seeing the body, hiding from the cameras, all the hope drained out of her. Stevie's parents look the same in the brief footage of them in Sandford.

289

For a few days last week, Destiny's mother wore a *#LetDestinyGo* T-shirt. Now, she thinks the person who made them strangled her daughter to death.

Everyone thinks that. There's no *#NateWasFramed* movement among *Gory Details* fans, or other opinions shared in the flood of YouTube videos. I check on the budget smartphone I picked up on that first night, loading pages at a snail's pace on the hotel's dodgy wifi.

Curtis already made me my own Wikicide page. For someone who's such a stickler for truth, he's speculated a lot. The news has gone wild with this, and people have come out of the woodwork – kids I fought with in boarding school; girls I slept with once and never called back. They're interviewed on podcasts and blogs and YouTube shows, they go viral on TikTok, and Curtis knits everything they say together on his website, making me out to be some shallow, insecure narcissist so desperate for attention that I killed to get it.

It's the exact theory Stevie and I had for the killer, but reversed back on to me.

I hate reading these lies about me, but I have to know what's going on. I wait for three days for something to change, but it doesn't. The YouTube titles are always the same.

True Crime Podcaster A MURDERER?? Exclusive reaction video

Stevie Knight: Is She Really Dead? CRAZY Conspiracy Theory

EVIL Podcasters in it Together? Gory Details MURDER DUO Killed for Fame!

Twitter is even worse.

weirdos i wouldn't let my kids listen to them scum absolute scum should be hung

Can't believe I bought one of those #LetDestinyGo T-shirts when she was dead under his bed this whole time.

um i know nate blackwell is a serial killer and all, but he's kinda cute, ngl. i'll be your accessory. hit me up

James Nash runs the gauntlet of respectable media, doing TV interviews in his casual suit, flashing his teeth, earning his living as a documentary guest star who has *James Nash, retired detective and true crime expert* flash up at the bottom of the screen every time he talks.

'*You were with him days before this news broke, James. How does that make you feel?*'

'*Awful. Truly, truly awful. As detectives, we develop a sixth sense over time. We can tell when something's off. And something was off. If you watch back over the interview, you can tell. I should have trusted my gut then and there, but I didn't. I wanted to give Blackwell the benefit of the doubt. Now, I wish I'd trusted my gut. If I had, I could have saved a lot of lives.*'

I sit in this dingy, damp-stained room with its leaky bathroom tap and a window that doesn't open, waiting for some breakthrough to make the police realise they've got the wrong person. But it doesn't happen. Every bit of news is about me – a possible sighting here, a lead over there. Psychoanalysing me to find a motive. Going through my past history to figure out where I could be hiding out.

For now, I'm safe. I have a stack of cash thanks to Dad's card and the wallet I emptied, and I could steal another wallet if I needed to. I have no connection to Southall – it's just where I happened to get off the Tube. Nobody knows I'm here. I haven't turned my phone on. I could hide out for weeks, months maybe.

But nothing will change. The police aren't discovering clues that point to who *actually* did this, they're only focused on looking for me. The frame was too good for them to doubt it.

The killer has Stevie's key to my flat – and her phone and tablet. I haven't dared sign into any of my social media accounts, because the police can track me if I do. But that hasn't stopped the Mimic from tweeting from the *Gory Details* official account.

Mimicking me.

Told you I'd get Destiny Davis back. Want me to do the same with Stevie?

Keep looking. You'll never find me.

Want to see me do it again?

Why haven't police shut the account down? How is it allowed to continue?

This tiny, creaky room is like a prison cell itself. I could stay here for weeks, but then what? Things will be just the same. Stevie will be missing or dead; no one will ever suspect anyone other than me.

I need to do something.

SIM card removed, I turn on my phone just long enough to jot down a few phone numbers from my contacts. Then I turn it off again. Can't be too careful. Then I scroll down the new numbers on my pre-paid phone.

In any situation – rain, shine, whatever – I'd call Stevie. Who else is there?

I stop on a name, and hit dial. After four rings, it goes to voicemail.

'*You've reached Charles Blackwell. Please leave a message.*'

I sigh, and try again. This time, it gets to three rings before he ends it. Then two. Then—

Answer the phone, you little turd, I text.

This time, he does.

'Charles, listen, don't hang up—'

'Why are you calling me, serial killer brother? Piss off!'

'I didn't do it.'

'Yes, you did.'

'I was framed. Someone put my DNA in those crime scenes. They had Stevie's key to my flat, they planted those things there.'

'The dead kid, you mean? The one tucked under your bed?'

'*Yes.* That was nothing to do with me, I swear.'

'I'm getting Dad.'

'No!'

'Yes! The police need to know about this. Where are you? You need to turn yourself in.'

'Don't tell anyone, Charles. Please. If I wanted that, I'd have called Dad. But I called you. Trust me, for once in your life. I didn't kill anyone. I've been framed.'

'And I've been a lawyer long enough to know that's what they all say, Nate.'

'This time it's true. I'm not trying to trick you. I didn't hurt anyone, and you should know that better than anyone.'

'What do you mean?'

'If I was going to murder anyone, it'd obviously be *you*, you smug git.'

He exhales. It sounds like he flops into a chair. 'Okay, yeah, that does kind of check out. Go on, then. Give me whatever speech you have planned. I'll listen.'

'Someone planted that DNA evidence. I don't know how they got it or how they did it, but it wasn't me. That means Mimic is still out there somewhere, but nobody's looking for him. They're too busy looking for me.'

'That's because you keep tweeting those weird threats from all over London.'

'That's not *me*, that's him! He has Stevie's login.'

'*Oh . . .*'

'What do you mean, from all over London?'

'You know Dad's got his contacts. They keep tracing the phone. It turns on in a different part of London, posts a tweet, then turns off again. Police go there, and no sign of you.'

'Because it's not me doing it.'

'Yeah. Wait, so why's the killer doing that, then?'

'I don't know. Trying to confuse them, somehow? Make it seem like I'm on the move?'

'Are you?' Charles voice changes a little. 'Where are you, by the way? Are you okay?'

'Fine, and I can't say. Charles, I *need* the police to stop looking just for me. Can you . . . I don't know, get a message to Logan?'

'Who's that?'

'DI Logan Jeffries?'

'Oh shit, *him?*'

'What do you mean, *him?*'

Charles whistles. 'Don't think he's going to listen to you. He's convinced you did it. He keeps coming round here, asking us about stuff. He thinks Dad let you go on purpose.'

'Well, he kind of did . . .'

'And he's saying you quit your job so you'd have more time for murder. Apparently you were lying about still working at some bar? So you've got no alibi?'

'I've been taking a fast-track journalism course, okay? Night classes, library research, that kind of thing.' My forehead is clammy. All of me is. 'The podcast was over and I wanted to make this true crime thing legit, and I couldn't stand that job any more, so I quit. I've been burning through the money my mum left me ever since.'

'Why didn't you tell anyone that?'

'I didn't want the pressure, or the expectation. I thought if I could get into journalism somehow, and in my own time, I could do a James Nash. I . . . I was never good at the school stuff like you. I *couldn't* be who Dad wanted me to be. I wasn't good enough.

But I thought if I could just get my shit together and have a career, Dad might still be proud of me, and . . . Ugh, it doesn't matter now anyway. Look, Logan is just doing his job. If I can get him to consider the framing theory, maybe—'

'Dad already mentioned it. I went with him. He said that before you ran off you were adamant you'd been framed and that you'd never hurt Stevie.'

'If you knew that already, why didn't *you* believe me?'

'Well, Dad didn't necessarily believe it either. There was a body in your flat. That one's hard to deny. But that Logan wouldn't hear it at all. Said Stevie had been worried about you anyway.'

'*What?*'

'Yeah. Something about some texts she sent? That were deleted?'

'He thinks they were about me?'

'And that *you* deleted them when you attacked her, yeah. Said that's why you disappeared her friend, too.'

'August? She went missing last week, two days after Stevie. She came to the house, and then—'

'Disappeared. Apparently nobody saw her again after she went to your place.'

'She *left* my place. I saw her.'

'But no CCTV did. And nobody can trace that taxi you say picked you up.'

'*I* didn't hurt either of them!'

'Yeah, but people think you did, and that's why. Logan's been saying Stevie must've told August something about you, and you found out about it so you got rid of them both. They think Stevie figured out what you did.'

I get up from the bed. The window is small and the curtain paper-thin. I twitch it, looking out at the tiny bit of street I can see.

One night, Stevie was kissing me. The next morning, she recoiled when I kissed her.

Why?

'They haven't said this in the news,' Charles says, his voice low, 'but they found her tablet at your place. Her blood was on it.'

I leave the window and sink back on to the bed. 'How much blood?'

'A bit, but that's not the bad thing. They found some images on it, ones she'd been looking at recently. Apparently there were photos from when you threw that house party. When that girl was murdered in our hometown.'

'Lauren Parker.' My voice catches. 'That DNA match on the knife isn't right. Someone planted that, too. I never—'

'And there were pictures of you and Lauren together at a different party. You're just in the background of another shot. Kissing or something. And it's at that creepy old farmhouse where they found her body. But you said you didn't know her, so . . .'

I cover my eyes. *Shit.*

'Nate,' Charles says slowly, 'be honest with me. Mimic has framed you, and I . . . I can believe that. But you were the one who killed Lauren, weren't you? I remember her friends searching for her the next morning, and you getting rid of everyone. You made me go over to a friend's house for the night, and then the police were there the next day. That's why we moved away from that town. Dad knew, and he took us away from there. That's what happened, isn't it? That's why you two don't talk any more.'

'No. I didn't kill her, Charles. I didn't kill anyone.' I set my jaw. 'And I'm going to prove it.'

'How?'

I pick up my phone, and click the SIM card back into place.

'I don't think those tweets are for the police. I think they're for me. I think whatever this guy's endgame is, he wants me involved in it.'

296

'Whatever you're thinking of doing, I'm going to assume it's a bad idea. Stay out of it, Nate. Stay wherever you are.'

'I can't. I think this is the only way to save Stevie.'

'And if she's already dead?'

I take a deep breath. 'Then hopefully he'll kill me, too. Goodbye, Charles. Tell the others that I didn't do this.'

'Nate, wait—'

I turn my phone back on, and immediately feel like there's a satellite camera targeted on the roof of the hotel. I get on to Twitter, log into my personal account.

The *Gory Details* official account is still up, the goading tweets still visible.

Good.

Usually tweets would be flooded with comments, but so far there aren't any – just lots and lots of retweets. The tweet settings have changed: *only people this account follows can respond*. I check our account's follow list: one person.

Me.

I was right. *This* is what he wants. I hit 'Reply'.

Is Stevie still alive?

I stare at the phone, nudging the screen every so often so it doesn't time out. Within a few minutes, there's a reply.

For now.

I type again.

Where is she?

Somewhere special.

It makes my skin crawl – not just to talk to him, but because it looks like I'm talking to myself. How quickly can this kind of thing be tracked? I have to be fast.

I'm the one you hate, not her. Let her go, and I'll meet you. Just tell me where.

There's a pause. I pace the room, thumb on the screen, nudging, nudging.

Come on. Come on!

A reply doesn't come – but there's a new tweet on the main feed.

Come and get me, cops. I'm going back to where this all started. Where I killed Lauren 17 years ago.

It's about time I was punished for it.

I rip the SIM card back out of my phone, grab the things I need, and rush out of the hotel.

Sandford.

I should have known this would take me back to Sandford.

EPISODE 194: OUR APOLOGY

'Hi, everyone. Almost four years ago, Nate and I started this podcast with a story from our hometown. The death of seventeen-year-old Lauren Parker.'

'We based the episode on the things we remembered from the time, and the assumptions we – and many of the other locals – made. This included repeating the rumour that Lauren had been murdered by her boyfriend, despite him never being charged by police.'

'This was wrong of us.'

'Although we never mentioned him by name, The Boyfriend, as we called him, could be easily identified by a simple Google search, which unfortunately is something many of our listeners did.'

'More unfortunately, this is something Nate and I encouraged. We should have shut down the jokes, memes, and eventual bullying that Mike Edwards – The Boyfriend – faced, but we didn't. We let it continue to a point where Mike's life was unliveable. We should have known better than to dangle his identity within such easy reach, and we should have shut it down long ago.'

'Recent DNA evidence on the murder weapon found during building work on the original crime scene has firmly ruled Mike out of the investigation, as the DNA on the knife belongs to someone else. Despite the rumours in our hometown, Mike had nothing to do with Lauren Parker's murder.'

'We would both like to apologise to Mike, his family, Lauren's family, and anyone else personally affected by the allegations we made in episode one of the podcast. Neither Nate nor I knowingly mislead you on this. We were just mistaken, and unprofessional in how we handled the hearsay of seventeen years ago.'

'Due to this, Stevie and I have decided that *All the Gory Details* will take a brief hiatus as we listen to your feedback and take steps to move forward with the podcast in a more responsible way. Out of respect, we've also pulled our *It's Always the Boyfriend* T-shirt line from our online shop, and replaced it with a charity design featuring an illustration of Lauren and Mike together. All profits from this shirt will go towards a fund for those falsely accused of crimes, to help the accused rebuild their lives after release.'

'When we recorded that first episode, we had no idea that anyone would listen to it. We had no idea of the damage we were doing to an innocent person. And for that, we're truly sorry. We also realise that we missed the opportunity to use our platform for good, and we want to put that right. If anyone, anywhere, has any idea who may have killed Lauren Parker in the small town of Sandford in 2006, please come forward. Anything you can tell us or the police will be invaluable to Lauren's family, and to Mike. This can't be solved without your help.'

'Thank you for listening, both to this and to the podcast over the years. Your support has been unexpected and wonderful, and we can't thank you enough for sticking by us for so long. We can't wait to come back in a few weeks with more of a content you – and we – love.'

'No, Nate.'

'What?'

'You can't leave that in.' Stevie leans back in her armchair, drawing Rosie up to her chest. 'I don't want to come back to this. And we can't end an apology with you gloating about how many fans we have – especially when they all hate us now.'

'They don't hate us. It's a vocal minority.'

She rolls her eyes at me.

'You'll feel differently in a few weeks, once all this dies down. And I don't want listeners to think this is the end for us, Stevie. Come on, let's end this in a hopeful way, and look to the future.'

'The future?'

'Yeah. When all this has been forgotten, and the podcast is top of the charts.'

'There's dreaming big and then there's delusion, Nate.'

'Nah, I believe it. We can come back from this. Wait and see.'

CHAPTER 23

Halloween has always been Stevie's favourite time of year. Even witchier jewellery than usual, the cult of black cats, crushing crunchy orange leaves beneath her boots like they did something to personally deserve it. We've celebrated all kinds of ways over the years: covering each other in special-effects scars and wounds for a house party; staying home to watch the goriest movies we could find; dressing as zombies and chasing after the trick-or-treaters in our street, them scream-laughing but never quite sure if it's a joke. It's her absolute favourite season.

But it isn't mine.

It's dark when I get to Sandford. I got off the train one stop early and walked the five miles over the hills – my phone slipped into the coat pocket of a random traveller I passed hours ago when I changed trains at Heathrow. I don't know if it'll help throw off the scent, but it's worth a try.

The police will be expecting me, I'm sure of it. Coming here at all was a risk, but there's no better night to slip quietly into town than when you can pull on a Ghostface mask and blend in with the rowdy, boisterous, costumed kids spilling out across the streets. I'm one of the crowd.

I leave the mask on as I work my way through the old, familiar streets. It feels different from when Stevie and I were last here: pumpkins flickering on doorsteps; fake cobwebs festooned in windows. Kids run from house to house with their parents, rattling plastic buckets of sweets, jumping as they see my scary mask.

Their parents would jump more if they knew the face beneath it.

Nobody looks at me twice. I make my way through the town centre, past the shops, and Lauren's grave in the churchyard. Some police officers lurk there, their jackets reflecting in the lamplight. I walk past them as though I'm the parent in charge of the gaggle of kids ahead, but turn down a side street once I'm past.

There will be fewer crowds from this point, and I haven't come this far just to be caught.

I can't take the main road that loops up and out of town, and I can't take the main rural footpath. I strike out through the woods instead, fighting my way through thorns and bracken in the dark, wishing I'd splashed out on a burner phone with a torch. I pocket my mask when I get nearer to where the farmhouse used to be – it's too white, and it might stand out in the dark. I tread carefully, giving the area as wide a berth as I can while still going in the right direction. There are voices, the flash of torches, and I jam myself behind a tree.

'Nothing yet,' an officer says to his colleague. 'He's a no-show so far.'

'Maybe he was just bluffing about coming back here.'

'Let's check the main path again.'

I wait until they're gone, then resume my journey – bypassing the old farmhouse area entirely.

Come and get me, cops. I'm going back to where this all started. Where I killed Lauren 17 years ago.

I'm one of two people on the planet who know where that is.

I cross the lane into the other side of the woods and head in quite deep, far enough to turn right and cut along the backs of the houses dotted along the road. It's quiet, here. Sleepy. There's enough space between properties that you can do things in secret without being noticed.

My old house looms into view, the white mock-Tudor walls sticking out amid the gloom. The house is double gated behind the sweeping driveway, but the back garden is only ringed by a lowish wall and a thick hedge. It's become wild now, stretching out, but there's still a specific gap in the corner where two bushes weren't planted quite close enough together.

It's the spot I said Lauren left the party through.

But really, she didn't leave the house at all.

A police car rumbles along the lane, slowly, and I force myself into the overgrown bulk of the bush. The officers inside the car stare at the house as they pass, then one shakes his head, and the car gathers speed as it continues along the road.

It's a routine check, not surveillance.

They aren't watching the house.

I force my way over the wall and through the bushes, the branches snagging on my clothes.

The garden, always more rustic than manicured, feels nightmarish now. It's not ridiculously overgrown – Dad probably has someone trim things a couple of times a year – but it's so obviously unlived in. Mum used to read in a hammock between trees on warm summer days, and she'd wrap up into the autumn to continue it. *'Once there are more spiders than sunshine, I let them have it for the winter.'* Later, Charles had a swing here, and equipment for every kind of sport. There are probably still balls stuck in the surrounding trees somewhere. But the things that made this garden feel lived in are long gone.

I approach the back door, and realise I don't have a key. I don't have a plan, either. I grab a rock to smash through the double patio doors with – but I don't need it. The door is slightly open, already unlocked, clicking slightly in the breeze.

Yep. Nightmarish.

I step in, scraping around for a light switch, still wishing I had that torch – but the switches do nothing. The power must be out. I wait for my eyes to adjust, tensing up. I'm still holding the rock.

This is a trap. I know it. But what can I do other than walk into it and hope for the best?

Dad never quite moved out of this place. Dust sheets are thrown over furniture, and ornaments still line up on the mantelpiece in the living area. It's as though he only meant to leave for a season, but never returned.

I wish he had sold it. I wish it had been razed to the ground like the farmhouse, the rubble ground up into dust and ashes. I wish I could do the same to the memories of this place.

I creak through the house, waiting for a jump scare like in the movies. I hated those movies. I used to grin at Stevie during them, laughing at the gory bits, when really I was looking just below the TV, my eyes unfocused, trying not to see.

It was the same with crime scene photos. I got better over time, but it was a struggle at first. I don't like gore. We pored over disgusting images that first night, here, seventeen years ago, her gleefully pointing out bullet exit wounds or bone sticking through flesh, while I nodded and tried not to gag.

I don't like blood. I've never liked blood.

But I always liked Stevie enough to pretend.

Over the years, I mastered the art of faking it. I could laugh on the podcast about guts hanging from trees or eyeballs being eaten raw – and after a while, my toes stopped curling in my shoes and I no longer needed to suppress involuntary shudders. I became desensitised to it. I enjoyed it, even – this creepy little hobby of ours, with its escalation of shocks and slaughter. Or I thought I did, anyway.

Seeing Anna Farley's body through that farmhouse window brought back the disgust.

I need light. Christine used to burn candles all the time – the big, overpriced ones in jars. I feel my way to the kitchen – *fuck*, why am I thinking about *Silence of the Lambs?* – and find the right drawer. Thin candles roll around as I open it, and I grab one – along with some matches. It takes a few goes, but I get it alight.

I get my jump scare – me in the kitchen window, pale and ghostly, stubble overgrown, wearing a stolen coat and a look of terror.

I put down my rock and upgrade to a knife instead, holding it up, combat style. I grip the candle in my fist, and leave the kitchen.

The door that connects the garage is at the end of the house.

I don't want to go in there. I haven't been in there since that weekend. I always made an excuse to avoid it. I mentally wallpapered over the doorway. It didn't exist. It wasn't there. What happened inside it that night was a bad dream, a nightmare, and as long as I didn't try to remember it, I could let it fade away, hazily, leaving only half-remembered flashes.

That's what I told myself, anyway. But it never really worked.

I check behind me, then grip the door handle.

Come and get me, cops. I'm going back to where this all started. Where I killed Lauren 17 years ago.

My dad's garage.

I push the door open and raise the knife again – but for a second, all I see is this room as it was seventeen years ago.

Sunlight streams in through the high strip windows, glinting on Dad's vintage Jaguar. That's the first thing I see: the perfect, untouched car, not smashed by the guys who broke windows, or stolen for a joyride by the ones who raided Dad's golf bag. Dad can punish me for the rest of it, but at least this car is . . .

Two feet stick out from beside the car, on the other side.

Is this where that girl was the whole time? Sleeping in the garage?

'Uh, Lauren? Time to wake up, now.'

She doesn't move.

'Lauren? Are you okay?'

I walk around the car, and wish I hadn't.

There's so much blood. It's soaked into her clothes, dirt-brown and dried against her skin, and pooling around her on the concrete. Her eyes are open, glassy, staring at the ceiling.

Dead.

I know her. I met her at a party, didn't I? It was a few months ago, over at that farmhouse I'd heard people talk about. I sneaked in with some of Dad's booze, trying to make friends, but they were all a year older. I pretended I was, too. It worked, because I got talking to her and we kissed. Just that one time. It didn't mean anything. I didn't even know her name.

But now she's dead. She's dead in my house. Dead with her chest hacked open like one of the women in Dad's crime scene photos.

I stagger away and vomit on the floor.

This wasn't an accident. She didn't fall and hit her head, or get too drunk and choke in her sleep. Someone did this. Someone stabbed her.

Someone *murdered* her.

And they did it at my party.

I grip shelves and door frames and stumble out of the garage, digging my phone out of my pocket. I need to call the police. I need to . . .

There's a big mirror on the hallway wall – cracked now, but still showing the discarded bottles, the broken glass, the wreckage of the party.

And me, phone in my hand, my Halloween costume still covered in the flaky fake blood I doused myself in last night. The costume of a murderer.

I met this girl once, and now she's dead. She's dead in my house – hidden away behind the car in the garage where nobody would think to look. I helped her friends search the house for her, but we didn't check here. I didn't even suggest it. I told them I didn't know her, because I didn't realise the Lauren we were looking for was the girl from the farmhouse. I sent them home saying she was probably back at her house. I said she'd turn up. I told them not to worry.

Stevie and I just spent all night being the weirdo true crime freaks who can't get enough of murder. We talked about it in the kitchen in front of everyone. We practically shouted about it.

And now someone's dead.

Someone's murdered.

Someone I knew.

What if they think I did this?

I didn't see a murder weapon. What if it's in the house? What if they used one of our knives, or a tool from the garage – something I've touched before? What if they put it back? What if they hid it, but it looks like *I* did? What if they search here? What if they find it? What if they don't believe I didn't know about it?

What if everything they find points back to me?

I can't breathe properly. Can't think.

I have to report this. I have to tell someone, it's the right thing to do, but . . . Sometimes killers do that, don't they? They call the police and say an intruder broke in and attacked their wife, or they walked in and found them already dead. Doing the right thing doesn't mean you're innocent. Sometimes it means you're guilty.

What if I call the police, and they don't believe that I found her? What if there's never another suspect and it's just me, *me*, the suspicious guy in a murderer's outfit with a dead girl in his garage? What if my DNA got on her somehow when I went in there just now? What if people at the party tell the police about the gory stuff I was telling Stevie last night? What if her friends tell the police I said I'd never met Lauren, but someone remembers that I did?

Suddenly that one meaningless kiss could look like a motive.

Dad already thinks I'm a fuck-up. I can't bring shame and scandal on him like this. He can't be the barrister with a son on trial for murder. He'll never forgive me for it. And I can't wreck my own future.

I wipe my face with my sleeve, and delete the three emergency digits from my phone.

Lauren's dead. There's no murder weapon around. Nobody knows she came into the garage. Everyone thinks she left.

If I can just get her out of this house, nobody will have to know it happened here. I can cut the link between her death and me. It can be investigated properly, without the wrong person in the frame.

If I stay calm and do this right, nobody can accuse me of anything.

I've revised enough true crime cases over the last few weeks to know what to do.

First, I have to get rid of Charles. He's still on the sofa, watching cartoons on a TV with a crack in the corner. I shove some things into his backpack and walk him along the street to a friend's house. Take the Xbox 360, take some pizza money. Just don't come back until tomorrow.

Then the house is empty. Empty except for her.

I cover up – plastic gloves, a shower cap, a black bin liner as a top, plastic bags over my shoes – and drag her body on to a shower curtain. Trying not to be sick again, I carefully wrap her up in it, and secure it with string. Then I haul her into the back of the car.

As I wait for it to get dark, I scrub at the floor, the suds turning pink beneath the brush. I can't get it clean. I squeeze on a load of neat bleach, and hope.

Night-time. When it's properly dark and deserted – 2 a.m., later – I open the garage and head out.

I can't drive. Not well enough to pass a test, anyway. I hit the gate on the way out, and nearly hit a tree as the lane twists in the dark.

Here will do. I pull to the side of the road and haul her out into the trees. People will think she was walking home, and didn't make it. I undo the string, and—

A car streaks past, lights shining. I'm hidden, but they'll have seen the car. Would they remember the make? The number plate?

Not here, not here.

Back into the car, the shower curtain flapping. Where? Somewhere safe, somewhere she can be found quickly. The farmhouse? I know how to get there. It'll be deserted tonight.

It's perfect.

I get her inside, my back aching from the weight, and put her on the floor. Her hand flops out from beneath the plastic, dried blood beneath her nails.

And I sink down and cry.

What the fuck am I doing?

I tear at myself through layers of plastic, gritting my teeth, hating myself.

I didn't want to be the one accused of murder – but how will the police be able to find who actually killed her now? I've destroyed the crime scene. Anything the killer left behind has probably been lost, either dropped en route or burned away by the bleach in the garage. I've trampled over the clues. Erased the evidence. I hauled her around like a sack of rubbish to be dumped on the street, like she was nothing. Like she didn't matter.

I stare at her still hand.

You didn't deserve this, Lauren. You deserved dignity. You deserved justice.

But I took that away from you.

I should tell the police. I should come clean about this, let them salvage whatever evidence they can from her, from the house. Give a statement and let them work out the truth from there. Admit to being such a selfish fuck-up.

But I can't do that.

Finding her body was one thing. If I admit to moving her like this, to bleaching the garage, it'll look like *I* killed her. Nobody will believe what really happened. They'll see a teenage boy who killed a girl, panicked, and tried to cover it up, then came crying to the police with a bad cover story when he realised he was in too deep.

I could have explained my way out of finding her in the garage if I hadn't panicked, but there's no explaining this. There's no excuse that will save me.

Innocent people don't dump bodies in the woods. Only killers do.

I'm fucked.

Nobody can ever know.

I move her on to the sofa, like she's lying down. Her feet – wait, there's only one shoe. Was there always only one shoe? – curled beneath her, and her hair spread out against the cushions. It's not enough. I look outside, in the old flower boxes from when this used to be a family home. Amid the weeds, something pretty. I pull them out and make her hold them, gagging as her hands flop unnaturally, and try to cover the gaping wounds in her chest.

It doesn't make me feel any less ashamed. It makes it worse, even. But it's too late to go back now.

It's too late to undo any of it.

I step out backwards, careful not to tread blood anywhere, and go back to the house. I wash the shower curtain with bleach and throw it in the bath – it'll look too suspicious if I get rid of it. The bleach hasn't worked on the floor. I try again, scrubbing and scrubbing, but the stain is still there. I have to cover it. I can't let all this be for nothing.

There are old paint cans in the garage, from when Dad had decorators turn Mum's art room into Charles' bedroom. Sky-blue paint. I pour it on the floor, covering the stain, and splash it over the car – and on the inside. Just in case. I take one of the golf clubs used to smash up some trees and bang out the lights, the wing mirrors. I make it look like this was another room destroyed by the party.

It's Sunday morning, and Stevie and August come. So do the police. So does Dad. He holds in his fury about the house and watches me silently, assessing my story like it's one of his clients. Looking for holes, but with no intention of pointing them out. I lie – '*I think I saw her leave that night, actually. From the attic*

312

window. Dark hair, right? She went through the gap in the hedge, over there,' – and I lie – *'We were up in the attic all night. I think she must've left about one a.m., or two?'*

Before all this, I let Stevie think I stayed in the attic all night because I didn't want her to know I couldn't keep all that whisky down. Now, I can't let anyone think I had the opportunity to kill Lauren.

But someone *did* kill her.

I've tried not to think about it, but I see so many faces from the party at the vigils and the searches. Mike crying over her, pleading with her to come home. Asking me about the party. Asking me what I saw.

But does he already know?

The only other person in the world who knows Lauren is dead is the killer. They know I never reported her murder. They know I moved the body before the police searched the house. They know I'm involved.

Mike seems to stare at me too long, too hard. The police do, too. I need them to look somewhere else.

One night, I take the keys from Mike's bag – I'm good at that after boarding school – and torch his van in a field.

Boyfriends kill their girlfriends all the time, don't they? It's everywhere in Dad's cases. He must be the killer.

And even if he isn't, at least the police will have a prime suspect who isn't me.

They find her shoe in the lane, where I was *going* to leave her, but nothing else. Whoever spooked me in their car that night doesn't remember me, or maybe they were just passing through. The days drag on, and nobody checks the farmhouse. I can't leave a tip – they might trace it back to me. She needs to be found. Her family need closure. The police need to be able to investigate this, properly. Surely there'll be the killer's DNA on her?

I have to go back. I go on foot after Dad's asleep, sneaking through the trees and fallen leaves. It smells different in there now. I can't look at her. I don't need to. I'll never forget it.

I tug her other shoe off and drop it at the end of the lane, at the turning to the farmhouse.

And the next day, she's found.

But the killer never is.

If I hadn't messed with the crime scene, maybe they would have been.

Now I raise my candle in the garage, casting its meagre light around. There's no car here any more, but there is something on the ground, near the stain that's since been painted over in white.

Someone has painted a dark outline of a body, just where I found Lauren seventeen years ago.

The candle shakes in my hand, spilling drops of wax on my skin.

For the past few weeks, I've known these killings were personal – but I didn't want to admit how deep. For seventeen years, I thought I was a stupid kid who panicked when he found a dead body and destroyed all the evidence, getting in the way of the truth and costing a family their closure. I thought the only link between the killer and me was that I'd inadvertently become his accomplice, disposing of all the evidence that pointed to him when I was trying to stop it from pointing to me. I helped someone get away with murder.

But that wasn't what Lauren's killer wanted that night, was it?

When the knife was discovered in the farmhouse ruins, I assumed the killer had played into the narrative I gave him, stashing it there years ago as a kind of sick joke: *thanks for the help, mate!*

But now my DNA is on crime scenes I never visited, and on a murder weapon I never touched. The killer didn't bury it seventeen years ago, did he? He planted it there six months ago when the dirt was freshly churned, hoping it would lead back to me – hoping I'd take the fall for the murder, like I was supposed to all those years ago.

I was right to panic that night: Lauren's body was left here to frame *me*.

The only person who knows about what happened in this room is Lauren's killer. The only person who could have lured me here today is Mimic.

It's the same person.

But who?

CHAPTER 24

There's a creak in the floorboards above me. I grip my kitchen knife a little tighter, and head for the stairs.

Other than that creak, the house is silent. Wax drips down my hand, burning my skin as I check room after room, eliminating them. I should have guessed where he wants me.

The attic.

From the main staircase, a door opens to another set, going straight up.

The lesson of every horror movie I've ever watched – half watched – tells me not to go up there, but I force myself. I didn't come all this way to be a coward.

It feels darker in here, somehow – the shadowy corners beneath the beams shrouded in a velvet black that nothing can penetrate. I glance around, raising the candle as I step further into the room.

Boxes. Old curtains. A figure hanging from a beam.

No. I rush over.

Stevie's hands are tied above her head, stretching up, while her body is slumped, her head hanging. I shove the knife under my arm and touch her face, raising her head.

She's warm. She's alive.

She's *fucking* alive.

'Stevie,' I whisper, hardly getting the word out through my smile. She doesn't wake. Her head lolls back down when I move my hand. I lower the candle. She looks okay. She's not hurt, she's all in one piece, she's . . . *covered* in blood from the knees down.

It's trampled into the floorboards beneath her, and all over her bare feet. I crouch down and check: shards of bone jut through the torn fabric of her trousers on each leg, oozing.

I cover my mouth, gagging.

This is what Mimic did to her in that recording. He broke both her legs so she couldn't run away.

I can't imagine the pain of being strung up like this – forced to hold yourself up with your arms, or rest on two shattered legs. This is torture. No wonder she wouldn't wake – her pain receptors probably won't let her.

I have to get her out of here. She should have had medical attention *days* ago.

I wedge the candle in the corner of an open cardboard box, and raise the knife to the rope.

'Don't do that,' someone calls at the other end of the attic.

I squint through the gloom, my heartbeat hammering. But I recognise the voice. 'August? Is that you?'

'Yeah, it's me.'

I touch Stevie's face again. 'Be right back, okay?' I grab the candle and head back towards the stairs. 'Are you tied up, too? Are you hurt?'

'I'm okay.'

I can't find her. It's too dark. I can't even locate her voice.

'Where are you?'

'Over here.'

What? That came from behind me, back near Stevie.

317

'Hold still, I'm coming.' I retrace my steps, avoiding the boxes. Stevie's pale arms come into view again, the blood beneath her glistening. I look around. 'August?'

'Here.'

She looms out of the shadows by Stevie, and I jump. She's like a ghost from a horror movie, a mass of dark hair and shadows and eyes that seem too big.

What's been happening in this attic?

'Are you okay?' I look her over, checking for wounds. She seems to be okay. 'What happened here? How did you get free?'

'I was too strong for him. I wouldn't let him tie me up like this. He tied me up, over in that corner. But I chewed through my rope.' She raises an arm: her wrists are raw and bruised. Stevie's must be, too.

'He hasn't been back since you got loose?'

'No, he was here.'

'What do you mean?'

She smiles a little, the candle throwing strange shadows across her. 'I chewed through my rope, and then I waited. He came at me with the hammer, but I was ready. And now I have the hammer.' She holds it up – blood crusted over it – and grins.

'You attacked him?'

'Yeah.'

'Badly?'

'Yeah.'

I grin, too. 'Good for you.' I glance around – as though I'll suddenly be able to see in the dark. 'Where is he? Did he leave?'

'No, he's still here.'

I tense up again. 'Where?'

'Close.'

I move nearer to Stevie, gripping the knife tight. 'I need to get you two out of here. Can you hold her, while I cut her down? I'll carry her out.'

I stash the candle in the box again and start sawing through the rope, checking behind me every few seconds.

'August, who did this to you?'

'Someone we know.'

'Who was it? Someone from Sandford, right? Someone who was at the party?'

'Yes.'

I saw through more fibres. 'Mike? Benkins? Someone else?'

'No. You know it wasn't any of them.'

Do I?

'Who was it then?'

'You already know, Nate. Don't play dumb.'

I'm almost through the rope. The last final threads.

'The killer kept us here, he attacked Stevie so, so badly, but I managed to fight him off us. I caved his head in with this hammer. He was hurting Stevie again, and I couldn't let him do that. I had to save her from him.'

'From *who*?'

'You.'

The rope breaks, but August doesn't catch Stevie.

Her weight smashes through her legs and she screams, her eyes bursting open, and I pull her to me before she falls. She looks at me – and screams more.

'Let go of her!' August shouts, raising the hammer. 'I won't let you hurt her any more, Nate!'

And she swings the hammer at me.

Metal connects, and it feels like my brain explodes inside my skull – but I can't let Stevie stand. I raise her up as I fall backwards, knocking into boxes, making sure her feet don't touch the ground before I slam into it.

She fights me, squirming like a cat, still screaming, screaming.

'Get out the way,' I hear August say – slurred, like slow-motion film. 'I have to hit him again to make sure.'

My eyes snap open. My face is wet, it feels like there's a shard of hot metal through my head, but I'm alert. I have to be. Stevie drags herself off me, crying, before I can grab hold of her properly. My hands are empty. I don't know where the knife is. But I can see the hammer coming down.

I roll into August's legs, throwing her off balance. She staggers, and I pull myself to my knees, searching around for the knife. Someone's turned on the light. I can see the spaces between boxes, the beams across the ceiling.

The fire raging in the corner.

We knocked over the candle. *Fuck*.

It's spreading.

August lunges for me again – but she only gets my shoulder this time. It's another burst of pain, but I can't let myself feel it.

Stevie tries to claw herself away from the fire, her broken legs trailing, dragging blood along with her. August swipes at me again. I push her back into a pile of boxes that collapse beneath her weight, and run to Stevie, grabbing her under her arms.

'Got to get you out,' I say, pulling her across the floor with one good shoulder. She fights me, trying to resist.

'Killer!' she screams, pain and terror choking her. 'You killed *everyone*!'

'No. It wasn't me, Stevie. I swear. It's August. She's tricked you. She framed me. *She's* Mimic.'

'Liar!'

'No. Listen to me, please. *She* killed Lauren in my garage all those years ago. I . . . I moved the body, I found her and got scared and moved the body, but I never hurt her. I should have told you, but I was a coward. I didn't want you to know that about me. That's the secret. Nothing else. I didn't do this, Stevie. Any of it. I promise.'

I blink, blood stinging my eye.

Stevie isn't screaming or struggling any more. She's looking up at me, a kind of desperate hope in her eyes.

She believes me. She knows I'm telling the truth.

She winces, tears mixing with the sweat on her face. 'Nate,' she says, clinging to my injured arm. I don't care that it hurts – I let her have it. 'I . . . I can't walk.'

'I know. But you don't need to, okay? I've got you. One, two, *three.*'

She cries out as I haul her up, my teeth gritted against the ache in my shoulder – and August stumbles out from the shadows beside us, already bringing the hammer down.

She's aiming for me – but the hammer cracks into Stevie's skull, shattering the bone, and the three of us slam on to the floorboards together.

'Stevie!' I scream, cradling her as I kick August away. Stevie's eyes are closed, and her hair is wet with blood. I clutch her head, pressing my palm to it – as though I can fuse the bone back together to stop the blood leaking out.

'Is she breathing?' August screeches, clawing her way to us. 'I was aiming for you. It was supposed to be *you*! You're ruining everything!'

She raises the hammer again, but I shuffle back, and kick out her knee. She slumps on to her hands, the hammer thudding – and before she can pick it back up again, I feel Stevie's pulse against my fingers.

She's alive. She's still alive.

I set Stevie down behind me and get to my feet, guarding her.

'How could you do all this, August? You've murdered twelve people. You killed a *child!*'

'No, *you* did. That's what everyone will think. Doesn't matter what happens here. It doesn't even matter what she remembers. This time, I've got you.'

'This time? Why did there have to be a first time? What did I *ever* do for you to want to ruin my life like this?'

'You ruined mine!' She shrieks it, something feral about her with her wild hair, her wild eyes.

'How? What are you talking about?'

'You stole her from me.' She points the hammer at Stevie's still body. 'I could see through you from the start. You didn't even like the same things we did, you just pretended to. You took her away from me because of a *lie*. We had plans, but you ruined them. I could see it happening. So I tried to stop it.'

'By killing an innocent girl who had nothing to do with anything? Why didn't you just kill *me?*'

'Because I don't want you dead. I want you *destroyed.* I want you to feel what I felt that night, while you two were locked away up here, replacing me.' She gestures to the attic. Flames lick up towards the roof, catching on the beams. The boxes behind her are ablaze. 'I want you on the outside looking in, all the time. I want you where I've been these past seventeen years.'

'You killed twelve people because you were *jealous?*'

'You stole my life from me!'

'I didn't steal anything! You moved away, and Stevie *chose* to stay with me. I don't control her. She makes her own decisions.'

'But you tricked her into hers.'

'No. Maybe I embellished my interest in true crime, but she made me love it. That's genuine. Our connection is genuine.'

'No, it isn't! It's a lie! You made her think you were her soulmate, but she already had one. She was mine. I've always been there. Always. And I'll still be here after you're gone. She'll see what a fraud you are. She'll see what you're capable of.' She laughs – unhinged, awful laughter. 'Nobody will believe you. You'll never be able to clear your name. I've destroyed you.'

My eyes flick to her hammer, and dart around the floor for the knife. I can't see it. I need to get Stevie out, but how can I when I'm unarmed?

'How did you do this?' I ask, stalling for thinking time. 'How did you get my DNA to frame me?'

'With my nails. Got you *twice* the same way. The first time, for when I planted Lauren's murder weapon at the farmhouse, I got you to serve me in the bar, and when you passed me my drink, I *accidentally* scratched you. Easy DNA. But I knew I'd need more for what I had planned. So I put on a wig, and found you in a bar when you were a customer. You liked me, then. You were all over me. And my nails were all over you. And your hair.'

Some memory I didn't think was worth hanging on to washes up in my consciousness: some ginger woman on some drunken night, back when Stevie and I weren't talking and I couldn't stand being alone. We kissed in an alleyway, her hands scraping up and down my back – drawing blood, I later realised. She tugged my hair *hard*.

Then she said goodbye, and walked off.

Was it that easy? *Really?*

'Seventeen years, Nate. That's how long I've waited. All so I could take from you *exactly* what you took from me. Tell me, was it worth it? Stealing all those years from me just to spend the rest of your life without her?'

The fire spreads nearer, engulfing a box of files. It won't stop. There won't *be* a rest of my life if we don't get out of here. Now.

I grab Stevie's body to drag her away, but August is too quick. She grabs one of Stevie's bloody legs.

'Don't do it,' she warns, digging her nails in. 'This break can be fixed. But another blow? Right about here? That's amputation. But you like that, don't you? You're *partial to dismemberment*. Or so you claim.'

Fuck it.

I jump up, going for the hammer – but August expects it. She flips it, and swipes at me with the claw side, again and again. I put up my arms to protect myself, and move towards her. She can't land a proper blow – the coat I stole is thick, the claw barely snagging on the threads with each hit. I take a risk, and grab for it.

She slashes across my cheek before I get my hands around the hammer. Screw the head injury, the blood, the face – I'm not letting go.

The things she's done . . . She's not going to let me walk out of here with Stevie. She's not going to stop.

Not unless I stop her.

It's a tug of war, but with consequences. We push and pull, fighting over it, snarling at each other, the flames starting to roar – and then she lets go.

I fly backwards with the hammer, and stumble into the fire.

Instinctively, my hands go out to break my fall, and the pain is instant. My palms sink through the ashy cardboard of a stack of my dad's old files, and it topples, sending paper and fire down the stairwell and across the attic floor. I pull my hands out, staggering away, shaking the burnt, shiny skin. Sparks fly around us, settling. Stevie? Where's Stevie?

There's smoke now. It's harder to breathe.

The old curtains are catching on the floor. The fire takes hold fast, burning them up in seconds. I get my bearings again, and see Stevie: still exactly as I left her. Is she breathing? Is she even alive?

Her head is bleeding so much.

I need to get her out. She can't die like this. I can't let that happen.

I swore I'd always protect her.

I search around the fire. Where's August? I see her, and then she darts away again, dancing around the flickers of the fire. Then I spot her beside me. Something glints in her hand. The knife.

She plunges it into my chest – just like she did to Lauren.

But she can't do it five times.

She tries to pull it out, but I grab her hand and hold it in place. I don't know where it is – lung? Heart? Am I a dead man walking? – but I don't let her hand leave. She does what she can, twisting the knife, making it hurt worse, but I don't care any more.

Her face – so smug, so delighted – starts to betray her, fear flicking in her eyes like the reflections of the flame. I force us away from the stairwell and deeper into the attic. Past the boxes, past the beam where she broke Stevie's legs, past the curtains where Stevie and I slept that night.

To the window.

But I don't think she knows this attic as well as I do.

I let go, and the knife instantly slides out – dragging a spurt of blood with it. It splashes over her face, and she grins.

'This is the last thing Lauren saw before *she* died, too,' she says. 'And this is the last thing *you'll* see.'

I grab her shoulders and charge with all the strength I have, and launch her into the round, latticed window.

The glass shatters behind her and she falls through, screaming, the fire gusting around her with the extra oxygen flooding the room. And then she's gone.

Stevie.

I cover my face with my sleeves and push through the fire, making my way to Stevie. I start to haul her up, but stop.

The stairwell is ablaze. The fire has spread downstairs, black smoke billowing in through the doorway. But it's the only way down – other than a vertical drop.

Stevie lies on her side, arms exposed in a tank top, legs broken, pain etched on to her bloody face even though she's unconscious.

I don't even think about it. I pull off my coat, lie it over her, and bundle her up in it, covering her face, her chest, as much as I can. Then I haul her up over my shoulder, her poor ruined legs tucked in close against me.

And I run.

Don't think about the heat, the cracking of the stairs, the fire ripping at skin. I get down to the first floor, choking, eyes streaming, searching around. The walls are on fire, but there's a path to the stairs. I can do this. We're nearly there.

The roof collapses. Beams smack through the house, missing us but sending sparks flying, spreading the fire on to the sheet-covered furniture, the plush rugs. They catch so fast. Another beam falls, taking out most of the living area. That's the way out, the open door.

I hold Stevie even tighter, checking she's still covered. Then I bury my face against her, and run through pure fire.

I stumble out the door into the garden, and collapse on the grass with Stevie. The coat is smouldering, patches of fire still alight. I pat it with my arm, protecting my hands by using my sleeve – but I don't have a sleeve. It's burnt away, the leftover threads stuck in raw, burnt skin.

Stevie's screaming. I pull the coat away and throw it off, getting her air, checking her.

She's still unconscious. She's not screaming.

I am.

I'm screaming.

I'm still on fire.

I pull the coat over myself and roll, but it doesn't help. The flames go, but the pain doesn't.

It's my hands, my arms, my legs. I shake uncontrollably, my nerve endings shredded. But I don't care.

I crawl back to Stevie. She's not moving. Can she breathe? Does she have a pulse?

I press my fingers to her throat, but I can't feel anything. I don't know if that's me, or her. I reach out and flick some of her hair over her face, my hands clumsy and weak. I stare, waiting, pleading, willing it to move.

And it does. The strands flutter up with a breath, and down with an inhale.

She's still with me, somehow. I did it.

I saved her.

I pull her to me on the cold grass, cradling her like we're back on my bed in those few perfect moments we shared together. I cup her head wound, applying as much pressure as I can with my numbed palm, feeling her gentle breaths on my neck.

Looking up, the trees and the fiery house both sway against the stars. I struggle to see them through the long, slow blinks. But then new things start to pop up.

Bright yellow jackets. People. Faces.

A pressure on my chest.

'Help her,' I say, my throat scorched. 'Help Stevie. *Please.*'

I'm being carried. There's help.

I vaguely recall, a lifetime ago, people driving past the house. And now they've saved us, because this house I hated so much became a beacon.

Lights. A ceiling sliding over me. A paramedic. A metallic click.

'Stevie,' I say, trying to look up. I turn my head. It's busy out there, outside my house. Police in those jackets. Flashing lights. Another ambulance, Stevie being slid into it – oxygen and medication and bandages ready for her.

She'll be okay. She's safe now.

A third ambulance. Dark hair on a stretcher.

August.

She didn't die from the fall. She can stand trial. Everyone can get justice. Everyone will know the truth.

It's over.

The doors bang shut, and I lie back on the bed, closing my eyes. Drugs numb me. I check out, the vibrations of the ambulance rocking me to sleep, voices murmuring, a heavy pressure on my chest.

'. . . will he make it?'

'I think so. There'll be some scarring.'

'Good. It's what he deserves.'

I know that voice. I pull on its thread, and blink until my eyes open.

DCI Gates stands by the paramedic, holding on to the edge of the bed. My arm – blistered and shiny and so unlike itself – is cuffed to the railing, her hands gripping either side of it. Protecting her kill.

She smiles at me.

'Kidnapping, attempted murder, twelve counts of murder, and now arson, too. Let's see how Daddy gets you out of this one, *Mimic*.'

I close my eyes, letting the drugs fully take me.

August's plan failed. Maybe not yet, but it will.

Because Stevie was there. Stevie saw it, heard it. And her testimony is all I've ever needed.

She's all I've ever needed.

And maybe now, after seventeen years, I'll be brave enough to tell her to her face.

EPILOGUE

It still feels weird to be recording in a proper studio.

I twist from side to side in the wide office chair, tapping my metallic nails against the armrests. Professional-grade mics sit on the desks, and headsets to hear each other as we discuss cases. It's so different from how my podcasting journey started out six years ago.

But not worse. A studio and a budget means production values, guests, even researchers if we need them. I've always preferred winging it, though. That's the Stevie Knight charm, right? Getting a bit too carried away, but having a co-host serious enough to rein it back in.

There's always that nostalgia, though. For the old days.

I fiddle with one of my rings – an ornate onyx gemstone with tiny silver bats flying around it. A gift to myself after all the surgeries and physiotherapy were finally over.

Even after two years, it's hard to reconcile the good with the bad; the memories of smiles and laughter against the horrors that came later. The unspeakable things done in my name – and done *for* me. It tarnishes everything. Taints it.

But the good is always there, waiting for me in a box in my head. I can never quite get it to stay closed.

The catchphrases and in-jokes. The knowing smiles. The Thursday nights.

The simpler times, before the darkness.

But things change, and I've changed. I didn't want to come back to this life at all, I didn't want to risk making the same mistakes again, hurting new people in new ways. But we agreed it would be different this time, and it is. We don't retell other people's stories – we invite them on the show to tell those stories themselves. We give a voice to the people so often silenced in these narratives, the victims whose names don't roll off the tongue as easily as the serial killers with Netflix drama series and flashy celebrity casting.

I don't like to think of myself as a victim. In a lot of ways, I could have been – but physical wounds heal, and for mental ones, there are always boxes. Industrial-sized, reinforced boxes.

No, I'm a survivor. We both are. Our scars prove it every day.

And what happened in the past can no longer hurt us.

'Largest mocha on the menu, here you go,' August says, setting it down for me. I smile up at her.

'Thanks. I definitely need it.' I cup my hands around it, enjoying the warmth. One downside to the studio is no Rosie to absent-mindedly stroke during discussions.

'You didn't sleep well? Again?'

I sigh, twisting in my chair. 'Too many dreams. But always the same ones.'

'The attic?'

'Yeah.'

The cup is too hot now, like fire. I shove my hands between my knees.

'Let's talk about it,' August says, settling down opposite me and resting her chin on her hands.

'We always talk about it. I don't want to always bring it up. It's not fair on you when we're both trying to forget it.'

'I don't mind, Stevie. Really. It's only been two years. Less for you, because of the coma. Nobody can heal from almost two decades of lies that fast. What's on your mind? We've got time before our guest arrives.'

I pull my legs up, crossing them in front of me and hugging them – gently, like they're made of glass.

It's stupid, but I always have the fear that they're going to snap again, even though I know they can't. There are too many metal pins for that. I have the X-rays and gnarly scars to prove it.

'It's just . . . I wish I could *remember* it.' I run my nails over the left side of my head – the part that's also now metal. 'I know, I know, it's better if I don't remember, and it's probably my mind blocking out trauma, but . . . It's just so hard to put the two things together. The Nate I knew, and the things he did to me. I *know* he did them, it's undeniable and proved, but . . . I can't picture it.'

'What was the dream?'

I shake my head. 'It's stupid.'

'No, tell me.'

'In the dream, he tells me he didn't do it. And I believe him.'

'Ah. So Dream Stevie believes the defence's argument about *me* being the criminal mastermind, huh?'

I throw her an apologetic smile. 'Sorry. I told you it's stupid.'

August crosses her legs, too. 'Don't ever apologise for how your brain processes trauma. He was your best friend for *seventeen years*, and all that time he was lying to you. That's a hard enough thing to work through *without* a traumatic brain injury thrown in. It's fine. Really.'

There are some parts I *do* remember from the attic – being blindfolded, the pain, the fear. And August on the other side of the room, drugged and bound like I was. But she got free, she overpowered him, and she saved us. She saved us both.

I wouldn't be alive today if it weren't for her.

What I feel about Nate is a confused blur of contradictions and impossibilities that I'm not sure I'll ever fully understand. But August . . . I know exactly who August is. I always have.

'You know, he wasn't *really* my best friend.' She frowns at me, and I pull the old friendship necklace from under my jumper. A puzzle piece, and *best*.

She smiles, and pulls out her own: *friend*.

Best friends forever. A pact made in childhood that turned into a stronger bond than either of us could have imagined.

'It's always been us, Stevie. You and me. And it always will be.'

Lights go out in the prison at 11 p.m. It's the only good thing that happens in here.

The days are too long. I used to count them, back before the trial. Back when I still had hope that they were finite, and this whole fabricated narrative would fall down around the prosecution somehow and I'd be exonerated with a full apology, and life would go back to normal.

But it didn't.

Stevie didn't wake up. Without her, there was only my version of the story, and August's – and August's was the one that fitted the evidence. It didn't matter that Dad's firm managed to find CCTV of me *not* killing when I supposedly should have been, or that August's role in forensics made the planting of DNA evidence a very real possibility. The jury didn't care about the inconsistencies. They took the fiction as fact.

Without Stevie, I was painted as a weirdo, a loner, a man so obsessed with one girl that he'd do *anything* to get her.

They used the last video I made of Stevie and me as evidence. The last time I saw her, kissing her on the sofa in her flat, and her pulling away, terrified, and shoving me back.

It's always the boyfriend – or the stalker who wants to be. Slam dunk.

She pushed me away because August had poisoned her against me, showing her old photos that I could have found a way to explain if she'd asked. But she didn't ask. She didn't trust me. And that video is damning.

They say I killed twelve people, including a five-year-old child. They gave me a whole-life sentence. No parole. I'll be in here for the rest of my life for crimes I didn't commit. I'll die in this cell.

I'm one of the famous ones, now. I get letters every day from *fans*.

Curtis writes to me, begging for his letter back. I won't send it.

I won't end up on his wall of curiosities in The Murder Emporium. I'm not another name to tick off his list, however much the world is convinced I am.

I do write to Stevie. Or try to. She doesn't answer. Does she still live at the flat? I send letters there, but get no answer. I write to her parents in Sandford, but no response either.

I wish she'd come to visit. If I could just talk to her, maybe she'd remember how she really got those injuries. Maybe she'd remember that moment in the attic before the fire got too wild, when I held her in my arms and told her the truth, and she believed me.

But she doesn't remember. She woke up too late for the trial, and by that time, the narrative was set. August was the hero who'd fought off Mimic and saved her best friend.

And I was the villain.

I curl up in my bunk, the mattress hard beneath me.

It wasn't supposed to be like this. I promised Stevie I'd be there for her and that I'd protect her, but I couldn't. August got what she wanted: the friendship that I had with Stevie. She made it so we could never go back, and she stepped into the empty vacancy she'd created for herself.

Dad told me they even podcast together now.

Does Stevie ever think of me? Is she awake now somewhere, Rosie purring on her lap, feeling like something isn't right? Does she ever wonder if I was telling the truth about everything?

Does she ever think of the kiss?

I do. I wish we'd paused that moment, and lived in it forever.

Because now I have to live forever without her.

I feel down the side of my mattress and fish out the old iPod Charles bribed a guard to sneak in for me. It's the only thing I wanted.

I put in the earphones and curl up, facing the wall, the light from the screen picking out the burn scars on my hands. I scroll through the MP3 files, back to the top of the list.

Episode 1: It's Always the Boyfriend.

Time to start over.

I close my eyes and hug myself, willing myself to be back there, on that sofa opposite her with her fidgety fingers, her wry smiles, the twinkle in her eye that I adored so much.

The twinkle that I'll never get to see again.

I click the 'Play' button, and smother my tears into my pillow.

'Do you like hearing about gruesome murders?'

'Good, because we love talking about them. This is All the Gory Details, *the true crime podcast . . .'*

ACKNOWLEDGEMENTS

On Wednesday, 7 March 2018, a young woman from Worthing named Georgina Gharsallah went to the shops, and never returned home. She disappeared without a trace, leaving behind two children, a family, and friends.

Five years on, she is still missing.

I never met Georgina. She and I are complete strangers whose paths never crossed, but I think of her often. I see her almost every time I leave the house – in the missing posters taped to lamp posts on the streets, and in the reward banners strung along the main roads. In a strange, uncomfortable way, she is probably the most famous person from my hometown.

Who is the Georgina from yours?

There's a certain guilt that comes from enjoying the crime genre. Unlike dragon attacks, alien invasions, or demonic possession, the horrors that humans inflict upon each other in crime fiction are entirely plausible. We hunger for sadistic serial killers, and feel toe-curling, disgusted elation when we get them – but the violence we read about for fun is within the realms of possibility. People are murdered every day, and it could happen to any of us. It could happen to you.

And yet . . .

I've spent two years bingeing true crime podcasts, and I've loved it. But sometimes – when I catch myself thinking, 'Really? Only ONE victim?' or 'No, no, don't leave out a detail because you think it's too traumatic!' – I feel ashamed of myself. The line between crime fiction and true crime has become so blurred in this age of podcasts and Netflix adaptations that it's easy to get swept up in the storytelling, and forget the real human beings at the centre.

Small Secrets is a love letter to my fascination with crime stories – and the conflicted emotions I'm sure we all feel when we consume them, whether they're based on a true story or not.

As with my previous novel *The Edge*, I have to thank my agent Hannah Schofield for whole-heartedly championing this book ever since it was a one-line pitch sent to her on a list of many others – and for holding my hand throughout my whole publishing career so far. Thank you to my editor Kasim Mohammed for stepping into a new job and almost immediately being hit by a messy first draft, and overseeing that draft's transformation into a novel we can all be proud of. Further thanks to Mike Jones and Sadie Mayne for editing, Melissa Hyder for proofreading, Molly von Borstel for the cover, and the entire Thomas & Mercer team for all they do.

Once again, thank you to my family for their never-ending support and love, and a special mention to Phil Goacher – my dad, who insists I mention him by name this time – for coming up with the idea for Carousel as we walked along Worthing seafront while the funfair was in town. He must be who I get my weirdness from.

I finished this novel in the feverish, sleepless first weeks of my debut novel *The Edge* being published. I'd go out for night walks in the pouring rain with *My Favorite Murder* in my ears, then return home to new reviews sitting on the Goodreads page, and kind DMs from readers.

When stress was high and completing this novel felt utterly impossible, I can't say how much it helped to hear one particular phrase from so many different people: 'I can't wait for the next one!'

I really hope that when you finish this book, you feel the same.

ABOUT THE AUTHOR

Lucy Goacher was born and raised in Worthing, and can often be found braving the windy weather on the seafront. She has an English degree and a Master's in Creative and Critical Writing from the University of Sussex, and was a finalist in the 2017 *Daily Mail* First Novel Competition. Her first novel, *The Edge*, was published in 2022.

Her time is split between writing, pampering her cat and photographing the urban foxes who visit her garden every night for dinner – much to her cat's annoyance.

You can follow Lucy (and her foxes) on Twitter and Instagram: @goachwriter.

Follow the Author on Amazon

If you enjoyed this book, follow Lucy Goacher on Amazon to be notified when the author releases a new book!

To do this, please follow these instructions:

Desktop:

1) Search for the author's name on Amazon or in the Amazon App.
2) Click on the author's name to arrive on their Amazon page.
3) Click the 'Follow' button.

Mobile and Tablet:

1) Search for the author's name on Amazon or in the Amazon App.
2) Click on one of the author's books.
3) Click on the author's name to arrive on their Amazon page.
4) Click the 'Follow' button.

Kindle eReader and Kindle App:

If you enjoyed this book on a Kindle eReader or in the Kindle App, you will find the author 'Follow' button after the last page.